BONE
HARVEST

Also available from James Brogden and Titan Books

Hekla's Children
The Hollow Tree
The Plague Stones

BONE HARVEST

JAMES BROGDEN

Titan BOOKS

Bone Harvest
Print edition ISBN: 9781785659973
E-book edition ISBN: 9781785659980

Published by Titan Books
A division of Titan Publishing Group Ltd
144 Southwark Street, London SE1 0UP
www.titanbooks.com

First edition: May 2020
1 2 3 4 5 6 7 8 9 10

A CIP catalogue record for this title is available from the British Library.

Printed and bound by CPI Group (UK) Ltd, Croydon CR0 4YY.

FOR JOHN AND GRETA

The dews drop slowly and dreams gather: unknown spears
Suddenly hurtle before my dream-awakened eyes,
And then the clash of fallen horsemen and the cries
Of unknown perishing armies beat about my ears.
We who still labour by the cromlech on the shore,
The grey cairn on the hill, when day sinks drowned in dew,
Being weary of the world's empires, bow down to you,
Master of the still stars and of the flaming door.

From "The Valley of the Black Pig" by William Butler Yeats

Theophagy (n.): the sacramental eating of a god

PART ONE

PREPARE THE GROUND

1

THE GREY BRIGADE

THE DESERTER RAN FROM THE BATTLE, AND HID IN A shell crater in No Man's Land.

By the time he felt that it was safe to move, the sun had disappeared in a crimson smear behind the shattered reek of sky. The thunder of the big guns had stopped hours ago, and the popping crackle of rifle shots was dwindling like rain, leaving only the evening chorus of screams, prayers, pleas and curses from men dying unseen, as if the churned earth were bewailing its own torture.

He was sprawled halfway down the slope of the crater, little more than a water-filled pit with the half-submerged corpses of three other soldiers for company. With their uniforms the same mud-grey as their flesh, it was impossible to tell which side of the line they had originally come from, and the mud also caked him from head to foot, making him one with the dead, all brothers together. He'd spent the hours waiting for nightfall watching the rats eat them, their sleek bodies cruising the crater's waters like miniature destroyers, graceful in their element. They'd avoided him once an exploratory nibble at his left boot had prompted a kick; there was no need to attack the living when they could glut themselves on the dead. One particularly bold fellow had sat by a corpse's outflung hand and taken his time to gnaw away the fingers, pausing every so often to look at the deserter as if inviting him to join them. *Plenty to go around, chum.*

And despite himself – despite the screaming and the stench of shit and bowels and rot – the deserter's stomach had been growling before long.

He wondered how he might go about catching one. It would not be the first time he'd eaten rat, but it might be the first time he'd done so raw, since he had no means of making a fire and to do so would be suicide anyway.

The attack had been at dawn, of course. The result had been butchery, of course. It was possible that one or other side had gained several yards of ground, but in the noise and tumult he had become so disorientated that he no longer knew in which direction lay his own trenches or those of the enemy. Not that such a distinction had meaning any more. All that mattered was that he had been lying in this crater from sunrise to sunset without food or water. He remembered (or tried to; it was hard, his thoughts darting to and fro like the rats), eating some kind of thin oat porridge in the pre-dawn dark before the attack. He had not eaten since, and what little water he carried had run out before noon. By evening he'd developed a nasty fever, which from the heat of it in his blood felt like it wasn't going anywhere soon.

The western sky grew sullen, and when he felt that it was safe to move the deserter began to inch his way down, lower into the crater, keeping his head below the rim. The rats squealed, reluctant to abandon their feast, and watched him with glittering eyes as he fumbled amongst the dead soldiers' packs and pouches. He found a few crumbs of salted pork that the rats had somehow missed and some lumps of a dark, waxy substance which could have been chocolate or the remains of a candle but which he ate anyway since experience told him that there would be little difference in taste. There was a letter from a loved one addressed to 'My darling Everett', which he kept since paper was good for lighting fires. He also found a leather case about the same size and shape as a large notebook, which contained a brush, a few blocks of watercolour paint, and a packet of daubings on pieces of thick cartridge paper. Anaemic landscapes, for the most part – pale hills and flowering trees – this trench-bound Constable's idyllic memories of his homeland. The deserter tossed them into the stagnant water at the bottom of the crater. None of that existed any more. They were lies. Lies got men killed. Lies like 'it'll all be over by Christmas lads!' and 'just this one last big push and we'll break them!' and 'for God and the King, boys!' He peered into the dead man's face – the half of it that wasn't a pulped ruin of skull and brain, all that remained of Everett's loves and artistic aspirations reduced to the one remaining eye rolled up so high in its socket that it looked like a boiled egg.

His stomach growled again.

He couldn't remember anything from before the trenches. Every time he tried to think further back than that – to home and family, assuming that he had either – he was met with the monstrous anger of the guns roaring continuously, like a great standing wave threatening to overtopple and crush him if he got too close. He had tried to point this out to Captain Milburne, but since his memory for killing was intact that was all that seemed to be required, and he'd been ordered to pick up his rifle and return to his post. Both post and rifle were long gone, obliterated by the enemy guns, along with his rank and his name, but they hardly mattered.

What mattered now were boots, lucifers, field glasses, weapons, and especially ammunition. He was going to need a sufficient tribute if he hoped to be accepted by those whom he had come in search of rather than simply killed out of hand.

The Wild Deserters.

The Grey Brigade.

The No-Men.

It was said that they lived in the remains of old dugouts and the cellars of shattered buildings in No Man's Land, and that they emerged by night to scavenge amongst the dead, even going so far as to eat the flesh. Some, it was whispered with ghoulish glee by veterans to wide-eyed new recruits, preferred it fresh rather than bloated and maggot-ridden, and would lure an unwary man away from his post to butcher him like a beast. Others told stories of them appearing like angels out of the drifting smoke to give mercy to the dying and rescue the wounded, returning them to their lines before disappearing. None, that the deserter had ever heard, had been ordered to march to their deaths in a hail of bullets and shrapnel by fat, complacent generals who sat safely distant having their cocks sucked by French whores and dining on three square meals a day. The Grey Brigade had no generals or officers, it was said.

The deserter shouldered his satchel of loot and set off, coughing like a hag, into the cratered waste to find his new company.

There was a purity to No Man's Land that the deserter admired, in the way that one might admire a piece of machinery engineered perfectly for its purpose, without fripperies or useless ornamentation. It was a landscape that could not have been better designed to take life, and in this it succeeded beautifully. One did not walk through No Man's Land – to do so would risk a sniper's bullet. You squirmed up the slope of one crater and peered over its lip into the other, trying to see what awaited you as you slid down into the next, often half-swimming in mud and blood, and sometimes, if you were lucky, on a more solid carpet of corpses. Every yard of progress was a negotiation with barbed wire, splintered wood and bone, mud so deep it could drown a horse, and scum-covered water that hid razor shards of metal. Entrails garlanded the wreckage. Dying men sobbed and implored him as he passed. Others dragged themselves blindly through the mud, shattered legs trailing behind them like worms. He ignored them all, just one more worm amongst so many. As night deepened, one side or the other would fire off the occasional flare, and in the shifting shadows of its descent the corpses seemed to move too, twisting like things rolling in deep ocean currents.

There was a place that had once been a wood – the trees now little more than broken, jagged pillars – and he aimed for this as it seemed as good a place as any. A flare was dying behind him, and as it fell with the wind its glare threw long spokes of shadow that swept the ground around him.

And then, without transition or warning, three of the stumps were men.

They hadn't moved an inch or done anything to signal their existence to him; one moment they were simply there, in the same way that a picture of a young woman will be that of a crone, or a candlestick becomes two faces. They were motionless in the light of the falling flare, and there was something breathtaking about the fact that they were actually *standing*, like men, not crouched and creeping like animals. For all that the No-Men were bearded, unkempt and dressed in rags, they claimed their ground with more authority than any groomed and pressed officer. Despite his earlier confidence, and the fact that he'd brought them tribute, the deserter nevertheless felt that he should drop to his knees, were it not for the fact that he was already lying on his belly. A worm. A corpse lacking the wit to realise it was dead. He could think of no reason why they shouldn't put a bullet in him and correct the mistake. He would have done so in their position.

Then the flare died completely, and the No-Men must

have moved, though how they could have tackled this terrain so swiftly didn't seem possible, because they were standing around him, three deeper shadows in the blackness, and he felt the prick of a bayonet pressed between his shoulder blades.

'What's your regiment?' The whisper was hoarse, and in English.

'Royal Warwickshire Territorials, sir,' he stammered in reply.

'Don't sir me.' The bayonet pressed harder. 'What do you think I am? I'll ask you again. Your regiment.'

'Who do you take orders from?' added a second voice, accented, probably German. A third voice sniggered, thick and low. They were mocking him. Testing him. Then he realised what the first voice had really asked.

'None,' the deserter answered. 'No regiment. No orders.'

'So, who are you, then?' asked the whisperer.

'*What* are you?' added the sniggerer.

'Nothing,' he said, and as soon as it was uttered he felt the truth of it lift its burden from his soul. 'I'm nothing,' he repeated more confidently, on an outrush of breath as if it were a confession of love. 'I'm a deserter. A coward. If they catch me they'll put me up against a wall and shoot me.'

'Funny, that,' replied the European. 'What do you think they have been doing to you all this time?'

The bayonet disappeared from his back, and hands helped him to his feet. It was such a simple act, but it ran counter to months of crouching that he cowered, convinced that a sniper would immediately blow his brains out, but nothing happened. There was no challenge or gunshot, just the screams and tears of the wounded all around them in the darkness. Then another flare soared into the sky, much further off than the last, and the hands that held him up began to guide him.

They led him deeper into the skeletal wood, to the shell-blasted ruins of what might have been a farmhouse. It seemed so obvious a landmark and rendezvous point for raiding parties that anybody trying to avoid patrols would go nowhere near it, and he said as much.

'Regulars have learned not to come here,' replied the whisperer. 'This place belongs to the Grey Brigade.'

There had been one large room which was now a courtyard with its roof gone, and in one corner a wide trapdoor made of heavy timbers. Two of the No-Men hauled it open to reveal stone stairs descending to what had presumably been the farm's cellar. Down here there wasn't even the meagre ambient light of the outside, and the deserter stumbled in absolute blackness. Then a fist thudded on wood, a rattling bolt was withdrawn, and a door opened into light, warmth, and the aroma of food.

The cellar was long and low-ceilinged, and even though it had collapsed at the far end it was still luxurious compared to the funk-holes he'd slept in and even some of the officers' dugouts he'd seen. Scavenged kit was stacked in piles all around – rifles, ammunition, boots, blankets, mess kits, tools – between which were makeshift cots for the dozen or so men who called this place home. It was humid with the reek of contained and unwashed men. They lay or sat, picking lice off themselves, mending or making gear, or any one of the dozens of small tasks that kept off-duty soldiers busy.

Some stopped what they were doing to stare as he entered, while others carried on as if he didn't exist. Four were sitting on chairs about a small table, playing cards. Their uniforms were a motley of German *feldgrau* with red trim and gold buttons, French horizon-blue and British khaki, salvaged and patched from either side of the lines. The only thing they had in common was the lack of any rank insignia – cuffs, collars, and epaulettes were all stripped bare. Light came from stubs of candles set around the room and at the far end where a crude fireplace had been made out of the rubble and the damaged ceiling allowed smoke to vent. Here a man crouched on his haunches by a large cast-iron pot, who turned from regarding the newcomer to resume stirring its contents. As he stood in the doorway gaping, the European and the Sniggerer pushed past him to their own particular corners and started stripping off their gear.

'Welcome to the Wild Deserters,' said his escort. Seen properly for the first time, he was younger than the hoarseness of his voice had led the deserter to imagine, dressed in the same assortment of gear. 'I'm Bill. You have a name?' His voice was still a guttural whisper, which served well enough for survival in No Man's Land, though it appeared he had little choice since his throat was a scrawled nightmare of scar tissue. Bill, then. No rank, no surname. Probably not even his real name.

'Everett,' he said, since it was as good a name as any.

'Lads,' said Bill to the room, 'meet Everett.'

There were grunts, a couple of tin cups raised in sardonic welcome, and one cry of 'Fresh meat!' which was met with chuckles.

'You're hungry,' said Bill. 'Come on.'

Everett helped himself to an empty mess tin and spoon and approached the cooking pot, inhaling deeply. The aroma felt rich and heavy enough to fill him on its own – something meaty, with pepper and rosemary that conjured up images of Sunday roasts and tablecloths and creamy white plates at a table with roses at the window, but the roaring noise at the back of his head overwhelmed that unbidden memory, and when he shook himself he saw that the cook, introduced only as Potch, had ladled his mess tin full of stew. Large lumps of meat and dumplings were drowning in a thick brown gravy. Bodies in mud. There was a space next to where Bill was unwinding the puttees from his calves, so he sat there.

His first mouthful stunned him. He'd been expecting some creative use of bully beef, salty and formless mush, but his tongue encountered flesh and gristle, and he chewed and chewed and finally swallowed. 'My God!' he grinned at Bill. 'Is this actual pork?'

Bill paused in unwinding the strips of cloth from his legs and eyed him. 'What do you care?' he asked.

The deserter became aware that the room had become very quiet, and that everyone was looking at him. In their eyes he saw the same flat appraisal that the rats had given him. *Plenty to go around, chum.* What did he care? The answer, he found, as he devoured his meal and then licked the mess tin clean, was that he didn't.

2

BILL

EVERETT'S TIME WITH THE GREY BRIGADE WAS IN many respects much the same as life in the regular army. There were long periods of intense boredom alleviated only by finding creative ways to gamble and the ongoing war of attrition against lice and damp, interrupted by outbreaks of nerve-shredding noise and terror when one side or the other made another futile attempt to break the stalemate and claim another few yards of No Man's Land. There were rifles to be maintained and latrines to be dug and the cellar ceiling was forever threatening to collapse and needed shoring up with pieces of timber.

In other respects it was a different world.

There was no command structure and hence no one to order that these duties be done, and so they were only ever completed haphazardly, or at the cost of sometimes brutally violent arguments about who should take responsibility for what. There was no stand-to at dawn, and no inspections. But there was no relief either. Before, he could have expected six days at the front before being rotated back to the reserve trenches and possibly even some home leave, but with the Grey Brigade there was nowhere to rotate to. And, because of the exposure to snipers during daylight, they led an almost entirely nocturnal and silent existence. Light and noise were shunned. He had hoped that the relative warmth and better diet might help his fever, but if anything it worsened, developing into a persistent cough. Long bouts would leave him with blood on his lips and unable to stand, and he felt something heavy swilling at the bottom of his lungs, like water in a shell crater. Almost certainly it was tuberculosis, fatal in the long term, but given that his life expectancy was likely to be a matter of days he tried not to let it bother him too much.

At times, sitting in his alcove in the cellar either mending a sock or cleaning a gun, he wondered if this was how medieval monks had lived. Before, it was not unknown for some of the men to comfort each other physically, but with the threat of court-martial and imprisonment such acts were scrupulously clandestine; amongst the Wild Deserters there were no such inhibitions and he quickly ceased to be shocked by the sight of men fucking.

Sometimes, regulars from one army or the other would try to use the farm as a staging point for a raid or recce, and then the Grey Brigade would hide, deep and silent. Taking the wounded, who were as good as dead anyway, was one thing, but to attack a fully armed squad of fighting men would attract reprisals. And the caution was felt on both sides. On one occasion a private discovered the cellar door and excitedly called to his sergeant while in the dark on the other side Everett and the others gripped their rifles tighter and readied themselves. The deserter tried to take slow and even breaths, as a coughing fit at this moment was the last thing they needed.

'Leave it, private,' they heard the sergeant grunt.

'But, sir!' complained the private. 'There could be all sorts down there! Bottles of wine! Brandy, even!' There came a murmur of interest from the other men in the squad at that.

The sarge's reply carried the low and intense anger of a man who was deeply scared. 'Now you listen to me, boy. The only thing on the other side of that door for you is death. You can go in and look for it if you like, but you're going on your own, and you ain't coming back.'

That seemed to do the trick for the curious private, and the squad moved off, but not before the sarge hawked and spat heavily at the door.

'Why didn't they come in after us?' asked the deserter afterwards.

'They don't know for sure that we exist,' said Bill. 'Or if we do, what our numbers are, how we are armed, what we are capable of. Hard enough to carry out your orders as they stand without going looking for trouble. They try not to believe that we exist for the simple reason that they can't comprehend our motives as being anything other than cowardice and the desire to save our skins. They think, why would a man who cares only for his own survival willingly put himself in the middle of conflict? For men such as they are, who are moulded by and perpetuate a system of fear and unthinking obedience, the notion that a man might flee them out of a refusal to have his spirit so enslaved and that the safety of his flesh and blood means nothing in comparison – it's beyond the scope of their imaginations. Easier for them to imagine ghouls and monsters than men with a sense of their own dignity.'

I am what the elders teach the young ones to fear, Everett thought proudly. *I am the thing in the cellar.* 'I'd like to get a full, proper Grey Brigade together out here,' he said. 'We could invade the world from No Man's Land. Imagine their faces!'

'Imagine their faces as they mowed us down with Lewis guns, perhaps.'

'So why did you join up, then? You don't seem very much the unthinking obedient type.'

But all Bill would offer him by way of reply was a wry smile and the response, 'Who says I joined up?'

It occurred to him that he should have felt sickened by the act of cannibalism, or at least guilty. But he found that after seeing so much of how human flesh and bone and viscera could be mangled and mutilated, the sacred vessel of the human spirit torn open and spilled into the mud with no revelation, it lost any sanctity it might have once held for him, and the taboo became as meaningless as trying to stay a virgin in a brothel.

This was not to say that he didn't retain some principles – he made it a point of pride to only ever eat from men he had killed as a mercy. The problem was that any kind of meat perished rapidly in such damp and unsanitary conditions, and when even the living suffered from gangrene the freshness of a carcass could not be relied upon. The balance, then, lay in finding a man so wounded that he had no hope of survival.

Everett's first kill was a young German *Gemeiner* that he and Bill found in a shell crater, semi-conscious and raving with infection.

His left leg hung in tatters, though he'd done a passable job of using his belt as tourniquet above the knee. Since bone was always awkward to cut through, and the explosion had already done that work for them, Everett decided to take advantage of this and moved in with a knife to cut through the remaining tissue and sinews; however, the sensation of being sawn at roused the private to such fresh pleading and screaming that the deserter felt something like pity and drew his pistol to put the boy out of his misery.

Bill pushed his gun down, miming *Noise*. As if the boy were not already making enough. But Bill was right; screaming was just background noise, easily ignored, whereas a gunshot in No Man's Land might draw the attention of snipers. So the deserter replaced the gun and used his knife. It whispered across the boy's throat and as his screams became gurgles and then finally stopped, Everett was aware that Bill was murmuring some litany and turning a bracelet that hung on his right wrist.

Later in the cellar, eating what the boy had provided, he remarked to Bill, 'If it's forgiveness you're after, I think you're looking in the wrong place.'

'Not forgiveness,' replied Bill in his hoarse choke of a voice. 'Blessing.'

Everett laughed. 'Even worse!'

Bill removed the bracelet with which he had been fiddling and passed it to him. It was a simple loop of something whitish-yellow that felt like ivory, with open metal-capped ends.

'What's this?' Everett asked.

'It's a boar's tusk, the symbol of my faith. I belong to the Farrow, the followers of Moccus.'

'Huh. Sounds Greek.'

'He's older than the Greeks. Moccus is the Great Boar, He Who Eats the Moon, much older even than your Christ.'

'He's not *my* Christ.' Although given the roaring blankness of his memory even that might not have been true.

'All the same. Moccus protects warriors and hunters, as well as bringing life and fertility to the land. Think of him as the patron saint of soldiers, if it helps.'

'Naw, that's Saint George,' said Geordie, one of the other Tommies.

'*Khuinya*,' growled Nikolai, the small Russian sapper. 'Bullshit. Saint George is patron of Moscow.'

Bill overrode them both before an argument could brew. 'Moccus was old when your city was a village of mud huts,' he said. 'He defended the people of the deep forests against the Romans. He's there still, for those who know how to look for him.'

'Then why hasn't anybody heard of him?' asked the deserter, passing the bracelet back.

'Why haven't you heard of him, you mean? As if the world will simply open its secrets to you like a whore because you're in it?' Bill shrugged. 'You're hearing about him now. That boy, the German with the leg, he was a soldier, and his death gave us something, so I hoped that Moccus might bless him for that.'

The deserter chewed slowly, wondering if he should be grateful, and if so to whom. The corpse he had left in the mud with its throat cut, indistinguishable from all the others? God? If He was there, surely He could regard such acts only with abhorrence. 'It seems to me,' he said, 'that if this Moccus of yours is a protector of warriors and hunters then he's doing a bloody awful job of it hereabouts.' This earned him some chuckles from the other Wild Deserters.

Bill simply nodded; if he'd taken offence he kept it to himself, but he raised his chin to expose the pink ruin of his throat. 'Do you think I would have survived this otherwise?' he asked.

'I don't know,' the deserter admitted. 'I've seen men survive some pretty horrible things.'

'I've survived a lot more than most. I was at Mafeking, where we were so hungry we ate our own horses. I was with the 90th Light Infantry at Ulundi when we broke the Zulus. Got this.' He pushed up his trouser leg to reveal a long, shining scar that curved down his calf and disappeared into his sock.

'But that was over thirty years ago!' Everett protested. 'You're nowhere near that old.'

'He's full of bullshit,' said Nikolai.

'The sound of their spears drumming on shields was like thunder rolling across the plain out of a clear blue sky,' Bill continued, as he stirred the stew in his mess tin.

'Next you'll be trying to tell me that you rode with bloody Wellington himself.'

Bill smiled at that. 'A bit before my time,' he admitted, and was quickly sober again. 'The favour of Moccus is not some deferred celestial reward if you say enough Hail Marys and eat fish on Fridays every week until you die. It is writ in the flesh and blood and muscle and bone of his worshippers, gifted from that of himself. He makes his followers strong.' He was still stirring his food, not eating, and the deserter caught the unspoken word hiding in his tone.

'But?'

'Strength doesn't count for much when a man is all scar.' Bill grunted a dry little laugh and put his meal to one side.

'Ah yes, the sword of righteousness and the shield of faith. Forgive me if those don't sound much help against a trench mortar and Jerry coming at you with a bayonet. No offence, Hans,' he added. The German lad picking lice out of his beard with the use of a candle and a mirror waved the insult away. 'Are there songs? Does your Moccus offer virgins in heaven?'

There was more laughter at this. Only Potch, the cook, who had known Bill longer than any of them, didn't join in. 'Don't provoke him,' he warned the deserter.

Bill drew out his knife.

Everett jumped to his feet and stepped back. 'Now hold on there a moment, chum...'

'I told you,' Potch murmured, watching with interest. Activity in the cellar had stopped; white eyes in the gloom turned their way, wary. It wouldn't be the first fight – or death – this room had witnessed.

But it seemed that fighting to defend his faith was not what Bill had in mind. 'There's this,' he said, pulling up his sleeve, and then drawing the blade across the underside of his forearm. The cut was shallow but bled in a quick, red flood. He winced a little, put the knife down, gripped the cut with his other hand and then wiped the blood away. Where it should have bled afresh, there was the shining pink line of a new scar.

Everett gaped while the other men, evidently familiar with such small miracles and uninterested in the conversation now that it seemed unlikely to become violent, went back to their business. He felt his lungs go into spasm and sat back down heavily as coughing wracked him. 'Well,' he wheezed, wiping blood from his lips with the back of one hand. 'You've convinced me. I could do with a bit of whatever you're selling. Consider me a convert. Where do I sign up?'

'It's not as simple as that. If this ever ends,' Bill said, with an upward nod that meant not just the outside but the whole war, 'and you're alive to see what comes next, find a village called Swinley, on the Welsh Marches in Shropshire. That's where you'll find us: the Farrow. It's where our god walks – you can make your case directly to him.'

3

SWINLEY

THE DESERTER WASN'T CONVINCED THAT THE WAR would end. With his past lost behind that wall of thunder, and along with it any clear recollection of a time of peace, it seemed entirely possible that no such state had existed, that slaughter and mud and mangled flesh had been the condition of mankind forever and would continue forever, war without end, amen. He wasn't persuaded by the way other men claimed to recall such a time and told stories about it. The members of the Grey Brigade rarely offered insights about their pasts, presumably fearing betrayal to the authorities and a firing squad, and it was easy to dismiss those that did talk about their lives before as madmen. There were plenty of men in the trenches who were shell-shocked and suffering from all manner of absurd fantasies – what more absurd than a world of green grass, trees, and birdsong? Then the Loos offensive was launched, and in the botched attempts to cut the German wire an artillery barrage brought down the cellar roof, killing half of the Brigade along with Bill, and his particular absurdity died with him. Apparently his unnatural healing couldn't do much in the face of several tons of stone and earth. The Allied offensive rolled over their position in a wave of steel and thunder, and while the surviving Wild Deserters tried to flee before it Everett let himself literally sink beneath it as it passed, reasoning that the world would have its way with him and there was little he could do about it.

When British arms pulled him out of the mud they found a man dressed in the rags of a British uniform but who, despite speaking English with an accent which sounded vaguely Midlands, claimed to have no memory of where he was from or what had happened to him. This in itself was not unusual, but the lack of any insignia, tags, or documents to give a clue as to his identity caused more suspicious voices to suggest that he was simply shamming and really a deserter. Nonsense, it was countered, who in their right mind would desert *forward*, into No Man's Land? And so he was declared to be suffering from shell-shock and sent to an army hospital at Langres, where the surgeons confirmed that diagnosis and added tuberculosis to the list, and he was invalided out to an asylum for enlisted men called Scholes Farm on the outskirts of Birmingham.

Here, for the first time, he felt truly afraid.

He saw strong men reduced to stammering and twitching puppets, jerked by invisible strings that tied them inescapably to the horrors that they had experienced – weeping, vomiting, pissing themselves like infants. Still, for them there was some hope, however thin, that their minds might be healed. Worse were the ones who retained their clarity of mind within mutilated bodies – who had lost faces, limbs, genitalia, and who knew that nothing would ever make them whole again – but even for them the damage was done, and as bad as it was, wouldn't get any worse. For himself, the consumption that ate away at his lungs was a death sentence by slow and insidious degrees. The best that he could hope for was a massive haemorrhage and a swift bleeding-out. At worst, the disease would spread into his bones and brain, causing meningitis and warping his spine, trapping him in the rotting corpse of his own body.

Through the winter of 1915, a cheerless Christmas and the hollow promise of the New Year he got used to being awoken in the night by the sound of running footsteps and screams, often his own, and so the first time that Bill came to visit him was peculiar in its absolute silence.

He could not recall the process of waking up; one moment he was asleep and the next awake with the stark clarity of a gunshot. At first he couldn't work out why. There was no noise from anywhere else in the building, just the ticking of his wristwatch on the bedside table, and then he became aware of the human silhouette watching him from the corner of the room. Something about the figure gleamed. He could make out no features and yet he knew instinctively that it was Bill, an understanding confirmed by the lighter shine of a boar-tusk bracelet around his wrist. The deserter waited for his visitor to say something. Then either he moved, or the thin light through the curtains changed fractionally because the deserter could now see the condition in which

Bill had chosen to visit him: he was naked and slicked with blood from huge wounds where his flesh appeared to have been gouged – no, not cut, the deserter realised, but eaten. Then he was gone as suddenly as he'd appeared.

Bill returned for the next two nights, but not again afterwards. It never occurred to the deserter that it might have been a hallucination. The bloody footprints that his old friend had left were real enough, though the deserter made sure that he cleaned them away so that the doctors didn't see them and think that he was up to anything unusual. Bill had simply, for whatever reasons of his own, chosen to visit him from the No Man's Land between life and death.

Time and again he dreamed of that conversation in the cellar, Bill drawing a neat scar across his forearm, and the boar-tusk bracelet on his wrist, while his cough grew steadily worse. He searched county maps of Shropshire for a village called Swinley, and found it hidden in a narrow valley amongst the tumbled folds of hills right on the border with Wales.

The locks and bars of Scholes Farm Asylum were no more effective as barriers against him than the barbed wire and craters of the Western Front had been. He stole clothes, money, and identity papers from the other inmates, who didn't need them and probably wouldn't notice their absence anyway. It was January, the worst possible month for a man with a lung condition to be travelling, but instead of convalescing by a warm fire he travelled by train out through Wolverhampton and the Black Country, enduring a series of draughty third-class railway carriages and long waits in damp station waiting rooms until he reached the market town of Church Stretton, which huddled below the sombre bulk of a hill called the Long Mynd. Despite being the low season, it was impossible to find a guest house vacancy for the night, since at the first sign of his cough the proprietors would close their doors to him, terrified of the disease he carried. It also meant that there were no brakes to be hired and he was forced to walk up the hill road and onto the unsheltered moorland plateau of the Mynd. It was not especially steep but with his lungs the going was strenuous. For a place that billed itself to summer day-trippers as 'Little Switzerland', he saw no majestic snow-capped peaks, just a succession of grey slopes looming out of the drizzle like waves of a cheerless sea, and the closest he got to a buxom blonde milkmaid was a fat dairy farmer called Jones who let him sit in the back of his cart amongst the rattling milk churns.

The countryside on the other side of the Mynd was a tangle of narrow lanes and high hedgerows running between farms and small villages, mostly without signposts since presumably the locals knew where everything was, but if he'd been alone and on foot he'd have soon become hopelessly lost. As it was, Jones the farmer deposited him at a junction with an even smaller road – little more than a track between close-crowded trees – assured him that it was the road to Swinley, and continued on his way.

It was cold under the trees. They pressed close on either side and tangled heavy limbs overhead like the fingers of hands steepled in dark rumination, while the undergrowth filled the space between their trunks, holly and hawthorn as thick with barbs as any coil of barbed wire. There was no wind, and yet he fancied that he heard faint rustlings, either of the trees themselves or something moving stealthily amongst them, keeping pace with him.

At a turn in the track he saw, blocking his way, an animal that he at first took to be a pig, covered in a dark, bristling hide with stiff hackles, and tusks curved both up and down either side of its snout. A boar, then. But surely extinct in Britain? It was statue-still in the middle of the path, staring at him, daring him to dispute its existence. There seemed no point in trying to hide his purpose, so he said, 'I'm looking for the followers of Moccus.'

The boar regarded him, almost as if it understood, then uttered a rattling, full-throated squeal and dashed back into the undergrowth. The deserter waited for any further reaction from the surrounding woods, but none came, so he took that as encouragement and pressed on.

Bill had called Swinley a village, but it was really more of a large farmstead surrounded by a cluster of satellite cottages and outbuildings hidden behind tall hedgerows and the coats of their own ivy, and separated from each other by a patchwork of small fields. There was even a church steeple rising from the midst. Beyond and above it reared the slope of another steep hill, wooded for the most part but bare where trees gave way to heather and the tumbled mass of a granite outcrop. Swinley appeared to be perfectly ordinary, probably unchanged since the time of Shakespeare, except that as he wandered its narrow lanes looking for someone to whom he could present himself, he saw no sign of people at all. Even in winter there should have been someone working the fields. He decided to make for the church: if the village had a centre it would be there, though if Bill had been telling the truth that the inhabitants of this place worshipped something other than a Christian god, he did wonder what kind of a church it would be.

Again, perfectly ordinary, as it turned out. According to a noticeboard by the lychgate this was The Church of St Mark's in the Parish of Swinley. *Mark's*, he thought. *Moccus*. Now more than ever he suspected that this whole affair was nothing more than the brain-fever of a man no saner than the rest of the madmen. He saw weathered stone, lichen-spotted headstones, and a stout oak door standing open to the church's porch. From inside he heard a woman's voice singing – not a hymn, but something with lilt and sparkle, something about a sailor and his bonnie bride.

The deserter entered. In the porch a waxed jacket hung above a pair of muddy wellingtons, and the singing, soft though it was, was picked up by the building's vaulted interior so that it seemed to come out of the very stones. As he opened the inner door the coolness of stone and the warm smell of furniture polish and old carpet folded around him. He saw ranks of darkly gleaming oak pews and a pulpit, a paraffin heater doing its best against the chill, stained-glass windows, and the singer, in the process of polishing the pulpit's brass fittings, turning in surprise.

She was young, with dark hair wound up in a chignon, and wearing a pair of bib overalls like a munitionette. Cool blue eyes regarded him with the kind of still, silent appraisal that reminded him oddly of how the boar on the path had watched him. He could well imagine how he must look to her: a scarecrow of a man, dripping wet, in a threadbare suit. 'Who are you?' she demanded. 'What do you want?'

Before he could reply, a fit of coughing wracked him, and when he could catch his breath replied, 'My name is Everett. I'm looking for the followers of Moccus. The, uh, the Farrow.'

She at least did him the courtesy of not feigning ignorance. 'Oh are you, now? And what makes you think you'll find them here?'

He told her a highly selective tale of how he had met Bill and what the other man had shown him. 'He must have been from here,' the deserter finished. 'Did you know him?'

'Come with me,' was all she said. She bundled her cleaning things into a bucket and edged past him down the aisle to the door, where she looked back to see that he hadn't moved. He'd just noticed that there was something very odd about the images depicted by the stained-glass windows. 'Well?' she said. 'Are you coming or not?'

'Sorry, yes.' He shook himself and followed.

'You look like you could do with a cup of tea and a hot meal, if nothing else. My name is Ardwyn.'

She led him out through the churchyard and to a neighbouring cottage – an ancient and rambling building with a humpbacked thatch roof and a chimney of granite. In the yard outside they passed an absolutely huge man with a slab of a jaw chopping wood, with whom Ardwyn stopped to have a few quiet words before leading the deserter on. The wood-chopper watched him pass with a frown of distrust.

'Afternoon, chum,' the deserter nodded.

The big man responded by baring his teeth in what could never have been mistaken for a smile. For a start, he had far too many of them; they crowded his mouth like headstones and looked more like tusks than human teeth.

'That's Gar,' said Ardwyn. 'He doesn't speak much.'

'I can see why.'

Everett was ushered into a kitchen with a ceiling so low that for a moment he was in the cellar again and Potch the cook was at the table with his knife, taking the meat off a man's shoulder, and the deserter swallowed against the sudden rolling hunger in his guts and clenched his eyes shut, and when he opened them again Potch was gone, replaced by a middle-aged woman in an apron, chopping nothing more contentious than parsnips.

'This is Mother,' said Ardwyn. 'Tell her what you told me.' So while Ardwyn busied about pouring tea and setting a plate of bread, cheese and, cold ham before him, he told the older woman the same story. She quizzed him closely on his description of Bill, nodded and said, 'Now tell me the rest of it.'

'I'm sorry, I don't know what you mean.'

'Yes you do. You've just described my son and told me that he died bravely and honourably in the trenches, but Bill wasn't his name. His real name was Michael.' Ardwyn was weeping with her arms tightly crossed but her mother's eyes were dry, her voice calm and steady. She might weep for her dead son but not now, not in front of him, a stranger. 'Why would Michael lie about who he was, especially if you were so close with him that he told you about his faith?'

'The Wild Deserters weren't exactly the sort of chaps you used your real name with,' he replied. 'I'm sure he meant to tell me eventually – probably here, when it was all over. But then artillery barrages have a tendency to be a nuisance to one's long-term plans, don't you know.'

She came around the table, wiping her hands on her apron and perched on the corner, fixing him with the same blue eyes as her daughter. 'So, what name did he know you by?' she asked. 'Who are you? If he told you such things he must have seen something in you that would flourish here, in our particular situation. But I hear nothing of that in the story you've told. If you want to enjoy the favour of He Who Eats the Moon, tell me who you are, really.'

The deserter pushed his plate away. 'All right, then. My name might as well be Everett, for all I know. As for the rest...' He shrugged, and told her all of it. He had nothing to lose; if they were revolted and threw him out, then so be it. It was a relief, in the end, not having to maintain a façade of respectability to protect the sensibilities of people who could not possibly comprehend what had been done to him and what he had done in return, in order to survive.

When he was done they did not throw him out, nor did they look particularly revolted. Mother nodded slowly. 'Thank you,' she said.

'You don't seem to be too surprised by any of this,' he commented.

'You'll find that our particular circumstances here mean

that we have to be a bit more open-minded than most. When you're washed and presentable I'll show you what I mean.' To her daughter, she added, 'Show him to Michael's room. His things should just about fit.'

'We're taking him in, then?' Ardwyn looked him up and down with evident distaste.

'You disagree, I take it.'

'He's scrawny, and sickly. And a liar.'

'Thanks,' the deserter muttered.

'And for all we know he could have murdered Michael himself. We've only got his word for any of this.'

'Now wait a moment…'

But the women carried on talking over him as if he wasn't there.

'That is true,' said Mother. 'But even if it were, so much the better that he take on the responsibilities that Michael abandoned when he left us.'

'But he—'

'Enough! We will give him the benefit of the doubt, for Michael's sake. If he proves incapable of living up to it, well then the Recklings can have him for their sport.'

'Wait,' the deserter repeated in sudden alarm. 'Recklings? Who are the Recklings? What do you mean, sport?'

Ardwyn was looking at him now with something approaching a smile, but he was not altogether comfortable with what it implied. 'Do you know what?' he said. 'I've been very rude. Thank you for your kind hospitality and for your food.' He got up from his chair and backed towards the kitchen door. 'I feel that I've imposed too much on your time already. You have a charming village. Utterly charming.' He was retreating towards the back door, and they were making no move to stop him. 'I would love nothing more than to stay longer but I must be getting back or I'll miss the last train.' He turned, opened the back door, and found himself face to face with Gar, who was cradling his axe casually across his great barrel of a chest. His eyes were entirely without whites, the tawny brown of his irises filling their orbits completely. 'Steady now, chum,' said the deserter. 'I don't want any trouble.'

Gar shook his head, and his mouth worked slowly, trying to fit the immensity of those teeth around the shapes of human speech. 'No truh-bull,' he growled.

'Gar is one of the Recklings,' said Mother from behind him. 'The children of Moccus. The servants of the Farrow. He's very helpful to us – does a lot of the heavier jobs around the village and looks after us. For example, if there are people who need keeping out, he keeps them out.'

'And if they need keeping in too,' added Ardwyn. He felt her hand slip into the crook of his elbow. 'Come on. When was the last time you had a decent bath?'

4

DE-TUSKING

MOTHER LED HIM OUT TO THE WOODS ON THE OTHER side of the village, which were even thicker, if that were possible, then along the entrance road. Here there was no road, just a well-worn footpath twisting uphill between ancient elms and oaks, their trunks moss-muffled and many times wider than a human armspan. Here and there outcrops of the granite bedrock erupted like half-glimpsed ruins. Birdsong was muted, and the light was dim. He knew that it was only a few hundred yards before woodland gave way to the heath and towering height of the peak known locally as Edric's Seat, but for the moment it felt like the forest spread unbroken and untrodden for hundreds of miles, if not forever.

'This wood hasn't been touched by human hands for over two thousand years,' said Mother as she led the way deeper. 'This was once part of the tribal lands of the Cornovii people – that's what the Romans called them, anyway, and even that word might be overstating it. They were more like a loose confederation of tribes who shared a similar language and beliefs. They revered Moccus, and when the Romans invaded the local Cornovii called on him to protect them. And he did.'

They came to a wide clearing, empty except for a single tall stone set at the centre. Although the clearing was grassy, the ground immediately surrounding the stone was bare and black, and the stone was carved with elaborate curvilinear knotwork and tableaux that he couldn't quite make out yet from this distance.

'Moccus is a protector of hunters and warriors,' she continued, leading him towards the stone. 'Especially hunters of boar, which was a sacred animal to those people, and still is. A cohort of soldiers from the Fourteenth Legion was sent here to suppress the locals, who led them to this spot, from which the Romans never returned. Moccus tore them apart – five hundred fully armed legionnaires.'

'You mean this clearing is one whole mass grave?'

She nodded. 'Their blood sanctifies this soil. It is a hallowed place for us. I take it that doesn't disturb you?'

He looked around at the green, level grass and the black soil surrounding the stone. 'I've seen worse.'

They were at the stone now. It reared ten feet high, carved on all sides with scenes of battle and slaughter in which one figure dominated repeatedly: a man of towering stature with the head and tusks of a boar. One image on the battle tableau showed a Cornovii warrior holding something that looked like a war-horn to his mouth, except that it was extremely tall, rising in an elongated S-shape like a striking cobra – if any cobra had the head of a boar.

'That is a carnyx,' Mother explained, when he pointed it out. 'The horn that summons Moccus.'

'Pretty useful god if he can just be summoned like that. Does he do tricks too? Roll over? Play dead?'

'He will heal your body and give you a lifespan many times that of a normal man – will that do for a trick?'

Bordering the scenes of carnage were images of crops and copulation: sheaves of wheat and vines entwined with phalluses and figures fucking in every conceivable position, some surely beyond the flexibility of human physiology.

'If you don't mind me saying so,' he said, 'Bill I understand, but you don't seem to be a village of Celtic hunter-warriors to me.'

'I was speaking simplistically, in terms that you would understand,' she replied, and he felt a dull flare of resentment at being patronised. 'Moccus is the hunter because he is the boar, which is the oldest of all sacred animals. His tusks are the crescent horns of the moon, which he holds between his jaws, and so like the moon he is both eater and renewer, death-bringer and life-giver. His favour brings us fertility, bountiful harvests, and good health—'

'That,' the deserter interrupted. 'I want that. You want blood – well, I've shed enough of that for other people so it's about time I spilled some of it for myself. You want my soul...' He laughed at the sky. 'You're welcome to it. I've no use for the wretched thing any more. My lungs are full of holes – the doctors say I'll be dead in a year, eighteen months at best.'

'In that case for your sake I hope that you're able to hang on until September.'

'Why's that? What happens in September?'

'The autumnal solstice. That is when, if you're worthy, you will meet him.'

'Meet him?'

'Unlike the Christian god, who defers his rewards until his worshippers are dead and unable to enjoy them, Moccus delivers his favour here, on earth. In the flesh.' She indicated the surrounding woodland. 'He's out there now, walking his domain. He populates the woods with his children, got sometimes on the wild boar that are still hereabouts, sometimes on the women of the neighbouring villages. You've already met one of them.'

'Gar.'

She nodded. 'He's probably watching you right now, curious about whether or not you have the strength of character to become one of us – one of the Farrow.'

'I do!' Everett strode to the trees at the clearing's edge and peered into their shadow. 'I'm ready to do this now!' he called. 'Whatever this is!'

'You don't honestly think it's that easy, do you? You need to prove yourself.'

'Fine. How do I do that, then?'

Mother regarded him with an amused smile. 'That depends. How good are you at catching wild boar?'

Not very good, as it turned out. It took him a good month before he was able to snatch a piglet away from its screaming, furious mother. In that time, he moved into one of the cottages that the war had emptied and set to repairing both it and himself. He met many of the other villagers, and discovered that they were all either women or children; even given the fact that the war had reaped so many such villages of their menfolk it was odd to find none at all. Other than Gar, he seemed to be the only adult male for miles around. As the weeks passed he put on weight, most of it muscle, and even his cough abated somewhat. He also made a number of advances towards Ardwyn, but was even less successful with this human quarry; although her opinion of him had warmed, she firmly but good-naturedly rebuffed him at every turn, leaving him in another No Man's Land of seething frustration. She was unshocked by his crude ways, treating him with an amused coolness which he found as infuriating as it was arousing. 'Catch your boar,' was all she said. 'And we'll see.'

'All right, then, now I've caught one,' he said, showing her the small, striped bundle of panic that was squealing and dashing around the pen he'd built in his backyard. It was tethered to one of the fence posts and going nowhere, but it didn't know that. He'd already decided to call it Nikolai. 'What do I do now?'

'You look after it,' said Ardwyn. 'You raise it until its lower tusk curves back on itself, and then you sacrifice it to Moccus and you become one of the Farrow. And I,' she added, twining her arms around and pressing her curves against him, 'become yours. After a fashion.' She kissed him, and she tasted of apples.

The grisliest part of looking after Nikolai was over soon, mercifully: the de-tusking.

The boar's lower tusks were called its 'cutters', he was told, and they would continue to grow throughout the animal's life, kept sharp and to a reasonable length by the grinding action of the upper tusks, called its 'whetters', and these were the ones that had to be cut short so that over time the cutters would grow unchecked and curve back on themselves in a loop. He would wear this as a bracelet once Nikolai was sacrificed and he was made one of the Farrow.

Everett, Gar, and Ardwyn had the piglet in a 'crush' pen with its backside wedged into a corner. A rope noose was looped around its upper snout and behind the front tusks, with Gar on the other end holding it steady. The animal was making a continual deep-throated squealing, mightily displeased by its situation.

'I notice you're not wearing one,' the deserter said to her. 'It seems to be only the men. Why is that?'

'Because we have nothing to prove,' she replied, flashing him an insolent grin. 'Boars are matriarchal. They group in sounders around a few dominant females. Males are solitary, meanwhile, joining the sounder only to breed. They have to demonstrate their worthiness.'

'We're not pigs, though.'

She looked him up and down. 'That's debatable. This small, angry animal is you; it is your masculine power which you must cherish, nurture, tend, and eventually sacrifice to Moccus, taking the tusk circle as a symbol that you have given yourself to him.'

'So how long will it take to grow?'

'This little chap should come to maturity in another two to three years.'

The deserter laughed so hard that it brought on a coughing fit, and he had to lean against the fence to catch his breath. 'I'm not going to survive the next winter, never mind three years.'

'You would be surprised what the favour of Moccus can do.' She gave him a cheesewire saw with sturdy wooden handles at each end. 'Come on.'

Somewhat nervously, he strung the wire saw behind one of Nikolai's whetters while Gar held its mouth open. The young boar's eyes rolled and glared at them both. 'I'm not enjoying this any more than you are, chum,' the deserter muttered, pulled back on the wire and began to draw the saw back and forth against the rear of the tusk.

Nikolai *really* didn't like this. The noise he made was like a drill in the deserter's skull. Ardwyn told him to hurry up, so he did, and smoke came from the saw along with the stench of burning tooth. Abruptly, the tusk sheared free, and the release of tension sent the deserter sprawling on his arse in the mud. Gar roared with laughter.

'That's one,' said Ardwyn, smiling.

Sighing, the deserter picked himself back up.

5

THE RECKLINGS

HE EXPLORED THE VILLAGE AND WALKED OFTEN IN the woods around Swinley looking for the god but without success. The only sighting of Moccus he had was in the stained-glass windows of St Mark's church: they repeated the images engraved on the obelisk in the woods. Where Jesus Christ would have stood in the central panel, boar-headed Moccus raised his hand in beatific blessing, showering fruits and corn onto the multitudes fornicating in the panels below, while to either side men were speared, decapitated, and disembowelled. The deserter often heard furtive rustlings accompanying him from the shadows beneath the trees. Gar's cousins, if he was to believe what he'd been told, but by then he was swinging back around to the conviction that this was all an elaborate hoax, or at best a collective delusion, and the creatures in the bushes nothing but rabbits, badgers, or just more boar.

In a black mood he sought out Gar, and found him hacking a tree stump out of a field with a huge mattock. His bare torso was shining with sweat, and a pelt of coarse black hair which might have belonged on an animal spread across his shoulders and narrowed to a point down his spine. With each blow, clods of earth and splinters of wood flew everywhere, and the deserter had to blink away the sudden vision of artillery explosions launching geysers of mud and human remains into the sky. The remembrance just made his mood fouler. There was only so long a man could be fobbed off.

'Gar!' he called.

Gar paused in his work, leaning on the mattock handle. He grunted.

'They say you're a child of Moccus, is that right?'

Another grunt.

'And all his other children are out there in the woods capering like pixies, aren't they? Though I'll be blowed if I've seen any of them.'

Gar shrugged and sniffed, picked up the mattock and prepared to swing.

'Well, I want to meet them.'

Gar put the mattock back down and looked closely at the deserter, narrowing his eyes. 'Mee hem,' he rumbled, drooling a little as the words struggled to emerge from around his mouthful of tusks.

'Yes, meet them. Because you're a big lad and all, but I'm having a hard time believing that's down to anything other than your mummy and your daddy's branches growing a little too close on the family tree, if you take my meaning.'

If Gar had taken offence, or even fully understood the insult, he didn't show it, but simply shrugged again and set off for the edge of the field with the mattock slung over one shoulder. The deserter hurried after.

Past the clearing with Moccus' stone the ground delved sharply into a gully carved by a stream from the hilly slopes above. It was treacherous with mossy boulders and dark with the dripping gloom of overhanging beeches, whose roots, snaking over and around the rocks, threatened to trip him at every turn. Gar stopped at a place where the tumbling water formed a basin, and his face split in a smile. 'You mee hem,' he repeated, then cupped his hands around his mouth and let loose a volley of barking grunts into the shadows, calling to his kin.

And they came, but if he'd expected the half-human spawn of a god to be something majestic or terrifying, he was wrong.

They were tentative, fearful, hiding themselves behind tree trunks or peering from under the arches of roots. No two were alike, though all carried with them in differing degrees the taint of something boar-like in their blood. He couldn't tell which of them were the products of Moccus' bestiality and which were from lying with human women. He imagined that some might feel it an honour to be visited thus by their god, but what must the mother feel as she came to term, wondering what might emerge from between her legs? Some were little more than animals themselves, though with human hands or eyes. Others were more human, though nowhere near enough as Gar to be able to pass as normal villagers. Some had limbs that were too short, or too long, or missing altogether, and dragged themselves along on stumps like some of the men in the asylum. He saw snouts, tusks, and the split pads of trotters for hands. Moccus might very well be a fertility god, thought the deserter, but evidently the seed did not always grow true. Seeing them, he felt no fear, only a rolling swell of pity for such creatures trapped in a No Man's Land of their own – one that was carried in their blood.

Something woman-shaped stepped forward, trying to stand upright on knees that bent the wrong way. She was covered in a pelt of light-coloured hair that became striped over her hips and dark below that, but was otherwise naked, and he tried not to stare at the twin rows of small breasts that descended her torso.

'New. Man,' she said. Her mouth was better shaped than Gar's for speech, though again, tusks got in the way.

The deserter nodded. 'Everett,' he said, checking the absurd impulse to hold out his hand. Her right arm ended in a thumb and half a trotter where the other four fingers should have been.

'Sus,' she indicated herself. 'Do you have food?'

'Oh, ah, no, sorry, I didn't think. I don't have any on me.'

Sus made a gesture of disgust and dismissal, and turned to leave.

'Wait!'

She turned back.

'Where is your father? Where is Moccus?'

She peered around, at the enclosing woods, listening,

sniffing. 'He walks,' she said. 'Soon he will come to the stone, and they will dance for him. We are his Recklings. His runts. We do not dance.' She disappeared back into the trees. Since he had no food, the others quickly lost interest in him too, and that being the sum total of all he was going to find out, it seemed, he followed Gar back to the village.

After supper that evening he asked Ardwyn about them. 'Isn't there something you can do for them?'

'Do? Like what? We put food out for them. We find work and homes for the ones like Gar who are capable of it and want it, and the ones in the woods provide us with some measure of security. What should we do instead, keep them as pets? Put them in pens and cages? Those that can think don't want that. They're wild, free creatures. You should understand that, being a Wild Deserter yourself.'

'I suppose so. They just seem so lost.'

'They are our brothers and sisters. We are all Moccus' children, more or less.'

'Some more, some less, it seems. One of them spoke to me.'

'Oh?'

'Yes, she said that he will come to the stone, and then they will dance for him. What does that mean?'

'It means that you're not one of the Farrow yet, and when you are you'll understand. In the meantime, look after your piglet.'

The deserter grinned. 'I'd rather you look after my "piglet",' he leered, and reached for her, but she skipped out of his reach, silver-quick as ever, laughing.

Denied the pleasure of her company once again, he

decided that the only reasonable alternative was to get blotto and so went in search of Gar, who he found in the barn mending some rabbit snares. 'While I am not normally given to self-pity,' he announced, plonking himself down on a crate uninvited, 'I find that on this occasion I am prepared to indulge myself. I have a terminal lung condition, a beautiful woman who refuses to fuck me until I convert to her religion, and my occupation now appears to be swineherd to one very small and angry pig. At times like this it behoves a man to get gloriously drunk with his chums and you, my terrifyingly huge friend, are the closest to it. So.' He produced from his coat pocket a bottle sloshing half full of brandy. 'What do you say?'

Gar pointed at the bottle. 'Wot.'

'Eh? This? You mean what is this?'

'What?'

'Oh my poor chap!' The deserter laughed. 'I didn't realise! You have it so much worse than me!' And he passed Gar the bottle.

Sitting by the fireside, Ardwyn looked up from her book. 'What is that horrible noise?'

Her mother, who was doing the household accounts, didn't look up. 'It's just the men, dear,' she replied. 'Just the men.'

6

THEOPHAGY

Towards the beginning of March activity in Swinley increased – cottages that had lain closed and empty were opened, swept, and aired. Cartloads of food arrived and were stored away in larders and pantries. Daffodils, primroses, hellebores, and hyacinths appeared in tubs under windows, beside front doors, and all along the path leading up to the great clearing. Then the first visitors began to arrive – on foot, by horse, and by motor vehicle – and the deserter realised that the Farrow were not a small and local group but had adherents all over the country. There were a few single, unattached men, all of them wearing tusk bracelets, but the majority were married couples, obviously very wealthy to judge from their clothes and large number of suitcases – some had even brought servants. Did Moccus' favour make them rich or attract the already well-off? If they all possessed the same sort of longevity that Bill had boasted of, maybe they'd simply had more time to accumulate their wealth. Too rich to be called upon for active service, that was for certain – no doubt working in sectors 'crucial for the war effort' and profiteering from it nicely besides. Far too busy to volunteer in the hospitals. These were the same type of people as the generals who sat in comfortable offices miles behind enemy lines and gave the orders to send thousands of young men into the meat grinder to gain a few yards of mud. He hated them instantly. He'd been hating them since before he met them.

Mother knew them all by name and embraced them warmly, along with her daughter. The only thing that made this bearable was how obviously deferential they were to her despite their trappings of power. Ardwyn was kept busy looking after the guests and she had little time to spare for his questions, but he caught up with her as she was taking delivery of a cartload of bread. 'It's the spring equinox,' she said. 'The most important celebration in our calendar.'

'Bit of a knees-up, is it? Bit of a sing-song?'

'Sort of. We summon the god, sacrifice him, butcher his flesh and eat it.'

'Ha ha, very funny. You should do music halls with that act.'

She gave him a withering look and continued ticking off a wad of receipts.

'No,' he said, realising that she was absolutely serious. 'No!'

'Is that so strange to you? The Christians have been doing it every Sunday for two thousand years.'

'I don't think that's exactly what the miracle of transubstantiation means.'

'Well, I'm afraid I don't really have the time for a long theological discussion at the moment.'

'But that's what keeps you strong and healthy, right? Stops you from growing old?'

She sighed. 'We enjoy the blessing of the first flesh – we take the strength of Moccus into ourselves, if that's what you mean.'

'That's what I want! It's what I've come for!'

'Out of the question – at least for now.'

'But—'

'No! It's the most hallowed sacrament of our worship! You can't just barge in here as a complete stranger and expect to take that kind of communion after only a couple of months!'

'Mother said that I could meet him in September,' he pointed out.

'And you will, but you still won't be one of the Farrow. You'll be a privileged spectator, at best. Every one of those men has completed what you've only just started: spent years raising their boar—'

'Been a glorified pig-keeper, you mean.'

'Yes! Except that you still think of it as a low, dirty animal, which is the first thing you've got to purge from your thinking. The first of so many. You don't understand what Moccus is. For women there's no danger because he doesn't see us as a threat. But if you, a soldier, and one who's eaten human flesh at that—'

'If you're trying to shame me, it won't work.'

'I'm not trying to shame you, you idiot, I'm trying to protect you! I'm trying to explain that if you approach

Moccus without due deference and humility – without having devoted part of yourself to caring for one of his creatures – he will rip you apart!'

'And I'm trying to tell you that I don't have however many years that would take still left in me! I'm not going to survive another winter, the doctors have told me that. So this whole tusk bracelet business is a total waste of bloody time! You want me here as much as I want to be here, we both know that. There's got to be something you can do!'

This tirade brought on a fresh bout of coughing, and he collapsed against the side of the bread cart, wiping blood from his lips. It stood out stark against the skull's pallor of his face. 'Deference and humility, is it?' he gasped. 'Fine then. I won't give it to him, whatever he is, if he even exists – not until he earns it. No god ever did anything for me. But I'll give it to you.' He slid to the ground and knelt in the road before her. He'd never begged for anything as far as he could remember; begging was simply an invitation to be kicked in the face. 'Please, Ardwyn, I'm begging you. I don't want to die. Help me.'

She hesitated for an age, then reached down and ran her fingers through his wild hair. 'You can't attend the sacrament,' she said softly. 'But there might be a way of bringing it to you. I'll talk to Mother.'

'Anything,' he whispered. 'Anything.'

On the evening of the equinox Ardwyn told him to wait in his cottage and be patient, but the deserter had no intention of sitting placidly at home while the Farrow performed their sacrament, and possibly she or Mother suspected as much because whenever he went anywhere near the woods on the eastern side of the village Gar was there, blocking his way. He saw armloads of blankets and firewood being taken up towards the clearing. He was permitted into the church where bundles of dried jimsonweed were being burned to produce a sweet-smelling smoke that made his head swim. He stood at the back and watched their liturgy. The celebrants arrived dressed in loose robes and wearing masks in stylised boar designs – some crude and plain, others gleaming with precious metals and gems like religious relics. They sang in a language he didn't understand; it sounded like Welsh, but he suspected it might have been that of the long-dead Cornovii. Eventually the celebrants made their way along the path into the woods, carrying burning torches, leaving him behind.

The deserter decided that he'd had enough pussy-footing around and strode brazenly up to where Gar was standing with his arms folded and his massive jaw set firm.

'No,' said the big man.

The deserter didn't say anything. He simply reached into his coat pocket and produced the replenished brandy bottle. He waved it at Gar, unscrewed the top, swigged, and then tossed it to the ground at Gar's feet. 'I think you know what I mean,' he said. 'All I want to do is look. Just look. I won't interfere, you have my word.'

Gar picked up the bottle and sniffed it. Then he took a quick step forward and grasped the deserter by the throat.

Shocked and choking, the deserter was positive that Gar's massive hand was meeting thumb-to-finger at the back of his neck. 'Wait…' he croaked.

'Uss ook,' Gar growled, his face inches from the deserter's, every peg-like tooth and tusk on display.

Everett nodded, unable to speak now.

'Uss ook, or…' Gar squeezed a fraction tighter, and black blotches began to crowd Everett's vision from the edges. Then he was released, and fell back, gasping.

'That sounds very reasonable,' he wheezed, and staggered past Gar into the trees.

The clearing was lit by flaming braziers set atop tall poles, which were burning the same jimsonweed as in the church, its smoke sweet and thick and heavy in the clearing. Beside the pillar a great bonfire had been built, and had obviously been burning for some time because it was by now a mound of glowing embers. The Farrow of Moccus had gathered in a loose circle around the stone pillar, having removed their robes but kept their masks. They stood naked and listened raptly – the men stroking their cocks, the women dipping between their legs – to a woman in the centre that he recognised as Mother from her voice as she declaimed to the congregation. Another woman stood close by who he assumed was Ardwyn; it was the first time he had seen her naked, and for a moment the sight of it blinded him to everything else. Then he realised that she was carrying a long, cloth-wrapped object which she unwound with reverent care and passed to Mother, who held it aloft.

It was a carnyx, the S-shaped war-horn of the Cornovii.

It was at least four feet tall, and it was made of bone. The upper end, the bell of the horn, was very definitely an actual boar's skull, but whether the rest of it was femur or vertebrae he couldn't tell. He could only think that it must somehow be decorated over an actual brass instrument because he couldn't see how that thing should be able to make any noise. Nevertheless, Mother raised the bone carnyx to her lips and blew a long, mournful note. It carried past the circle of worshippers, into the woods, through him, through his very bones, and every sinew, muscle fibre, and blood vessel sang in harmony with it so that his whole body felt like a tuning fork drawing the resonance out of him. His hair stirred on his scalp, his skin shivering with gooseflesh, his cock rigid in his pants. It was all he could do to stop himself from answering that call, breaking cover and running to prostrate himself before Mother.

She blew a second time, and the worshippers fell on each other. Some literally so – thrusting, grasping, sucking – in pairs and groups, copulating in combinations that in some cases he struggled to make sense of. For a man who believed himself incapable of being shocked by human depravity he was astonished – not by the acts he was witnessing, but by the energy of the participants. Most of them were middle-aged, with drooping breasts and flapping scrotums, yet they were going at it with all the fervour of dogs in the street. He understood the blankets spread out on the ground now, and he tried to follow what or who Ardwyn was doing, but it was impossible amidst the tangles of writhing limbs. Their gasps and cries filled the clearing. The smoke grew heavier and sweeter, and his head was swimming, sweat blurring his vision. The firelight that gleamed on backs, buttocks, and breasts began to resemble that of the flares drifting over No Man's Land, and the rutting figures were churning the grass to mud, in places so deep that they were sinking and stirring up objects long buried in the earth as if out of a cauldron: sandbags, duck-boards, barbed wire, and bodies. Pale limbs in rotting uniforms, rats and rifles. The orgiasts fucked the cadavers as eagerly as the living in anywhere that gaped, or filled themselves with death-stiff fingers. He saw a woman straddling the face of a corpse with half its skull blown away, and a man held aloft by barbed wire wrapped around each limb, being sodomised with a bayonet. The deserter reeled away, head and stomach both churning, his damaged lungs in revolt, coughing and vomiting over the bushes.

A third time, Mother blew the horn. Now, however, it seemed that she didn't so much create the sound as pull it out of the air, a note that had always been there unheard in the background, like the song of blood in the ear, from a time far down in the immeasurable well of the years when there was only woodland in whose shadow humanity crept fearfully, hunting aurochs with flint blades. The bone carnyx drew it out of the past and through the human bodies contorting around it, clothing itself with sound in the world, summoning.

And the god came.

The deserter heard it, something huge moving through the trees, pushing aside branches that stood higher than his head.

What emerged from the edge of the clearing walked like

a man, if a man ever grew to ten feet tall – naked, its limbs and torso busy with tattoos and the raised ridges of ritual scarification in spirals, stripes, and complex knots. From the shoulders up all semblance of humanity ended in a boar's head, its amber eyes reflecting the firelight back in twin points of yellow fire above a snout from which tusks curved like scythes.

But it was old, this thing. Peering harder through the stinging smoke, the deserter saw that its eyes were filmed with cataracts, its tusks were cracked and yellow, its once-broad chest was sunken above a sagging belly, and its wizened limbs shook with geriatric palsy as it regarded its worshippers. The black hide of its head and the hackles that ran down its spine were streaked silver-white. *How could this be their god?* he wondered. Moccus looked like he barely had the strength to keep himself upright, never mind any to spare for his faithful. The deserter's initial awe was quickly overtaken by disappointment and even a kind of pity.

He stepped over the rutting figures and closer to the stone, where several men who had remained aloof from the orgy were waiting, but instead of them making obeisance to the beast, Moccus knelt to them. Mother resumed her intonations as many pairs of hands grasped the god's outstretched arms and pulled, bringing his head lower, to within closer range of a great knife with a black, crescent-shaped blade that was held by one of the men. The sickle-wielder plainly had never done this before; he was nervous, the blade trembling in his hand, and at the height of Mother's chanting Moccus threw back his head with a roar that made the very flames sway, but the butcher made such a half-hearted and shallow sweep of the killing stroke that the beast was more maddened than hurt, and the other men struggled to hold him. If he hadn't already been so weak with age he'd have broken free and wrought carnage about the clearing. As it was, the only carnage was visited upon his throat – a messy, amateur hacking that the deserter found infuriating to witness. The least they could have done was make it quick. They tried to catch as much of his blood as they could – *cruor*, he heard them calling it – in three great bronze bowls but a lot of it was lost to the ground. Mother was saying: 'He Who Eats the Moon, we thank thee for this, thy bounty,' and in his memory the deserter saw Bill praying for the German boy that he'd killed for his leg.

As Moccus' convulsions ceased the orgiasts slowed their frenzies and gradually disengaged from each other, coming forward to cup their hands in the bronze bowls and ladle the god's cruor over their bodies, painting the stone with the rest. The butcher and his assistants prepared the carcass; certain items of the viscera were set aside (the heart and liver, he presumed) while the unwanted offal was taken into the woods for Gar's kin and the flesh was parcelled up in leaves and set amongst the bonfire's embers. He was watching them bury the head, hide, and bones at the foot of the pillar when he felt a tap on his shoulder, and whirled. It was Gar.

'Ee-nuff now,' he said. He was chewing on something, which rendered his speech even more indistinct than usual. 'Go.'

The deserter's sigh of relief deflated him. 'You know you move very quietly for a big lad,' he said.

Gar bunched a ham-sized fist in the front of his coat. 'Ee-nuff. Now. Go.'

'Fine, I'm going, I'm going.'

The only other people remaining in the village were the few servants and drivers, with whom he had no desire to make small talk, so he hid himself away in his cottage until Ardwyn came to find him a few hours later. She was dressed and clean and if he hadn't seen with his own eyes what she'd been doing up in the woods he wouldn't have believed it. Far from being revolted by her participation in the orgy, the thought of who she might have had between her legs only made him want her more. She produced a charred, leaf-wrapped bundle. From it arose the smell of roast pork, but it was richer than that, a deeper aroma that was familiar and set his mouth watering.

'I've persuaded Mother to let you have this,' she said. 'You have no idea how unprecedented it is. She must really want you to stay.'

He unwrapped it and looked at the handful of cooked meat. 'So, I just eat it, then?'

'You could try wearing it as a hat but I don't think it would be particularly effective.'

'No, I mean, do I need to say a prayer or anything?'

'That which you would pray to, you hold in your hand. What would be the point of prayer? Show your gratitude by accepting what is offered.'

So he ate.

It was heavier than pork, somewhere between that and man, though its effect on his system was much more immediate and pronounced. It reminded him of the one time he and Bill had found some dead stretcher-bearers and scavenged from their pockets the tins containing phials of morphine and ether. A dreamy languor spread out from his belly and into his limbs, and the tightness in his chest eased – a tightness that he'd lived with for so long that he'd become unaware of it until now, as it passed, and he drew in a huge lungful of air and laughed it out without coughing for the first time in as long as he could remember.

'My God, this is incredible!' He beamed at her, then took her around the waist and twirled her around the room, laughing.

'Your god indeed!' She laughed with him. 'So, does it taste like man? I've always wanted to know.'

'You want to know what man tastes like?' He grinned, pulling her towards the sofa. 'Let me help you find out.'

7

REPLENISHMENT

'NOW THEN,' SHE SAID AFTERWARDS, STRAIGHTENING her skirt as he sprawled naked beside her. 'I'm going to tell you something that you're not going to like hearing, but you're going to keep your mouth shut and not interrupt me and at the end of it you're going to agree with me, otherwise you leave here tonight and never return. Are we clear?'

He propped himself up on one elbow and frowned. 'Do I have a choice?'

'I've just told you what your choices are. Weren't you listening?'

'Then we're clear, I suppose.'

She reached between his legs and cupped her hand around his balls, caressing, and he grunted with pleasure. 'Tomorrow night, before everyone starts to leave, there will be a small dinner party at my mother's home, quite private, to which you will be invited as a courtesy.

Our guests will be my fiancé and his parents.'

The deserter opened his mouth. She tightened her grip on his balls, sharp nails digging, and he closed his mouth again. She relented, nodding approval.

'The Farrow who have come to our celebration are from all over the country, and it's not just for a bit of fun in the woods, or even an encounter with the sacred. We are not a cult, Everett, not a bunch of inbred country bumpkins or bored aristocrats. We are a church, and a church must be maintained financially, and for that a church must grow. Do you remember how I told you that the Farrow are matriarchal, like boar themselves?'

He nodded while trying to keep as still as possible, which wasn't easy. 'Males are solitary,' he said. 'They mate and they're off again. Right now I'm thinking they've got the right idea.'

She laughed a little, but didn't loosen her grip. 'Well, we may not be boar, but the principle is much the same; the other reason for our gathering is so that young, eligible, well-resourced young men can ally themselves with the daughters of influential families, who will leave to establish new churches, and so we grow. He provides the material security, she provides the spiritual leadership.'

'Seems fair,' he said. 'Listen, is there any way I could...'

'Shh,' she replied, and he shushed. 'The timescale is obviously longer than you might expect – the flesh of Moccus doesn't grant immortality but we tend to be extremely long-lived. The match that Mother made for me with Gus – that's his name – happened before you were born, and some year soon, when he is in a position to support a new church, we will be married and I will leave Swinley. Until then, you and I may do as we please, as long as you understand that I am not yours. I'm telling you this now because young men, like boar, tend to become territorial when a rival male appears, and, well, I like you, and I would hate for you to do something stupid and get yourself thrown out. Now, before I let you go, are you going to say something annoying or are we going to be grown-ups about this?'

'Believe me,' he said, 'the last thing I intend to do is annoy you.'

She let him go and he hurried to put his clothes back on.

'I don't know what you think I'm going to do about it,' he said, buttoning his shirt. 'Challenge him to a duel for your affections?'

'Hmm,' she replied, pretending to give it serious consideration. 'Which would you prefer: pistols at dawn or mounted lances in shining armour?'

'While you watch from the top of your ivory tower? Sorry, my lady.' He laughed and shook his head. 'You women. How it flatters you to think that we're all dripping hard and squaring up to compete for the privilege of rutting with you. You wave us off to fight with tears in your eyes. You love us when we're heroes, home on leave or wounded somewhere that doesn't turn us into stammering eunuchs, and you dole out white feathers to the chaps who won't or can't live up to your fairy-tale ideal. If I wanted to challenge this well-heeled beau of yours, whatever his damned name is, I'd bite his throat out in his sleep. But I'm not. I have no interest in him. I came here for me first and foremost, and while you've been a pleasant enough bit on the side, please don't imagine that I intend to endanger that by pandering to your romantic delusions.' He finished buttoning his shirt. 'I hope that wasn't too annoying.'

For a moment he thought she was going to slap him, but instead she took his face in her hands and kissed him full on the lips. 'Perfect,' she murmured against him. 'You're absolutely perfect.'

The last thing Everett wanted to do was sit down to dinner and make polite conversation. He wanted to take this newfound vitality and run with it into the night – run to the top of Edric's Seat and howl at the stars, or find Sus in the woods and see what it was like to fuck something nearly human, or get drunk with Gar and fight him until neither of them could stand. He almost told her that her dinner could go to the devil, but found that he was curious to see who or what she had been allied with, so he agreed.

His curiosity was not justified. Augustus Melhuish and his parents were no more or less than he'd expected: self-assured in their privilege and generous with their facile opinions about the war. While he found nothing threatening about the young man, Gus obviously found some in him, because he kept making arch comments about what a good *sport* Ardwyn was, and wasn't she such a *sport*, and didn't Everett think that she was a *sport*, as if to stake his claim over her, and because an annoying fly must eventually be swatted, the deserter found himself responding with, 'I'm curious as to what kind of *sport* you think she is, exactly, Gus. Something involving balls or one that requires a spirited mount?' which shut him up – at least until they were leaving.

When Gus found him, he was smoking a cigarette by Mother's sty of prize Welsh pigs, enjoying the darkness and the ability to draw a full lungful of smoke again without choking. The deserter was surprised to see that they too had participated in the feast; they were nosing in one of the great bronze bowls, and had licked it clean. These beasts were obviously more important than he had first thought. Then Gus arrived, interrupting his train of thought as he looked the deserter up and down with a contempt that he obviously practised on the lower orders.

'What are you, Everett – if that even is your name?' he sneered. 'What's a strong, healthy young man like you doing skulking out here amongst decent folk, instead of serving your King and country?' Wealth and breeding did not confer an overabundant sense of irony, it seemed. 'I bet you're a deserter, aren't you?'

The insight took Everett aback, and he looked at Gus more closely. Maybe there was something more going on behind those soft eyes than just self-regard.

'Yes, that's it, isn't it?' Gus persisted. 'I might have a bit of a word with some people my father knows at home. War Ministry folks, don't you know. Have them send some constables out here to find out who you really are.'

The deserter took a final drag on his cigarette and flicked it to the ground, extinguishing it beneath his heel. Then he leaned closer to Gus and sniffed. 'You smell of cloves,' he murmured, and sniffed again. 'And pepper. It must be whatever mouthwash or cologne you're wearing. Under that...' He inhaled more deeply. 'You've tried to wash off the smell of sex but it's still there.'

'What the bloody hell are you on about?' The other man flinched away from the deserter's proximity, but he followed, sniffing close to the line of Gus' jaw where it met his neck in the densely clustered trunk of veins and arteries.

'And talcum. Or flour. And lard. Lots of lard. Why, I bet if I killed you and boiled you down I could make some halfway decent dumplings out of you.'

'If that's your idea of a threat—'

'It's not a threat. It's more of a menu option.' Everett winked at him.

Gus stormed off and the deserter found that he was being watched by amber eyes. Mother's swine chewed, unimpressed.

'And you lot can shut up too.'

He slaughtered the first of them a month later.

'Let's face it,' Mother said to him. 'You're no farmer. You didn't seek us out to spend the rest of your long life digging turnips and milking cows, and I wouldn't be so foolish as to think if you ever did become one of the Farrow that you would stay with us for long afterwards. Fortunately, there is an important role that you can perform for us which doesn't require you to do so – in fact, it makes perfect sense for you to take it up since it was Michael's role too. You've replaced him in our community, you might as well replace him in our rituals too.'

It sounded ominous. 'What was his job?' the deserter asked warily. They were standing at her sty, watching her Welsh grunt and wallow contentedly.

'He was our slaughterman.'

'Of course, he was.' He almost added *and you bloody need one, after that botched mess at your orgy*, except that he wasn't supposed to have seen it. 'But I still haven't passed my initiation, or whatever you call it. Is that allowed?'

Mother's smile was thin, but not entirely humourless. 'What is allowed is what I judge best for the Farrow. It's why I'm going to overlook your threats towards Ardwyn's intended. This is a role for which it seems to me your skills and personality make you ideally suited, but don't worry if you don't feel up to it straight away. It will be twenty-six years before Moccus returns and you are needed, which gives you plenty of time to practise and for us to find a replacement if you turn out to be unsuited.'

'Why twenty-six years?'

'Because that is the duration of the cycle of Moccus. Do you want to spend years here learning about the lives of the stars and the planets, their correspondences with human souls, and the majestic mathematical balance of the universe? I can teach you the answer to that 'why' but I doubt you'd find it rewarding. You're even less a priest than a farmer.'

'Fair enough. But I'll be...' He stopped, realising that he had no idea how old he was. 'In my forties,' he finished.

'You won't feel it. Nor will you look it. You'll continue as strong and healthy as you are for a long while yet. But nothing is immortal, not even a god. Moccus takes on the burden of birth, ageing, and death so that we don't have to. For a while.'

She told him that the six months after Moccus' sacrifice between the equinoxes was a time of replenishment, when that which had been given was repaid. Replenishment came in the form of one perfect swine, sanctified by consumption of the first flesh, to be sacrificed to Moccus each month just after the new moon, when the waxing crescent formed the great boar-god's tusks. It was taken up to the clearing and slaughtered in a much smaller ceremony, which the deserter much preferred the sound of – anything instead of watching a bunch of middle-aged toffs humping each other.

When he'd killed the boy for his leg, the deserter had been starving, sick with neuralgia and barely aware of what he was doing. The first time he killed one of Mother's swine it was with absolute clarity. He felt the life of the creature thrumming through it as it was held, like a bowstring drawn back tight and ready to let fly, or a bullet in the breech, an explosive release waiting for just the slightest pressure of his fingers. It wasn't the sense of power that he experienced because the power wasn't his – it belonged to the arrow, the bullet, the creature, and the blood of the god that it had eaten. It was the sense of control over that power, the ability to unleash and direct it, to destroy or reorder the world with it at his whim, the intoxication of finally, *finally* not being at the mercy of vast forces beyond his comprehension but for once possibly being in charge of them. For the first time he thought he understood those fat generals issuing their orders, and it should probably have made him humble but instead all he could think was *More. How do I get more?* The animal squirming in his arms was just a pig; imagine spilling the lifeblood of a *god*.

The knife they gave him was an ancient thing, its sickle-shaped blade black and pitted with centuries of bloodletting, but the edge was as keen and bright as a slice of moonlight. It bit into the pig's throat with almost no resistance – he only knew how deeply he'd cut when he felt the blade scrape against vertebra. The blood pumped onto the bare, black earth at the foot of the obelisk where Mother had buried Moccus' head – pints of it swallowed up instantly as if the very earth thirsted for it.

'Moccus, be replenished,' the congregation around him intoned. 'Moccus, be renewed. Moccus, be reborn.'

Afterwards, he butchered the carcass – with the help of some of the older and more experienced men – and there was a hog roast on the village green, with music and dancing by firelight. A clay jar of cider kept over from last year's harvest was opened and he was given the first pint as a gesture of respect. All throughout the evening people kept coming up to him and congratulating him on a job well done, the first time in his damaged memory that he could recall anyone ever doing so. It made him profoundly uncomfortable at first, but he found that if he just smiled and nodded and said thank you, that was all they seemed to need and they went away happy again. Nobody seemed to mind that he wasn't yet wearing a tusk bracelet. Nikolai was growing well but his tusks were barely a quarter circle so far. He had never imagined that it could be so easy to make other people happy, or even that it was a thing he would value. He danced with Ardwyn, enjoying the way her eyes flashed and her hair smelled and her body moved beneath his hands in a way that wasn't sex.

That first time he was, admittedly, clumsy, but by the time September came and the harvest was being gathered in he had refined his technique month by month such that the beasts barely knew what was happening before it was over. Mother had been right, this suited him. In the meantime, he surprised himself by settling into village life quite comfortably. He made repairs to his cottage, fixing the roof and front door as best he could, and enjoyed sitting out on the lingering summer evenings, watching sparrows bickering in the honeysuckle, smoking or getting drunk with Gar. Beyond taking care of his own hearth and the monthly sacrifice, he didn't have to do any more work to earn his place in Swinley; the Farrow fed him, and there was plenty to go around.

8

THE SIXTH SACRIFICE

FOR THE FINAL REPLENISHMENT SACRIFICE THEY HAD adorned the obelisk with harvest bounty: barrels of apples and pears, crates tumbling full of marrows, onions, and a dozen other fruits and vegetables in abundance that he couldn't name. Sheaves of corn were stacked in pillars on either side of the stone. It was an obscene amount of food given that men fighting in the trenches were suffering from scurvy and malnutrition, but most of it would go on to be sold at local markets or to the War Ministry eventually. The little knowledge he could glean from newspapers and gossip in the surrounding villages suggested that, as impossible as it seemed, the same offensive that he had seen the start of was still grinding its way through young lives. As the solstice approached there was a buzz of excitement in the village – not on the same scale as the sacrifice-orgy, but in that September of 1916 the waxing crescent moon came almost a week after the solstice itself, a delay which caused Mother some anxiety.

'Don't linger,' she said. 'Once you've bled the vessel, step to the outer circle as quickly as you can. When Moccus returns he'll be confused and disoriented at first, and has been known to lash out at whoever is nearest. That's why we form a circle to welcome him back into the world. It's for our own safety.'

The deserter did as he was told. Mother blew the carnyx to summon the god to life, and Everett's knife whispered its song, and this time the earth gave it back. He felt tremors in the soil through his feet as he stepped back to rejoin Ardwyn in the circle. The tremors became shudders and throbbing pulses, as if a great heart were beating just below the surface, or else something was pounding its way out. The black, blood-soaked earth at the foot of Moccus' column heaved and subsided repeatedly, a little higher each time until cascades of soil were pouring down the sides of a long mound that was slowly, painfully pushing itself out of the ground.

Then a hand broke free, clutching at the air. It was followed by a second, thick fingers pulling apart and widening a well within which something huge stirred. The torchlight gleamed on tusks and straining muscles. Moccus screamed in the high, full-throated bellow of a boar as he raised his head clear and glared with burning amber eyes around at the assembled worshippers. Then he planted his hands either side of the hole and hauled himself into the world.

This wasn't the ancient and crippled thing that the deserter had seen being so ineptly butchered in the spring. Moccus rose before them in the full swell of strength and vitality. His broad chest and limbs were thick with muscle, the pelt that covered his head and continued down his back in a crest of hackles was black and lustrous, and his cock swung between his thighs like a club. His smell filled the clearing, thick and rank. He roared again, but it wasn't entirely an animal's squeal; it seemed that there might have been human sounds buried in it. Several of the Farrow faltered back, and Moccus' head swivelled to track them, watching, alert. Instinctively, the deserter raised his blade in self-defence, and Moccus' attention snapped onto him, the burning eyes narrow.

'No,' whispered Ardwyn, easing the knife down. 'Don't make yourself a threat.'

Everett did as he was told. Moccus grunted, apparently satisfied that there was no challenge here, then in an explosion of movement he was racing past them and into the trees, crashing sounds diminishing towards the stream gully and the thickest part of the woods.

During the customary hog roast on the green, Mother took him to one side. 'Your work has been better than I could have hoped,' she said. 'You have a gift for bloodletting.'

'Thank you, Mother. I'm sensing a "but", though.'

She nodded. 'But now is the time for you to go. Moccus will go out into the wild places of the world to hunt and mate, and there's no place or purpose for you here until he returns.'

The deserter was surprised at how distressing he found this sudden change of plan. 'What about Nikolai? My pig, I mean. I still need to complete my bracelet, don't I, to become one of you properly?'

'You already are one of us. The last six months should have proven that. I think sitting around here twiddling your thumbs for the next two or three years waiting for that pig to grow would be an unnecessary delay.'

'I might get too comfortable, you mean.'

'Something like that, yes.'

'Too comfortable with your daughter.'

Mother sighed. 'Ardwyn has told you what her part in the Farrow is, I take it?'

'Yes, she has, to shack up with some stuffed shirt and set up a happy little coven of her own, which if you ask me—'

'I didn't,' Mother cut him off, and the flatness of her tone was absolute. 'And I won't. You won't be consulted. Your approval is neither required nor wanted. I am Mother, just as she will become Mother of her own sounder, you're right, and she will have the final say over the fate of the males that come to her, just as I have over mine. Over you. You are a soldier. You're accustomed to obeying orders. Well, obey this one.'

'I'm a deserter,' he reminded her. 'I gave up taking orders. And I've never taken them from women.'

She met his gaze, and there was not one hint of indecision or mercy in it. 'Then desert,' she said. 'Leave us. That's exactly what I'm telling you to do, in case you weren't paying attention. But if it satisfies your masculine pride to tell yourself that you're going on your own terms and not because some woman told you, then I'm not going to argue.'

'And come back in, what – 1942?' He couldn't keep the

scepticism out of his voice. For all that he had seen and done, the horizon of his future had only ever been, at best, months at a time. To ask him to plan twenty-six years ahead, she might as well have been asking him to fly to the moon.

'Yes,' she said.

'But I like it here,' he replied. 'This is as close to a home as anything I can remember. I can be useful here in other ways.'

'You mean farming? Building barns? We've already had this discussion. It's not what you are, and you'd cease to be what we need if you tried to be anything else. In a quarter of a century you are going to have to sacrifice a god, and for that you will need the kind of strength that you won't get from ploughing fields. You need to be out in the world, fighting it, letting it harden you. Moccus will be old, but his spirit might still be too much for you to cope with.'

'You don't know that.'

'I know that Michael wasn't fighting in that war for the sake of King and country. Or possibly I'm mistaken and you're made of sterner stuff than he was?'

He had no answer to that.

The deserter went to where Nikolai was tethered in his pen. The boar was quite a bit larger than when he'd first been caught, his piglet striping beginning to fade and his lower tusks were curled halfway back on themselves, longer than natural but maybe not too long for him to survive in the wild. He eyed the deserter with undimmed suspicion. 'Looks like you're off the hook, young man,' Everett said, and paused before untying him. 'If you bite me I'll bloody well leave you here.'

Nikolai let himself be untied without protest. The deserter held the gate open but the pig hesitated, possibly suspecting that it was a trap. 'Look,' said the deserter. 'I know we haven't exactly got on but I've tried to do all right by you. You've got a nice sty here – bit of clean straw to sleep on, some yummy old slops to eat if you want. It's up to you.'

As he moved away from the gate there was a flash of movement behind him and a small dark shape bolted over the lane, through the hedge and off across night-darkened fields towards the woods that surrounded the village.

'Yes,' he said quietly. 'I suppose so.'

And he went inside to pack.

9

1942

IT WAS WITH A MIXTURE OF EXCITEMENT AND apprehension churning his guts that Everett hiked down from the slopes of the Long Mynd and into the woods surrounding Swinley in late winter of 1942. It was like the feeling before battle, except worse, because this time he actually gave a damn about the outcome.

He'd done as Mother instructed and let his appetite for blood lead his feet out into the world. The Great War had finished not with a bang but with a whimper, and the mess of its aftermath had left plenty of opportunities given that there were so few men of fighting age left alive. Closest to home there had been the Irish to put down, and then half a dozen squabbles between the fragments of the old world's broken empires as they fought to cannibalise each other. He rarely cared who he fought for, just relishing the irony that the whole of Europe had become No Man's Land – as if that nightmare territory had leaked out like a swamp once the levees of the trenches had been dismantled, and had expanded to flood the continent, drowning everyone who had escaped the immediate fighting. He broke heads during the General Strike of '26, and then for balance joined the International Brigades in Spain in '33, from which catastrophe he retired to lick his wounds in Gibraltar. When, lo and behold, the Second World War broke out with all the inevitability of a toddler shitting itself, he enlisted with the 3rd Infantry and deployed to France to kill Germans again. He never once met another man wearing a boar-tusk bracelet, but he always kept the date of the Farrow's equinoctial orgy firmly in mind – the 21st of March – and when the time came he deserted again, trading his uniform for a refugee's rags and making his way home.

He didn't know what kind of welcome to expect. He imagined that by now Ardwyn would have long since taken up with her rich young man, Gus, but for all these years he'd deliberately avoided trying to find out. It was easy enough; her social circle was unlikely to overlap with his, and he wasn't much for reading the society papers or the financial news.

The rutted cart track through the outlying woods of Swinley was a gravel road now, with electricity and telephone lines strung on poles alongside. Presumably they had motor vehicles and lightbulbs. The Farrow could perform their blood-soaked rituals and then settle down nice and cosy to listen to the Light Programme on the wireless.

And all of a sudden the deserter knew he couldn't do this.

It was all too big. He had no place amongst such people and he'd been a fool to ever think so. He turned to leave.

He heard Gar bellowing and crashing through the trees a moment before the huge man exploded onto the path, grabbed his shoulders and slammed him up against a tree. Gar roared in his face, spittle flying, his breath rank.

'It's me… you idiot…' Everett gasped.

'Yes!' Gar's mouth was split in a grin like a boulder-filled crevasse. 'YES!'

'Pleased to see you too, chum, but would you mind putting me down?'

Gar dropped him, and while Everett brushed himself down and picked up his kit bag, demonstrated his glee at seeing his old friend again by whacking a nearby tree-trunk with a log and whooping. 'Drink!' he shouted.

'Sorry, chum, but I don't actually have—'

Gar shook his head and stabbed a thick forefinger at his own chest. 'Drink! *My* drink!' He tugged at Everett's arm.

'Your drink? You have drink? You're offering it to me? Well, that's very generous but I really can't stay. I've just remembered that—'

But Gar was insistent, a twenty-stone toddler. It seemed that desertion was no longer an option. Gar dragged Everett along the narrow lanes of Swinley – away from Mother's cottage and towards the half-derelict barn where he lived, except that it too had changed with the years. The window holes had proper shutters and there were tubs of flowers by the door, which was decorated with animal skulls. The deserter didn't have time to remark on Gar's house-husbandry or his carpentry skills, because the big man led him inside to proudly display the thing that he'd built inside. Everett saw a copper vat, rubber tubes, and a glass demijohn, and smelled a familiar sweet reek.

'Is that…' he breathed. 'My God, Gar, is that a *still*?'

Gar nodded wildly, and even jumped up and down a little. He picked up the demijohn in one hand as easily as if it were a hip flask and poured a little clear liquid into a tin cup and passed it to Everett. 'Drink! I make!'

'Well, you certainly are a clever old stick and no mistake.' But then he supposed twenty-six years was a long time for someone even like Gar to learn a few new things. He took the cup of moonshine, sniffed the contents, and tried a wary sip.

When he'd finished coughing and his eyes had stopped watering enough to be able to see again, he handed the cup back. 'That is brutal,' he gasped. 'You're an evil man and you must be stopped.'

Gar topped up his cup and handed it back. 'Drink!' he insisted, and swigged from the bottle to demonstrate. He shuddered, and howled.

'Oh, all right, just a quick one, then,' Everett replied, swallowed a mouthful and howled right back at him.

The hangover that followed was almost as brutal as the moonshine itself, but the equinox still wasn't for a few more days so he had time to pull himself together and make a proper approach to Mother. She interrogated him long and hard about his adventures over the years before she was satisfied that his spirit was strong enough to cope with sacrificing Moccus.

'He is an ancient thing,' Mother told him. 'One of the very last of an elder race who shaped the world when humanity was hunting aurochs with flint spears. But that which shapes creation is inevitably shaped by that creation. The begetter is begotten. We take Moccus into our bodies and souls, and something of us is taken into him. With each replenishment sacrifice it is not just the life of the vessel which goes into him but something of the man wielding the knife, the way that a great work of art will carry some flavour of the artist's soul. And with each rebirth, Moccus' spirit is shaped by that man's character.'

'In that case I think you've made a huge mistake,' he replied, 'because my "character", as you call it, is atrocious.'

'But that's exactly what makes you perfect! Not the fiddling details of what you've done, but the fact that you know exactly what you are, and are unapologetic about it. It's that purity which we need. You must hold on to that when it comes time to kill him. Even as aged as he will be now, he's a potent force and though he may not mean to, in death he'll try to take you with him.'

'He wouldn't be the first.'

'Just try to maintain a clear sense of your own self. There are certain prayers and meditations that I can teach you—'

'No,' the deserter cut her off. 'None of that. If I need my head to be clear I won't want to be filling it with that sort of nonsense.'

'Well, don't go filling your belly with Gar's moonshine,

either,' she said. 'You'll need to choose four men to help you. The god might need restraining. Choose from the unwedded men. It'll be a great honour for them.'

As he'd expected, Ardwyn had left Swinley long ago, barely a year after himself, taken the married name of Melhuish and become Mother of her own small congregation in Cirencester, supported by her husband's money. He looked for her as the Farrow began to arrive from all over the country during the following days, imagining how she might have changed and whether, God forbid, Gus had spawned his limp-chinned progeny on her. It was a relief, then, when they finally arrived, to see that she was virtually unchanged from the autumn of 1916, and unencumbered by brats. Maybe the planes of her face were a little more defined, or maybe that was just the combination of make-up, a more modern hairstyle, and his own faulty memory insisting that she must have looked younger because so much time had passed. Her clothes were smarter – the kind of wasp-waisted suit he'd seen in American films – but her spirit, to use Mother's terms, was just as bright and scornful, if her laughter at Gus and his scowl in response was anything to go by. They arrived in a burgundy MG VA Saloon, a beast of a car, so fuel rationing obviously wasn't a concern, and the moment she saw Everett she gave a shriek of delight and rushed to embrace him, mashing his lips with her own.

'You look appalling,' she said, when she pulled away and properly took in his lean and scruffy appearance.

'What have you been doing all these years?'

'Oh, you know, the usual,' he said airily. 'Bloodying my soul with as much death as possible to prepare myself for killing a god.'

'Still, it can't have been all fun, surely.'

By this time Gus had marched over, but Everett noticed that as angry as he obviously was, he didn't try to pull Ardwyn away or touch her at all. 'That'll do,' he snapped. 'Winnie, we have a thousand things to do before tomorrow…'

Everett choked. '*Winnie?!*'

Ardwyn winced apologetically. 'He thinks it's endearing.' To her husband she said, 'Given what we're all going to be doing the day after tomorrow, you can hardly complain about me showing a bit of affection for an old friend.'

'Friend, is it?' Gus looked him up and down. The same contempt was there but it was better hidden now. More controlled. Augustus Melhuish had grown up, it seemed, and the deserter began to think that he had the makings of a dangerous man. 'Well, since you are my wife and what is yours is mine I suppose that means he is my friend also. Let me shake your hand, friend. Let's let bygones be bygones.' He put out his hand to be shaken, and Everett saw that his tusk bracelet had gold finials. Obviously.

Amused, Everett obliged. Gus didn't attempt anything so obvious or adolescent – or futile – as to test his strength against Everett's grip, but held it just a little too long, turning his wrist over and inspecting it in mock surprise.

'What, no tusk? That's funny. I thought you were one of the Farrow. I must have been mistaken. And yet I hear that you are to perform the sacrament. Possibly I'm mistaken about that too.'

'Darling,' said Ardwyn, somewhat frostily, 'you're mistaken about quite a few things.'

'May I have my hand back?' asked the deserter. 'Or do you intend to propose? Your wife might not like that.'

'My wife is more than capable of deciding what she likes, as I'm sure we both know. That being the case.' Gus stepped back a pace and bowed. 'Darling, please accept my apologies for interrupting your reunion. I will see you later, at your convenience. I need to talk to some people to clarify my understanding of Saturday's celebration.'

Ardwyn and Everett watched him go.

'He's going to try to turn the other Farrow against you,' she said.

'I know.'

'You don't seem especially worried about it.'

He shrugged. 'I'm Mother's choice. At the end of the day there's nothing he can do about that. Plus, he won't cause a fuss on an important occasion like this. It's more likely that he'll wait until all of this is over and try to have me quietly killed.'

She laughed. 'Oh, you boys! You know I almost want to see you two fucking each other on Saturday just so that I can see you fighting to be the one on top.'

It was his turn to laugh, then. 'God, I've missed you.'

'Really? Care to take me to your cottage and show me how much?'

So he did.

10

THE SACRAMENT OF THE FIRST FLESH, 1942

IN CONTRAST, TWO NIGHTS LATER WHEN HE STOOD BY
Moccus' column with the knife in his hand, naked in the
firelight and surrounded by rutting figures, it stirred no heat
in him. He was not witnessing a display of desire. Their
grunts and squeals, their sweat and spit – it was all a part
of the summoning, like Mother blowing the bone carnyx,
but there was something desperate about their frenzy, like a
child throwing a tantrum to get its parent's attention.

When the aged figure of Moccus emerged through the
veils of smoke and shadow, he gripped the knife tighter
in a fist that was suddenly sweating, and found that he'd
involuntarily stepped back a pace. *None of that*, he chided
himself. Deserter he might be, but he'd stand firm here at
least. He laughed aloud at the paradox, and maybe it was
the sight of him laughing, but the god stopped and shuffled
warily. It couldn't see him, of that he was sure, with its milky

blind eyes, but its sense of smell was just as sharp, judging from the way its snout wrinkled around its tusks, huffing as it scented him out. How could so few years age it so much, especially when the Farrow aged barely at all?

'Now then,' he said, trying to sound the way he'd heard sergeant majors cajoling their belligerent or terrified men. 'Let's have this nice and easy, shall we? I mean to make this as quick as I can, if you'll let me.' He could feel the four men he'd chosen as back-up tensing behind him, and the weight of Mother's attention.

Moccus came right up to him, still tall despite his stooped age so that the deserter's face barely reached his chest. The god reached out a hand towards his face; he shifted stance and flexed his fingers around the knife haft but Mother said, 'Steady, Butcher. Be still. The god seeks only to know you,' so he forced himself to stand immobile as it took him by the jaw with arthritic fingers and turned his face this way and that. Its snout was only an inch away, its thick tongue rolling, nostrils quivering, its breath hot and wet. He could see the hairs in the ridges of its skin and the cracks in the yellowed ivory of its tusks – they looked razor sharp, even with age. It could bite the face off his skull like an apple if it wished. It was insane that he was just standing here without defending himself. He was in a perfect position to disembowel the beast.

He angled the knife slightly and prepared to strike.

To his surprise, Moccus released him. It stepped back, dropped to its knees and bared its throat. There was a collective sigh of relief from all around.

'The god accepts you as his deliverer,' said Mother. 'Do

your duty before he changes his mind.'

'First flesh, first fruit,' he said, and did his duty, opening the creature's throat in a single swift sweep, and as he did so he saw the German boy's face and remembered the taste of his flesh. The memory was so vivid that it blotted out everything else – he was back in the shell crater with the dying boy, only this time he was drowning in mud. It closed over his feet, then his knees, thighs, and hips, and he struggled against it but he was pulling against the sucking weight of the earth itself. As it reached his chest he felt arms slip beneath his from behind, elbows curling around his armpits, holding, steadying. Mother's voice was in his ear: 'I can't pull you out on my own. You have to help me. You have to push. Come on, Butcher, push!' So he pushed as hard as he could, until the sinews in his knees and back screamed, and the sucking weight relented a bit, then a little bit more, and then relinquished its hold all of a sudden and he flew backwards and found himself back in the clearing. He was sprawled in Mother's arms and the other men were catching Moccus' cruor in those great bronze basins.

He lay back against Mother's breast, panting, exhausted. 'That is what the death of a god feels like,' she said, stroking his brow, and she kissed the top of his head. When he had caught his breath, she patted him on the shoulder and gave him a helping shove upright. 'Please, Butcher,' she said. 'Will you prepare the first flesh for us?'

'Yes, Mother.' He retrieved his knife and set to work.

* * *

As far as everyone else seemed to be concerned it was all a tremendous success, but when Ardwyn came to him in his cottage afterwards he couldn't bring himself to touch her.

'What's wrong with you?' she asked, re-buttoning her blouse and making no attempt to hide the fact that she was upset and irritated.

'Nothing,' he said.

'Really? Are you going to tell me that you're "just a bit tired" or that you've "got a headache"? Because if I want that rubbish I'll go to my husband.' When she saw that her anger didn't move him she softened her approach. 'My darling, you achieved something awe-inspiring today. You should be proud of yourself! We should be celebrating!'

'I find it hard to celebrate when…'

'When what?'

He flailed, trying to find words to express something that he was struggling to understand. 'Mother keeps calling me Butcher, but I'm still just a deserter,' he said. 'When things get too big, I run. I almost didn't come back here at all. I wouldn't have, if Gar hadn't waylaid me on the road and got me drunk. I'm glad you're married because it means I don't have to try too hard with you; if you were after something permanent from me I'd run a mile.'

'I know,' she replied. 'That's why I'm with you, you dolt, don't you understand? You have no idea how wearisome it is being surrounded by men who are always *trying*. I find them so, well, trying.'

He smiled at that, but it faded as quickly as it appeared. 'Moccus, he submitted to me. Something that powerful, bigger than wars or history, that I have no right to approach – it knelt to me and let me kill it. What do I do with that?'

She scrutinised him, her lips pursed.

'What are you thinking?' he asked.

'I'm trying to make up my mind whether you're aiming for false humility or just melodrama.'

'Ha. Maybe I should be humble. If he – *it* – is really a god, then no god should kneel to a man. It feels wrong.'

She laid her hands on his chest. 'How does it feel here, in this heart that hasn't aged for nearly thirty years?'

'To be honest with you? It feels like theft.'

She laughed, her scorn bitter in his face, like smelling salts. 'As if you care! Murderer? Cannibal? Why, even your name is stolen! Yes, you're a deserter. Things too big, you say? Then run from death, because there's nothing bigger than that. Even gods must die. None of us can escape it completely but you and I can run a while longer and further than most. Let me run with you! Or at the very least...' She snuggled closer and slipped her hand under his shirt. Her fingers were cool and sure where they stroked his nipple. 'At least let me enjoy a bit of light jogging.'

As always, he found it impossible to refuse her.

All the same, when it came to the replenishment sacrifices he couldn't bring himself to stay for the whole six months. Something about sitting comfortably in his cottage drinking whisky and reading the newspapers felt like an insult to the god who was dragging himself slowly back from death once again. So Everett took himself off into the world in the meantime, returning at each tusk moon to slaughter one of Mother's pigs, and when Moccus birthed himself from the earth that September, the deserter didn't have to be ordered to leave this time. His satchel was already packed.

11

ATTENUATION

He was almost late for the sacrament in the spring following the Summer of Love, having discovered that psychotropic substances were an ideal method for deserting from reality altogether. But he got his shit together, as the saying went, and arrived in time to perform his duties. The sacrament and replenishment sacrifices went smoothly, and there were no signs that anything was going wrong – or if they were, his senses were still too battered to notice. It was during the sixth and final replenishment on the autumnal equinox in September of '68 that the catastrophe became evident.

Moccus was too weak to arise.

As the blood of the sixth and final swine soaked into the earth and the earth began to heave, the assembled Farrow readied themselves for Moccus to break free and be reborn, but it just continued to heave, and nothing emerged – no reaching fingers, no gleaming tusks. The tumult in the earth was even diminishing, as if the god was weakening from his exertions.

Murmurs of unease and disbelief gave way to exclamations of dismay, until Mother ordered several of the congregation to run back to the village for shovels. When they returned with the tools, they set about digging their deity out of the ground, and were able to remove enough weight of earth such that Moccus was finally able to grasp the edges of the hole and haul himself into the world. He stood there, soil-streaked and panting, glaring around at his worshippers in the way a man caught in the act of some foolishness might seek to disguise his embarrassment, before staggering off into the woods.

Quite what had happened was the only subject of conversation in Swinley for days. Ardwyn's husband, who was there to make sure that no opportunity to undermine Everett was missed, made his opinion that it must be some fault in the butcher known often and loudly. Everett himself was almost sure that it had nothing to do with the fact that he was stoned a lot of the time, but quit cold turkey all the same. Everyone assumed that Moccus had gone out into the world and that he would not be seen again until the sacrament of the first flesh in 1994.

Then the body was found in Mother's pigsty.

It was the corpse of a poacher, still in his long coat with pheasants in his pockets, and disembowelled so utterly that his torso was virtually an empty sack propped open by his ribcage, but with no signs of his viscera anywhere.

Everett went up into the woods to see if the Recklings had played any part in this, and found them huddled by the stream with Gar, chewing on what the poacher had left behind.

'Did you do this?' he asked Gar.

Gar shook his head. 'Moccus,' he replied, with his mouth full.

'But why would he kill a man and then dump his body in the village? Is it meant to be some kind of a warning?'

'Man is stronger,' said Sus, who was squatting on her haunches nearby and licking her bloody fingers. She had learned to wear clothes since the last time they'd met, but the way her dress rode up over her thighs seemed to make her more feral than if she'd been naked.

Everett prodded something gristly with his toe. 'Well, he obviously wasn't strong enough.' He was about to leave when he got a proper look at what Gar was actually eating. 'Is that his liver?'

Gar shrugged. Anatomy was not important, it seemed, for the enjoyment of this meal.

The deserter hesitated. Liver had always been a delicacy in the Grey Brigade, usually reserved for the one who provided the meat. He found that his mouth was watering in a way that it hadn't done in the more than fifty years since he had tasted human flesh.

He glanced around to make sure that Ardwyn hadn't, for some reason, followed him. She was tolerant of a lot, but he didn't think she'd find it easy to accept this. 'Here, pass us a piece of that,' he said.

Gar narrowed his eyes and clutched his prize tighter.

'Now then, I'm only going to have a nibble. You can't begrudge me that, surely, can you, chum? After all the whisky I've brought for you over the years?'

Reluctantly, like a child giving up a favourite toy, Gar handed over the half-chewed organ. The deserter took his penknife, pared off a thin slice and tossed it back. Gar continued munching while Everett placed the morsel on his tongue and savoured the rich heaviness. Just a taste for old time's sake. When he opened his eyes again he found that Sus was gazing at him speculatively.

'You are like us,' she said.

He laughed. 'A runt and a cast-off? How right you are.'

Everything went wrong in '94.

The year before had been good for killers, cannibals, and fanatics – eastern Europe was tearing itself apart all over again, Waco burned, and the World Trade Centre was bombed – and as if in response to that, Moccus did not submit peacefully to the sacrament of the first flesh. When Mother summoned him with the bone carnyx he came unwillingly, snorting and roaring in the peculiar throaty squeal of a mature boar, and if he hadn't already been weak with age and the unaccountable malaise that had afflicted him in '68, it would have been impossible to subdue him at all. As the Farrow held him on his knees, the deserter looked into his blind eyes with concern.

'What's up, old chap?' he murmured. 'You're not yourself these days.'

Moccus had merely snarled at him, so he'd done the only thing he could do which was to put the god out of his misery and hope that the replenishment sacrifices restored him better than they had last time.

But he didn't even get around to the first one before the Farrow realised that something was wrong. A week after the feast of the first flesh Everett awoke with a familiar weight in his lungs, and when he got out of bed he was seized with a fit of coughing. It wasn't as bad as it had been in '16, but it terrified him, nonetheless. The rest of the Farrow were similarly afflicted. While the scars of old physical injuries remained healed, illnesses and disabilities were creeping back – arthritis, gout, deafness, blindness – not drastically so, but just the first twinges which warned them that whatever was wrong with Moccus hadn't been remedied, and was in fact getting worse.

The first flesh was losing its potency.

Urgent debates were held.

'We must hold to our faith,' said Mother to the Farrow assembled in St Mark's. 'We must trust that he will grow strong again, and bless us once more.'

'As a plan of action goes, I have to say it stinks,' said the deserter. 'The only thing that we will get by sitting around waiting on the off-chance that something spontaneously improves is very bored and then very dead.'

Gus Melhuish sneered. 'I'm amazed that you have the audacity to even open your mouth, Butcher. If this is anybody's fault, it's yours.'

'How do you figure that, chum?'

'Nobody else is wielding the knife.'

'That's very true. You'd best remember that in case I decide to wield it in your direction.'

'Oh, this is ridiculous,' said Ardwyn, likely meaning both the situation and their squabbling. 'Whatever we're doing, it's obviously not enough. We need to modify the ritual in some way to make our lord stronger.'

'There will be no modifications,' asserted Mother. 'We will worship as we always have. If there is a fault it lies in us – in our doubts and weaknesses. We must look to our own souls for the answer.'

Stronger. Everett remembered Sus' words in the woods after eating the poacher's viscera. The poacher that Moccus had killed and dumped in Mother's sty, which everyone at the time had interpreted as some kind of cryptic warning – against what, they still had no idea – but which the deserter was now starting to think might not have been a warning at all, but a demand. *Man is stronger*, Sus had said.

'I think I know what we need to do,' he said, knowing too that it wasn't going to go down at all well with the Farrow, and least of all Mother.

'Really?' scoffed Gus. 'Give us the benefit of your deep theological insight, please.'

'Human vessels,' he replied simply. 'The swine that we used last time obviously weren't enough. You remember how weak he was, and how we had to dig him out of the ground. I think the poacher was a message to us. Moccus put his body in the sty where the vessels are kept for a reason. Man is stronger.' He gave a little laugh. 'I think our lord wants a change of menu.'

A babble of consternation and outrage broke from the congregation, over the top of which Mother's voice came ringing: 'Unthinkable! Absolutely unthinkable! What do you think we are, Everett – savages? We do not perform human sacrifice! Would you go into a Christian cathedral and suggest that they begin eating their infants? The very idea is an abomination!'

'Maybe, but it didn't used to be, did it?' he replied. 'Two thousand years ago, when the Farrow were Cornovii tribesmen? Do you think they shied away from giving the hunter of the first woods their blood? At some point since then the practice has switched to swine, which is more civilised, obviously, but what does Moccus care for civilised? He is a hunter and a killer – he wants what he wants, and it's been denied to him for so long that it's not surprising he's finally starting to sicken from the pale substitutes that you've been offering.'

Mother fixed him with a look of steel. 'We. Are. Not. Murderers.'

'No, but he is,' said Gus, pointing at the deserter.

'What's your point, chum?'

'The beast takes on something of the butcher, isn't that right, Mother?' Gus asked.

She nodded. 'With each rebirth he is created anew, shaped by the man with the knife.'

'Well, forgive me if I'm mistaken, but the man with the knife in this case is a murderer and a cannibal, isn't that so?'

'You're saying this is my fault?' asked Everett. 'You might

want to be very careful there, Gus, because it seems like you're questioning the wisdom of Mother in choosing me as the god's butcher.'

'Whatever the cause,' Ardwyn interrupted, 'we are still left with the problem.'

'We will hold to the ways of our faith,' said Mother. 'Everett, if you feel that you are unable to perform your duties with the replenishment sacrifices, I will understand and find a replacement.'

'No, that's all fine,' he replied. 'With your leave, Mother, I'll continue to bleed your swine. Six months is not such a long time after all. But if the equinox comes and Moccus is reborn even weaker than before, none of us will live to see the twenty-first century. Gus is right about me, so take it from a man who knows: if you want to survive, you're going to have to make some unpalatable decisions.'

Ardwyn came to his bed the night she and her husband were due to depart, but she was too agitated and angry for sex. Instead, he watched her pace around the room like a caged animal, her face haggard and her arms crossed tightly across her belly. He guessed that some old illness which Moccus' flesh had held at bay was making itself felt again, and not for the first time wondered how old she really was.

'How can she be so bloody blind?' she raged. 'How can she not see what's happening right in front of her?'

'Oh, she sees, all right,' he said. 'She's just scared like the rest of us.'

'The worst of it is, I thought I knew her! I thought, she's looked after us for so long and guided us all this time, surely she'll recognise the danger and act on it. I knew that the old traditions were important to her but I never imagined that she could be so – I don't know – so close-minded. Damn her! *Damn her!*' Ardwyn was almost in tears. He moved to embrace her but she shoved him away. 'No!' She turned from him, smearing the tears away with the heels of her hands. 'Don't. That's not what I need from you.'

'Well, for God's sake what *do* you need, then?' he replied, stung.

'Something real. Something more than just words.'

'Fine then. What do you want me to do?'

'What *can* you do?'

He laughed. 'Oh I could do all manner of things. I don't know about you, but I mean to survive. The question is how far are you prepared to go? What are you prepared to sacrifice? Your husband and your church?'

'*Church*,' she snorted. 'A banker, his screeching wife, and a defrocked priest: hardly a huge congregation. I'm sure Cirencester can survive without us, and I'm damned sure I can survive without Gus.'

'Swinley?' he pressed. 'Mother herself?'

He watched her wrestle with this and eventually square her shoulders as if ridding them of an uncomfortable weight. 'If at the end of the day she refuses to see reason, then yes. Everything,' she said. 'All of it.' Ardwyn moved into his arms and laid her hands on his chest. 'All of it,' she repeated. He felt his heart swelling with some large, churning sensation that was quite new and uncomfortable. Then a coughing fit gripped him, and he decided that it had simply been a bronchial spasm.

'What do you want me to do?' he repeated.

She told him, and as he listened his grin grew wide.

12

SCHISM

Six months later, Gar's Reckling kin met Ardwyn's car on the road to Swinley two days before the final replenishment sacrifice. The lane had been blacktopped many years previously but not widened, so that trees still grew closely down to the roadside, and it was easy for the Recklings to get close to the vehicle without being seen when Gus was forced to stop it at the sight of Everett and Gar standing in the middle of the lane.

'What's this about?' He frowned, opening the door.

It was wrenched out of his hand by Sus. As he stared at her in astonishment, other Recklings appeared and hauled him out of the car.

'What are you doing?' he yelled. 'You can't do this! I won't allow—'

But then a hand that was mostly fingers closed over his mouth and they never did find out what it was that he wasn't going to allow. He was dragged into the trees, twisting and making muffled noises of protest.

'You'll look after him?' Everett asked Gar.

Gar shrugged.

'I mean, will he still be alive by tomorrow night?'

'Alive, yes.'

Ardwyn got out of the car and joined them. She was moving slowly, with a hand pressed to her abdomen low down.

'It's getting worse?' Everett asked her.

She nodded. 'And your cough?'

'Still bad. And it's not just us. Swinley is looking like a geriatric ward. He's had nothing but pig's blood since March.'

'Then let's do something about that,' she said.

The Farrow assembled in the clearing around Moccus' pillar and the sixth swine was brought to him for sacrifice. He could feel the slow life of the god churning in the ground beneath his feet, and the responsibility he owed to it. At a nod from Ardwyn he took the blade from the beast's throat and pushed it away.

'No,' she said, stepping forward. 'We will not perpetuate this travesty any longer. Gar?' she called, and out from the darkness beyond the clearing stepped Gar and Sus, pushing Gus ahead of him. The man was tied at the hands and gagged, and his eyes rolled like terrified white marbles in his face, just like every other man the deserter had seen die over the long years.

'What is the meaning of this?' demanded Mother,

outraged. She stepped forward, but Everett pointed the sickle at her and she stopped, paralysed almost as much by fear as fury, he hoped. Others of the Farrow made moves as if to intervene, but from around the clearing the other Recklings appeared to stand between them and the deserter. They stopped, wailing and cursing. One or two even ran.

'You can't do this!' Mother cried. 'It's sacrilege!'

'No, Mother,' said Ardwyn. 'It is the beginning of a new covenant between the Farrow and He Who Eats the Moon. But I don't blame you for resisting. Rebirth is always painful.'

'Ardwyn!' she wept. 'Daughter. I beg you to reconsider!'

Ardwyn didn't reply, but gently took the bone carnyx from her frozen hands.

Gar brought the new vessel before him and forced it to kneel. For the first time, Everett realised how much it resembled the young German soldier. 'Nothing personal, chum,' he said, as he took the new vessel by the hair and bent its head back. It was weeping and screaming behind its gag. 'First flesh, first fruit,' he whispered, and the knife made a whisper of its own, and the vessel emptied onto the black soil. Then Ardwyn blew the bone carnyx to summon their god back to life, and the ground began to heave.

This time, Moccus made it on his own, and stepped out of the pit to tower over them in something like his former vitality. His amber eyes locked onto Everett's.

He nodded, once.

Then he was gone, loping into the trees, and the Recklings too disappeared in their father's wake, to leave the Farrow alone in the clearing, shocked and weeping.

'What have you done?' whispered Mother, her voice hoarse and utterly distraught. 'Oh, my children, *what have you done?*'

'Survived,' said Ardwyn. From the way she was rubbing her belly he could tell that she was feeling better already, and he could feel the heaviness in his lungs clearing too. 'And so have the rest of you. You're welcome, by the way.'

'Get out,' said Mother. 'All three of you.'

'Gladly,' Everett retorted, and tossed the knife at her feet. 'But one day you'll come to see the necessity of all this, and you'll want me back.'

'Never!'

'Try not to take that long. You've got another twenty-six years to change your mind or find someone else.'

By February of 2020, she hadn't changed her mind. The old wooden farm gate that had once opened from the road onto the lane into Swinley had been replaced by a pair of tall wire mesh security gates attached to razor-wire-topped fencing that disappeared into the trees to left and right, a sign that read NO TRESPASSING: THESE PREMISES PROTECTED BY PRIVATE SECURITY and, as if to prove that this wasn't a bluff, a CCTV camera set on a pole a little further in.

Everett parked the RV that they'd picked up in Frankfurt and looked at it all. 'Do you ever get the impression that you're not welcome?' he said to Ardwyn and Gar.

The lock on the gates was too strong even for Gar to

break, so he tore a hole in the chain-link fence to one side and they walked instead.

'Maybe we should try the Recklings first,' he suggested. 'Get the lie of the land, so to speak. See what other surprises might be in store.'

'No,' said Ardwyn. 'This is our home. Mother can't keep us out; we're Farrow, the blessed of Moccus, just like her, and we have a right to worship him. I won't sneak in like a thief and I won't hide with the beasts.'

Gar grunted, but whether it was in agreement or displeasure at being called a beast was hard to tell.

'Fair enough,' Everett said, and checked that his officer's Webley was fully loaded before they set off. They managed no more than a few hundred yards before they heard the sound of a vehicle approaching, and a Land Rover Defender appeared around the corner, slewing to a halt across the lane diagonally in front of them. Two men in dark, nondescript uniforms were inside; while the driver said something into his radio, his passenger got out and approached them. He was wearing a utility belt with all sorts of things clipped to it, including what looked like pepper spray, a baton and something in a pistol-shaped holster.

'You need to leave now,' he said. He was very large and there was an earpiece with a coiled wire running behind his collar. 'This is private property. That's your one warning.'

'My name is Ardwyn Hughes,' she replied. 'This is—'

'We know who you are. All three of you. You were ID'd when you pulled up outside the gate. The owners have made it clear that you're not welcome. Leave. Now.'

'If I could just speak to—'

The guard's hand reached for something on his belt, but never arrived at its destination, as Everett produced the Webley and shot him in the face. There was a cry of 'Shit!' from inside the Defender and the driver slammed it into reverse, trying to turn around in the lane, but all that accomplished was to bring the driver's window side on to Everett, who shot him twice through the glass. Then he went back and put another in the first guard just to make sure.

'So much for the diplomatic approach,' he said. 'There's no point in trying to be stealthy about it now; there'll be more of these goons and the longer we hang about the more chance they have of nailing us. Ardie, where does Mother keep the knife and the carnyx?'

'In St Mark's,' she replied, looking down at the bodies. 'It's a shame it had to be this way.'

He looked at her. 'Second thoughts?'

She shook her head. 'No.'

'Good.' He went back to the Defender, opened the door, dragged the dead driver onto the road and climbed into his still-warm seat. 'Come on, you two. Chop chop.'

They climbed in and the vehicle drove away towards Swinley, leaving the winter morning sunlight to seep through the trees' bare branches, dappling the bodies of the two men who lay on the road. The watches continued to tick blank and busy on their wrists, and the voices in their earpieces squawked and crackled with increasing urgency. Birdsong returned. After a while, a pig-like creature with a long, human torso crept out of the underbrush and sniffed at the scene. It approached the nearest corpse slowly, ears and nose a-twitch for any scent or sound of an intruder. With small and oddly finger-like trotters it worked at the baton that was attached to the man's belt. It came free, and the Reckling snatched its prize up in its mouth and fled back into the bushes. The bodies had not begun to cool appreciably when the sound of a vehicle grew again and the Defender reappeared, swerving erratically from one side of the lane to the other. It pulled up short and hard before the bodies with a squeal of brakes and a chorus of complaints from inside.

Everett kicked one of the rear doors open and got out, helping Ardwyn after him. She was bleeding from a cut on her forehead and clutching a long cloth-wrapped object in her arms. Gar jumped out of the driver's side and ran for the gate.

'Who the hell taught you to drive?' shouted Everett after him.

'You!' Gar shouted back.

'Well, that's the last bloody time!'

They scrambled through the hole in the fence and back to their own vehicle, which started up with a roar and disappeared into the labyrinth of small country lanes.

Sometime later the small pig-creature returned, and began to sniff around the Land Rover.

PART TWO

SOW THE SEEDS

1

DENNIE

DENNIE KEELING WOKE TO THE SOUND OF A LARGE dog whining.

Viggo was on his feet in the darkness beside her, his tail down, ears pricked forward, and nose within inches of the inside of the shed door; he was such a huge dog and the confines of her shed were so narrow that this put his head directly next to and above her own. She reached up and scrunched him at the back of the neck where he liked it.

'Hey you,' she murmured. 'What's your problem? Is it the Great Rabbit Uprising?'

Viggo licked her face with his great shovel of a tongue, but then resumed staring at the door. The noise he was making sounded pathetic for such a big lad.

'Now that was just unnecessary.' Dennie wiped the slobber off her cheek with one corner of the sleeping bag and batted about for her glasses which lay on a small shelf above her head. Putting them on, she peered at the luminous hands of her watch. It was a little after three in the morning. 'Seriously?'

Viggo whined again and raised a paw to scratch at the door. Someone had once suggested to her that she install a dog-flap so that he could get in and out as he liked, but the Great Dane was so bloody big it would have been easier just to take the hinges off the side of the shed door and fix them to the top. Besides, her sleep was so thin these days that it was no great disturbance to let him out for his nightly manoeuvres. Dennie swung her legs out of her folding camp cot to sit up, and fumbled for the switch on the battery-powered lantern that sat beside her glasses. Then her hand froze, because Viggo wasn't whining any more.

He'd started growling.

It was a low, loose muttering from deep down in his barrel of a chest which meant that he wasn't scared – not yet – but there was something out there on the allotments that he wasn't at all happy about. Something that wasn't the usual kind of vermin.

She patted him again, the heavier kind to reassure him. 'Good boy, Viggo, good boy,' she whispered. 'What is it, hey?'

Burglars, most likely. It wouldn't be the first time that thieving little shitbags had decided to help themselves to the contents of her neighbours' sheds. It would be unusual for February, though. Come spring, when folks were waking up their plots there might be some newly bought tools worth nicking, and then in autumn it wasn't unknown for folks to have had entire shedloads of harvested produce stolen, but in Dennie's experience your average thieving shitbag wasn't too keen on going out in sub-zero temperatures in the early hours during the depths of winter.

It was none too warm in here either, now that she was sitting up, despite her thermal long johns. Fifteen years ago she'd insulated the shed with Styrofoam panels, carpeted it and double-glazed its one window with Perspex, and the combined body warmth of herself and Viggo meant that she didn't have to mess around with heating, but outside of her sleeping bag it was chilly all the same. She reached for and found her down jacket and her trousers; she knew the location of every item in her shed by touch and didn't actually need any light. Still, she was helped by a thin glaze of ambient town light that seeped between the curtains, picking out the tools hanging on the walls and the shelves cluttered with a lifetime's bric-a-brac. She shuffled her feet into unlaced boots and picked up a two-foot length of broom-handle. Any thieving shitbag who wasn't going to be deterred by a hundred and ten pounds of Great Dane certainly wasn't going to be bothered by his sixty-five-year-old owner either, but it couldn't hurt.

Viggo was still growling. Dennie shushed him and gritted her teeth against the flaring of old pain in her lower back and left hip as she stood up and clipped the leash to his collar. It was purely psychological; there was no way she could physically restrain him if he chose to go for whoever was out there. *Or whatever is out there*, she thought, and wondered where that thought had come from.

Dismissing it, Dennie unbolted the shed door and eased it open.

'Where is it, hey boy?' she whispered. 'Show me.'

Viggo licked her hand and padded off, tugging her after him. The other plots spread out around her in a jumbled shadow-patchwork of sheds, polytunnels, water butts, cold frames, fruit cages, and wired enclosures, their silhouetted shapes glittering with frost. Few of them were actively worked at this time of year, and many were blanketed in sheets of plastic to keep off the worst of the cold. Some were in better condition than others. There was the Pimbletts' place, its big oblong planting beds made with old railway sleepers. There was the Watts' place, all foil pinwheels and plastic streamers from last year's attempt to keep the pigeon hordes at bay. There was Shane Harding's plot laid out like a Viking longboat, complete with a mast and sail that had been built by his partner Jason, who made narrowboats at the marina in Kings Bromley. Caz the Dragon Lady grew plants for dyeing rather than eating, and her plot was festooned with streamers and pennants around a large junk-metal sculpture of a dragon. Briar Hill Allotments were not all that large, bounded on three sides by suburban streets and the open Staffordshire countryside on the fourth, but in the silent darkness they seemed to stretch for miles. At first she didn't recognise the plot that Viggo was leading her towards, but when she did she stopped dead, frozen by a chill deeper than a February frost.

It was the Neary allotment.

Calling it an allotment was quite generous, though, since it was little more than a length of overgrown waste ground, tangled with weeds and brambles and heaped with piles of rubble, rotting fence panels, old tyres, broken tools, rusted garden furniture, and empty plastic sacks flapping like the wings of dying birds. For the twelve years since Sarah Neary had gone to prison no new tenant had ever taken it on and so it had become little more than a rubbish tip for the neighbouring plots – though Dennie had never dumped anything there herself. Nothing would induce her to go an inch closer to it than she absolutely had to, and right at this very moment she wished she'd stayed in bed and told Viggo to shut up.

Because there was someone crawling about on the Neary plot, and it was no common garden-variety thieving shitbag. She had no idea what this was.

The figure was little more than a deeper shadow against the background, and even though it was stooped over as it worked its way to and fro through the weeds, she could tell that when it stood upright it would be huge. It – *he*, she told herself, *it must be a man* – was tearing out clumps of weeds, snuffling at them and tossing them away again. Then it – *he* – scooped up a handful of soil towards his face and she distinctly heard the sound of chewing.

'What the...?' she breathed.

Its head snapped up, then it reared to its full height, and she heard it sniffing in her direction, catching her scent. It started to move towards her, its gait shambling, but Viggo, who had been very well behaved up until this point, was having none of it. His growls became full-throated and furious barks, slobber flying from his jaws, and even though she could feel him quivering through the leash that strained in her hand, he stayed with her since she hadn't yet given him permission to attack.

The figure hesitated, obviously having second thoughts. Then it turned and was gone.

She let Viggo lead her back to the shed, and with hands that fumbled on autopilot lit her little camp stove for a cup of tea. Then she bundled herself back up in her sleeping bag and sat in her old wicker chair, sipping and staring into nothing while Viggo whined and thumped the floor with his tail, trying to reassure her. There was no chance of getting any more sleep tonight. At her age a decent six-hour stretch was a bonus anyway. It briefly crossed her mind to pack up and go back to the house, because what if it – whatever it was – was still out there and decided to come back? But it felt safer in here; she wasn't surrounded by empty rooms where anything could have been hiding. She would have spent the rest of the night wandering around like a madwoman, convinced that she'd heard something in her children's bedrooms, or the kitchen, or the study, or any one of a dozen other places. Here in the shed it was simple. Always had been.

She must have dozed off at some point, though, because she became aware of two things simultaneously: a grey morning light was sifting through the curtains, and the fact that she was as stiff as a board. Dennie groaned and levered herself out of the wicker chair. Her hip felt like there was ground glass in the joint. She swallowed a couple of ibuprofen with another cup of tea, fed Viggo, and when she couldn't put it off any longer went to have a look at the Neary plot.

If she'd expected it to look harmless in the thin light of day, she was mistaken. It was fringed with a veil of white winter-dead rosebay willowherb whose stalks rattled and whispered to each other in the chill breeze. Further in, knots of black-red brambles curved amongst the piles of rubbish like tangled loops of shoulder-high razor wire, some of the stems as thick as her wrist and all crowded with thorns capable of piercing the thickest gardening gloves. Past them and towards the bottom end of the plot was a copse of skeletal hawthorns and orange crab-apples. The plot obeyed the standard dimensions of a council allotment – five yards wide by fifty long – but was so overgrown that it was impossible to see its full extent, giving the impression that it was much larger on the inside than it should have been, as if anyone careless enough to trespass over its boundary might find themselves lost in a wilderness of thorns. Absolutely impossible to tell if someone had really been here during the night. But if there *had* been, if it hadn't all just been the product of her half-sleeping imagination, then it would have been up here, at the top end near the access track.

The end where Sarah Neary had buried the body of her husband.

The police have erected a blue evidence tent over the top end of Sarah's plot, and officers in disposable white overalls have been bustling in and out of it all day. The allotments have been closed and uniformed officers are at the gates to stop gawkers from interfering. There is a forensics van on the access track with its rear doors open for the investigators in overalls to transfer the remains that they've been excavating, and the driver has tried to park as close to the tent as possible to shield their activities from ghoulish eyes, but that doesn't stop Dennie from watching through the chain-link fence in the field behind the allotments and seeing what they are carrying out. Colin Neary's remains are removed in several black plastic body bags, each small enough for a single investigator to carry unassisted. Colin had been a big man, too big for Sarah to move in one piece. Dennie hopes they find all of him.

She came back to herself with a shake and a shiver. Viggo was licking her hand and whining.

'I'm okay,' she told him, and scratched him between the ears. 'Just wool-gathering, that's all.'

She checked her watch. Ten minutes lost. Not so bad this time.

She clicked her fingers and Viggo fell to heel as she headed for the Pavilion to talk to Angie.

The largest and only permanent structure on Briar Hill Allotments had been given its ironic nickname because of its total lack of any similarity to a quaint old-fashioned cricketing pavilion. It was low and squat, its roof mostly moss and its panels sorely in need of a new paint job, and despite being made from a pair of old demountable portacabins joined together which housed the committee meeting room and a members-only bar one side and the allotments offices on the other, gave the impression that it had sprouted out of the earth like a large rectangular fungus and was going nowhere. Over the years efforts had been made to replace it with something more substantial – or at least hygienic – all of which had been resisted by the committee members who loved their ramshackle clubhouse and didn't see the need to replace it just because the wiring was a bit dodgy and it tended to wobble in a strong wind.

Dennie found Angela Robotham in her office doing the accounts. Angie was almost a decade younger than Dennie, though her hair was iron grey and her face lined and tanned with years of working as a grounds team manager for the National Forest. Like most of the allotment holders, her work for Briar Hill was voluntary and part-time, undertaken on weekends and holidays. This being a Saturday, Angie was in early to catch up on the admin that nobody else wanted to do. She was sitting at her desk with a laptop open in front of her and wearing a heavy fleece jacket, since she also had a cigarette on and the window open next to her. A small electric heater whirred away on the other side, making a brave but doomed effort to alleviate the chill.

Dennie shivered. 'You know it's warmer in my shed,' she pointed out.

'Stinkier too,' Angie replied without looking up. 'With that great farting animal in there. Not to mention the dog.'

'Ouch. At least he doesn't smoke like a French soldier.'

Angie darted a bright blue eye at her. 'Does he do anything else like a French soldier?'

Dennie laughed. 'God, you're foul!'

Angie grinned, a topography of contour lines shifting in her cheeks and around her eyes. 'Morning, Dennie.'

'Morning, Angie.'

'Cup of tea?'

'No thanks, I'm swilling.'

'So, what can I do for you then? You haven't come here for the dazzling repartee.'

Pinned to a noticeboard beside her desk was a large map of the allotments, most of the plots labelled with the name of their tenants with the exception of a few blank spaces such as the one where the Neary plot lay. Dennie tapped it. 'I think we might have had a burglar last night.'

Angie closed the laptop and stared at her. 'What do you mean?'

Dennie gave her an edited version of her encounter with the strange figure, leaving out some of the more problematic details such as its abnormal size and the way it had seemed to be eating handfuls of the soil – details which would have made it sound like nothing more than the nightmare of a senile old woman. Angie listened with mounting anxiety, but not for the reasons that Dennie had hoped.

'And you thought you'd just go out and, what? Confront him? Jesus, Dennie, what if he'd had a knife? Or a gun?'

'I had Viggo with me,' she protested, scratching Viggo's head. He thumped the floor with his tail, pleased to be part of the conversation.

'Oh, so now he's bulletproof, is he? Why didn't you call the police?'

Now it was Dennie's turn to be scornful. 'Oh, come on,

Angie, you know better than that. The police don't bother with places like this. Remember when the Whites had that break-in? The buggers were in their home with their baby asleep upstairs and the best the police could do was tell them to lock themselves in the bathroom while it took them half an hour to get a patrol car out to them. You think they're going to send anyone to help *us*? We have to look after ourselves, because nobody else will. Let's face it, I'm the closest thing we've got to a security guard.'

Angie hmphed. 'That scares me more than the idea of burglars. You need to look after *your*self. You can't be sleeping in your shed, Dennie. We've spoken about this. It's against the by-laws, for one thing – and don't start with me,' she added, as Dennie opened her mouth to interrupt, 'because I know exactly what you think of the by-laws. Besides, it's just not safe. You'd have either set fire to yourself or been carried out with hypothermia long before now if it weren't for that big hairy lump there.'

Viggo thumped the floor again and grinned, tongue lolling.

Dennie sighed, and the sigh turned into a yawn. 'Look, Angie, I know you mean well but I didn't come here for a lecture and I'm too knackered for an argument. I just came in to let you know what I saw, so that you can tell everyone else to check their security. That's all.' She flapped a hand at the laptop. 'So just put it on your app thingy and I'll toddle off safely back to my proper bed, where I promise I won't be a nuisance to anybody.'

Angie smiled. 'Until next time.'

'Obviously.'

She left Angie to it and went home.

Home was on the other side of town, but since Dodbury was quite a small town – not much more than a large village, to be fair – it was only a half hour's walk. Nowhere near enough of a decent stretch for Viggo, but she promised him a good run around in the park that afternoon just as soon as she'd had a chance for a bath. She wouldn't normally have one in the morning, since an overnight in the shed was nothing unusual and she was way past the age where she felt the need to be fragrant for anyone, but being so close to the Neary plot had left her feeling itchy and unclean.

Briar Hill was a sunny rise on the north side of the village, so it was a pleasant amble downhill past the older and well-established houses of Greenlea to the crossroads which marked the top end of the High Street. There she stopped at Partridge's Butchers, their sign boasting that they were the oldest family butcher to still be 'preparing' their own meat in the county, and picked up a bone for Viggo as he'd been such a good boy. She endured the standard banter from Phil Partridge about whether he could tempt her from her vegetarianism with his pork buns. Further down the High Street, past where it became pedestrianised and every other doorway was a charity shop, the street market traders were setting up under their green-and-white-striped council awnings. With Christmas long over and Easter a distant dream, they were resigned to trade being thin. There had once been a proper indoor market right at the bottom of High Street where it became fast-food outlets and hairdressers – a part of town known as Dogtown for no reason that she'd ever been able to discover – but that had been demolished in the age of austerity to make way for some urban regeneration project that had never got further than an enthusiastic councillor's PowerPoint presentation. The resulting and perpetually empty lot was still called the Marketplace, and from time to time different enthusiastic councillors would propose revolutionary schemes to 'revitalise the flagging fortunes of our once vibrant market town' but nothing ever got built. Still, at least it gave the old men who wrote to the local newspaper letters of frothing indignation (and dubious grammatical accuracy) something to complain about other than fly-tipping and outrageous car parking charges foisted upon old-age pensioners.

Nothing was going to revitalise Dodbury, Dennie knew, for the simple reason that there had never been anything particularly vital about it in the first place. It was why she and Brian had chosen it as a home to raise their family. It was unexciting, quiet, and safe – for the most part.

Why the Neary plot, of all places?

She shifted uneasily in her clothes and scratched.

Left, then, at the top of High Street, past St David's with its blocky Norman tower, and then the pub that wasn't a pub – it had been the Hundred House for years before her time but when the brewery had gone to the wall it had been bought and transformed into an Indian restaurant called the Imperial Mint. Brian had hated it. Complained about how ugly the green neon and the Asian-style lettering sat against the old Victorian brickwork. 'I like a curry as much as the next man,' he'd said. 'But why can't they serve them up somewhere more appropriate?' By which he didn't just mean the architecture.

It was the Handsworth riots of '81 that had been the final straw for him. From their first flat just off the Lozells Road they'd been able to watch the fires and hear the police sirens screaming for three days, trying to explain what was happening to seven-year-old Christopher and his five-year-old sister Amy (little Lizzie was two at the time and only interested in chewing clothes pegs). Afterwards Brian had found Chris playing riots by smashing one of his toy cars into a Lego building; he'd cut out some tiny paper flames and coloured them in and stuck them to the car with Sellotape, and that was that. Within six months they had moved to a nice ordinary semi-detached in Dodbury which was quiet, safe, and came with a hefty mortgage that they had both worked hard to pay off, though to give him his due Brian had shouldered the heavier burden of it – a burden which had obviously been too much for his heart, however. A month to the day of their final payment he suffered a massive cardiac arrest and dropped dead in the middle of their driveway while taking the bins out.

Up that driveway now, past the spot where she'd found him, his face grey, but don't think about that, it's not for now, through the side gate (never the front door, not with Viggo's feet), tossing the bone to him in the back garden so that the great lolloping idiot could enjoy it in peace, and through the back door and into the kitchen. She stripped right there and stuffed all her clothes into the washing machine, and who cared if anyone in the houses behind her back fence was in a position to get an eyeful of this stringy old bird? Let them look. Then she went upstairs to run a bath.

While the water was running she quickly checked in each of the upstairs bedrooms. Not that she was checking *for* anything, she told herself, because of course nothing would have been changed or disturbed. How could it, when she was the only living soul here? There wasn't much to disturb anyway. The children's rooms had been stripped back to a spartan utility – no toys, books, posters, or clothes. She'd made sure that when each of them had left home they'd taken anything of sentimental value with them and given the rest to charity shops, and when Brian had ventured the opinion that this seemed a bit cold she'd told him, 'It's an empty nest, not a bloody shrine. They've got their own lives now and that's the way of it.' On the rare occasion when they all came back – Christmases, birthdays, Brian's funeral – she happily let their bustle and mess flow over her while it lasted, and then when they were gone again she replaced the bed linen, hoovered up, and shut the doors. To keep the warmth in and the dust out, she told herself, but she really knew it was because of the echoes.

There was a particular kind of echo to her children's empty rooms that she found unnerving. It wasn't an echo in the strictest sense of the sounds being repeated – more like the way the noise she brought in with her, even the whisper of feet on the carpet or the click of the latch, would resonate a little more, as if bouncing off extra corners in the room that shouldn't be there. More than once in the long, dark months after Brian's passing, before she'd learned to close the doors, she'd fancied that the sounds she made just moving around on her own might get caught in those odd corners and be amplified, feeding on themselves until they took on a life of their own and started whispering to her.

That was another good thing about the shed: it was too small and cluttered for echoes.

She quickly popped her head into each of the rooms to check that of course they were okay, closed them again and went to settle into her bath. She lay back with a sigh of contentment, letting the heat seep into her old bones. Just a quick one to scrub off the unclean feeling, not a long soak; it was only ten in the morning, after all.

It couldn't have been more than five minutes before she heard Viggo making a fuss at the back door, scrabbling and whining to be let in.

'Sod,' she grumbled. 'Couldn't you have waited…' But as she moved, and the bathwater sloshed around her, she realised her mistake. Viggo *had* waited. The little carriage clock on the window ledge told her that it was nearly eleven, and the water in which she'd been lying for nearly an hour was barely lukewarm. Viggo whined and scrabbled, scrabbled and whined. If he hadn't, how long might she have gone on sitting there?

Shivering with more than just the cold, she got out of the bath, wrapped herself in a towel, and went to let him in.

2

NEW NEIGHBOURS

DENNIE KEPT AWAY FROM HER ALLOTMENT FOR THE rest of the weekend but went back again on Monday morning because she needed to get a start on chitting her potatoes. It was comforting and repetitive work, picking out the unwanted eyes in the little seed potatoes and setting them with their sprouting ends uppermost in some old egg boxes by the shed window, and it allowed her to forget about the strange events of Friday night. Every so often she would pause to lob Viggo's slobber-sodden tennis ball down to the end of her plot, and he would make a great fuss about hurtling to retrieve it and then drop it at her feet.

When she spotted Angie through the half-open shed door walking on the Neary plot she thought at first that the secretary of the allotments association was following up on her report about the intruder, but then she saw that Angie was accompanied by two other people – a man and a woman, neither big enough to have been the huge figure from that night.

Both looked to be in their twenties, and were obviously a couple. The man was normal-sized, dressed in jeans and boots with his hands stuffed into the pockets of a long winter coat. His hair was dark and close-cropped, but not shaven like a thug, and probably good looking if you liked your men a bit dark and angular. Every so often he would kick at the soil a little, as if inspecting it. She was the taller, dressed in a style that would have been dismissed forty years ago as hippy chic: heavy boots, a tie-dyed gypsy shirt and denim jacket covered with patches, swathes of tasselled and glittering scarves over a loose-knit burgundy jumper that hung past her hands in ragged cuffs. She was also extraordinarily pale, with an oddly square jaw framed by masses of curling dark hair tipped over to one side.

They were chatting and smiling with Angie, standing right on the Neary plot as if they were just passing the time of day on a normal allotment like any other.

Journalists, Dennie decided. They popped up from time to time like weeds whenever they found out about the murder for the first time and thought they could unearth a unique new angle to an old story, but they never did – mostly because of what Angie was doing right now. Not warning them off, exactly, just making it clear that there was nothing more to be found.

'Shall we go and give her a hand?' Dennie asked Viggo. 'Shall we? You can bite him if you like.'

Viggo picked up his ball and trotted after her, but they weren't even halfway there when he started growling.

'I wasn't serious about the biting,' she said. 'Shut up, you big idiot.'

He subsided, but with her hand on his collar she could feel the tension bristling in him all the same.

When she was close enough to hear their conversation, it turned out that they weren't talking about the Nearys at all. They seemed to be having a conversation about, of all things, the optimum growing conditions for kale. Dennie approached the Neary plot as close as she was going to, but no further.

'Morning, Dennie,' said Angie. She wore a pleasant enough smile of greeting but something about the intensity of her eyes – a little too starey – came across as a warning. 'This is a nice surprise,' said her mouth, while her eyes said *Shut up. Whatever you were about to say, just shut it.* 'Let me introduce you to your new neighbours. Mr Everett Clifton and Miss Ardwyn Hughes, Mrs Denise Keeling. They'll be taking on Plot 27. Isn't that nice?'

Plot 27. Not 'the old Neary plot' which was what everybody called it. Not 'the plot where a terrified young woman had buried the remains of her brute of a husband after enduring years of beatings and abuse before finally snapping and killing him with a kitchen knife'. Not that place.

'Since when?'

If Mr Everett Clifton found her curtness rude, he didn't show it. He actually looked faintly embarrassed. 'Well,' he said, 'since yesterday, as a matter of fact. And it's just Everett, please. None of that "mister" silliness.' There was a hint of a Welsh accent in his voice. He put out his hand to shake hers, but that would have required her to step onto the Neary plot to reach him.

'Everett and Ardwyn were telling me that they've recently just moved into Dodbury.'

'Well, we're renting a little place just outside town,' said the young woman, whose accent was much more pronounced. 'We were having a nice lazy Sunday afternoon stroll, looking around, and we spotted this place and I just fell in love with it at first sight, so we called to make an appointment to look at it.'

Everett stepped forward, hand outstretched, and Viggo began to growl.

'Okay.' He stepped back a pace. 'He's a protective chap, I see.'

Dennie shook his collar. 'Be nice!' and the dog subsided. 'Sorry about that. He's a rescue dog – doesn't take to strange men too well. This is Viggo.'

'As in the actor,' put in Angie. In response to his blank look, she clarified: 'Viggo Mortensen? *The Lord of the Rings* films?'

'Yes, of course, I love those.' The easy smile was back, and Dennie thought *You're lying. You've got no idea what she's on about, have you?* But why would he bother to lie about such a trivial thing? She put on a smile of her own and gestured at the wild growth of the Neary plot. 'Well, you've certainly taken on a challenge. I'm surprised Angie didn't suggest something a bit tamer.' She turned to Angie. 'There are one or two other vacant plots, aren't there?'

Ardwyn shrugged. 'I know, and I can't explain it, but this one just seemed to call to me. Growing things – crops, I mean – it's all about transformation, isn't it? Seed to shoot, shoot to fruit, fruit to earth, earth to seed, round and round.

Something about changing this barren plot into a garden feels more meaningful than taking on one which is all clear and ready to go, do you know what I mean?'

'Well, if you can transform brambles into lentils or whatever it is you're thinking of growing on this, power to you.'

'Oh, I quite like the brambles,' said the young woman, turning to gaze speculatively at the head-high tangles. 'I bet they produce some incredible blackberries in the autumn.'

'They do,' said Dennie. 'But we don't eat them.'

'What a waste! Why ever not?'

Dennie looked at her youth and enthusiasm, the energy she was apparently prepared to pour into the hopeless task of turning this haunted wreck of an allotment into some kind of Edenic garden-of-plenty, and found herself feeling desperately sorry for her. 'Has Angie actually told you about this place?' she asked.

'I was just about to do that,' Angie interrupted, and Dennie thought *Like hell you were*. 'As a matter of fact, I was just going to pop back to the office and get all the paperwork. Dennie, could you come and help me please?' To the young couple she said, 'We won't be long.'

Everett smiled. 'That's fine. We'll just survey our new empire a bit more.'

Dennie plucked Angie's elbow once they were out of earshot. 'You haven't told them, have you?'

'Told them what? There's nothing to tell.'

'Angie—'

'There is nothing. To. Tell.' The other woman shook her arm free and walked on without looking at her.

'They deserve to know.'

Now Angie stopped and faced her squarely, arms crossed. 'Deserve to know what, Dennie? That something terrible happened there probably before either of them was born? What good would it do them? Or us, for that matter? We need new young people, Dennie. I don't know if you've noticed but the average age of our tenants is "geriatric old fart" years old and we need to do something about that before we're all compost. So what if they're a pair of starry-eyed millennials who'll give up after six months when they find that they can't grow avocados? It's going to be hard enough for them as it is without you telling them bloody ghost stories. For once, will you just please leave it?'

'What about the intruder I saw?'

'You mean the one you think you saw after a broken night's sleep in a draughty old shed?'

'It's not draughty! I've made sure that it's perfectly well…' She stopped. The word wouldn't come. She wanted to refute the accusation about her shed and tell Angie that it was this other *thing*, she'd put this *thing* in the walls to keep her shed warm, this thing that she couldn't say because it wasn't that the word was stuck, it was actually gone, like a fish slipping between her fingers; it had fallen into the empty space in her mind where bits of time sometimes went, the place where the echoes came from. She stood there with her mouth open like an idiot, groping for it, more confused than scared. 'Fine,' she managed to reply, and patted Viggo's neck. 'Come on, you.' She left, and he trotted after her.

'Dennie?' Angie's irritation had given way to concern,

and that was worse. 'Is everything—'

'No, it's fine!' she yelled back without turning. 'I won't say anything. I won't scare them off. But I'm not wrong! I'm not seeing things!'

She went back to the shed and spent the rest of the afternoon chitting her potatoes, because they didn't care about who was right or wrong, who died or who lived, they were going to need planting out all the same.

'Insulated,' she whispered to them, to Viggo, to the world, but mostly to herself. 'It's perfectly well *insulated*.'

'Will it do?' asked Everett as they left the allotments.

Ardwyn shrugged. 'It'll have to. There's no time to find anywhere more suitable.'

'I don't like the number of people around. There are other places with blood in the ground that are a lot less conspicuous. Battlefields, like that one we passed at Hopton Heath.'

'You read the same report that I did,' she reminded him. 'The Neary woman didn't just murder her husband, she dismembered him. That's ritual, whether she intended it or not. Moccus' spirit is strong here. Gar tasted it. He agrees.'

'Gar was right about the dog,' he said. 'It's an absolute monster.'

'Shh, baby,' said Ardwyn, and took his hand in both of hers as they walked towards the allotment's offices. 'Leave the monsters to Mother.'

After signing the necessary papers they drove back to their new home.

He Who Eats the Moon had provided for them in the form of a semi-derelict farm a mile outside Dodbury. A solicitor's notice posted in one of the windows of the farmhouse indicated that the Council had issued a closing order on it due to some kind of long-running legal wrangle, but that was the first thing to go on the fire when they started clearing out. The last inhabitant had obviously been a hoarder; they found teetering piles of yellowing newspapers and magazines blocking the hallways and staircase, rooms full of plastic bin bags stuffed with old clothes and crushed lager cans, and a kitchen rancid with rotting takeaway containers and crawling with vermin. The owner obviously hadn't been able to get into his own bathroom for years because he'd been washing in one bucket and shitting in another in one of the outbuildings, which were in an even worse state.

'Oh, darling!' gushed Ardwyn, all dewy-eyed and clutching Everett's arm in mock adoration. 'It's perfect! Our very first home!'

He carried her over the crumbling threshold and they collapsed into the hallway, laughing like drains. Gar looked on, bemused, then shook his head and went to look for some food.

Their ability to undertake any repairs to the place was going to be limited by the necessity to prepare the ground at the allotment first, but after fleeing Swinley and sleeping in a stolen van for two weeks in the depths of winter, a slightly mouldy mattress was positively palatial, and a small sacrifice to make in the cause of a much, much larger one.

3

THE SHED

Dennie first meets Sarah Neary in the spring of 2003, three years before Brian will be found dead in his own driveway. The Iraq War has ended and even though Dennie swore that she would never vote Labour again, not after the Winter of Discontent (having to keep two toddlers clean and fed in the middle of electricity blackouts and blizzards is a thing she said she would never forgive them for), in her opinion Saddam Hussein was a bullying bastard who deserved what he got. Christopher is twenty-nine and living the hedonistic lifestyle of a chartered surveyor in Burton-on-Trent – which is to say he's left home and hasn't asked them for money yet so he must be doing all right for himself – while Amy is sofa-surfing around America 'finding herself', and Lizzie has got herself an NVQ in Hospitality and Catering and is sharing a flat in Brighton with a nice young woman called Niamh on a basis that Dennie suspects *is something more than platonic; Dennie herself is still only in her late-forties, with the children allegedly able to fend for themselves and enough of her life ahead of her, she hopes, to think about training as a social worker. But it is daunting. Her schooling finished at about the same time that Neil Armstrong set foot on the moon, and studying for a diploma-level qualification seems just as remote. The textbooks are huge and expensive, she has to read them with a dictionary to look up every other word, and Brian makes no effort to disguise his disapproval of the cost but tolerates it because he's convinced she'll never stick it out.*

Between this and keeping the household, the allotment provides a welcome respite. The fruit trees have established themselves and she's got herself into a nice seasonal rhythm which means that she really only has to keep things ticking over. Brian doesn't bother her here, of course. He has his own routine built around a calendar of the four sporting seasons: cricket, football, rugby, snooker.

So it is that in May of '03 she sees a young couple exploring the vacant plot which is nowhere near as overgrown as it will be. Sarah is slim and blonde and heavily pregnant, while Colin is large, verging on overweight, and maybe it's the fact that he's wearing glasses which gives her the appallingly wrong first impression that he's basically harmless. Dennie doesn't introduce herself because they're wandering away even as she notices them, but they seem nice, she decides. It'll be nice to have new neighbours.

* * *

That Friday her new neighbours Ardwyn and Everett turned up with a van, a wheelbarrow full of pickaxes and shovels, and a helper: a tall slab of a man with a lantern jaw that made him remind Dennie of that big American actor from *Sons of Anarchy*. Big enough to be the hulking figure she'd seen – or dreamed – chewing the soil, although the more she thought about it the more likely it seemed that Angie had been right, so she tried to keep her head down and mind her own business. He didn't say anything – not to his friends and certainly not to any of the locals who stopped by to pass the time of day or offer advice – he just got stuck into the work of hacking back the forest of brambles with a silent intensity that was almost monomaniacal. She heard through the gossip in the Pavilion that his name was Gareth and that he was Everett's brother.

Over the next three weeks the new tenants of Plot 27 made a favourable impression with the neighbouring allotment holders by keeping largely to themselves and not changing anything too much. There was so much litter and overgrowth that it took them that long to clear and level the first few metres. Everett was often in the Pavilion making small talk with the old-timers and picking their brains for tips, though they told him he'd be lucky to get that wreck of an allotment into a fit state for planting by next spring, never mind this year. If any of them told him the Neary story he didn't seem to be bothered by it, because he and his 'brother' kept right on hacking and digging. He didn't make small talk with Dennie, though, and she wondered why.

Then their shed appeared, and first feathers began to ruffle.

It wasn't just that it seemed to spring up overnight – it was the kind that you bought as a kit from a garden centre and put up in a few hours with a drill and an extra pair of strong hands, if you knew what you were doing. It was the size of the thing. The Briar Hill Allotments by-laws stipulated that a shed could be no larger than six feet by eight, which was more than enough for most purposes, including the occasional illicit sleepover. The newcomers' shed was half that again, a size which caused much shaking of heads and muttering in the Pavilion about 'that bloody aircraft hangar'.

The first Friday of the month was Committee Night at the Pavilion, and more often than not there was so little allotment business needing to be sorted that it was not much different from an ordinary Friday night's drinking and chatting, but on this occasion Angie and the other committee members were pressed to Do Something About It. The loudest voice belonged to Hugh Preston, a grizzled man in his sixties and former Welsh Guard with one eye. He claimed to have lost its partner in a hand-to-hand scrap with an Argentinian soldier in the battle for Port Stanley in '82 armed only with a spatula, and whether this was true or not his undisputed military credentials gave his opinions the weight of authority. 'They might very well be a nice couple,' he said to Angie. 'But if you let that sort of thing slide at the start then who knows where it will end up?' He was playing darts at the time and was being given a wide berth by the other drinkers; despite claiming that his lack of depth perception didn't affect his accuracy in the slightest, the wall to the left of the dartboard was pocked with holes that suggested otherwise. 'They'll be having raves and orgies before you know it.'

'Chance would be a fine thing!' said Edihan 'Big Ed' Rimedzo, to general laughter. He owned the Turkish barber shop in town and was so called because he stood only a little over five feet tall. 'It's just a shed, Hugh, not a massage parlour.' Big Ed was deep in a game of dominoes with Ben Torelli, himself a veteran of three tours of Afghanistan, who made no secret of his disdain for Hugh's pronouncements and usually avoided the Pavilion altogether.

'Don't worry,' Angie replied. 'I'll have a word with them about it.'

But she didn't have to, because later that evening Everett came in with a home-printed A4 flyer that he pinned to the Pavilion noticeboard beside the bar. He cleared his throat a few times to get everyone's attention. 'So, just to explain,' he said, nodding at the flyer. 'Ardwyn and I would like to invite you all – and your families too – to a barbecue that we're throwing as a way of saying thanks to you all for welcoming us here and being so generous with your time and advice. It's next Sunday, and it's mostly going to be kind of a hog-roast thing, though of course there will be other options if pork isn't your thing. And it's all on us. Just bring your own good selves. And a big appetite,' he added with an embarrassed smile as if it were a lame punchline that he'd been rehearsing. 'Anyway, the details are all there. Hope to see you.'

He ducked out, leaving a murmur of surprise rising in his wake.

'They can't be short of a bob or two if they're offering to feed everyone,' said Torelli. 'Hey Angie, are you going to throw the book at him before or after he treats the whole allotments to a free hog roast?'

'I told you they seemed like a nice couple,' said Hugh, with a wink of his good eye that raised laughter from the room.

Viggo was growling again. Dennie twisted in her sleeping bag, consciousness trying to fight its way clear of a smothering weight of sleep that gummed her eyes and chained her limbs. 'Brian,' she murmured. 'The dog's going off again. See what he wants.' But Brian didn't answer, and when she rolled over to prod him her hand whacked against something hard and wooden and the pain was like a cup of cold water in the face.

She sat up. Past and present swirled around her like different coloured dyes in water, making it murky. Brian didn't know who Viggo was because she'd got him as a puppy a month after her husband had died. Brian was gone. Shed. She was in her shed. There was a man eating soil on the Neary plot. Colin Neary. No, Colin was dead too, buried in pieces under the earth.

She whacked her hand again on the shelf above her head, deliberately this time. 'Wake up, you stupid cow,' she growled at herself.

Then Viggo licked her face and that did the trick.

She cradled his head in her hands and scrunched his ears, partially to tell him that she loved him and she was all right, but mostly so that he would stop slobbering at her. He whined a little, appreciating the gesture, but was soon growling again. The sense of déjà vu was so strong that even when she checked her watch and confirmed that yes, it was 3:07 in the morning of Saturday the 14th of March – exactly the same time she had woken up to see the soil-eating man, which was a funny coincidence – the act of getting up and putting her boots on had a dreamlike quality to it, as if she were not entirely in control of her own actions.

She shushed him and followed him outside. Heavy cloud had insulated the ground from the frost, and this time when he led her to the Neary plot the bulk of her new neighbours' shed was a square shadow against the night. A thin strip of light showed under the door, and from inside she could hear the low murmurs of soft conversation between a female and male voice. In the weeks that they'd been clearing the ground and after the structure had appeared she hadn't bothered herself with interfering, because as far as she was concerned they could have any size shed they liked. And if the figure she had seen that first night had just been Everett's brother Gareth then, bizarre and terrifying though it might have been, it hadn't been burglary and no crime had been committed. If anything, she was in the wrong now, sneaking around and spying on them. So what if they were having an illicit overnighter? She could hardly accuse them of breaking that particular by-law. They weren't playing loud music or being a nuisance. She should go back to bed; live and let live.

Then came a sound she knew intimately well, but one that she had never heard coming from inside a shed: the scraping of shovels and the digging of earth.

'What?' she whispered to Viggo. Digging at this time of night? And how were they managing it inside – did their shed have no floor? It was so nonsensical that she listened more closely, trying to find an alternative explanation for the sound, something that her old ears had misinterpreted, something that made sense. Maybe they were mixing potting compost. It was still a chilly night; maybe—

And then the door opened, and Gareth stood framed against the light, having to duck his head under the frame, stepping outside with a shovelful of soil. He saw her, tossed the shovel to one side and came for her, just like before, except this time he opened his jaws and snarled. No human face could unhinge so widely or boast such close-clustered and overgrown teeth, like the business end of a construction digger, and the noise that came from it was like nothing she had ever heard out of a human throat: and the shock of it paralysed some tiny, terrified animal part of her brain. The figure – *it's no man, whatever that thing is it's not a man* – came for her, and Viggo went absolutely berserk.

Dennie screamed and ran, only realising that she had forgotten to lace up her boots until the moment her feet tangled and she was pitching forward, hands outstretched, and her head smacked into something so hard that—

Viggo was licking her face and whining, but the whining was also coming from inside her skull, rising and falling with a throbbing headache that filled it like a festering sore about to rupture. She groaned and dragged herself slowly into a sitting position, wincing as the headache shifted and sloshed with her movement. Wooden floorboards were hard beneath her hands. Morning light stabbed at her through the window, making the headache worse.

She was on the floor of her own shed, half-covered by the sleeping bag that had slithered off the folding camp bed which was tipped on its side next to her. *Finally done it, idiot*, she chided herself. *You've finally gone and fallen out of bed and given yourself a concussion. Now they'll all know that you're going gaga. Happy now?* She inspected herself with her fingers – there was a lump the size of a golf ball above her left eye but no blood, it seemed. That was some relief, but the bruising was going to be spectacular, and the pain in her head nothing compared to the 'I-told-you-so's' that she was going to have to endure from her children, from Angie, and from the other allotment holders—

A strip of light under the door.

The sound of digging.

A mouth with far too many teeth.

She levered herself to her feet and yanked the shed door open, squinting into the glare of daylight. It should have been bolted shut from the inside, but it swung freely. *Unless you just forgot to bolt it yourself last night.* Or unless someone had dragged her in and dumped her but been unable to bolt it after themselves when they left. The combination of headache, bright light, and suddenly being upright threw her guts into revolt – nausea twisted her, and she was nearly sick on her own threshold, but she held it back. *No. Not in front of other people. Have some dignity for once.* She staggered outside.

It was Saturday morning, a busy time of the week, and all around she could see her neighbours clearing the winter rubbish, preparing cloches, planting out seedling crops. Over on the Neary plot Everett and Ardwyn were digging away just the same as everyone else, but no alleged brother. She marched over, a little unsteadily on account of the nausea and the fact that she was in her socks.

'Just what in hell do you people think you're playing at?' she demanded.

The pair of them paused as she approached, expressions of confusion turning to concern.

Ardwyn's hand flew to her mouth. 'Oh my God, Dennie! Your head! What's happened to you?'

'That looks like a nasty bump,' said Everett. He stuck his spade in the ground and took out his phone. 'You need an ambulance. You could have a concussion.'

'Don't give me that bollocks!' Dennie retorted. 'And you'd better put that thing away or I'll stick it somewhere you'll need a spade to get it back out again.'

'I don't understand,' said Ardwyn. 'Dennie, what's happened?'

'At least let us get an icepack on that,' Everett offered, putting his phone away. He gestured back to their shed, the door of which was shut. 'Why don't you come in and sit down? We'll make you a cup of tea and have a look at that.'

'Icepack my arse!' she snapped. 'I'm not setting one foot on this plot, and I don't know what's wrong with that "brother" of yours, but if I see him around here again I'm having the police on him for assault. Do you understand?'

'Dennie,' said Ardwyn, 'you've obviously had a fall. I don't think you're thinking clearly. Is there anyone we can call?' She was talking in the gentle tone and making the placatory hand gestures of a person who has realised that they're dealing with someone drunk or mentally unstable, but behind the concerned frown there was a sparkle of amusement in her eyes that just made Dennie even more angry. *She's enjoying this, the little bitch.*

'Oh, piss off!' she yelled, and now she was drawing the attention of those nearby. Heads came up, digging paused. If any of the neighbouring sheds had net curtains, they were twitching. 'Just keep away from me and my dog, got that?'

'Did we get that?' asked Ardwyn as they watched the old woman totter away.

'Loud and clear,' Everett replied. 'As did I think most of the neighbourhood.'

'Good. Honestly, this is the best way.'

'I know, and I agree, but try telling Gar that. If that dog comes for him again there's no telling what he'll do.'

Ardwyn kissed him, stroking his hair. 'If you think about it,' she said, 'she's actually doing us a favour – anything she sees will be dismissed as the ravings of a crazy old bat. Who knew she actually slept here? Does she even have a home, do you think? Maybe she eats out of bins.' She chuckled at the thought.

'It's a problem,' he insisted.

'Not if properly managed,' she replied. 'Assuming that she comes to the feast, we'll have nothing to worry about.'

'And if she doesn't?'

She took up her spade and resumed digging over the ground. A worm appeared, pink and squirming, and she chopped it in half with the blade, watching it writhe as its juices oozed out, fertilising the soil with its death. 'Then we might have to let Gar off the leash.'

4

BRUISES

OVER THE NEXT FEW DAYS THE LEFT SIDE OF DENNIE'S
face came up in a livid rainbow of yellows, purples, and
greens. The neighbours were too polite to say anything, of
course, which was just as well with her. Despite the drinking
and camaraderie in the Pavilion, when it came to the actual
allotments themselves people were a lot more solitary.
For many of them, like Dennie herself, their allotment
was a welcome distraction from the stress and noise of
everyday life, a place of solitude and calm where each was
king or queen over their own tiny kingdom, and so they
were reluctant to disturb each other, happy to potter and
dig in companionable silence. So when, on a bright and
breezy Wednesday afternoon, Dennie saw Becky Pimblett
coming towards her with a tentative smile and a plastic
Tupperware container, she was surprised, alarmed, but also
a little pleased.

Rebecca Pimblett was red-haired and rail thin, with high, birdlike cheekbones and a wide goofy smile that she lavished on the world, though Lord knew the Pimbletts had little enough to smile about.

'Hello, Dennie!' she called. 'I hope you don't mind me dropping by. I heard you had an accident and I thought I'd bring you a little something to cheer you up.' This was exactly the thing that Dennie liked about Becky: a straightforward and complete absence of pussy-footing around and a refusal to wallow. If Dennie had told her to sod off and mind her own business, she'd have given a chirpy 'Fair enough' and tried again some other time.

'Becky,' she replied, 'don't tell me you've gone and actually baked something for me.'

'Well,' Becky drawled, as if it wasn't a big thing. 'I was making some biscuits anyway and it wasn't any trouble to throw in an extra batch.'

Dennie took the offered box but didn't open it straight away. 'Can I ask how the little one's doing?'

'Alice?' Becky's smile sobered. 'About as well as can be expected, thanks for asking. This last round of chemo has really knocked her for six. But David has the day off so we've brought her out for some fresh air. It's going to be spring soon and I want her to see things growing instead of spending all her time surrounded by tubes and wires. I mean the house is clean but it's a cold clean, you know?'

'I know exactly what you mean.'

'Listen, why don't you come over and say hi to her?'

'Oh no, I don't think—'

'What, you've got something more important to do than meeting my family?'

'No, it's just…' Dennie gestured at her face. 'I must look a fright.'

'My little girl is a Pimblett, and we don't scare easily. Besides, you've got a way to go to be scarier than a man in a white coat with a big needle. Come on.'

Dennie gave in and let herself be led, Viggo trotting by her side. She glanced towards the Neary plot as they went; the newcomers hadn't been seen since the Saturday when she had confronted them, and she hoped that they had enough of a sense of shame to be keeping their heads low for a bit. She'd debated whether or not to tell Angie, but not for long – Dennie knew exactly what she'd say. *Are you sure you didn't dream it, Dennie? Been having more of those blank moments, Dennie? Do you really think it's safe to be on your own so much of the time, Dennie?* She went with Becky mostly because she genuinely just liked the young woman and her family, but there was also a way in which she thought they might be able to help her.

Becky's husband David was a printing engineer by trade, running the big machines at a company in Stafford that made menus and local newspapers and the endless stream of glossy junk mail that seemed to be the only things that the postman delivered these days, but with that industry going down the tubes along with pretty much every other one, he'd been forced to go part-time, lucky to have not lost his job altogether. The opportunity to spend extra time with his sick seven-year-old daughter might have been a godsend to some fathers, but David Pimblett was one of those vanishingly rare individuals, in Dennie's experience, whose sense of community spirit was almost as strong as his love for his family, and he'd volunteered to use some of that newly freed-up time as a Special Constable for Staffordshire Police's Needwood Neighbourhood Team. The police station in Dodbury had closed over ten years ago, with the nearest station now being four miles away in Rugeley and only five full-time officers employed to look after nearly twenty square miles of isolated rural farms and villages, most of whom had only a Neighbourhood Watch scheme as their front-line defence against the increasing amount of farm theft and 'county lines' drug gangs. Dodbury was no different. David's shifts riding along with the regular officers rarely saw him in the village itself, but even when he was off-duty there was a sense that at least they weren't completely on their own. With his time taken up in this way it was Becky who looked after their allotment, which like its owners was straightforward, no-nonsense, and cheerful.

The planting beds were simple rectangles formed out of old timber railway sleepers painted in bright colours – a bit weathered, but still solid. At one end they had a few small fruit trees which were just starting to bud and at the other a timber shed with a bit of decking out front and a water butt to catch rain run-off from the roof. David was digging over the soil in one of the beds, his breath pluming in the cold. He was the sort of man she would ordinarily cross the street to avoid, with his closely shaven scalp and tattoos covering both arms, which just went to prove how wrong first impressions could be. On the deck, their daughter Alice sat in a folding picnic chair reading a book, wrapped up thickly in a hat, coat and gloves, and a surgical mask which made it hard to see how thin Dennie guessed she must be, but the pallor of the girl's face and the dark circles under her eyes said enough.

'Hallo, the workers!' called Becky as she and Dennie approached. 'Get the kettle on! I've brought a guest for morning tea.' Alice looked up and waved. Her father set his spade in the ground with a sigh of relief.

Alice was staring at Viggo, open-mouthed with delight. He grinned back at her, tongue lolling. 'Can I pat him?' she asked her mother.

'Sorry, honey, no. Germs.'

'If it's not safe, we can always go,' said Dennie.

'No, it's okay. The doctors have said that she's making good progress but her immune system is going to be a mess for a while yet. So a few hours in the outdoors should be okay, just as long as bits of it don't lick her.'

Meanwhile the girl had noticed the bruise on Dennie's head. 'Were you in a fight?'

'Yes I was,' she replied. 'With a huge ogre! But I kicked him up the bum so hard my shoelaces came out of his nose.'

Alice giggled in horror, her eyes shining.

David filled a small camping kettle and set it to boil on a portable gas stove while Becky brought out an extra folding chair, and they sat on the deck. Dennie complimented them on the upkeep of their allotment and David asked her advice about onions while they watched a robin inspecting his handiwork, and then tea arrived, accompanied by Becky's home-made biscuits. The Pimbletts were further away from the Neary plot than herself, with more allotments between them, so Dennie couldn't tell whether the newcomers were there or not.

'How are things in the neighbourhood watching business?' Dennie asked him. 'Quiet, I hope.'

He nodded. 'Nice and peaceful. I think all the troublemakers have migrated south for the winter.'

'Nothing from the OWL?'

'Nothing from the OWL,' he confirmed. 'As you would know, if you had a smart phone.'

Dennie hmphed. 'And have Siri or Alexa or whatever it is following my every move? No bloody thank you.'

'Where's the owl?' asked Alice, looking around.

'It's not that kind of owl, honey,' said her father. OWL stood for Online Watch Link, an app-based service which allowed members of the local community to report concerns to the police and for the police in turn to inform the Neighbourhood Watch, through David, if there might be suspected criminal activity in the area. Dennie had asked Angie to log her first encounter with the 'intruder' on it, but was beginning to suspect that she hadn't done even that. 'It's a thing on my phone that helps me to hear when there might be bad people around.'

'Can I have a phone?'

'No,' said her mother and father at the same time.

The robin continued to hop and flutter, peering for worms and beetles in the overturned earth. Viggo watched it intently, but behaved himself.

'So, nothing at all, then?'

He turned to look at her. 'Why? Are you expecting something?'

She tried to laugh it off. 'No, of course not. It's just that old saying, you know, about it being too quiet.'

'Well, I like it quiet,' said Becky. 'Though chance would be a fine thing with this monster rampaging around my house all the time,' she added, and pulled Alice's hat down over her eyes.

'Mummy!'

'Although,' Becky added, 'there is that big hog roast on Sunday, which sounds like it should be fun. I take it you're going?'

'I don't know. I haven't decided yet. I'm a bit busy this weekend. I'm also a vegetarian, so hog roasts aren't really my thing.'

Removing meat from her diet had been another of those changes after Brian that she couldn't have made while he was alive. He'd liked his Sunday roasts. He'd also liked his Sunday morning fry-ups, and his Friday evening sausages – in fact there hadn't been a day of the week which hadn't included meat on the menu, a factor which had probably gone a long way towards explaining his heart condition.

'Well, my family's Jewish but it doesn't make any difference to me,' Becky said. 'I'm sure there will be other options for us social outcasts, and for heaven's sake we can take something along anyway to help out. It would be lovely if you could come. I think there should be more occasions like that, getting everybody together for a big celebration.

161

You know, like a proper little village within a village.'

'Have you met our new neighbours, then?'

'Only to chat to, in passing.'

Dennie sipped her tea carefully and tried to keep her tone neutral. 'And what do you make of them?'

Becky shrugged. 'They seem nice. She's obviously got him wrapped around her little finger, but he's a bit of a charmer himself.'

'Easy, woman,' growled David in a mock yokel voice. 'Don't you be staring at no other menfolk, or I'll beat you.'

Sarah tries to laugh it off but Dennie can see that it's a fragile and shiny thing, that laugh, like a glaze over something brittle that might craze and crack into pieces at any moment.

'Don't be silly, Dennie.' She laughs. 'I was taking Fred for a walk and he saw a bird and charged off after it, and I had the lead wrapped too tightly around my wrist, that's all.' She tugs the sleeve of her jumper down from where it has accidentally ridden up to expose the bracelet of bruises around her forearm – they are an angry purple, thunderclouds threatening to break out from under her skin. Dennie doesn't say that she has seen a matching bracelet on her other wrist, because then Sarah will have to elaborate upon the lie with something about how she transferred the lead to her other hand and then, wouldn't you know it, the silly dog did the same thing again. Dennie doesn't point out that she's noticed over the past year how Sarah's t-shirts have gone from short to long-sleeved, and how she's gone from wearing low-cut blouses to turtle-neck sweaters even when working on her allotment in the heat of summer.

Dennie doesn't think her brittleness could survive that. But she can't say nothing, because if she says nothing she may as well be inflicting the bruises herself.

Sarah's baby boy, little Josh, is eighteen months old and trundling around the allotment in tiny overalls and rainbow wellies, using a plastic beach spade to help Mummy dig. Dennie watches him potter and chatter happily to himself, and experiences a deep upwelling of sadness for what this boy will have to grow up seeing.

'Sarah,' she says. 'You know that if you ever need, you know, a break. A rest. You can always... there's always room... now that my lot are gone...'

'I'm sorry, if I need a what?' Becky was frowning at her in concern. Not Sarah. David was pretending to be helping Alice break part of a biscuit into crumbs for the robin, but Dennie could tell that he was listening too. Viggo was on his feet, whining.

'Oh no,' she whispered, struggling to her feet out of the folding camp chair. Her mug clattered to the deck and spilled lukewarm tea. 'I'm so sorry, I didn't mean to...'

Becky was rising to her feet too, now. 'Dennie, are you okay? Do you want me to call someone?'

Dennie waved it away. 'No. Thank you. For the tea and... No, sorry, I just. I need to...'

Muttering more vague and half-coherent apologies, she wandered back towards the safety of her own allotment, Viggo close beside, leaving the Pimblett family staring after her.

5

THE SUMMONING

A FRESHLY PAINTED SIGN ON THE GATE THAT OPENED onto the main road proclaimed that this was now Farrow Farm. Preparations for the equinox rite were as complete as they were going to be, but the deserter was still nervous.

'You're sure we don't need to do this at the allotment?' he asked.

'I told you, we only need to raise him there,' she said. 'We are the new Church of Moccus, and we can perform the rite in any way we see fit. He can be killed anywhere, which is just as well, considering the noise.'

'Aren't there not quite enough of us? You know, for an orgy?'

'The sex was always in celebration rather than summoning. Still,' she added, with a teasing smile, 'if it makes you feel better, you and Gar could always—'

'No, forget it. No way.'

'Well, then maybe you and I can celebrate afterwards.'

As mother of her 'church' Ardwyn had controlled the purse strings but she hadn't wanted to take any chances on how quickly the Farrow might have been able to convince the police to track the use of credit cards, so part of their four-day flight from Swinley had included a long detour south along the M6, emptying her account in a series of transactions that she hoped would encourage pursuers to follow a false trail. During their short time in Dodbury some of the cash had been spent on a suite of skinning and butchering tools, a stainless steel cattle trough, a chopping table, a chain block hoist and a sturdy extendable tripod, hooks, a mincing machine and a sausage machine, and a large chest freezer – but he didn't know how long the rest of it was going to have to last them. He didn't know if he and Gar would be enough to hold Moccus, assuming that the god would be able to find them at all.

The rite would be after moonrise at five in the morning, barely a couple of hours before dawn itself, and after checking and re-checking everything there was nothing else to do except fret, so he fell back on a soldier's habits and tried to grab a few hours' kip while he could.

When Ardwyn woke him she was naked, and she held the bone carnyx.

'It's time,' she told him.

He removed the clothes that he'd slept in, took up his knife, and went out to join her and Gar in the farmyard, where a bonfire had been lit.

Moccus – Eater of the Moon – had shown his favour by

blessing them with clear skies, though this made it chilly. The waning moon was low in the east, a fingernail sliver which would soon disappear into darkness, only to be reborn like the god himself. Virgo was on her back on the opposite horizon, and between them Mars and Jupiter were in conjunction, so close that their overlapping brightness outshone everything else in the heavens. 'War and wisdom combined, see?' she said, pointing it out to him. 'As his tusks die she opens her legs to him that he may be reborn inside her.'

She raised the pale bone of the carnyx to her lips.

'Wait!' he said. The horn dropped, and she stared at him. 'What if I'm wrong? It's not too late. Maybe we could...' he trailed off, irresolute.

She didn't try to reassure him; that wasn't her way. 'Are you wrong?' was all she asked. 'You've killed him three times already. I imagine that means you know him as well as any mortal can. Besides, what's the alternative? You're wrong about it not being too late, I'll give you that. We can't go back. Mother would feed us to his children. When I first met you, you were a deserter, and that was ideal for what the Farrow needed, but I don't need that any more. I need someone who will stay and make a stand. So, are you wrong?'

Gar added an interrogative grunt.

Everett sighed, deflated. 'No. I'm not wrong. Do it.'

'Good then.' She put the carnyx to her mouth again and blew, and its mournful note rolled across the night-shrouded fields.

'Moccus!' she cried. 'Great boar! Dagger mouth! Hunter's bane! We summon thee!'

She blew a second time.

'Ninurta! First farmer! Law giver! Healing hand! We summon thee!'

She blew a third and final time.

'Saehrimnir! First flesh! God's feast! Divine blood! We summon thee!'

A mile away, the people of Dodbury stirred in uneasy sleep. David Pimblett dreamed of being chased through the cathedral spaces of a primeval forest by something huge that ran on two legs but panted like a beast. Angie Robotham dreamed of harvesting root crops on her allotment, only instead of carrots and parsnips she found herself pulling up hunks of raw flesh, dripping red and twitching. At home, downstairs in the kitchen, Viggo woke Dennie with his howling.

Moccus, ancient and weary, stepped into the firelight. His nearly blind eyes squinted around at the farm buildings, and his nostrils flared as he took in the scents of this strange new place. He snarled, confused and displeased.

'I know,' said the deserter. 'It's not what you're used to. But it will be better, believe me. The offerings of Swinley were weak and their flesh thin fodder to keep a god under their heel, but here we will deliver you from that. Here you will be free, to finally enjoy human blood as you were always meant to. Only submit to us, one more time. Once more, that we may deliver you and earn your favour.'

Aged though Moccus was, the beast-god still towered over him, and though his tusks were yellowing they were still sharp enough to disembowel him with a single toss of the head. Everett held his breath, waiting for the deity's response. Next to him he could feel Ardwyn's tension like a bowstring thrumming in the air.

Moccus' snout began to wrinkle in a snarl, and he lowered his head to charge.

With a roar, Gar leapt onto his back, slamming both knees into the base of his spine while simultaneously curling his arms into the crooks of Moccus' elbows and pulling the god's arms back, bending his torso skyward even as he was driven to his knees. Everett leapt forward and plunged the black-bladed knife deep into Moccus' breast even as the god managed to rip one arm free and swat him. Everett went reeling, his head full of ringing chaos. He was aware of Gar and Moccus both roaring and tearing at each other, then a great concussion in the earth nearby and then silence.

When he shook his head clear and looked around, Moccus was lying on his back, feebly clutching at the ground, his chest heaving, the blade still hilt-deep. Gar was picking himself up painfully from where he'd been flung.

Then the heaving stopped.

The deserter spat out dirt. 'Get the chain block,' he said, and went to retrieve his knife.

They rested after hoisting Moccus up into the apex of the tripod slaughtering frame and bleeding him into the cattle trough. Gar, nursing several bruised ribs, disappeared on his own business. Ardwyn dipped a finger in the cruor and marked Everett's mouth with it. It tingled, like salt sherbet. She sucked the rest of it off her finger and said, 'You have a busy night before you, slaughterman. But first we celebrate.'

She used her hands to paint him with the blood of Moccus, putting feral striping along his face, flanks, and thighs. He did the same for her, decorating her breasts and belly with swirls and whorls which might have been fruiting vines or serpents. She slicked his cock with cruor and lay back to take him, and he fucked the blood of their slaughtered god into her beneath the light of a dying moon.

6

BARBECUE

SUNDAY WAS THE BUSIEST DAY OF THE WEEK AT BRIAR Hill Allotments, and there were plenty of eyes to watch the preparations for the much-anticipated barbecue. The weather had set in overcast but it wasn't actively raining, which was the most anybody could expect from late March. The first surprise was when the newcomers' battered blue van arrived around mid-morning, because most people had assumed that they would simply buy a hog roast in from Partridge's or a catering company – and when the young man and woman started hauling out trestle tables, bags of charcoal, boxes of disposable picnic supplies, crates of beer and soft drinks, trays of bread rolls, and three large red cool-boxes, a few muttered that they'd bitten off more than they could chew but the general feeling was one of approval. The new neighbours weren't going to dazzle them by flashing their cash on something slick and corporate. They were doing it old school.

Within ten minutes they had offers from half a dozen pairs of willing hands who, between them, made short work of digging a wide, shallow pit for the charcoal, putting up the tables, and setting out the plates, cups, bottles, and napkins. This attracted satellite hangers-on in the form of friends and relatives, and in half an hour a sizeable crowd had gathered. Meat came out of the cool-boxes in large foil-wrapped joints that were placed directly onto the charcoal once it had died down to white embers, more embers were shovelled over the top and then turves from the pit were laid on top of that to keep in the heat.

Everett popped the top off a bottle of beer, dumped himself into a camp chair, smiled around at the crowd and said, 'And now we wait. You know this is going to take about six hours to cook, right? Did anybody bring a pack of cards?'

People brought more than a pack of cards. From sheds across the allotments came outdoor games and toys that had been stashed away for the summer: giant Jenga, swingball, and cricket sets. Shane Harding brought a set of juggling balls, causing hilarity and chaos by substituting them with increasingly improbable objects like potatoes, cushions, and – to cries of delighted disgust – even Hugh Preston's false eye. The festivities drew out even the recluses like Ben Torelli and dour old Marcus Overton, a decommissioned grammar school headmaster who was using retirement to enjoy his twin hobbies of gardening and misanthropy. While the kids played, the adults stood around in groups and chatted, comparing notes on what they were growing, arguing about sport and avoiding politics because a dispute over football statistics was one thing, but a conversation about Brexit could end friendships. Most went and brought back some contribution or other to the occasion – salads, snacks, more bread, more drinks. Over the next six hours they came and went, some stayed for a few minutes, some an hour, some went home to do the laundry and came back again later, some went back to work on their plots, but as the afternoon lengthened and the time for the pit to be opened drew near, the numbers gradually increased.

Dennie watched the day unfold from her own plot. She couldn't see any sign of the brother, but that still wasn't any kind of incentive to join in with the festivities. She watched Ardwyn and Everett being the perfect hosts – chatting, mingling between the various groups, playing swingball with the kids, and saw nothing to suggest that there was anything underhanded about them. The door to their shed was wide open, and as far as she could see from here it looked absolutely normal, stocked with the kinds of tools and gardening odds and sods that she would have expected to find in any of the other sheds. Looking at its solid wooden floor it seemed ridiculous to think that she had heard digging coming from inside; it was much more likely to have been a dream or another episode, but the one thing that she was absolutely rock-solid sure of was the mockery she had seen in Ardwyn's eyes. The young woman's solicitous concern for Dennie's health had been a mask behind which she was laughing at her. Worse, she was now laughing at all her friends and neighbours. Dennie watched Ardwyn chatting with Becky while David helped Everett check the cooking pit, then hunker down to say something to Alice which made the girl giggle, and thought *Right, that's it*. Whatever game the couple were playing, they weren't going to play it with the Pimblett family.

But that didn't mean she had to march over there and make a big fuss like last time. They'd caught her off guard, and she'd made a fool of herself. Worse, she'd alerted them to the fact that she knew they were up to something. They wanted to pretend that she was just a doddery old fart. Well that was a part she was more than happy to play.

'But you stay here, my big hairy hero,' she told Viggo, and put him on his leash in the shed. 'I don't need you picking any more fights on my behalf.'

He thumped his tail and whined as she left, not at all convinced that this was a good idea.

'I think it's incredible what you've done with this place,' David said to Everett as they strolled towards the end of the allotment. 'Especially in so short a time.'

The bottom half of their plot was still an unreclaimed wilderness of brambles and nettles growing through heaps of debris, but the space between that and their over-sized shed – roughly ten yards of the overall length – had been cleared, dug over, and marked out with sticks and twine.

Everett waved the compliment away with his beer. 'Thanks, but this is mostly Gareth's handiwork. He's an absolute fiend for digging.'

'So, come on then, what are your plans for it? When you sit on your deck at the end of a long day and you gaze across your empire, what will you see?'

'Mostly heritage varieties, you know, streaky tomatoes, purple carrots, that sort of thing. I want to bring something old out of the ground.' He gave a little laugh.

'Ah, going for the millennial market. Too bad avocados don't grow in this climate.'

'Give it time. But no, not really. This isn't a style statement – it's the exact opposite, as a matter of fact. A hundred years ago, farmers and gardeners grew vegetables to be sold at local markets for greengrocers that were just around the corner instead of flying them halfway around the world, and they grew varieties that they liked the taste of. Somehow we've lost that. I just think, here I have this opportunity to make something of my own, why am I going to grow the same crops that are cultivated over thousands of square miles and bred to be wrapped in plastic so that they can sit in a fridge for two weeks?'

'I know exactly what you mean.'

'I have a particular fondness for the Hutton Wonder Pea.'

'What's that?'

'Genuinely, I have no idea. I just love the name.'

They walked on for a bit, passing the tangled wilderness, the sounds of merriment fading behind them as they headed towards the very end.

'And yours?' asked Everett. 'What's the Pimblett Project?'

'Nothing as ambitious,' David admitted. 'As organic as we can be, I suppose. We took the allotment just after

Alice was born because we wanted her to grow up eating something not so much full of pesticides and antibiotics and shit like that. Then just to prove that the universe has a sick sense of humour she was diagnosed with acute lymphoblastic leukaemia—'

'Ouch.'

'Yeah. And we haven't been able to keep it up, obviously. She's still not out of the woods but she's slowly getting better, so I've tried to give it a bit of TLC. Maybe I can pay your fiend of a brother to come and have a go at it.'

Everett smiled. 'Well, I genuinely hope that we can arrange something like that.'

They passed the end of the allotment and walked back up the other side to rejoin the party.

At around teatime the turves were removed, the cinders raked away, and the half dozen large foil parcels brought out to be unwrapped. The aroma that rose from them was rich and warm, gravy and rosemary and apples and cloves, drawing murmurs of appreciation from the guests, and despite Dennie's fourteen years of vegetarianism even she found her mouth watering.

'Now before I do this,' said Ardwyn, holding a corner of foil between finger and thumb like a magician about to whip away a handkerchief, teasing her audience, 'I just want to say on behalf of myself and Everett that we never expected to be lucky enough to find ourselves in a place with so many new friends and neighbours. In the short time that we've been here we've been bowled over by your helpfulness and generosity. I'm not a religious person—'

Everett suppressed a snort of laughter.

'—but I do believe in coincidence and good timing, and I don't think it's an accident that this is the spring equinox, or as near as, a time for renewals and new life. I mean look who I'm talking to!' She laughed. 'You're all gardeners, you know this. This is a new beginning for me and my partner, but I hope that maybe this can also be the start of a new tradition, because I'd love to have one of these parties every year.'

'Hear hear!' came a shout from the back, to general laughter.

'Now,' she continued, peering at what was under the foil. 'Having said all that about timing, I hope this is done...' and she whipped it away to reveal a joint of pork studded with cloves and gleaming in its own juices. The meat was so tender that she didn't have to carve it – it fell apart beneath a pair of forks that she used to pile it onto bread rolls that were passed out amongst the crowd who watched her, rapt. *It's like she's feeding the five thousand*, Dennie thought. It was a performance. Ardwyn Hughes knew exactly what she was doing.

And then she is bathed in bright sunlight and it is 2007 and Sarah has invited her to a late summer picnic on their allotment. Little Josh is four and about to start Reception at school next month. Brian has only been dead a year and Dennie hasn't yet made the resolution to go veggie yet, so she's looking forward to one of the burgers that Colin is pushing around on the cheap disposable barbecue in its silver foil tray – ideally with a side helping of the salad made from lettuces and tomatoes that Sarah has grown herself. Colin has insisted that he do the cooking as it is the man's job (and here is a thing she's never been able to fathom: why they won't go near the kitchen cooker but get them outside with a pile of charcoal and they think they're Jamie bloody Oliver), but the problem is that Colin has been drinking steadily since the morning and he's burning the burgers, and is becoming increasingly aggressive to Sarah when she tries to warn him.

'I know what I'm doing, for God's sake,' he growls. 'Don't you tell me how to cook a fucking hamburger. They need to be well done. Or do you want to get fucking food poisoning, is that it?'

'Darling,' Sarah murmurs. 'We have a guest.'

'Oh, have we?' he replies with withering sarcasm. 'Is that who I'm doing this for?'

'Maybe I should go,' Dennie says to Sarah, and gets up to leave.

'No—'

'Yes,' says Colin. 'Maybe you should go, and maybe you should stay gone.'

She knows she shouldn't say anything, that there's nothing she can say that will help. Sarah has confided in her that Colin received a redundancy letter in the mail earlier this week from the Indesit factory in Blythe Bridge where he's worked for the past five years making cooker parts. No, anything she does say will only make things worse. But she says it anyway: 'What's that supposed to mean?'

'What that's supposed to mean,' he sneers, and she can

smell the beer on him even at this distance, 'is that maybe you should stay the fuck off this allotment and out of my marriage.'

'I'm not—'

'Dennie, please—'

'Like fuck you aren't. I know why she spends so much time up here rather than at home. Don't tell me that you two don't sit here and gossip about me while I'm at work, making shit up. Well, enough. I'm putting my foot down.' He waves the spatula that he'd been cooking with in her face. 'Keep away from my wife, you old witch, or I'll give you the slapping that your dead husband should have given you years ago.'

It is so vicious, so totally and utterly out of order that it shocks her into silence, as is doubtless the intention. Very quietly, trembling slightly, Dennie gathers her things together and goes, leaving Sarah weeping.

Then the present reasserted itself and Dennie staggered a little with the sudden rush of remembered fear and impotent fury. She found an empty chair to sit on while her breathing steadied and her heartbeat slowed.

Obviously she declined when a pork roll came her way, and she wasn't the only one – she was in a sizeable minority who were enjoying the alternative halloumi burgers and veggie kebabs – and almost regretted it, seeing how obviously delicious it was. People were chewing, lost in savouring the texture and flavour, making little murmuring noises of enjoyment; they moved like sleepwalkers or drug addicts, with their eyes slightly distant as meat juices streaked their fingers and chins. She saw David enjoying one, though Becky politely declined one for herself and Alice. Meanwhile Everett and Ardwyn stood hand in hand and watched with beatific smiles.

Dennie was sure that quite a few of the people queuing up weren't allotment holders but residents of the neighbouring houses who had heard that there was a free meal on offer. For example, there was Matt Hewitson and his mates; Matt was the youngest son of Shirley Hewitson, whose garden backed onto the allotments. Technically she wasn't a tenant, though she was close enough friends with Carole and Geoff Bennett, who owned the plot behind her house, that the Bennetts let her use the few yards directly behind her back fence – which in practice meant that Matt and his friends were often hanging out there. There was the occasional grumble about noise and mess, but it all fell into the grey area of the by-laws about 'guest use' and was never serious enough for a formal complaint. Matt, his girlfriend Lauren and a handful of their friends – who were very definitely *not* allotment tenants – were queuing up for pork rolls, but Everett and Ardwyn didn't seem to mind. They were served as generously as everyone else.

The only crack that appeared in the new neighbours' façade came during the one incident that cast a shadow over the afternoon. Ironically, it was a heated argument between Matt and Lauren. Matt was nineteen, long enough out of school to have been able to get a job by now, if there had been any going, while Lauren was a few years older with a flat of her own and a job at a travel agency in town, which anybody who paid attention to the local gossip could see put her out of his league – anybody but Lauren, apparently, and her friends had given up trying to tell her and were just waiting for the penny to drop. Apparently it dropped that afternoon, and dropped heavily, because Matt went looking for her and found her behind a shed snogging one of his mates, Darren Turner. Darren was the son of a local farmer, but had a motorcycle and a Deliveroo contract. There were shouts, accusations, and, inevitably, fists. Matt took a swing at Darren, missed, and put his fist straight through a small window – if the shed hadn't been so old, the pane would have been Perspex and his fist would have just bounced off, but it was glass, and he went straight through up to the wrist. Then there was blood and screaming, and Ardwyn leapt forward with a tea towel to staunch the wound, and that was when Dennie saw it: for a flash of a second, Ardwyn grinned. Probably nobody else noticed it, their attentions fixed on Matt's bloody fist, and even if they had, would have dismissed it as a grimace. But Dennie knew delight when she saw it.

The fuss attracted his mother, who stopped just long enough to accuse Ardwyn and Everett and the Briar Hill Committee as a whole of unspecified health and safety violations before rushing her son away to Accident and Emergency, and Dennie took the opportunity to establish her own mask a bit.

'That was quick thinking, there,' she said to Ardwyn. 'Poor boy. I hope he's all right.'

'I think it was just a scratch,' Ardwyn replied. 'These things always look worse than they actually are. Plus, you know men: big drama queens. How are you doing, anyway?'

Dennie rubbed her forehead. 'Quite a bit better, thank you. Listen, I just wanted to say how sorry I am for the way I acted last week.'

'Oh, honestly, look—'

'No, no, you and Everett have been nothing but kind and generous, and the last thing you need is a doddery old neighbour yelling at you. Please, will you accept my apology?'

'Of course. You're sure I can't tempt you with one of Everett's pulled pork rolls?'

'Not me, I'm afraid, but you might be able to tempt Viggo.'

She did accept a wrapped-up portion of meat to take back for Viggo, as both reward and apology for leaving him at the allotment. 'There you go,' she said, setting it down in front of him. 'That's for being such a good boy.' Viggo, who had never been known to refuse a treat, including many that he was not technically supposed to be able to digest, sniffed at the meat but then turned away and curled himself into a corner, looking at her reproachfully over one paw. 'Really? Do not try to tell me that you've gone veggie too. Frankly, my dear, your farts are bad enough as it is.' She tried again later, but he wouldn't touch it – wouldn't even sniff it at it. In the end she threw it in the bin.

'That went well, then,' Everett said.

'Better than we could have expected,' Ardwyn replied.

They were driving back from the village with debris from the feast rattling around in the back. Everett was happy but exhausted, and night had fallen, and he was working his way slowly along the twisting country lanes, headlights picking out details of the hedgerows. Hawthorn branches were just coming into bud but they still had the stark, skeletal beauty of their winter thorns.

'It's just a pity Gar couldn't be there,' she added.

'He's better off at the farm, out of sight. I think we might have been a bit complacent letting him be amongst people so soon. He's not used to it, poor chap. How many of them ate the first flesh?'

'At least a dozen.' Ardwyn squeezed his arm lovingly and leaned her head against his shoulder.

'You were magnificent. That speech – the bit about not being religious? I nearly choked. Did you find out their names?'

'Mm-hm. I mingled, I chatted, I caught up on all the local goss. I was the perfect Mother.'

He nodded, relieved. 'And we only need six. That gives us the rest of the month to check them out and pick the ones who won't be missed.'

'As well as the ones who can be useful,' she added. 'I'm afraid you're going to have to put up with a few dinner parties at home over the next few weeks.'

'I promise I'll be on my best behaviour.'

'Good lord, that bad? I might have to make you eat out in the shed with Gar.'

They drove on in silence for a while. 'Pity about the old woman,' she said eventually. 'I would have liked for her to join the new church, then we wouldn't have to worry about her sniffing around so much. But, if she will insist on refusing to eat meat...'

The van lurched as Everett twisted the steering wheel violently and slammed on the brakes. Something heavy slid up the inside and whacked the back of their seats.

'What—?' Ardwyn gasped.

Standing in the road in front of them, paralysed by the headlights, was a small tawny-coloured deer. Its head was narrow and triangular, it had no horns, and it only stood about three feet high. Its flanks were heaving and its nostrils flaring. They stared at it through the windscreen, equally transfixed. Then it bolted, the hedgerow quivered, and it was gone.

'Steady,' Ardwyn breathed. 'You nearly killed that poor creature.'

They looked at each other, and then burst out laughing. Everett started the van and they drove home.

7

LIZZIE

ON THE WEDNESDAY AFTER THE BARBECUE, DENNIE'S youngest daughter Elizabeth paid her a visit, and that was when she really got pissed off with Angie.

The potatoes had been chitted, she had two rows of strawberries under plastic to force them into an early fruiting for the summer, and her current job was mulching her broccoli with bunches of shredded newspaper as part of the annual war of attrition against the great slug horde. In the Watts' pond, three plots over, frogs were beginning to spawn, desperately shagging each other and leaving great gelatinous puddles everywhere. In contrast, fruit trees all over Briar Hill Allotments had come into blossom like pink and white clouds of candyfloss, and the bees were going crazy. There weren't as many of them as there had been in the past, but that was the way of things, she supposed. Even the strange new neighbours were keeping themselves to themselves. She found that the less time she spent interacting with other human beings the fewer blank moments she had, and that was just fine by her.

The only conversation she'd had so far that day had been first thing in the morning, heading in with Viggo and her tools, when she'd been surprised to see Marcus Overton humming and whistling to himself as he pottered away, weeding. He'd been much less active on his allotment in the last few years as his arthritis had worsened, but she'd seen him at Sunday's barbecue tucking into a pork roll as rapturously as the rest of them. She certainly hadn't expected to see him here again, so early in the morning, and especially on his hands and knees pulling up weeds.

'Someone sounds happy,' she commented as she passed.

Overton looked up and waved. 'Good morning, Denise!' He smiled. 'I thought it was about time to give the family estate a bit of TLC. How are you?'

'Can't complain. How are the knees?' On the rare occasions that he was seen out of doors, it was usually making his painful way to the shops on a pair of walking sticks.

'Do you know, it's incredible!' he said, straightening up in a single, smooth action. 'They are absolutely fine! There's no sign of swelling at all!'

'And when did this happen?'

'Almost overnight! I hesitate to use the term "miraculous", but...' He grinned and did a little dance. Seeing the old chap capering, Dennie had to stifle a giggle. 'Well, I'll let you get on,' he said. 'I've left this far too long. It's like a jungle here.'

'Well, don't you overdo it, now.'

'Never do.'

And she went on her way. As far as having to play nicely with others went, that was it until mid-morning, when Lizzie appeared. Her arrival was heralded by Viggo's head shooting up like a meerkat's and him hurtling off to throw himself, barking joyously, at a figure who had appeared at the allotment gates. She came over, laughing as she fended off the huge dog that was capering around her, trying to lick her face.

'Viggo! For God's sake will you just—'

'Viggo!' Dennie snapped. 'Get a grip!' He subsided and Lizzie ambled the rest of the way, wiping her face with the cuffs of her jumper.

'Hi, Mum. I went by the house first but there was nobody in so I guessed you'd be here.'

'Lizzie, my darling, what on earth are you doing here?' Her daughter had progressed from waiting tables to co-owning and running her own café-bakery in Bristol with her partner Niamh; it took a lot of time and energy and left little of either for visiting her mother, especially from such a distance. Christopher still lived a lot closer in Burton, but the prodigal son was too busy with his own life, and Amy was working for a disaster-relief NGO somewhere in India. 'Don't tell me you were just passing and thought you'd drop in.'

'Nice to see you too.' She gave Dennie a hug and a peck on the cheek. She smelled like bread and cigarettes. 'Mum, can we talk?'

'Are you in trouble? Do you need money? Is it the shop? Oh, it's not Niamh, is it?'

'No, Mum, I'm not in trouble but I will be if I don't get a cup of tea soon. Can we go home first?'

'Of course.'

She packed her things and Lizzie drove them home in the battered little yellow Micra that she'd parked outside the allotments. Lizzie looked well. She'd let her hair grow out a bit and there was some colour in her cheeks. It was while Dennie was sitting in the passenger seat that she noticed the overnight bag on the back seat, but didn't say anything until they were in the kitchen on either side of the breakfast bar with two steaming mugs in front of them.

'Well, this is a nice surprise,' she said, 'though I do wish you'd called first. Are you planning to stay over? I'll make your bed up.'

'Mum, I did call, but you're never here to pick up and you never check your messages.'

That was fair. She glanced at the phone on the counter by the microwave. A small red LED was flashing. Bugger. 'Well, I'm a very busy person, you know,' she said in her best Edina Monsoon voice. 'Social life is absolutely hectic these days, sweetie darling.'

It should have raised a laugh, but Lizzie just smiled. 'Yes, I'd like to stay for a few days, if that's okay.'

'What about the shop?'

'Oh, Niamh has all of that under control.'

'So, what is it you wanted to talk about?'

Lizzie fidgeted with the ring on her right hand, the one with the garnets that Dennie's own mother had given to her youngest granddaughter as a keepsake before she died in

187

'91. 'Mum, I don't want you to get upset, okay? But I had a phone call from the lady that runs the allotments—'

'Angie.'

'Yes—'

'I knew it. I bloody *knew* it. That interfering cow. And she doesn't *run* the allotments, she—'

'Mum. Please. She said that she's worried about you.'

'Fine bloody way of showing it—'

'She said that you've been having… episodes. That people have seen you just stop and stare into space for ages.'

'Daydreaming. Wool-gathering. It's not a symptom of anything, you know. It doesn't mean I'm going gaga.'

'Nobody's saying that you're going gaga,' said Lizzie, but as far as Dennie was concerned that was exactly what it sounded like. 'This Angie woman said that you had a big blazing row with the people on the plot next to yours a couple of weeks ago. That you've been hearing and seeing strange things there. That you've been sleeping in your shed, for heaven's sake.'

'Angie's given you a nice comprehensive report, hasn't she? Had she told you what my diet's like? The frequency of my bowel movements?'

'Mum!' Lizzie twisted harder at the ring. She was obviously uncomfortable having to say all of this and Dennie suddenly felt foolish and cruel for picking on her when it wasn't Lizzie she should be angry with. 'You can't sleep in your shed, Mum. It's not safe. It's cold, there are sharp things…'

Dennie laughed. 'You sound like somebody's mother!'

'Funny, I wonder where I get that from.'

'Darling, I am sixty-five years old. I am not...' And it was gone again. The word. Erased from her memory – no, not erased, become a slippery fishword, squirming away from her the closer she came to grasping it. 'I'm not...'

'Not what, Mum?' Lizzie was frowning at her in concern. She put down her mug and laid both hands across her mother's, which Dennie only just now realised were twisting on themselves, her fingers making little pinching motions as she tried to catch the term that wouldn't come. She pulled herself together and took her hands away.

'Listen,' she said, 'there are women older than me that climb Mount Everest and run marathons. For heaven's sake, the Queen's nearly a hundred and she runs the whole country!'

Lizzie frowned. 'I'm pretty sure that's not how it works. Also,' she pointed out, 'the Queen doesn't sleep in a potting shed.'

'Not as far as we know.'

Lizzie peered at her as if she really had gone mad. 'What?'

'I mean the royals. Very strange people. You never know. I bet the Queen could sleep in a potting shed if she wanted to, though. Who's to stop her? "I'm the Queen, and I'm sleeping in this shed and if you don't like it you can fack awf".'

Lizzie laughed at that.

'Finally, she cracks a smile.'

'I'm serious, Mum.'

'I know, darling, you have always been one of the most serious people I know. I love you for it. And I love you for coming all this way up here to tell me to stop being such a silly old cow.'

'You're not a silly cow. And I love you too.'

'Moo.'

'Stop that.'

Dennie made up the bed in Lizzie's old room and Lizzie came to help her on the allotment for a few hours. She took Viggo on a long leg-stretch along the country lanes outside the village where they had walked as a family on Sunday afternoons, and in the evening cooked them a vegetable stir-fry for dinner which they ate while watching *Emmerdale*. And when Dennie went to bed that evening she didn't have to listen for strange echoes because the noises in the house came from her daughter moving around, brushing her teeth, coming in to kiss her goodnight, and for the first time in a long time the house felt like a home again.

Marcus Overton was also having an unexpectedly good evening. He was up in the attic looking for his passport. Admittedly, this might not have seemed to be anybody's idea of a fun evening, let alone a septuagenarian ex-schoolmaster, but Overton hadn't been able to climb a ladder for the best part of ten years. Come to that, he hadn't been able to get upstairs comfortably for the last two. The carer woman who came around every week had helped him set up the downstairs study as a small bedroom so that on really bad days he didn't have to make the painful attempt at all. But this morning he'd awoken with the swelling in his joints gone, and the feeling of being pain free after so long was like slipping into a pool of clear calm water after a long day's hike in the hot sun. He had expected to find that he'd overstretched himself on the allotment and that his knees would punish him for it, but they hadn't. He'd taken himself out for a meal in town, then a drink at the Golden Cross – sitting at an outdoor table with a pale ale and a copy of Professor Beard's *SPQR: A History of Ancient Rome* and not having to worry about the effects of damp or cold – and then walked all the way to his home in Greenlea later in the evening with a literal spring in his step, wondering how long this miraculous respite could last and how much further he could exploit it. It was as he stepped through his front gate and between the mock Doric columns of his front porch that the answer came to him: he would go on a holiday. To Italy.

In his long career at the chalk-face one of the most rewarding aspects of teaching young men and women had always been the opportunity to take them on overseas excursions to show them the treasures of antiquity that they would otherwise only read about or see on the tiny, ugly screens of the phones to which they seemed perpetually glued these days. Mr Overton's Overseas Trips (or MOOTs as they became known), had been legendary fixed feasts in the school calendar, always heavily oversubscribed and spoken of with fond remembrance at Old Pupils' reunions. The cruel irony of retirement had been that at just the age when he had found himself free to travel for his own pleasure, his body had decided that it was no longer willing to get him upstairs to the main bathroom let alone to the Mediterranean.

Yet now, it seemed, it had changed its mind, and he was determined to take advantage of this situation before it changed back again. *Carpe diem*, and all that. *Carpe patellam*: seize the knee. He chuckled as he climbed.

His passport had ended up in a packing box in the attic when the study was being modified and he'd had a clear-out of his old desk. Of course, it would have expired by now, but you still needed the old one to apply for a renewal. All the boxes up here were carefully labelled, and it was exactly where it should have been. He tucked the passport into his trouser pocket, closed the box, climbed back down to the upstairs hallway, retracted the loft ladder and pulled the cord that shut the loft hatch.

All without so much as a twinge.

He was so excited by the idea that he completely lost track of time googling destinations, flight options, hotels, and jotting itinerary notes, and when the front doorbell rang he looked up in surprise and realised that it was one in the morning.

'What on earth?'

He put the door on its chain because you never could be too careful, even in a quiet place like Dodbury, and opened it to see that nice young lady who had organised Sunday's garden party. Arwen – no, Ardwyn, that was it. A peculiar name but quite lovely, much like the girl herself. She was looking anxious, however, as she stood on his doorstep. It was raining lightly, and she looked damp and cold.

'I'm very sorry to trouble you so late, Mr Overton,' she said, 'but I've got a bit of an urgent problem and I wonder if you could help me, please?'

'Why my dear, of course!' He took the door off its chain

and opened it for her. 'Whatever can I help you with?'

Behind her, a huge shape detached itself from the shadows of his front garden and rushed at the doorway. He glimpsed a giant of a man, a mouth snarling impossibly wide, and then a fist that hit him in the face so hard that he actually flew backwards down the hallway and cracked the back of his skull on the floor. Too stunned and utterly bewildered to be afraid, Overton could only watch as the young woman stepped into his house. Her hulking companion had to duck under the lintel to follow her.

'Well,' she replied. 'I was wondering if you might very kindly pass out for me.'

Fear came then, and he tried to scream, but then the fist hit him again and he had little choice but to oblige.

The deserter kept a sharp eye out through the windscreen as Gar loaded the unconscious man into the back of the van and climbed in after. The narrow road behind these big properties was dark, and the large trees of their established gardens meant that it had been relatively easy to park somewhere that wasn't overlooked, but he was determined not to be undone by complacency.

The van doors were eased shut – Gar had been instructed very firmly not to slam them – and Ardwyn climbed up into the passenger seat next to him.

'All set?' he asked.

'Yes,' she replied. 'Let's go.'

He started the engine and drove them to the allotments.

8

TUSK MOON

THE VESSEL HAD BEEN STRIPPED, TIED AND GAGGED securely, so when it woke all it could do was wiggle slightly and stare around at the inside of the shed with wide, terrified eyes. Everett would much rather that it remain unconscious – just as with the swine vessels and the German boy before that, he had no desire to inflict any more distress than was absolutely necessary – but neither he nor Ardwyn had any knowledge of how to keep a human being drugged and Gar could be a bit heavy handed. The vessel already had a broken nose, and there was a very real possibility that if Gar continued hitting it to keep it unconscious he might actually kill it by mistake, and they couldn't risk that. Dead blood held no power. The big man was currently on sentry duty outside. Fortunately, it seemed that the old woman had decided to behave like a normal human being and sleep in a proper bed tonight, which was a relief. There were enough wrinkles in this new liturgy without the extra complication of unwanted spectators.

Ardwyn was praying, her soft voice soothing him with a sense of peace and the righteousness of this night's work. It was somewhat undermined by the smell of piss coming off the vessel, which was a lot more pungent in the enclosed space instead of the open clearing above Swinley.

Yes, this was going to take some getting used to.

He took the knife in his right hand and the nape of the vessel's neck in his left and bent the vessel into a kneeling position over the pit. The shed's false floor had folded back on hinges to expose the bare earth below, the pit that had been dug in it and the remains of Moccus that had been placed there, ready for his rebirth. The vessel's eyes goggled as it saw, and it began to weep and scream in muffled bleats from behind the gag. Everett wondered if he should say something to it – thank it, possibly, the way Bill had thanked the German boy. There wouldn't have been any point when the vessels of replenishment had been swine, but then he thought what would be the point now? Nothing he could say would alleviate its terror. Best to simply get it over with as quickly and painlessly as possible.

The deserter's elbow bumped against the wall and he had to shuffle a bit to get into a position where his arm could move freely. Then he opened the vessel and held it as it thrashed, angling it carefully so that the blood jetted directly into the pit rather than up the walls because apart from the waste nobody wanted that clean-up job.

'Moccus, be replenished,' he and Ardwyn intoned

together. 'Moccus, be renewed. Moccus, be reborn.'

Afterwards they wrapped the empty vessel carefully and put it back in the van, shovelled a foot of earth into the pit and put the floor back over it, then locked up and drove back to the farm. The tusk moon would not rise until after dawn, but they would stay up to toast its appearance as it journeyed out from under the shadow of mother earth and celebrate the first replenishment ceremony of their new church.

Only five more to go.

3:07

Dennie stared at the display of the bedside radio clock, trying to feel surprised, and failing.

She couldn't recall waking. It hadn't been Viggo this time; he was downstairs as normal, shut in the kitchen. As far as she knew she might well still be asleep. It would make sense if she was, because how else was she to explain the fact that Sarah Neary was sitting in the chair in the corner of her bedroom?

Sarah hadn't moved or said anything since Dennie had become aware of her. The chair was just a tatty old piece of wicker furniture that she'd inherited from her own mother and which had followed them in the move from Birmingham; it was for dumping rogue pillows and underwear, and she wasn't sure it would support the weight of a human being. But then Sarah had been dead for a little over ten years. She was wearing the same t-shirt, sweatpants, and pink slippers that she'd been wearing on the one and only visit

Dennie had made to see her at HMP Bronzefield – and the last time she'd seen Sarah before she committed suicide. For some reason she was also cradling in her lap an old rag doll that had belonged to Dennie as a girl. Sabrina. She hadn't thought of that doll since before she married Brian. What was Sarah doing with it?

'I don't know what you want,' she whispered. 'I helped you as much as I could. Please, leave me alone.'

Sarah neither moved nor replied. One moment she was there, and the next she, along with Dennie's childhood toy, was gone.

'You want me to drive you where?' Lizzie's toast froze halfway to her mouth in disbelief.

'Stapenhill Cemetery.'

'Yes, I thought that's what you said. And that's in…' She waved her toast for Dennie to repeat it.

'Burton, yes.'

'Because…?

'Lizzie, you asked me if there was anything you could do to help. This is it. Honestly, it's not that far.' She hadn't been able to get back to sleep after Sarah's appearance and so had tiptoed downstairs and sat in the kitchen drinking tea and listening to the World Service on Radio 4 until she knew what she needed to do. When she heard her daughter moving around she'd roused herself and got breakfast ready as if it were any normal day.

'I understand that, but I was thinking more along the

lines of cooking you a nice meal, perhaps, or doing a couple of loads of laundry. Not driving you to visit the grave of a convicted murderer who hung herself in her cell.'

'Her victim was a monster of a man and she killed him in self-defence, remember.'

'Yes, and then she cut him up and buried the bits in her allotment!' Lizzie shouted. 'It's not the same as taking a bunch of flowers to Dad's grave!'

'Lizzie, I know that it doesn't make much sense, but part of what's been happening over the last few weeks is that for whatever reason, Sarah Neary has been...' *appearing in waking memories and now visiting me at night* '... on my mind. I thought that if I visited her grave it might help to settle it a bit. I understand that it's not what you planned to do, and you probably need to get back to the café, and I'm more than capable of driving myself, so if you really don't want to...'

'No,' Lizzie sighed. 'It's fine. Of course, I'll help. I just need to make a couple of phone calls, that's all.'

Lizzie made her calls and Dennie convinced Viggo that it was only a half hour drive and she'd be back well before lunchtime, and they left. Stapenhill was a modest-sized council-run cemetery on the other side of the River Trent from the town proper; up from the river's broad sweep there was a green bank crowded with daffodils and a tree-lined walk and then the cemetery's gateway of three tall gothic arches. Lizzie left her to her 'morbid bloody obsession' and took herself off for a walk along the river. The cemetery grounds themselves were broad and open, and it was easy to locate the Nearys' cremation plot – it was towards the back, in the modern section away from the old Victorian graves, and close to a neighbouring housing estate. The funeral arrangements had been left to distant relatives who wanted shot of the whole horrific business as quickly as possible, and so in a final act of cruel irony after everything that Colin had done to Sarah when alive, her remains had been interred next to his. Even so, nobody was so thoughtless as to have their plaques engraved with standard platitudes like 'Loving wife' or 'Devoted husband'. There was simply a pair of names, and a set of dates. There were no flowers, not even withered remains. Dennie wasn't sure what she was expecting to see; it was just a simple patch of gravel with two low stone blocks and their metal plaques. It was as she was looking around, wondering what on earth had made her think this was a good idea, that she saw – through a line of thick trees and a heavy wrought-iron boundary fence – a familiar glimpse of plastic sheeting, small wooden structures and tidy vegetable patches in neat rows. There were allotments bordering on the cemetery. Colin Neary's remains had been exhumed from one allotment only to be buried within sight of another, and she laughed. Serve the bastard right.

The first thing Dennie notices about Sarah, before she even takes her seat in the prison visiting room, is how far along her second pregnancy is. She's not allowed to give Sarah a hug so she simply squeezes her hand and asks. Seven months, is the answer. Dennie's instinctive reaction is to feel sorry that the father will never see his new child, but she squashes it because it was the fact that he tried to make her lose it which led to her killing him in the first place.

Are they treating her well in here?

Fine, thank you, Dennie.

And little Josh?

He's with her sister, Michelle, and her husband. She hopes to God that he's too young to understand what's happening.

Dennie thinks that Sarah would probably have put up with the abuse for years more, decades, and possibly the rest of her life if it hadn't been for the imperative to protect her babies. Dennie can well understand this. Brian was nothing like Colin, but his childhood had its own problems and she'd had to set firm boundaries for him when Christopher was little. It had been the time that Brian had come home from work, tired and irritable, and found that Christopher had got into the laundry basket and 'coloured in' his Daddy's favourite shirt with wax crayons, and he'd given the child a good solid wallop – the first and only one ever. Dennie had gathered the squalling child in her arms, fixed Brian with a look and told him that if he ever laid a finger on any of the children like that again, she would take them and leave. She meant it, and he knew it. He knew that she wouldn't go to the police or try to divorce him, he would just never see his children again. She had known that the single worst thing for Brian Keeling – the fault-line which tracked right back into his troubled childhood – was to be abandoned, and she'd felt cruel to poke a finger in that crack but she'd done it without hesitation. Colin Neary had been more riddled with cracks than a badly laid pavement, and Dennie couldn't begin to imagine how Sarah must have had to tiptoe through their marriage until the point came where it wasn't just her that was threatened but her children. She hadn't had to poke anything; Colin had crumbled beneath her feet all on his own.

Is there anything she can get Sarah?

No, thank you. She has everything she needs in here.

There is something about her calmness, her placidity, which frightens Dennie deeply. 'Sarah, please, if you'll just let me tell them—'

This gets a reaction. 'No! We've been over this! What good will it do? I'll still be in here whether it's ten years or twenty, not that it will make much difference anyway because after the little one arrives I won't be here at all.'

'You need to stop talking like that. They'll let you keep her. They'll—'

'In a cage? No, Dennie, I can't allow that. I grew up in locked rooms. I won't have that for her. I won't.'

One of the prison officers notices that Sarah is becoming agitated, and comes over. 'I think that's enough for today, Miss,' she tells Dennie. Her eyes and voice are both steel. There's nothing Dennie can do – nothing except the one thing that she promised Sarah she would never do, and that deep down she is too scared to do, and so she leaves in a fog of tears and shame at her own cowardice and her head ringing with the confession she can't make.

I helped.

For a moment Sarah was still there when the world came back. She was sitting in her prison clothes at that small table on the grass next to her own grave, except this time instead of a round belly she held Dennie's old rag doll Sabrina on her lap, and then she was gone.

9

GRAFTING

APRIL ON BRIAR HILL ALLOTMENTS CAME IN A tumbling cloud of blossom and gauzy sunlight. The days warmed and lengthened, the weather woke up from winter and began falling over itself with sprees of hot sun followed by days of drenchings. From its elevated position the allotments had a view of the river ribboning along the valley, through a patchwork of fields, gleaming with pools, meres and wetlands. Curlews had arrived for the breeding season even earlier this year, and the grasslands echoed to their looping cries. The soil seemed hungry for planting – a crop sown would be springing shoots in a matter of days. Bean poles and netting were going up, tomatoes were coming out of greenhouses, and the ground was being prepared for courgettes, pumpkins and asparagus. Even the old Neary plot was defying the pessimistic older timers' predictions and starting to green up. But the excitement was tempered with caution; there was still the threat of a late hard frost, and everybody remembered last April's Storm Hannah that had wrecked people's fruit cages and bean trellises and threatened flooding all along the Trent.

For Dennie it was time to graft her tomatoes. After a run of several bad years in which blight had taken a heavy toll on her harvest she had decided to learn how to graft the fruiting 'scion' of the plant onto a hardier and disease-resistant rootstock. The seedlings had been doing well in her little greenhouse since mid-March, and on the first warm day in April she sat out with some plastic bags, grafting clips and a wickedly sharp craft knife. She'd let them settle for a week or two before planting them out, and hopefully get a better crop this year, if the god of slugs looked favourably on her.

The Association meeting in the Pavilion bar on the first Friday of the month was particularly well attended and had only one item on the agenda: that of the upcoming VE Day celebrations. This year the government had moved the May Bank Holiday, which would ordinarily have been on the 12th of May, back four days to coincide with VE Day on the Friday before, so that the country could celebrate the 75th anniversary of the end of World War II with a three-day weekend. The topic had been raised in Association meetings now and then since the change had been announced last June, but typically it was with only a month to go that any sense of urgency began to be felt. Angie led the charge, of course, having been asked by Dodbury Village Council to come up with ways in which the allotments could contribute to the festivities, and she spent the meeting begging, cajoling and browbeating anybody who showed even a hint of interest into forming subcommittees for the production of bunting, vintage costumes, cakes, and even sandbags to give it an authentic feel. Hugh Preston and Ben Torelli were excused on grounds that, being ex-servicemen, they would be participating in the wreath-laying ceremony at the cenotaph on the village green. Then Margaret and Fred Pline, another pair of married old-timers, announced that they were going to build an actual Anderson shelter on their plot this year so that the younger generation could get a sense of what it had been like to endure the Blitz, which caused much excitement.

With all this activity it wasn't surprising that it took a good fortnight for Dennie to realise that Marcus Overton hadn't been working his plot. To be fair, he hadn't been working it for the last few years anyway, but after seeing how vigorously he'd been attacking the weeds back at the end of March she'd thought to have seen him around the place a bit more. The chances were that whatever respite he'd been enjoying from his arthritis had been short-lived and he'd probably gone and made it worse for himself by overdoing it, but if that were the case then maybe someone should have been looking in on him. He was known to be something of a recluse, usually only seen hobbling into the village for his morning paper. It was unclear whether he had a partner or relatives, or even a carer to look after him. She asked around but nobody seemed to know.

Angie took a bit of persuading to give her his address, which was one of the larger, posher houses in Greenlea – a bit out of her way but the extra exercise would do both her and Viggo good.

They were all detached properties along here, separated from their neighbours by thick hedges and high walls. Overton's car – a sky-blue Audi – was in the drive but when she knocked on the front door and called there was no reply. Viggo went for an exploratory sniff in the bushes while she peered through the letter flap.

'Mr Overton?' Her voice echoed down an empty hallway. 'Marcus?' She could see a glimpse of a darkly polished parquet floor with an ornate Turkish carpet runner and, if she angled her face just so, a drift of mail on the floor inside the front door. Most of it was glossy junk, but there were enough white and brown envelopes in the pile to tell her that wherever he was, he hadn't been collecting his post.

Now she was genuinely worried. She had visions of him lying dead, maybe having fallen out of the shower on unsteady knees and slippery tiles, cracking his head and starving to death, calling for help from someone who would never come.

Dennie dug out her phone and dialled 999.

Matt Hewitson was sitting on the swings in the kids' playground on the old Marketplace smoking a cigarette and necking a can of Red Bull when the guy from the barbecue came up to him.

'You're Matthew,' he said. It wasn't a question, and it pissed him off straight away because nobody ever called him Matthew except his mum.

'Fuck off,' he said. So what if the bloke had treated everyone to a free hog roast? That didn't give him the right to go around using people's names.

The bloke grinned, and Matt didn't like that either. It was a piss-taking grin if ever he'd seen one, the kind he'd like to punch. 'I'm Everett,' he said, as if that mattered. 'I've come to offer you a job.'

'Digging potatoes?' he sneered. 'I told you, fuck off.'

'It starts now,' Everett continued, as if he hadn't heard, and then just as Matt was about to get up and in his face, the guy pulled out his wallet and offered him a twenty. Just like that. 'This is your first pay cheque, and all you've got to do is let me buy you a beer and listen while I explain the terms.'

Matt looked at him closer. He didn't seem like a homo, and this didn't feel like a come-on. He wasn't old, wasn't young, with dark hair and weird eyes. He dressed a bit better than the locals – a dark shirt and jeans over boots rather than a hoodie, sweatpants and trainers – and he must have a bit of money if he could afford that meal. 'Make it forty,' he said.

'You can have forty if you like,' said Everett, still smiling, 'but for every pound over that twenty I'll pull a tooth out of your head and make you swallow it, how about that?'

Matt flinched backwards and the man in the dark shirt laughed. 'Oh, I'm just fucking with you, don't worry. But twenty's it. You can negotiate when you've got something to negotiate with. In the meantime, beer?'

They went to the Golden Cross where Everett bought him

a Stella and sat down opposite with a pint of ale. It wasn't especially busy in the pub, but there were a few faces he recognised, so he made sure they took a table that was well hidden because he didn't want people to think he was gay. He could feel the guy watching him as he drank. 'What?'

Everett gestured to the bandage on his hand right that had been there since he'd put his fist through that shed window. 'I was just wondering when you were going to take that off, that's all.'

'What do you mean?'

'I mean it's healed, hasn't it? It's been healed for a long time, if I'm right. Maybe a day after you did it? Two? Three? It's a bit hard to tell – it's slower the first time but it gets quicker as your body gets used to it.'

Matt felt himself grow shivery and hot all at the same time, and his pulse began to beat heavily in his head. There was no way this guy could have known that. No way. He hadn't even shown his mum. She taken him to Accident and Emergency straight after and a nurse had put five stitches in his hand, and the next morning they'd been lying there in his bed next to freshly healed skin. He'd been so freaked out that he'd wrapped his hand up again and tried to pretend that nothing had happened, because it was wrong, wasn't it? It was unnatural and there was something wrong with him.

'Just who the fuck are you, mate?' he demanded.

Everett sipped his ale. His smile had gone. 'I am the man who is going to help you make something of your life, Matthew Hewitson,' he said. 'I know what is in your veins, and I can show you how to use it. I will give you strength, and long life, and power over your enemies. Oh look,' he added without sounding surprised in the least. 'There's one now.'

Later, it would occur to Matt to wonder whether Everett had known all along who was in the pub and had deliberately set this up, but by then it was too late. He looked over to where Everett was indicating, and saw Lauren sitting at a table with her new boyfriend (and his ex-mate) Darren, along with two other lads he didn't know. She was dressed in her work suit and looked smart and sophisticated. It was humiliating. 'Fuck,' he muttered. 'Let's get out of here.'

'Oh no,' said Everett. 'That's not how this works at all. You never move for someone else again.' He took another swig of his pint, stood up, and Matt watched in horror as he went over to Lauren's table with a big shit-eating grin on his face. He tried to shrink further into the corner as words were exchanged, faces turned his way, and Everett came quickly back towards him with an apologetic shrug and four furious-looking people close behind. 'Sorry, Matt!' he called. 'I tried to tell them but they're just too stupid to listen!' Everett plonked himself back down in his chair, took a drink, and winked at him.

Lauren's face was like thunder as she stormed up to their table. 'Who the fuck do you think you are, giving orders?' she yelled at him.

'What? I—'

'And who's this twat you've got delivering your messages?' By this time Darren Turner and his two mates had arrived, and they were both bigger than him.

'I think it's his new boyfriend,' sniggered one of them.

Everett tipped him a salute with one finger, still smiling serenely.

'Your fucking pub, is it?' Darren shouted. '*Your* fucking pub?'

'Listen, Daz—'

Then Daz grabbed a fistful of Matt's t-shirt and instinct took over. He was hardly aware of what he did next. This wasn't one of those choreographed fight scenes from films, this was the ugly, free-for-all scrapping that he'd learned in the school playground, all flailing fists and lashing feet. If it had been a Friday night and the bouncers had been there he'd have stood no chance. Even so, outnumbered three-to-one, he should have been getting the shit kicked out of him but, impossible as it seemed, he was winning. Fists came at him and he felt nothing. Someone's nose crunched beneath his forehead and he laughed at their squeals. Someone else was on the floor, curled up around his foot and vomiting and Lauren was screaming at him to stop but this felt good, for the first time in his life he felt like he could dole out some of what he'd always had to take and *it felt good*, and then Everett was pulling at him and they had to leave before the pigs were called.

'You're stronger now,' Everett said, as he pulled the van into the farmyard and killed the engine.

'No shit.' Matt had blood all down the front of his t-shirt and covering his hands, but he was grinning like a loon. 'Want to tell me why that is?'

Everett shook his head. 'You need to come in and meet Mother. She'll explain everything.'

He led Matt towards the farmhouse, past a couple of old farts that Matt recognised from the allotments, who were painting one of the outhouses.

'What are they doing here?' he asked, pointing.

'They're doing here what we hope you will be doing here: helping us to build a new church.'

Church. So, they were a cult. That explained a lot. He was led into the living room, where a young woman with dark hair was sitting at the big table, working at a laptop. He recognised her from the barbecue, though he couldn't remember her name – she'd been the one handing out the food. She closed her laptop as they entered, rose and embraced Everett. 'My darling!' she beamed. 'Have you found him?'

'Yes, Mother, I have. This is Matt. Not Matthew.' He called her 'mother', but the way they kissed was not any way a son should kiss his mum. There was some seriously fucked-up shit going on here.

She turned from Everett, and welcomed Matt with a little bow of the head. 'Matt. We have so longed to meet you,' she said.

'Who are you people? What is this place?'

'With respect, those aren't the questions you most want an answer to, are they?'

'I'm pretty fucking sure they are.'

'How about "why can I do what I can do"?'

'Okay, yeah, let's go with that.'

'You are blessed, Matt. You have been sanctified through

the consumption of the first flesh, and it has made you strong. Do you like being strong?'

'Well, I have to say,' he said, looking around at the huge fireplace in its naked stone wall, the massive ceiling beams, and the kitchen counters busy with pots and pans, 'it makes a pleasant change.'

'We've made you strong, and you can strengthen us in return. We need people in the community who can be our eyes, ears, and hands. In return, we can offer you money, power, influence, girls.' She shrugged. 'Or boys. We have room here for you if you want, unless you like still living at home. More importantly, we can offer you purpose. You can help us to build something truly great. When have you ever had any of those things that you didn't have to fight for?'

'Not very often, that's for sure. I got to be honest with you, though, whatever religious thing you've got going on here, I'm not into that. So, if you're thinking of going all *Wicker Man* and dancing around naked and burning cops and shit, you can count me out.'

'Don't worry,' she smiled. 'We don't do that kind of thing. We're really very normal people once you get to know us. We've been watching you for a while, and we think you're just the sort of person we need.'

'Right.' He looked around some more, spotting a shelf crammed with bottles of fancy-looking booze. He turned back to her. 'Can I have a car?'

'Everett will go shopping with you tomorrow.'

He grinned. 'Great. I'm in.'

10

INFECTION

DAVID MET DENNIE KEELING AT THE ALLOTMENTS ON his way back from work. The message that he'd got from the regulars at Rugeley police station had said that she'd called in a report of a missing man, and uniforms had checked his address but found no sign of him. Could he, as the Neighbourhood Watch Liaison, have a follow-up chat with her and ask around for friends and relatives of the missing Mr Overton? Not a problem, he'd replied. Usually it would have been the last thing he'd have wanted to do after a long shift at the works, but he didn't feel as fatigued as normal. In fact, for the last couple of weeks he'd been feeling great – he was sleeping well, that niggling shoulder trouble from the old rugby injury had gone, and he was even thinking of taking up running again. He put it down to the effects of an early spring, and if this was climate change then fair enough. One thing about it that frustrated him was that his shift times meant that he couldn't help Becky care for Alice much more during the day. The other thing – which was entirely selfish, he knew – was that as the sap of the world seemed to be rising, well, so was his. He hadn't felt this horny since he and Becky had first started going out, maybe even since he was a teenager. Their sex life had tailed off naturally after Alice had been born and then much more dramatically since she'd fallen sick, but it hadn't been a major problem because they were both exhausted most of the time and if the spirit hadn't exactly been unwilling the flesh certainly had. Recently, though, he woke up some mornings with the warmth and the smell of her lying next to him and an erection so hard that he could have used it to plough a field.

He stowed that line of thought firmly away as he parked at the allotments and met Mrs Keeling. She repeated for him what had happened the day before. 'Has there been any word yet?' she asked. 'I've asked around here but he didn't say anything to anybody about going away – but then he was never down here very much.'

'Things like this always take time,' he said. 'More so these days, what with all the cutbacks. The regulars are going through his things, trying to track down any relatives. What we can do right now is have a quick look in his shed, just to make sure.'

Her hand went to her mouth. 'Oh God, you don't think…'

'No, I don't think. It's just something to cross off the list for the investigating officers, that's all.'

He'd already called Angie Robotham, who met them at

Overton's plot with a pair of bolt-cutters. It wasn't likely that the missing man would be in there if it was locked from the outside, but David liked to be thorough. From the frosty way the two women greeted each other there was obviously something going on between them, but that was their business. Overton's shed had seen better days; the tar-paper roof was mossy and torn in several places and the windows were green with mould. Hard to see what was inside, whether it was empty or if, God forbid, the missing man was lying in there. His plot wasn't in a much better state – mostly overgrown with weeds except for the one patch that he'd started to clear. Angie cut the lock free and David pushed the door open, bracing himself for the smell of rotting flesh.

The shed was empty – if shelves teetering with towers of old flowerpots, a ragged cane chair with a mouldering cushion, boxes of slug pellets, and cobwebs garlanding rusty rakes and trowels could be called empty. On the chair was a book, its pages open and bloated with damp, over which a large black spider ambled. *My place now.*

'Well, that's a relief,' Dennie said.

'Except that we still don't know where he is,' Angie replied.

'Okay, well,' said David, closing the door. 'I'll put a message out through the OWL for people to keep their eyes open and tell us if they know anything. Realistically it's all we can do at the moment.' And he still had to get home to help Becky with dinner. He'd messaged her that he was going to be a bit late, but he didn't want to push it.

* * *

There were no silver linings to his daughter having acute lymphoblastic leukaemia, none whatsoever. She was into the maintenance phase of her treatment which meant that at least she was being treated on an outpatient's basis and able to come home, and was utterly exhausted and in bed by eight in the evening – but the fact that this left David and Becky with some time on the sofa to catch up with each other's day wasn't much of a consolation.

'Her white cell count is still a bit down,' she said. 'So, Dr Barakhada has said that he's going to up her antibiotics just in case, but apparently her MRD results are good which means that she's on track for the summer. I told her that she might be able go swimming again, and you should have seen her face.' Becky snuggled up against him, resting her head on his chest, and he stroked her hair.

'Maybe I should book some time off and take us to the beach,' he said. 'I wonder if Cornwall is still there.'

'I would hope so! I can't wait to be able to do normal family things again.'

He hadn't meant to take the conversation in that direction, except maybe he unconsciously had because now all he could think about was that Cornwall holiday when it had just been the two of them, in their twenties, spending long days in the sun and Becky had worn that backless one-piece swimsuit that had slipped off so easily.

'I've got an idea about a normal family thing that we can do right now,' he suggested, moving his hand down to stroke the back of her neck.

She sat up and looked at him in amazement. 'Seriously? I'm

thinking of what a relief it's going to be not to have to take my daughter into hospital to have drugs pumped into her stomach and your take from that is "take me now, big boy"?'

'Becky, that's not what I meant—'

'Well, it sounded like that to me. I'm knackered, David, I can barely keep my eyes open. And you should be too, the shifts you've been pulling. How you can have the energy to want... I just don't know.'

'I know, I'm sorry, love. Look, let's just forget it and have an early night – not that kind!' he added hastily, wondering how hard it would be to fit his other foot in his mouth. 'A nice, clean, vanilla-flavoured early night. With reading and pyjamas.'

A small smile quirked the corner of her mouth, and he thought he might have got away with it. 'Vanilla-flavoured?'

'I don't know,' he mumbled miserably. 'I just know I'm a shit, and I promise I'll keep my hands to myself.'

He was as good as his word. Becky was asleep and snoring moments after her head hit the pillow, and he stayed up reading an Ian Rankin thriller. It wasn't even eleven o'clock when he heard the shuffling of tiny bare feet on the carpet in the hall outside, and then Alice was in the doorway, her hair mussed and her face red and puffy with sleep.

'Daddy?' she murmured. 'I don't feel well.'

It was as if invisible hands had placed defibrillator pads either side of his naked heart and hit him with a million volts. A little over two years ago he'd taken her for a swimming lesson at the leisure centre and been helping her get changed afterwards when she'd said those exact same words: *Daddy, I don't feel well.* He'd dismissed the slight temperature and the bit of a rash on her tummy as the results of the heat and humidity in the changing rooms, and given her some Calpol when they'd got home, but at teatime she'd said it again, *Daddy, I don't feel well*, and this time she'd vomited – the milk that had come up had been pink, but she hadn't been drinking strawberry milk that time. It had been blood. His baby's blood. She'd been rushed to hospital, and within hours had been diagnosed with acute lymphoblastic leukaemia, was on a drip and surrounded by friendly but urgent-faced people in white coats, and the nightmare had begun for all three of them. He was told that even if he'd taken her straight to hospital the moment she'd said it the first time, those few hours wouldn't have made a difference, but he didn't believe it.

Now, those words now bypassed his rational brain completely and jerked him out of bed in a panic sweat.

'Becky, wake up,' he said, shoving her, and at the same time falling out of bed to kneel down in front of Alice. 'Honey, what's wrong? Are you in pain?'

'David?' Becky was sitting up in alarm. 'What's going on?'

He put a hand to Alice's forehead. It was like touching the side of a furnace. Her hectic colour had nothing to do with sleep.

'Hurts here,' she murmured, touching the place high up on her chest where the port for administering her chemo had been installed, just under the skin.

'Jesus, Becky, she's burning up. I'm going to call an ambulance.'

Infection. Next to the actual cancer itself, it was the thing that they dreaded most. Alice's immune system had been levelled by the same methotrexate that was taking out the cancer cells, so any infection could become life-threatening very quickly, and places like her port were especially vulnerable. She was on preventative antibiotics anyway, but it seemed that on this occasion they hadn't been enough.

'Come on, Wondergirl,' said Becky, sounding calm and controlled. 'Let's get you back to bed.' She turned haunted eyes to David and whispered, 'Just get them here fast.'

Becky took her back to bed and he heard her running cold water as he picked up the house phone and dialled 999. He stammered through his answers to the call handler's questions, and was told that an ambulance had been dispatched and would be with them in ten minutes.

'Ten minutes,' he told Becky. She had pressed a cold, damp hand towel to Alice's forehead and was stroking her hair. 'Do you want to, uh, get dressed and get her stuff together, or, uh, maybe should I…?'

'I don't really care, David,' she said. 'Just as long as they get here.'

But by the time he'd thrown some clothes on and taken over from her while she did the same, ten minutes had passed. Then eleven. Then twelve.

'Why aren't they here?' he growled, staring out of the window at the road which remained stubbornly empty of blue flashing lights.

'Call them again.'

'I'm sure they'll be here...'

'*Call them again.*'

So he called them again. He was put through to a different dispatcher who said, 'I'm very sorry about that, sir. We've received a high number of call-outs this evening, but I can see that an ambulance is on its way to you and should be with you in three to five minutes.'

'Well, is it three or is it five?' he snapped. 'My wife, who's looking after our daughter – you know, the one I told you about? The one with leukaemia? She'd quite like to know.'

'All I can say, sir, is that I'm very sorry, but I can see—'

David slammed the phone down.

Three minutes became five, and five became seven.

He marched back into Alice's bedroom. 'I'm taking her,' he said.

'No you're not,' she said, and she was right; he knew as well as she did that it was at least a half hour drive to County Hospital in Stafford before Alice could get treatment whereas the ambulance crew could get an IV line into her the moment they got here. He'd seen the quality of emergency services deteriorate terribly in rural parts of the country like this as he'd grown up – it was part of the reason why he'd volunteered as a Special in the first place – but he couldn't bring himself to believe things were so bad that it would take nearly an hour for the ambulance to arrive.

But they had to arrive first.

It couldn't have been more than a minute or two, but it felt like geological ages, watching the sweat breaking out on his baby's forehead and seeing her twist and moan with discomfort as the infection rampaged unchecked through her already beleaguered system. Eventually there were flashing lights outside, and a heavy knock at the door.

11

SNARES

WITH SPRING CAME RABBITS, INCLUDING IN THE fields around the Farrow's farm, and Gar was showing Matt how to make and set snares. Matt had not been keen about the idea to begin with because as far as he was concerned rabbit trapping was for pikeys and gyppos, plus Gar scared the absolute shit out of him, but Mother had insisted, and he had quickly come to learn that when Mother snapped her fingers everybody at the farm jumped. And it turned out that it was actually quite fun.

He had to admit straight up that he had no idea what Gar was. Everett had claimed that they were brothers, and Matt had shrugged okay, whatever, but he wasn't sure that the pair of them were even the same species. He was like something off one of those programmes about conjoined twins. He had hair growing down his back. Not long like a girl's, but as in thick black hair growing out of the skin down past his shoulder blades. And there was definitely something wrong with the guy's head – maybe it was in his genes or maybe he'd had an accident or something, because who had teeth like that? But that was only on the outside. Gar was a man of few words, conveying all the meaning he needed in just a few grunts, and he appreciated that. Gar listened instead of delivering speeches, and Matt appreciated that too.

For most of his adolescence the countryside had simply been miles of fuck-all between where he was and where he wanted to be, navigable only by sucking up to mates with cars or spending what little he had on Ubers – but never the bus, not that there were any, and only under the most dire of circumstances begging a lift from his mum. He walked when he had to, with headphones in and face to his phone. It never occurred to him that there might be anything worth looking at on the other sides of the hedgerows.

Gar took him out into the field behind the stone barn just before dawn. The air smelled clear and damp and dew soaked his ankles as they walked, Matt hurrying to keep pace with Gar's enormous strides. But he slowed down as they approached a stile in the hedge, turned back and mimed *shh* with a finger to his lips, then indicated that Matt should go first over the stile. Matt eased himself slowly through the gap in the hedge, and as he saw dozens of furry shapes bounding away with their white tails flashing he felt a surge of childlike joy that he hadn't experienced in a long time. Gar joined him, and showed him the trails that Benjamin Bunny and his mates had made coming through hedgerows, and the burrows where they were hiding.

'Supper,' Gar had said, pointing, but since his mouth couldn't form p's correctly it had sounded more like 'suffer'.

Matt didn't know how Everett's group was funding itself but it seemed that there was a genuine need to feed quite a few mouths. Sometimes people stayed to supper, but none of them were accorded the privilege of being allowed to live at the farmhouse like Matt was, and he appreciated that most of all. So when Mother said that Gar was to teach him how to snare rabbits, he hadn't complained.

The first time he'd got bored and started checking his social media, Gar had slapped the phone out of his hand and grunted: 'No.' The second time, Gar had grabbed it off him and squeezed it until Matt could see it actually bending, and when Matt had pleaded with him to stop he'd given it back and repeated: 'No!' and Matt stashed it away.

But Gar's heavy fingers were also oddly delicate when it came to the practice of setting snares. It was a lot easier than he'd expected: a wide slip-knot of wire with its free end tied to a stake and hammered into the ground on one side of Benjamin's trail, and hanging loosely on a smaller stake on the other side of the trail, so that the open mouth of the snare's loop covered the trail itself, about half an inch above the ground. Mr Bunny came hopping along, popped his head through the snare, strangulating himself as he tried to escape, and hey presto – rabbit stew. Together he and Gar set a dozen of these around the farm, and then came back the next day to see if they had worked. There were three rabbits, one of them in a snare that Matt had built and set completely on his own, and he felt another swelling of a long-forgotten feeling. This one was pride.

The rabbit was still alive, having got a forepaw through the snare too and so prevented itself from strangling, and it kicked and thrashed in exhausted panic, its eyes wide and rolling, as he knelt down beside it. Having only ever seen them as roadkill, he marvelled at how soft and fluffy its fur actually was.

Gar grunted, and mimed a twisting motion with both hands.

'Really?' he asked. 'We've already got two. Can't we let this one go?'

Gar repeated the motion.

Matt sighed. 'Sorry, chum,' he murmured. It was a word he'd heard Everett using, and it sounded nice and retro. The rabbit froze in terror as he pinned it to the ground with one hand, feeling how warm it was and its tiny heart hammering away, as he loosened the snare with the other. Without trying to think too much about what he was doing, and trying not to get bitten, he grabbed its head and twisted it sharply a hundred and eighty degrees, hearing the sharp crack of its neck breaking. The hammering heart stopped.

Gar's heavy hand clapped him on the back, and there was that feeling of pride again. Matt looked at the small grey corpse in his hands. Snares were one thing, it was like fixing a punctured bicycle tyre or rolling a spliff, but he hadn't been sure that when it came to it he could actually kill another living creature.

Turned out he could.

'Cool,' he said.

* * *

Later that day, Everett showed him how to use the tractor's back-hoe to dig a trench behind the big tool shed. He assumed it was for burying rubbish, and Everett said, 'In a manner of speaking, yes.' It was a lot fiddlier than making a snare, as there were levers and gears to deal with, and he nearly took out a fence by mistake. It was only a short trench, a little over two metres long by half a metre wide, and he saw that one had already been dug and refilled nearby. The long mound of earth looked weirdly like a grave.

'Hey, who are we burying?' he joked.

Everett smiled and said, 'Haven't decided yet.'

'Is everything set for Torelli?' asked Ardwyn, a week before the second tusk moon.

'All set,' said the deserter. 'I still think it's a shame, though. I quite liked him.'

He'd chatted with Ben Torelli a few times at the allotments. Torelli grew things that didn't need an awful lot of looking after, like spinach and chillies, and his plot seemed to be mostly an excuse for him to sit out on clear evenings smoking dope. Everett had joined him once or twice out of politeness, but also as a way of sounding out how useful Torelli might be to the Farrow; he'd been at the barbecue and eaten the first flesh, and thus was hallowed. The discovery that he was also ex-army had led Everett to feel that there might have been the possibility of a connection based on shared experiences, albeit within reason. Anecdotes about the Great War were obviously off-limits, and Everett's own apparent age meant that he probably didn't look old enough to have served in anything much before Iraq, Bosnia at a push. He also knew that a confrontation with the authorities was inevitable at some stage and fighters were always useful.

But Torelli was another loner like Overton, and the fact that he was unlikely to be missed was more useful to Mother, it seemed.

Torelli rented a small flat in a new housing development on the western edge of the village, which had been built on the site of an old colliery. Thirty years after the miners' strike had killed the industry it had been sold off and the pits back-filled with concrete, but there were still areas that surveyors had marked as too unstable to build on and so these had been left to grow wild – not open countryside, not park, but edgeland; a loosely connected archipelago of untamed places known locally as the Links and used by dog-walkers, teenagers, courting couples and residents like Torelli taking a shortcut between the village high street and home.

He worked driving forklifts for a distribution warehouse near Lichfield, and his habit, rain or shine, was to get home from his shift, head out to the allotments for a peaceful spliff where there was less chance of nosy neighbours causing trouble, and then saunter home again, usually via one of the village's fast-food places to pick up something for his dinner.

On the day of the tusk moon Moccus blessed them again with rain, because it made it so much easier for the deserter to pull up beside Torelli as he was walking home, head down and hood up against the weather, water streaming from the plastic carrier bag that swung at his side. Everett had timed it so that he caught the man on an empty stretch of narrow lane running through the Links overshadowed by trees; another few yards one way or the other and Torelli would have been on a footpath and Gar would have had to get out for him, making things potentially a lot more complicated.

He slowed and wound down the passenger window.

'Ben!' he called. 'Hey, Ben!'

Torelli looked up, and his face lit with recognition.

'Give you a lift? It's pissing down.'

'Really?' Torelli replied drily. 'Hadn't noticed. Cheers, mate.' He opened the door and climbed up into the van, bringing with him the smell of doner kebab and marijuana. 'You're a life saver.'

'You'd better believe it. Where do you live?'

'I'll direct you.'

He had no intention of doing this on an open road, no matter how narrow, where anybody might happen along. For the first 'wrong' turn he was able to claim driver error. For the second, that he knew a quicker way to correct the first mistake. By the time he'd taken a third wrong turning he could tell that Torelli was becoming suspicious. The vessel was no fool, no slow-witted beast like Overton, and the deserter found himself beginning to enjoy this. Torelli might actually prove to be a challenge. There was a wire fence and a gate that they'd cut the chain from earlier in the day, which led into a wide, derelict area of old gravel piles overgrown with weeds, between which ran the long-rusted rails of a narrow-gauge track that had once been something to do with the old colliery.

Torelli didn't express surprise or confusion, and he didn't demand to know what the fuck was going on. If he had, which was what Everett and Gar were expecting, the whole thing would have been over quicker and with a lot less mess. As it was, Torelli simply ripped the passenger door open and legged it.

The deserter grinned. 'Gar!'

But Gar was already moving.

He burst from the back of the van like a bull at a rodeo, and powered after Torelli who had chucked his carrier bag away and was angling between two of the large conical piles of overgrown spoilage. Torelli wasn't wasting his breath in screaming or trying to attract nearby help because he probably knew there wasn't any, and again Everett felt that grudging respect. He floored the accelerator and the van's wheels spat gravel as he steered between two other heaps in an attempt to head the runner off. Torelli by now must have seen that the whole area was fenced off because he started slogging it up the slope of the nearest pile, either because he thought somehow he could jump over the fence from there or maybe just because his soldier's instincts told him to gain higher ground.

They were good instincts. Gar was starting to huff a little as his feet slipped and dug into the loose surface; being significantly heavier than his quarry, it must have been like trying to run up a sand-dune for him. Torelli paused, picked up a lump of sharp-edged concrete about the same size as his head with both hands, and lobbed it at Gar. Gar tried to dodge, but he couldn't move very far to either side and the missile bounced off his right shoulder, cutting it open in a red splash. Gar roared in pain and fury.

'Not happening, chum, sorry,' said the deserter. He slewed the van to a halt on the other side of the small mountain on which Torelli was currently playing king-of-the-castle, leapt out and sprinted up the slope. Torelli turned to meet him; his eyes were wide and his nostrils flaring, and wet hair hung in his eyes.

'What the *fuck*?' he gasped, and just kept repeating, 'What the *fuck*?'

Some part of Torelli was enjoying this, the deserter knew, but he didn't have the time to indulge this luxury, and he drew his Webley. He'd had it since the trenches and it had done him good service ever since. He kept it in perfect working condition even though he'd rarely had to use it in the last few decades; these days mostly just showing it to someone did the trick, as it did now. Torelli's hands went high, and he stepped back.

'Hey, wait, man, I don't know what this is about, but—'

Then Gar slammed into him from behind. Torelli went down hard. Gar roared and stamped on his lower leg, and the brittle snap of breaking bone was almost as loud as the gunshot would have been. Torelli twisted and howled. Before Everett could stop him, Gar stamped on the other leg and broke that too. Everett had heard most sounds that a human being in agony could make, but this was loud even so.

'Gar! For God's sake man! Muffle that noise!'

Gar clamped a hand over Torelli's mouth but the screaming just went on behind his fingers. Between them they dragged him back down to the van, tied him up and gagged him, then looked at Gar's shoulder. It was a deep gash, and his arm was already red down to the elbow.

'You'll survive,' Everett said, and it was true, the blessing of Moccus would ensure that this would heal in a few days, but in the meantime it was bleeding abominably so he did his best to wad it up with some old dust rags that were in the van. When he'd finished he nodded at Torelli, who was semi-conscious with shock, moaning and writhing, and said to Gar, 'You're going to have to carry that now.'

Gar indicated his wounded arm and made an indignant sound.

'I don't care. It serves you right for losing your temper.' He started the van and drove them back to the farm.

That evening the weather improved enough for them to see the tusk moon in a narrow band of clear sky low down on the western horizon, chasing the setting sun into darkness, and as if that were a sign from Moccus the replenishment rite was completed in the early hours of the following morning without complication. Unlike the first vessel, who had just wept and trembled, Torelli fought right to the end, which the deserter found satisfying; Moccus would need something of that defiance when he rose anew.

Another piece of good news was that the old woman seemed to have taken the hint and was not sleeping in her shed. So too, the others that they had brought into the periphery of the new church had been sent home, including the boy; it was one thing to ask them to sweep floors and dig holes, but quite another to expect them to accept the necessity for the use of human vessels in the replenishment. Once they had seen Moccus arise with their own eyes, however, things might very well be different.

Ardwyn, Everett and Gar returned in high spirits, but as they approached the farm gate Everett peered through the windscreen at a pale blur which had formed in the very periphery of the headlights.

'What's this?' he murmured.

The blur resolved into a human figure: an old woman, wearing only a nightdress, standing barefoot in the middle of the road by their gate.

The deserter cursed. It was Denise Keeling, and she had that damned dog with her.

12

SOMNAMBULISM

SABRINA IS BOUGHT FOR DENNIE FROM A CRAFT FAIR IN Loughborough in the winter of 1960, when she is six years old, and quickly becomes her favourite toy. She is a rag doll, with mitten-shaped hands and round feet, golden hair in a long pony-tail and large friendly eyes. She wears a pair of baggy knickers and the fabric of her body is printed so that it looks like she's wearing a vest too, and a white blouse under a pink pinafore dress, which fastens up the back with pink flower-shaped buttons. She does not have any fancy lace, ribbons or flowery patterns. She looks happy, calm, sensible, and down to earth; the kind of no-nonsense friend that you can rely on in a tight spot, who will keep your secrets, and never shirk from telling you the truth, even though it might sometimes be a bit painful.

Dennie's mummy and daddy enjoy watching her play with Sabrina, having tea parties and conversations, but they never suspect that Sabrina might be actually talking because Dennie is the only one who can hear her. And Sabrina always tells Dennie the truth.

Most of the things she tells Dennie are helpful, like where Mummy's spectacles are when she loses them, or what the weather is going to be like before a family trip to the park, or that Daddy's car is just about to appear around the corner at the bottom of the road. Dennie quickly learns not to tell her parents everything that Sabrina says because Dennie sometimes forgets and does things like telling her mother who is on the phone while it is still ringing and they give her some very odd looks that she doesn't like.

Sometimes she and Sabrina go for walks in the night. Sabrina shows her magical things like fairy rings of toadstools in the moonlight and a woodland clearing where baby badgers play. When her parents find out about this they do not like it at all. Her daddy starts sleeping with the house keys under his pillow and her mummy takes her to see the doctor, who says not to worry, it's just a phase that she'll grow out of.

As she gets older, some of the things that Sabrina tells her are confusing, like the feelings behind the words that her mummy and daddy say to each other, or the reason why the lady from next door had to leave suddenly in the night with just a single suitcase. One time Sabrina even saves her life and that of her brother and parents, as they are driving to see her Uncle Robert in Norwich. They are going smoothly and steadily along the road when all of a sudden Sabrina starts shouting We have to stop! over and over, and her *voice is so loud that it starts to come out of Dennie's mouth too – Wehavetostop!Wehavetostop!Wehavetostop!Wehave tostop! – so her Daddy pulls over to the side and while her mummy is fussing and her brother is teasing, they all notice the big cloud of oily black smoke from in the road up ahead. It later turns out that there has been a six-car pile-up with multiple fatalities, which would have killed them too if her Daddy hadn't listened to her.*

But as she gets older, Sabrina begins to fray. The print on her clothing fades and becomes threadbare, the buttons on the back of her blouse keep falling off, and her cotton stuffing starts to show. This is especially distressing when it happens to Sabrina's face. Mummy does the best job she can with big strips of Elastoplast, but eventually they have to take Sabrina to a dressmaker who stitches a completely new face on her, reproducing her eyes and smile exactly. Dennie can tell that Mummy is worried that she won't think it's the same, but by now Dennie is old enough to understand that Sabrina's voice comes from somewhere inside her, not her face.

It will be years yet before Dennie recognises that Sabrina's voice is actually her own voice, and that it isn't coming from the doll at all but from inside herself. The day she realises this is the day that Sabrina stops talking to her. Then all too soon Sabrina will be spending more and more time on her bedroom shelf while she discovers the toys of adulthood, and then Dennie will have her own children and that voice will fade as it finds expression in her love for her family, and she will forget that Sabrina ever spoke to her, and in the end she will forget even Sabrina herself.

Which was why it was with such mingled homesickness and dread that Dennie saw her old rag doll clutched in Sarah Neary's arms as she stood in the corner of the bedroom. It was 3:07, just like last time, which couldn't have been a coincidence. She closed her eyes, counted to ten, and opened them, but the apparition was still there. The house around her seethed with echoes, like restless birds' wings.

'Having a moment,' she said to herself. 'You're just having a moment, that's all.' It would pass, but she had to make sure that she was in the here and now. Trying to ignore Sarah, she got out of bed and went downstairs to the kitchen, where Viggo greeted her with a worried lick. 'It's all right, I'm just having a moment, boy, that's all.' She drank a glass of water, and switched the television on to a rolling news channel. It was the same litany of wars and scandals, but at least they were up-to-date wars and scandals rather than the regurgitated fragments of her unstable memory. She hadn't thought about Sabrina in years, and couldn't even remember whether she still had her. It was possible that she'd gone during one of the clear-outs when the children had left home. One would have thought that a toy so precious couldn't just slip out of the world unnoticed. The water was helping to clear her head, and she thought maybe the moment had passed. 'No,' she told a hopeful Viggo. 'It's not breakfast time and I'm not letting you upstairs with your stinky dog farts.' She patted him, put a few dry biscuits in his bowl anyway because she was a soft touch and he knew it, and Sarah was standing by the back door.

Dennie shrieked and dropped the box, scattering dog biscuits all over the floor.

'What do you want from me?' she whispered.

Neither Sarah nor Sabrina replied.

'I did everything you asked. You can't do this to me. It's not fair!'

Then somehow Sarah was outside the back door and walking away, carrying Sabrina so that the doll's face appeared over her shoulder, looking back at Dennie as she receded into the shadows of the garden like a drowned person sinking into deep water.

Dennie's sense of clarity drained away. She wasn't just having a moment – she was in the moment, always had been and probably always would be until she found out what it was that Sarah, or her own mind, or whatever was responsible for this, wanted. She opened the back door and followed Sarah out into the night. After a quick pause to take advantage of the unexpected floor feast, Viggo followed.

The moment folded around her again and held her in its bubble, making the outside world dim and hard to see. Some part of her knew that it was night, it was cold, and she was walking barefoot in her nightie along wet pavements, but that part felt like it was dreaming. The only thing she could focus on with any certainty was Sarah, who maintained a constant distance in her slippers that didn't seem to get damp at all, with Sabrina continuing to peep over the shoulder of her pink hoodie, either encouraging her to follow or warning her not to.

The village streets gave way to country lanes, hedgerows

dripping and rustling with the furtive movements of small animals. Then there was a gap, and a wide wooden gate with a freshly painted sign that read 'Farrow Farm'. A bright light grew behind her, sending her own long shadow skewering ahead, and Viggo began to bark.

Sarah was gone, and the moment burst.

'I could run her down,' the deserter suggested. 'Nobody would ever know.'

Gar grunted in agreement.

Ardwyn considered it for a moment. 'No,' she said finally. 'It's still too soon. And she's too easily missed, not like the others. Let's stick to the plan. She's an annoyance at best, and that's not a reason to kill her.'

'But what's she doing here?' the deserter insisted.

'What does it matter? She can't do anything. I mean, she's done us the biggest favour she could have by coming out here like this. They'll have her taken away if we choose to tell anyone, and we can hold that over her. She still might be useful.'

'I think you're being complacent.'

'I don't care what you think. I am Mother. Gar, get out of the van. And take the remains with you.'

'Why?' he growled.

'Because Everett is going to take nice, confused old Mrs Keeling back home and we don't want to be driving *that* back and forward all night, plus her dog wants to kill you. That's why.' There was unhappy muttering from the back and then the sensation of the vehicle shifting on its suspension as Gar opened the back doors and hopped out, carrying the empty vessel. Then he slammed them again and Everett heard him trudging back along the road.

Ardwyn got out and approached the old woman. 'Mrs Keeling? Are you all right?'

The old woman shook her head as if waking up, and shushed her dog. 'I'm sorry,' she said, her voice stumbling. 'I'm not quite sure what I'm doing here.'

Ardwyn took off her coat and draped it over the old woman's shoulders. 'Well, why don't we get you back home, hey, before you catch your death? What's your address, dear?'

Keeling looked at her, obviously suspicious.

'Or, if you like, I can call someone to collect you? Your daughter, perhaps?'

'No,' said Keeling immediately. 'No, that's fine. You don't have to call anybody. I'll... a lift would be very kind. Thank you.'

Keeling told her where she lived and Ardwyn helped her into the van. The dog balked at getting into the back, growling and whining and obviously not at all happy about what it could smell in there, but the old woman coaxed him in and they set off. She still seemed distracted and he didn't attempt to make conversation. It would have been the easiest thing in the world to take care of her off in the fields somewhere – there were plenty of small pools and reservoirs in this part of the Trent valley, not to mention old pit workings, quarries, and any number of other places to dispose of a body. Ardwyn was Mother, and he might still be nothing more than a deserter, but he'd fixed his colours to her for good or ill and he would stay loyal to that, at least.

So he saw the old lady safely back home and returned to the farm, where Ardwyn was waiting for him in bed with warm arms, but there was something that needed to be done first.

Gar was waiting for him. He had lit a fire by the hole where they would soon be burying the empty vessel. It lay partially wrapped in a tarpaulin, awaiting disposal.

The deserter looked at it and shook his head. 'What a waste,' he said, taking out his butcher's knife.

The deserter cut two slices from the vessel's flank and tossed one to Gar, then removed a large flat stone that had been sitting in the embers and placed his slice on it. It began to sizzle, and the smell of cooking flesh made his mouth water in a way that the meat of no other animal could. 'First flesh, first fruit,' he murmured, watching it sear and shrink, muscle fibres contracting in the heat. 'Thank you, Ben.' Gar ate his raw, chewing noisily.

The deserter missed the monthly replenishment feasts in Swinley, where the vessel swine would be thanked and eaten with celebrations, dancing and music, light and fun. It was different now, he accepted that; reforming the worship of Moccus to include human sacrifice meant that certain practices would inevitably have to stop. Emptying a vessel was one thing. Feasting on human flesh was entirely abhorrent. Ardwyn would certainly never understand. There was no danger that Gar would tell her what they were doing, he reflected as he turned his strip of flesh over to cook on the other side, because in this he was of the same mind: that there were some forms of worship even older than praying to gods.

Sometimes he wondered if Ardwyn appreciated that.

13

A NICE NEIGHBOURLY CHAT

IT TOOK DENNIE THE BETTER PART OF SATURDAY TO recover from her not-quite-sleepwalking adventure, but by Sunday she was feeling enough of her old self to start asking the older folk on the allotment what they knew about this 'Farrow Farm' place. She was pretty sure she'd never heard of it before, at least by that name. Sian Watts, who had once been a postal delivery woman, said that it sounded like the old Harris place. It was too small to be called a farm, only a dozen acres, but Harris hadn't even been able to manage that properly once his kids escaped the gravity of its black hole grip on their family. When his wife had died he jumped into a bottle with both feet, and had only ever been seen in town to pick up his pension and his daily ration of Special Brew until his liver finally had enough and quit on him as well. His kids had tried to sell the property, but found that the land had never been officially registered since Harris' own grandfather bought it back in the '40s, and now the Turner family, descendants of the original landowner, were claiming it had been rightfully theirs all along. This was a legal fight that nobody could afford, and so the impasse had resulted in the Harris place being left to rot in conveyancing limbo for years. Which meant that Ardwyn Hughes and Everett Clifton were squatters, and not the respectable, well-heeled young millennials that they presented themselves as.

When she'd put this to Sian, the ex-postie shrugged. 'None of our business,' she said. 'Unless you want to get mixed up in a lot of legal wrangling that could take years to drag out. Besides, they're a nice young couple. And you can't blame them, really, can you, property prices being the way they are? If you ask me, they're doing the village a favour by fixing that place up and not letting it get used by one of them "county lines" gangs to sell drugs to our kids.'

Armed with this knowledge, Dennie took a box of some early pickings from her plot – spring cabbages, broccoli and asparagus – and set off for a Monday afternoon stroll to pay her respects to the residents of 'Farrow Farm'.

The farm gate was timber and wobbling with age, but the sign nailed to it was very fresh and proudly painted with the name FARROW FARM in curling letters. Presumptuous, she thought, as if they could lay claim to a place simply by declaring it so arrogantly. Mortifying, too, to think that they had seen her out here in her nightie, as if it had been anything other than her own stupid fault. Why *had* Sarah led her out here, anyway? *She didn't, because she's not real. It's just you. You're going bonkers.* Whether or not that was true it wouldn't hurt for Miss Hughes and Mr Clifton to keep believing it, especially since she'd confronted them so belligerently after smacking her head, so Dennie put on her best doddery smile, let herself through the gate, hoisted the box of veg in her arms and walked along the muddy track to the house.

Despite the promise of the sign, she was not impressed. She saw overgrown hedges and tumbling stone walls, piles of rubbish and rusting farm equipment lying in weeds, and a crumbling outhouse where the ancient terracotta roof tiles had slid away to reveal warped trusses. A rust-streaked tractor was parked in a wide farmyard which was mostly mud and puddles, and she was surprised to see Matthew Hewitson just getting down from its cab, dressed in tattered blue overalls and wellingtons. The boy scowled when he saw her.

'Why hello, Matt!' she said cheerily. 'I didn't expect to see you here.'

'I'm working here,' he replied. His arms were crossed tightly over his chest as if she'd accused him of something. 'It's a proper job. They pay me.'

'I'm sure they do. Is Miss Hughes in?' She hefted the box. 'I have a present for her.'

'Miss Hughes,' he smirked. 'Yeah, she's in.'

'Can you please tell her I'm here?'

He laughed. 'They don't pay me for that. She's round the back.' He stuck his hands in his pockets and squelched off across the yard in the opposite direction.

Charming boy. His mother must be so proud. Dennie made her own way around the farmhouse, assuming that was what he meant by 'the back'. For all that the yard was a mess, someone had paid attention here, at least. The window frames and front door were freshly painted, there were tubs of daffodils and crocuses set beside the path, and it looked like several roof tiles had been replaced. There was a long stone structure that might have been a barn or a cowshed that looked like it had been given a new coat of paint, with some very large and shiny padlocks securing the doors, and past this she was into a field full of thistles and ragwort where she saw two figures standing by one of the tumble-down stone walls. One was Ardwyn, but she hadn't expected to recognise the other. It was Shane Harding, who along with his partner Jason had built their allotment in the shape of a Viking longship. He had the beard and brawn to match, but he ducked away when he saw her approach as if ashamed of being seen here.

'Sorry for just barging in like this,' she said. 'I would have called ahead but I don't have your number. I can see you're busy so I'll just drop this off and leave. Morning, Shane!'

'Morning, Dennie,' he replied, turning red. He was wearing thick working gloves, and it looked like he was getting set to rebuild this part of the wall.

'Mrs Keeling, so good to see you!' Ardwyn turned, beaming with welcome, but Dennie had been on the receiving end of enough surprise visits by well-meaning friends and relatives to know a fake smile when she saw one.

'Oh God, Dennie, please.'

'Dennie, then. What brings you here?'

'I'm not going to say that I was just passing, but I've come to say that I can't thank you enough for the other night, and to say sorry for the trouble, and to bring you a present.' She held out the box. 'First pickings from my allotment.'

'That's so lovely of you!' Ardwyn replied, taking the box and examining its contents. 'Thank you! You will come in for a cup of tea, I assume?'

'I thought you'd never ask.'

Ardwyn turned back to Shane. 'You're okay with what needs doing here?'

'Mm-hm.' He nodded and bent to work, picking up a large lump of stone and hefting it.

'Bye, Shane!' Dennie said, even more brightly than she'd greeted him, because it obviously made him uncomfortable and she couldn't work out why. He was acting like a guilty teenager. This wasn't like him at all. 'See you at the Pavilion some time?' He mumbled something in response.

'You seem to be gathering quite a little army of helpers,' she said to Ardwyn as they walked back to the house. 'I saw Matt Hewitson just now, looking like a regular member of Young Farmers.'

'I know, people are so generous with their time, offering to help. It's exactly the sort of village community spirit that Everett and I were hoping we'd find.'

'Well, Matt's mother will be pleased that he's doing something constructive with his time, anyway.'

They laughed together.

Viggo was given a bowl of water outside the back door and leashed to the pole of the rotary clothes hoist. There didn't appear to be any livestock nearby but it was lambing season and an unsecured dog, even one as well behaved as Viggo, was asking for trouble.

'He's gorgeous,' said Ardwyn. 'What breed?'

'He's a Great Dane. Six years old. Not a youngster, but not over the hill yet, just like his owner. They were originally bred for hunting boar, I believe, but all he gets around here is rat.'

'I bet he's great company for you.' Ardwyn squatted down in front of Viggo and took his ears in her hands, scrunching them playfully. 'Are we going to be friends, Viggo?' she said. 'Are we?' She scrunched his ears and scratched the fur beneath his throat and he panted, adoring the attention. Dennie found herself surprised and even a little jealous. *You big traitor*, she thought. 'Yes, I think we are, aren't we?' She turned back to Dennie. 'Can I give him a treat or something?'

'Oh, now if you do that he'll be your friend for life.'

She disappeared inside and came back a moment later with some plain biscuits that Viggo made short work of.

'That's it,' said Dennie, throwing her hands up in mock despair. 'I may as well leave him here now.' Maybe she had got the wrong idea about this young woman after all.

Ardwyn led her through the back door and into the kitchen, which was clean and orderly, though quite old-fashioned. There was a heavy wooden table, lots of mixing bowls and ceramic jars, and pots and utensils hanging from the walls, but no microwave or even an electric kettle; Ardwyn put a metal one with a whistling cap on the hob of a large black-leaded cooking range to boil. It smelled of flour and lard and pepper, and reminded Dennie of her grandmother's kitchen. She supposed it was the fashion amongst the younger generation to go for 'retro' things – in other words the clapped-out stuff that her generation had thrown out decades ago in favour of things that did the job better.

'This is all very embarrassing,' she said. 'I thought I'd come during the day this time, and in clothes. Honestly, what must you think of me?'

'Actually, what I'm thinking is would you like some walnut cake?'

'Very much so, thank you.'

Ardwyn took down and opened a square tin, and cut them each a slice of walnut cake that was heavy, loaded with walnuts, dried fruit and ginger, and easily the best she had tasted for a long time. Fair play to the young woman – she could bake.

'I used to sleepwalk when I was a girl,' Dennie admitted. 'I'd wake up in the living room with no idea of how I'd got there, and once or twice I was even found outside, miles away. One time I scared the life out of our poor old milkman who was doing his rounds early in the morning, when he found me sitting in the back of his little electric cart drinking one of his pints. My parents were at their wits' end. And then one day it just stopped as suddenly as it started. I'm really so—'

'If you apologise to me one more time,' Ardwyn interrupted, 'I'll take your cake away.'

'You monster!'

Ardwyn laughed again. 'I'm sure it's nothing serious – unless you find yourself obsessively washing your hands to get rid of imaginary bloodstains, that is.'

'That was Lady Macbeth, wasn't it?'

Ardwyn nodded. '"Out, damned spot", and all that. I don't know, I had a lot of respect for her up until that point. She had the spine to do what she thought was necessary, but then of course Shakespeare has to go and have her lose her mind like some typical feeble woman.'

Sarah is staring down at Colin's body on the blood-slicked floor of her kitchen. Her hands and arms are red to the elbow. She raises eyes like screaming black holes to Dennie and whispers, 'What are we going to do with him?'

Dennie jerked back into the present, shaking her head to clear it. *For God's sake, not now.*

'Are you all right?' Ardwyn was peering at her in concern.

'Yes, I, uh…' Dennie faked a small coughing fit. 'I think I might have breathed in a piece of walnut or something.'

'Oh no! Let me get you a glass of water.'

While Ardwyn was busying at the sink, Dennie hunted around for something to change the subject. 'You know,' she said, 'I've been living in Dodbury for nearly forty years and I had no idea this place was here. I love what you've done with it.'

'Thank you. The countryside is full of odd little corners and forgotten gems like this. We were lucky to find it.' Ardwyn returned with a glass of water, and Dennie sipped.

'If you don't mind my asking, why do you need an allotment if you've got a whole farm?'

'This place was so badly run-down when we found it that we worked out it'd be cheaper to level it and start again from scratch, but farming's a long-term investment and we just don't have the kind of cash to jump-start this place to make it a going concern. The allotment's the next best thing – a bit more manageable.'

'I'm impressed that you have time for both. If you don't mind my asking, what does Everett do?'

'He's a security consultant,' Ardwyn replied smoothly. 'He works from home a lot and can pick and choose his hours. We're both so lucky not to have to deal with the whole nine-to-five rat race.'

'And you?'

'Oh, I manage this place, which is more than enough of a full-time job, believe you me.'

'It must get lonely, though.'

'Well, I do have plenty of visitors!' she replied with a little laugh that was meant to sound playfully teasing. 'And the village is only just down the road. Plus, I like my peace and quiet. It gives me plenty of time to read and draw.'

'Oh! Is that one of yours?' Dennie pointed to a pencil sketch that had been pinned to a noticeboard next to the fridge. 'It's very good.' The image was a statue of a woman with loose robes draped over the shoulders of her otherwise naked form, with a crown on her head, a necklace about her throat, her right hand on her hip and holding a staff like a shepherd's crook in her left. She was gazing off to one side in imperious disdain, and there was nothing as far as Dennie could see to distinguish it from a thousand other similar classical statues except that the woman's right foot was resting on the severed head of a boar.

'It's Circe,' said Ardwyn. 'The statue of Circe at the Louvre, actually, sculpted by Charles Guméry in 1860.

Do you know the story?'

'Not really, no,' Dennie replied, surprised – this wasn't the kind of conversation she'd expected to have in a farm kitchen in rural Staffordshire.

'Circe was a sorceress, the daughter of the sun-god Helios, and Hecate, mother of all witches. She lived on an island called Aeaea where she perfected her skills in magic and herb-lore, bothering nobody, until Odysseus came sailing on his way back from the Trojan War. Faced with a crew of battle-hardened Greek sailors who were likely to gang-rape and then kill her, she used her powers to turn them into swine – all except Odysseus, of course, who had to resort to help from the god Hermes to defeat her. Hermes gave him a magic herb called "moly", which we know as the snowdrop, that would make him immune from her magic. And so basically he raped her at sword point, made her restore his crew to their human forms, then lived on her island for a year, forcing her to bear his children while he was supposed to be trying to find his way home to his loyal wife in Ithaca. Meanwhile Circe, of course, has been written as the enchantress and temptress in all of this.'

'No big surprises there,' said Dennie.

'No. But here's an interesting thing. The transformation of men into swine has been interpreted by some as a parable of the way that drink and drugs can degrade a person's capacity for rational thought. The bulb of the snowdrop contains a substance called galantamine, which is prescribed by doctors for the relief of certain forms of mental dissociation such as Alzheimer's.'

Dennie felt her blood run cold and did her best to cover it with a laugh. 'That's incredible! How do you know all of this?'

'I told you, I like to use the peace and quiet to read as well as to draw.' Ardwyn went over to a Welsh dresser that was crammed with bottles and jars of every shape and size, selected one, and brought it back to the table. Rattling around inside were what looked like a handful of dried peas. 'These are dried snowdrop bulbs. Now I don't want to interfere – I'm not a doctor and I'm certainly not judging – but, if you don't mind my saying so, there have been a couple of times like Friday night when you seem to have been a bit, oh, I don't know...'

'Off my trolley? Gaga? Ready for the men in white coats?'

'I was going to say "confused". These might help with that, is all I'm saying. Dennie, the last thing any of us wants is to see you hurt or in hospital because of another incident like that. I mean we nearly ran you over! I feel terrible!'

When had Ardwyn come to be one of 'us' along with Lizzie and the rest of Dennie's friends and relatives, she wondered, instead of 'them'? It was all said with such solicitude and care, but Dennie couldn't help feeling the iron of a threat lurking under the fleece of her soft words.

What she actually said was, 'That's very kind of you, but I think I'll trust to the traditional remedy of tea and gardening for the moment.' She finished her tea, pushed her plate away with a sigh of satisfaction and got to her feet. 'I'd better be on my way,' she said. 'I feel like I've imposed on your time too much already. That cake really is wonderful.

Enjoy the veg, and don't worry about the box.'

Ardwyn saw her out of the back door where Dennie untied Viggo from the clothes hoist. 'Just out of curiosity,' she said, as she wrapped his leash around her hand. 'Which estate agent found this place for you? I have a sister; she lives in London and the big city's not healthy for her and she's been looking for something a bit more rural. Somewhere like this would be perfect for her.'

Ardwyn gave a breezy smile and flapped her hand. 'Do you know, I'm so useless at that sort of thing? I left it all to Everett to sort out, so I don't actually know their names, but I'll ask him when he gets home and be sure to pass it on to you.'

'I'd love that.' She waved and set off down the track towards the gate and the road. 'Thanks again for the cake!' she called.

Ardwyn waved back. 'Any time!'

'Snowdrop bulbs my arse,' Dennie muttered to Viggo as they walked. 'What does she think I'm going to do, crush them into a line and snort them off a mirror through a rolled-up banknote?'

Viggo grinned at her and licked her hand because she was talking to him.

'Don't try that one, you traitor,' she grumped. 'What was all that about, anyway – letting her fuss over you like that? Bloody shameless, you are.'

He whined and licked her hand again.

Dennie sighed. 'Come on, my furry Viking boy, we've got a phone call to make.'

Early that evening, Farrow Farm had another unwelcome visit from another of their neighbours. Everett, Ardwyn and Matt were sitting down to supper when there came a thundering knock at the front door.

'Little pigs, little pigs,' said Everett, getting up. 'That was quick.'

'I'll give her this,' Ardwyn replied. 'She doesn't hang about.'

'I'll get Gar,' he said, and headed for the back door.

'Matt,' said Ardwyn. 'Get your phone out. Record everything.'

'Yes, Mother.'

She stood, drew herself up a little taller, and went to open the front door – putting it on the latch chain first.

'Hello? Can I help you?'

The belligerent glare of a man she didn't recognise pressed close up against the gap. He was jowly and swivel-eyed. Behind him there were two more – one bearded, and one wearing a snapback with the logo of an agricultural supplies company pulled down low over his eyes as if he didn't want to be recognised, as well he might not. It also sounded like there was at least one dog out there, maybe two.

'Who the fuck are you?' snarled Farmer Jowl. Leaning against the slope of his shoulder was the long barrel of a shotgun.

'I don't think I want to tell you that,' she replied. 'You don't seem very friendly.'

'*Friendly?* I'll give you three seconds to open this door and get the fuck off my property, or I'll show how fucking friendly I am!'

'Just so you know, my friend here is videoing all of this, aren't you?'

Behind her, Matt held up his phone in one hand and gave a little wave with the other. 'Hi, Daz,' he said.

The kid in the snapback slumped even lower.

She turned to Matt. 'You *know* these people?'

Matt nodded, and pointed them out. 'Darren Turner. His dad, Mark. And I think that's Rory, his foreman. Their farm's just on the other side of Drake's Hill from us.'

She turned back to Mr Turner, beaming. 'Oh, well then we're neighbours! How lovely! Well, Mr Turner, as I was saying, Matt here is recording this in case you were thinking of doing anything violent. Three big men threatening to hurt a woman in her home? With guns and dogs? I don't think the police would like that.'

Turner thumped the door, but not as hard as he could have done. He seemed to be getting the message. 'This is *my* property, and you're trespassing. *Squatting*, that's what you are. I've got every right to turf out the lot of you.'

'Actually, no you haven't. And no, it isn't. When we moved in, there was a helpful sign in the window that said this property was secured by bailiffs under order from Staffordshire County Council until court proceedings regarding ownership were resolved, and I don't think that's happened, has it? When it does, *if* it does, whoever the eventual owner is can start proceedings to have us evicted. In the meantime, I'm going to finish my supper. Good night.'

She started to close the door but his fist slammed it open again as far as the chain would allow.

'Smarmy bitch!' he shouted. 'I don't give a fuck—'

She never did find out what Mark Turner didn't give a fuck about, because that must have been the moment Everett and Gar appeared behind them. There was a lot of scuffling, shouting and barking, then the barking turned into whines and yips of pain. She took the chain off and opened the door fully to watch. Turner's four-wheel drive was parked in her yard and his bearded foreman was sprawling on his arse next to it. The boy Darren was on his knees with one arm stuck straight out at an angle that could not have been comfortable, his hand twisted in Everett's grip and Everett's knee in the small of his back. Gar had a dog's throat in each fist, pressing them to the ground; they whined and scrabbled helplessly while he snarled, every one of his tusk-like teeth on display.

'You're welcome to try and evict us, as and when,' said Everett. 'But in the meantime, we're all going to be nice neighbours and you're going to leave us alone to get on with our lives. Otherwise my brother is going to kill your dogs and your boy here is going to end up in a wheelchair.' He twisted Darren's arm a little and dug his knee in a bit further, and the boy howled.

'Of course,' added Ardwyn, 'you can be all pig-headed about it and call the police about us "trespassing", as you call it, but they won't intervene in a civil matter like that. And I'm certain that you don't want them to know you came here threatening violence.'

'Plus, you'll still have no dogs,' Everett said. 'And young Daz here will still be eating through a tube and shitting in nappies. What do you say, neighbour?'

Turner's eyes swivelled and rolled in panic, and his mouth chewed on curses that were too terrified to utter themselves. Eventually what emerged was a strangled, 'I'm... you can't...' and then a terse, resigned nod.

'Good, then.'

The boy and the dogs were released, Turner collected his wounded little vigilante mob together, and they helped each other into the four-wheel drive. He started the engine with a roar and zig-zagged down the track to the open gate, out onto the road, and was gone. Everett and Ardwyn strolled down in its wake, with Matt and Gar behind. She picked up the 'Farrow Farm' sign which had been ripped off and thrown into the mud, and brushed off as much of the filth as she could.

'This place is *ours*,' she said, with an intensity that surprised even herself. 'This is our *home*. Do you think he understands that?'

'In all honesty?' said the deserter. 'No. He's had a shock, but a shock isn't a lesson. He's been the big man around here too long, and he'll do what all big men do when they're beaten. He'll make excuses for himself – how it was unfair, how we cheated and so on – and once he's a got a few drinks in him he'll decide that he needs to hit us harder next time.'

'It's all very tiresome,' she said. 'Frankly I've got more annoying people to worry about. I want this resolved as soon as possible. This place is *ours*,' she repeated. 'Do you feel that, Matt? Do you feel that this your home?'

'Yes, Mother.'

'And what would you do to protect it? To protect me?'

'Anything, Mother.'

'Anything is a very big word, Matt. I wonder, can you live up to its promise?'

He squared himself. 'I can, Mother. You can count on me.'

'I hope so.' She turned back to the deserter. 'A poet once said, "good fences make good neighbours". Everett, I would like you and Matt to please show Mr Turner where the boundaries of acceptable behaviour lie, and demonstrate to him what happens if they are crossed.'

'Yes, Mother.'

PART THREE

PLANT OUT SEEDLINGS

1

BOUNDARIES

'ARE YOU SURE THIS IS A SHORTCUT?' SAID KATE.

'Of course, I'm sure.' Suzie threw her rucksack over the wall.

'I don't think this is even a proper footpath.'

'Look,' said Suzie, pointing at the map. 'We just follow this fence line here. It cuts off this big triangle here and saves us a good hour. We can be at the Laughing Goose by lunchtime.'

'But what if there's a farmer?'

'Then we just claim that we're a pair of idiots who got lost because they can't read a map properly. Which in your case is true.' Suzie glanced up and down the lane to make sure that there weren't any passing cars to see them, then climbed over the wall and into the field on the other side. 'Come on, twinkle-toes!' she called.

'We are so going to get arrested,' Kate grumbled, and tossed her rucksack over the wall too.

'Hey! That nearly hit me!'

'Did it? Oh, I'm so sorry, must be because I'm an idiot.' She climbed over the wall and dropped down next to her friend.

'Cow.'

'Moo.'

They grinned at each other, re-shouldered their bags and set off along the fence that ran perpendicular to the wall, uphill and into a copse of trees.

It had been a last-minute decision to go out for a day's ramble through the fields and down to Fradley Junction, where the Trent and Mersey Canal met the Coventry Canal. Suzie had gained an unexpected day off because some workmen renovating the offices next door had sliced through a power cable and cut the electricity to the whole building, and Kate's planned trip with her on-off boyfriend Gethin had fallen through because of some football-related thing, so Kate had messaged her to say why don't we do something – thinking an epic shopping spree – and Suzie had come back out of nowhere with it's a sunny day why don't we go for a walk in the countryside and to her own enormous surprise Kate had said sure, why not? Apparently Suzie had fond memories of a childhood holiday cruising the canal and had stopped at this place called the Laughing Goose Café, which sounded fun. So Kate had gone into the loft and dragged out the dusty old rucksack that she hadn't used since failing her Bronze Duke of Edinburgh expedition at the age of fourteen, bought some sandwiches from the Co-op across the road and then it was now.

According to the map this was called Drake's Hill. There was no path following the fence and the grass was long and still wet from the rain, and pretty soon Kate's jeggings were wet to the knee. 'I'm getting soaked here,' she complained.

Suzie laughed. 'Not that I'm trying to distract you in any way, but ooh look, babby lambs!'

She pointed to the field on their left, on the other side of the fence, where sheep were grazing accompanied by the tiny white dots of very new lambs. The nearest she could see were feeding, with their heads butting their mother's underside and their tails waggling voraciously.

'Oh, that is so cute!'

'Yeah, but imagine breastfeeding something that's headbutting you in the tits all the time. Respect, mama sheep.'

They carried on walking, and soon found themselves amongst the trees, having to step over roots and duck to avoid low-hanging branches that were just coming into leaf. The girls had to concentrate more on where they were putting their feet, so when Suzie stopped suddenly, Kate almost ran into her.

'Hey,' she said. 'You okay?'

Suzie continued to stare straight ahead at whatever had made her stop, and slowly raised her hand to point with a shaking finger. 'What's that?' she whispered.

Kate moved to one side to get a better view. Further ahead of them, half-hidden by the swaying branches of a birch, was something that looked like a red and white coat draped over a fence post. Then a stronger breeze stirred the branches more, and they parted fully to reveal the severed head of a lamb impaled there, facing back into the field where its living cousins were feeding quite happily. Its tiny, eviscerated corpse hung on the barbed wire below, limbs spread-eagled above a glistening pile of intestines. Flies were crawling here and on the lamb's staring eyeballs.

Kate jammed her hands to her mouth to stifle the small noises that were trying to escape. If they escaped, they would become huge, and might not ever stop. Suzie was whimpering, 'Oh my God, oh my God,' over and over.

'Who... what kind of sick fucker would do something like this?' said Kate.

Suzie swallowed thickly. 'I don't know. Let's go. Let's just go.'

So they just went, skirting the scene of carnage and holding their breaths against the stench of blood and shit, but Suzie stopped again a few minutes later, moaning, 'No, no, oh please God *nooo*...'

There was another one. This one had some black colouration in its wool. Its tongue had also been cut out and hung below its throat. This time Kate and Suzie ran, and in a few moments they were out from the trees and downhill into the open field, following the straight line of the fence on their left towards the hedgerow where the path lay, the path that they should never have left, and they could see another butchered lamb, and then another, one every hundred yards or so, maybe a dozen of them, all with their dead eyes gazing at the pasture from which they'd been snatched. At the very bottom there was a man pulling the remains of one from the fence and throwing it into a trailer attached to a quad bike. There were already several small corpses in the trailer already. The farmer glanced at the girls as they ran past but didn't stop them or say anything to them, obviously not caring that they were trespassing, and they saw that there were tears on his face too.

Kate and Suzie threw themselves over the wall at the other end and onto the lane. They completed the rest of their walk in shocked and trembling silence, and found the canal junction colourful with boats and laughing families. They sat at a table outside the Laughing Goose with cups of tea going cold in front of them and ducks cackling around their ankles, but if there was a joke neither of them could see the funny side.

David got back late from the hospital, chucked a frozen lasagne into the microwave and then sat on the sofa, flicking through the TV channels and wondering why he wasn't more tired. Alice had been transferred to Birmingham Children's Hospital, an hour's drive away, and he'd stayed until the end of visiting hours at seven, so he should have been exhausted.

The oncologists on the Ward 18 had diagnosed an infection of *staphylococcus aureus* in Alice's chemo port, which they removed, and put her on a week's course of IV antibiotics. Yesterday they had replaced it with a new port and were planning to keep her in for another four days to monitor how her body accepted it. Nobody could tell Becky and David how the infection had got in there – it could have been a slip-up in the way her port was cleaned and her chemo administered, or it could have been a miniscule flaw in the device itself. Becky blamed herself for not looking after her little girl better, second-guessing every decision to take her outside or let her play with something that hadn't been scrupulously disinfected first. David suspected that it was simply nature's way of reminding them who was in charge and punishing them for having had things go so relatively smoothly with her treatment. As if any of this had been easy.

To help keep her isolated, Alice had an en-suite cubicle which had space to let one parent stay overnight, sleeping in a chair which folded out into a narrow bed. David and Becky had been taking turns, and tonight it was hers. Both the print works and the police had been as generous as ever in letting him have the time off, but it meant that when he got home he had nothing to do but brood. He called Becky to let her know that he had got home okay, said goodnight and I-love-you to his brave baby girl, and then faffed around on his phone to keep himself distracted while the microwave worked its magic.

There was an alert on the OWL about two young women who had reported that they'd seen mutilated farm animals while out walking, the day before yesterday. The regular police had gone out to check on the landowner concerned – a farmer called Turner – who told them that it had just been a fox that had taken two of his lambs, nothing had been mutilated. The incident was actually being flagged as a case of trespass; Turner didn't want to press charges but the police put it up on OWL in case it happened again to anyone else who did. Lambing season was a sensitive time, and nobody wanted stroppy ramblers exercising their 'right to roam' and stressing their animals. It was done and signed off, nothing to see here folks, please move along.

But something about it nagged him.

It was the farmer's name: Turner. He scrolled back through the last few weeks' reports, and the name came up again. There had been a fight in the Golden Cross; Darren Turner and two of his mates had got seven colours of shit kicked out of them by Matthew Hewitson in an argument over a local girl called Lauren Jeffries. David hadn't been volunteering that night so he hadn't seen what happened, but he had seen the start of it at the barbecue two weeks before. Darren and his friends were no lightweights either, they were farmers' sons and used to a lot of hard physical work, so how did Matt Hewitson go from getting seen off by one of them to handing all three of them their arses in a fortnight? It was no surprise that they didn't want to make a thing of it with the police. There had been no serious injuries, so the regular cops had written it up as a Friday-night scuffle, handed out cautions to all concerned and got on with worrying about more important things.

Which was exactly what David himself should have been doing, he told himself. The microwave pinged and he went to collect his meal. He prodded the radioactive sludge around his plate before eventually abandoning it. It was tasteless and he had no appetite anyway. He took care of the ironing, vacuumed the house and then sat on the sofa again, feeling twitchy and restless. He scrolled through the OWL reports again.

'Fuck it,' he muttered, grabbed his jacket and his car keys, and went to have a word with Matthew Hewitson.

* * *

Matt wasn't at home, but his mum was, and she wasn't happy. David eventually managed to convince Shirley Hewitson that he wasn't there to get her son into trouble with the police, but it didn't improve her mood appreciably.

'He's off at that bloody farm again, I'll bet,' she complained. 'Spends all his time there now. I hardly see him these days!'

'What farm?' he asked.

'Oh, the one owned by that bloody pair of millennials. You know she actually came here to help him collect his things? The woman, the one with the Welsh-sounding name. I said to her, he's a legal adult and can make his own decisions but you're taking advantage of him and it's not right. And she says to me, she says that I don't need to worry about him any more because he's got a new family. Well I thought, that's bloody cheeky, isn't it? She says, "He's got a new mother now," looking all pleased with herself. So I says to her, love, you ain't somebody's mother until you've sat up with him vomiting all the night in hospital—' Mrs Hewitson stopped and slapped her hand across her mouth. 'Oh my God I am so sorry, I didn't mean… how is your little one?'

'She's improving,' he said. The last thing he wanted to do was talk about his daughter. 'Tell me about this farm where he's moved to.'

2

THE ABATTOIR SHRINE

By THE TIME DAVID ARRIVED AT FARROW FARM, FULL night had fallen; the sky was clear and dusted with stars. The first thing that he noticed when he pulled into the yard was how many other vehicles there were – and not farm vehicles. Ordinary cars. It wasn't unusual to see yards like this full of rusting old motors, but these weren't wrecks. It looked more like Mr Everett Clifton and Miss Ardwyn Hughes were hosting a bit of a get-together.

That impression was strengthened when he got out of his car and approached the front door. There was bright light behind drawn curtains and from inside he could hear what sounded like a dinner party: laughter and chatter and the sounds of cutlery on plates. David had no intention of interrupting; however odd the couple might be, they were entitled to their social life, and if Matthew was here then now wasn't the time to be asking him awkward questions.

David would come back another time. He turned to go.

The front door opened and Ardwyn was standing there with a tide of light and warmth and the noise of a boisterous dinner party flowing out from around her.

'Why, David!' She beamed. 'What a pleasant surprise! Please, come in!'

'Oh, no thank you, it's fine. I don't want to disturb. I'll just—'

'You'll just nothing of the sort.' She stepped to one side and beckoned with her head. 'In.'

It would have been rude to refuse.

She led him along a cluttered hallway, past closed doors to left and right, and then into a high-ceilinged kitchen where a group of people were sitting around a heavy table chaotic with the remains of a large meal. Matthew Hewitson was in the process of swigging from a can of lager when he entered, and chatter stopped as they all turned to look at him. David recognised them as fellow tenants of Briar Hill Allotments; he saw Angie Robotham, Shane Harding and his partner Jason, 'Big Ed' Rimedzo, and Hugh Preston, who winked at him. There was something weird about Hugh's face, but before he could look more closely, Everett was handing him a can of beer.

'Drink?'

'Oh,' he said, surprised. 'No, thank you. I'm driving.' Admittedly his own life had been somewhat hectic lately, but he was sure that he hadn't seen Hugh since the day of the barbecue, which was another strange thing because Hugh's allotment was his pride and joy and he would ordinarily have been working on it every day.

'Well, we can't have that,' Everett replied. 'You'd have to arrest yourself. Cup of tea it is, then.'

Ardwyn resumed her seat at the head of the table and murmured something to Matthew, who replied, 'Yes, Mother,' and immediately got up and started clearing the dirty dishes. 'Please,' she said, indicating his now empty chair. 'Have a seat.'

David sat, looking around at the faces of his neighbours, seeing nothing but smiles and friendliness. For some reason it scared the shit out of him.

'So, to what do we owe this honour?' asked Ardwyn, smiling. 'I mean, we would have invited you and Becky of course but we assumed that you were a bit preoccupied at the moment.'

Everett returned from having put the kettle on, wiping his hands on a tea towel. 'Yes, how goes the Pimblett Project?' he asked. 'How's Alice doing? We heard, you know, jungle drums and all that.' He shrugged.

'She's getting better, thanks. The infection's mostly gone. She's not out of the woods yet, but the doctors are optimistic.'

'Doctors always are, until they aren't!' Hugh laughed.

Angie winced slightly. 'Hugh,' she murmured.

'Sorry,' he said, subsiding.

When David had been a kid there had been a craze for those 'Magic Eye' pictures – those visual puzzles designed by computer, something to do with fractals, in which an image was hidden amongst the noise of a set of repeating patterns or shapes. He'd been terrible at them. 'Couldn't see the wood for the trees,' his father had said, and it was true. David was very good at honing in on specific details but found it hard to widen his focus to see the big picture. It was what made him good at spotting flaws in a print run but atrocious at spelling. There was something about the big picture in front of him around the dining table that was subtly, ever so slightly wrong, and it lay in a detail that he'd missed, just like in a magic eye picture...

'Hugh,' he said, frowning, 'is there something wrong with your eye?'

'My eye?' Hugh asked. 'What, this one?' He brought out of his pocket something that looked a bit like a marble and rolled it along the table towards him, and winked again, with the eye that used to be glass and moved sluggishly, if at all, but which now rolled in its socket as nimbly as its partner. An eye which, impossible as it was, had grown back. His old glass eye rolled to a stop against a cork, and peered blindly up at the ceiling.

'Hugh, what the *fuck*?' He turned on Ardwyn. 'What's going on here?'

She spread her hands. 'You tell me.'

'His eye! It...' He was not going to say *It grew back*, because that was impossible. He must be mistaken, obviously more fatigued than he'd thought. Prosthetic eyes could be very convincing, with veins and everything. The thing on the table must be a spare; this was obviously just one of Hugh's tasteless jokes.

Hugh got up from his chair and approached David. 'Come on, David lad,' he said gently. 'Come and have a look. It's real, I swear. Don't be afraid. It's not going to leap out of its socket and choke you.'

Cautiously, David peered closer. He might have been able to dismiss it as a particularly realistic prosthesis, complete with hair-like blood vessels in the sclera, and the fact that it moved could have been put down to it fitting particularly snugly with the muscles in Hugh's eye socket. But no prosthetic eye, however realistic, had an iris that expanded and shrank like this as Hugh turned his head to and fro. It was impossible, and yet it was literally staring him in the face.

'I know, lad, it's a bit of a shock, but you get used to it.' Hugh patted him on the shoulder and resumed his seat.

He turned to Everett. 'How...?' he whispered.

'Wrong question, chum. The question is who. Angie?'

'I've had Type 1 diabetes all my life up until six weeks ago,' she said. 'Then it just disappeared overnight. Poof!' She snapped her fingers.

'Edihan?'

'In 1997 I was in a car accident,' said the Turkish barber. 'They had to pin my spine back together.' He tossed onto the table a handful of metal pins and screws that clinked and glinted.

'Peanut allergy,' said Shane Harding. 'Put me in a coma when I was ten.'

'Which is no excuse for polishing off the pecan pie!' said Everett, and the others laughed.

'Me?' said Jason. 'Oh, I'm just here because Shane's here. But I did spit out all my fillings and found my teeth fixed. Nothing very dramatic, sorry.'

'Miracles,' said Ardwyn, 'don't have to be big and flashy and dramatic. They can be as small as a smile or a tooth filling, or they can be as huge as the ocean. Or your daughter's leukaemia.'

'Shut up!' David shouted. 'No! Just shut up! That's not... that's not...'

Acute lymphoblastic leukaemia is very treatable and the survival rates are high, they'd been told. *But you're looking at two to three years of treatment – that's chemotherapy which will feel worse than the disease itself, and very likely some painful surgical procedures. There's no miracle cure and absolutely no shortcuts, and if one single cell escapes the treatment the whole circus could start up again. There is treatment, but nothing to stop it from happening again, and the sooner you accommodate yourself to that fact the better.* Well, he and Becky had accommodated themselves to it, made all the concessions, taken Alice to all the treatments, held her hand while she cried with the pain of lumbar punctures and the nausea of chemo. To offer the hope of a cure after all of that – however impossible – was just unfair.

'I don't care,' he said, trying to make himself believe it. 'It's not possible. This must be a trick.'

Big Ed turned to Jason, puzzled. 'Was he not paying attention just now?'

'Why would it be a trick?' asked Everett. 'There's nothing set up here. We didn't even know you were coming, remember?'

Ardwyn looked disappointed. 'There's a fine line between scepticism and a stubborn refusal to accept the truth, David. Personally, I don't care which side of that line you choose to

274

live on, but just ask yourself whether you have the right to make your sick daughter go with you.'

David swallowed. 'Okay, let's for the moment assume that I'm not going insane and that everything you've all told me is true. What about the how?'

Ardwyn stood. 'Come. I'll show you.'

Feeling like he was sleepwalking, he let Ardwyn and Everett lead him out through the back door and across the yard to a large outbuilding, the door of which was secured by a huge padlock. He expected some kind of illegal medical clinic – something with stainless steel tables and trays of surgical instruments like in one of those horror movies – but as Everett unfastened the lock and opened the door, he saw nothing like that. It was an empty, cavernous space lit by bare electric bulbs. Hanging from the ceiling at the centre was a complicated arrangement of chains, pulleys and large metal hooks. Directly below this, the concrete floor was stained black. Close by the door was a large, white chest freezer, its compressor humming, and on the wall above this...

'Fuck me,' he breathed.

It was a skull, but not the skull of any creature a sane man had seen and lived, he was sure of that. It resembled a boar in its elongated jaw and curving tusks, but the eye sockets faced directly forward, like a human's, and it was much bigger than either man or beast. Hanging below it was something that looked like a long trumpet or horn made of bone that flared out to a normal-sized boar skull at the wider end. Below that hung a knife with a curved, black blade. Surrounding all of this, scrawled on the wall in paint, chalk, mud, blood and pigments more obscene than that, were hundreds of crescent moons.

The whole place looked like someone had made a shrine of an abattoir.

Behind him, the door closed and he found the exit blocked by a huge man dressed in stained overalls, chewing something nosily and glaring at him with amber eyes.

'Right now, it's going to occur to you to run,' said Everett as David stood open-mouthed. 'That's a perfectly natural reaction, and nothing to be ashamed of. But just ask yourself where you're running to. Home? Fair enough. The hospital where your daughter is being treated, perhaps, to make sure that she's safe?' As he was saying this, Ardwyn had opened the chest freezer and taken out a small parcel wrapped in ordinary white butcher's paper. She handed it to David, and he accepted it with trembling hands.

'What is it?' he whispered.

'It is the flesh of our god,' she said simply. 'It will heal your child, just as it has healed your neighbours. Just as it has already healed you, in fact.'

He stared at her, then at the parcel in his hands. Then he realised. 'The barbecue!'

She nodded. 'You've felt different ever since, haven't you? Healthier. Stronger. You don't get fatigued as much as you used to. Possibly you've had some niggling medical conditions that have cleared up mysteriously.'

'Your sex drive has increased,' added Everett. 'How's the wife finding that?' He closed the chest freezer.

'Deny what you saw at the dinner table just now all you

like,' said Ardwyn. 'You can't deny the evidence of your own body. Tell me that you believe this.'

'Yes,' he said. 'I believe it. I've got no choice, have I?'

Everett had taken the black sickle from the wall and was testing its edge with his thumb. Now he looked up at David, his gaze narrow, considering. 'No,' he said curtly. 'Too easy. Gar?'

David's arms were grabbed from behind by the huge man, and he dropped the parcel. He'd been half-expecting something like this, and slammed his head backwards, hoping to catch the big bastard in the nose, but his attacker was simply too tall and David only hit his shoulder. It felt like headbutting a sofa. Still, it made the guy twist his head to one side and David flailed backwards with one outstretched thumb like a desperate hitch-hiker, and got luckier – his thumb went somewhere soft and wet and the giant bellowed and threw him away. David skidded and spun, looking wildly for the door. The big bastard was staggering away, hands clutched to his face.

'David?' said Everett. He was pointing a gun at him. An actual pistol.

It was so utterly surreal that all David could do was gape. 'Wait, please—'

There was the ear-splitting crack of a giant firework going off and the sensation of being punched hard in his left thigh. The leg collapsed, pitching him to the concrete floor. In the frozen moment before his shocked nerve endings could start screaming, he stared at the ragged hole in his jeans and the blood welling there, then reached around to the back where there was a bigger hole and his fingers came away crimson and dripping.

Shot, he thought. *I'm shot. He shot me.* It was incomprehensible.

Then the pain hit, and he howled. His whole leg was on fire.

'Well, look at that,' said Everett, coming to stand over him. 'Straight through.'

'You could have killed him,' said Ardwyn, with just a hint of reproach in her voice.

'Oh poppycock. If I'd wanted to kill him I'd have put one right here,' and he tapped David in the middle of his forehead with a finger. 'You understand that, don't you?' he said to David directly. 'If we wanted you dead, you'd be dead. I doubt if you're even still bleeding. Have a look for yourself.'

'What,' David gasped, 'the *fuck*?'

'Fine. Let me show you.' He took the black sickle and for one terrified moment David thought that Everett was going to cut his throat, but instead he used it to slash open the jeans around the bullet wound – a wound which was no longer bleeding. There was still a hole, oozing slightly, but not bleeding as freely as it should have. Even the pain was nowhere near as bad as it had been a moment ago. As he watched, the hole in his leg closed over into a puckered scar.

Ardwyn and Everett helped him to his feet, and he stood, tottering slightly. His leg was prickly with pins and needles, but otherwise undamaged.

'Now then,' she said. 'What did that? What healed you?'

'I don't know,' he stammered.

Everett cocked the hammer of his pistol. 'Do you need another lesson, chum?'

'No!'

'The first flesh healed you,' she continued, and placed the wrapped parcel of meat back in his hands. 'The blessing of Moccus, He Who Eats the Moon. What other explanation is there?'

He had thought that such a confession might be difficult – he was a rational, logical human being, after all, who respected other people's beliefs without having to share them and absolutely didn't believe in magic or miracle cures – but he found that it was actually the easiest thing in the world. It was like scratching an itch that he'd resisted for too long, or giving in to a reflex that he'd been trying to suppress.

'None,' he said.

'Good,' she said. 'You've told me. Now tell him.' She pointed to the skull on the wall. 'Tell Moccus that you believe he exists and that his flesh can cure your child, just as he healed you.'

This was harder. But he was holding it in his hands. It was there on the wall in front of him. He had eaten it, and it had healed him. He'd been shot in the leg, and could still walk. How could it not be true?

'Moccus,' he said. 'I believe that you exist and that your flesh can cure my child.'

'Good,' she said again. 'Now. On your knees and beg.'

This was hardest of all. 'What? No! I'm not going to kneel down in front of that thing.'

Her face clenched and she inhaled sharply, but Everett

laid a calming hand on her arm. 'It's all right,' he murmured to her. 'Let me take care of this.' To David he said: 'I bet you've never knelt to anything or anyone in your life before, have you? And you have no intention of starting now.'

'You're right there.'

'I understand that, I really do. It cuts straight to the heart of your dignity as a human being and your masculine pride, doesn't it? In the words of Meat Loaf, you would do anything for love, but you won't do that?'

'If you want to put it that way, yes.'

'Tell me, David, how effective is a dose of masculine pride in healing leukaemia?'

He couldn't answer that. There was no answer to that, and there never had been.

'David, take out your phone and find a picture of Alice.'

'What? Why?'

Everett sighed with exasperation. 'I'm not going to steal your phone or profane the image of your child. Just take it out and look at it. I'm honestly trying to help you here.'

He did so, scrolling through the images until he found one of Alice on the allotment when she must have been five or six years old, before she had become sick, standing with a kiddie-sized shovel and wearing dungarees and pink wellington boots, tremendously proud of having helped with the digging. He showed it to Everett. 'How about this one?'

'It's fine. She's a lovely kid. I can't imagine how traumatic the illness must have been for her and you and Becky. Would you kneel to her?'

'Of course.'

'Then do it.'

Feeling like a complete idiot, and hating the fact that they were watching him do something so submissive, never mind that it was to one of the two people in the world he would gladly give his life for, he put the phone on the concrete floor and knelt down in front of it.

'See?' said Everett. 'That wasn't so difficult, was it?' Before David could react, he quickly stepped forward and took the parcel from his hands again.

'Hey…!' David started getting to his feet.

'*Stay down!*' Everett roared, so suddenly and loudly that David obeyed mostly out of surprise. The man's face was thunderous, and he seemed to have grown taller, like an Old Testament patriarch delivering judgement. Even Ardwyn stepped back. 'If you stand up a *moment* before I give you permission, then we are done here!' he promised. 'You can go back to the hospital and watch your child writhe and cry for her mummy and her daddy and know that the one thing you could have done to help is forever beyond your reach because you were too *proud* to beg.' His voice was barbed with scorn, and he pointed at the phone. 'Look at her. *Look at her!*' David obeyed, and found tears coming at the sight of his baby, so happy before she became the pale and forlorn shadow that the illness had turned her into.

Everett held out the package with his other hand. 'Do you want this or not?'

'Yes. Please.' He was weeping freely now.

'Then do as you are commanded, and beg, like the worm you are.'

'Please, I'm begging you...'

'Oh no, not me. I'm just a servant.' Everett pointed to the skull. 'The god. Beg Moccus for the gift of the first flesh that will heal your child.'

David turned to face bone and tusk and the black holes of eye sockets. 'Please,' he sobbed. 'Moccus. I beg you. Give me your flesh so that I can make my girl well again. I'll do anything. Anything.' He collapsed, and all the misery that he'd bottled up to stay strong for his family, two and half years of pain, fell in a flood of tears and snot between his knees.

They helped him to his feet. Ardwyn hugged him while Everett patted his back and said, 'There there, chum.' They ushered him from the building, locked up, and walked back across the farmyard towards the house.

'She didn't eat any,' said David, wiping his face with the sleeve of his jumper. 'At the hog roast. Neither of them did.'

'And that is an oversight that you can put right,' Ardwyn replied. 'Simply provide the first flesh for your loved ones.'

'But Becky doesn't eat pork.' It felt ridiculous even as he said it.

'Then don't call it pork!' Everett answered.

David stopped at the back door. 'Just tell me why. Why the hog roast? Why give this to everyone? And why not say anything about it?'

'We just want to help people,' said Ardwyn. 'But you know how this looks, you've experienced it for yourself: people can't bring themselves to believe in the miraculous even when it is actually happening to them. We let them find their way to us, like you have, and on occasion we go out and seek them when we feel it's necessary. I don't know what kind of a marriage you and Becky have, but I suspect that you might not want to tell her about this until your daughter is actually well again.'

'I don't like the idea of lying to them.' He especially didn't like the idea of sneaking pork into Becky's food. She might never forgive him even if Alice was cured by it.

'Of course, you don't. But it's for the right reasons, and you can tell them the truth when they're in a position to understand and accept it.'

Ardwyn returned to her guests while Everett led him around the side of the house and back to his car. As he got in, Everett put his hand on the door and leaned down. 'We'll let you know when we're having another get-together,' he said. 'Hopefully by then you can bring the whole family. In the meantime, we might ask you for the occasional small favour. Don't worry!' he laughed. 'Nothing criminal! But nature is a balance; you've been given something and I assume that you'll be happy with giving something in return.'

'Nature has already been unbalanced enough, as far as my family is concerned,' David replied.

'Exactly.' Everett grinned. 'Let's not exacerbate that situation, shall we?' He patted the bonnet of the car as David reversed away down the farm track, and stood unmoving in the beams of his headlights until David reached the road, shifted gear and headed for home. He tried not to look at the pale parcel sitting on the passenger seat beside him and instead focussed on the road ahead, but every so often he caught a glimpse of his own face in the mirror: his eyes red and haunted.

When he got home he put the meat as far back in the freezer compartment of the fridge as he could, hiding it with some packets of frozen peas and chips. Then he changed his trousers, threw his ruined jeans into the rubbish and sat down with his laptop, trying to find out as much as he could about Ardwyn Hughes, Everett Clifton, and the thing that their group worshipped.

The group to which he now belonged, whether he liked it or not.

'I can't believe that just fell into our hands,' said the deserter, when everybody had been sent home. He and Ardwyn were sitting by the fire enjoying the peace and a nice bottle of red, in her case, and a single malt in his, and he was glowing just as brightly with a sense of achievement. 'I know he was high on the list to approach, but the fact that he came here voluntarily, it makes me feel like we're on the right track.'

'Never doubt that, my love,' she replied, and sipped her wine. 'You broke him wonderfully, I thought.'

Everett accepted the compliment with a tilt of his whisky tumbler. 'The old parade ground bark is good for reminding the troops of who's in charge. Absolutely essential for a new recruit.'

'He will be useful in keeping the local authorities from taking too close an interest, but I wouldn't want to have to rely on that before I was sure about the strength of his loyalty.' She watched the embers shift and sparks drift up to die in the chimney. 'All the same, let's have no more until after the next replenishment. Maybe not until Moccus rises, even.'

'That long? With each replenishment the chance that someone's disappearance will be noticed increases, and the more people we have on-side the easier that is to conceal.'

'Yes, and the more chance there is that they will realise what the replenishments actually involve. I'm sorry, but we can't risk that. It doesn't matter what they're healed of, they'll never accept the necessity of human sacrifice, not until they see the god with their own eyes.'

Everett thought about this, swirling the liquor around in his glass. 'Matthew might.'

'Really? Is he so far along?'

'The boy's a natural. What he did with those lambs was inspired.'

'Hmm.' She drained her glass and poured another. 'Do it. Have him assist you and Gar on the next abduction. Let's see if he has any qualms. But test him first.'

'Yes, Mother. Who is to be next?'

She took out her little notebook, opened it, and smiled at him. 'Ooh, let's have a look, shall we?'

3

THE WILD SIDE

MAY ARRIVED IN A WHITE INCANDESCENCE OF hawthorn and blackthorn blossom in the hedgerows, raucous families of house martins settling in to the eaves of barns and swifts slicing the slow haze of the lengthening evenings as they hunted for insects. It was peak growing time on the allotments, and Briar Hill buzzed with activity. The majority of plot-holders who only ever came on the weekends now popped down for an hour or two after work, planting out seedlings from their cold frames, repairing fruit cages, putting up bean-pole trestles, digging in compost and weeding, weeding, weeding.

It also brought another visit from Lizzie.

This time she didn't bother coming to the allotment first; Dennie got home and found her car in the drive. Lizzie had let herself in and was in the kitchen, going through the contents of the freezer and checking the expiry dates.

'Hello, darling! This is a lovely surprise!'

Lizzie waved a packet of frozen butter at her. 'You know this expired in January, don't you?'

'It's lovely to see you too.'

'As in January *2015*.'

Dennie took off her boots, dumped her trug in the utility room and put the kettle on. 'Oh, butter keeps forever.'

'No it doesn't! You've heard of salmonella, I take it?'

'I think you're overreacting.'

'I think you're going to give yourself food poisoning one of these days.'

She gave her daughter a hug. 'I love you, darling.'

'I love you too.'

They had tea. Lizzie took Viggo for a walk while Dennie made a pizza from a frozen base (use by: Mar 2017). As it cooked she had a quick look in Lizzie's room and discovered that she'd packed for a longer stay this time – a week, probably.

'How are you feeling, Mum?'

'If I were any fitter I'd be dangerous. Why? What have you heard?'

'What makes you think I've heard anything?'

'Oh, come on, darling. I wasn't born yesterday. From the size of that bag in your room you look like you're moving back in.'

Lizzie chewed. 'Maybe that wouldn't be such a bad thing?'

'Someone told you about the sleepwalking thing, didn't they?'

'Mum—'

Dennie banged her glass down hard on the table. 'Why can't people just mind their own bloody business?'

The gentleness in Lizzie's voice was more maddening than her anger would have been. 'You are my business, Mum. And when you turn up outside someone's home at four in the morning in your nightdress, it becomes their business too.'

Dennie could feel her face burning red with mortification. 'She said she wouldn't say anything, that two-faced bitch. With her walnut cake and her bloody sketches from the bloody... thing, you know. Place.'

'What place?' Lizzie was looking at her in concern, and that only made it worse because Dennie knew that she was right to be concerned.

'You know! The place with the pictures! Paris! The *Mona Lisa*!'

'Do you mean the Louvre? Mum, why are you talking about the Louvre?'

'It doesn't matter! The point is that she and that boyfriend of hers are squatting. They've got no right to be there.'

'She's as concerned about you as all of us.' Lizzie took a deep breath. 'Mum, I've made an appointment for you to see Dr Fielding.'

'Have you, now?'

'Yes. It's for next Tuesday, which is why I'm staying for longer.'

'To make sure I actually go, is that it?'

Lizzie put down her half-eaten pizza crust and fixed her with a look that had the granite stubbornness she'd inherited from her father. 'As a matter of fact, yes. I'll physically drag you if necessary. I'll leash Viggo like a husky and have him pull you there on a sled if that's what it takes.'

'You think I'm losing my mind, don't you?' There had been no more visits from Sarah, and the echoes had been silent enough for her to have been able to sleep comfortably in her own bed since the sleepwalking.

'No, actually, I don't. I'll admit that I was worried, so I did a bit of reading up on it, but you're not confused or getting lost in your own home, you're not exhibiting obsessive and repetitive behaviour—'

'Other than hoarding butter...'

'—and you *definitely* don't have trouble communicating. Disturbed sleep patterns, sleepwalking, things like that, they could all just be the symptoms of stress or anxiety.'

'Well, I'm more bloody stressed now than I was before you turned up, I'll give you that. Darling, I'm not suffering from anxiety. What have I got to be anxious about? I'm retired, my husband's in the ground and my kids have left home. The only thing I've got to be anxious about is this great idiot and his farting.' She scratched Viggo between the ears; he was looking between the two women, concerned by the tension that had settled over the table.

'I don't know, but there's something. Going to that cemetery doesn't seem to have helped. I want you to see Dr Fielding. She might be able to suggest someone that you can talk to, or give you something to help you sleep, if nothing else. Remember when I had those beta blockers to get me through exams?'

Knowing when she was beaten, Dennie relented. 'Darling,

if it will set your mind at rest, and stop you interfering with my fridge, of course I will.'

Lizzie heaved a huge sigh of relief. 'Thanks, Mum.'

Her meeting with Dr Fielding was predictably inconclusive, the only concrete benefit being that it had put Lizzie's mind enough at rest that she was happy to go home. Fielding was a thin, harassed-looking woman who had made brusque and efficient use of the ten-minute appointment slot. She asked Dennie about her diet (vegetarian, avoiding sugar where possible but not averse to the occasional Bounty bar), alcohol intake (Malbec ideally, Shiraz if she had to really slum it, no smile there), smoker? (non) and exercise (walking to and from the allotment most days was a Good Thing). She took Dennie's blood pressure, which was a bit high but nothing to worry about too much, and said that she could prescribe a mild sedative if Dennie thought that would help. No thanks. In that case here was a leaflet listing various local support groups and national helplines for people coping with stress and anxiety. If the disturbed sleep persisted or she had any further sleepwalking episodes she should make a follow-up appointment immediately. Thank you and good afternoon.

Dennie still didn't know what the new couple's game was, but she had to give them credit: the top half of the Neary plot that they were cultivating was coming along well. One might even say it was burgeoning. She eyed their rows of perfect and apparently pest-free crops enviously, wondering whether they used any special kind of fertiliser. One or other of them worked it most days, though there'd been no sign of their huge friend for over a month. Maybe he'd run off.

On the days when it was left unattended she risked a closer examination, and on a bright Tuesday morning in the middle of May she was passing by on her way to the Pavilion when she caught a glimpse of glossy red peeping out from the nettles and brambles. It seemed that even the overgrown tangle of the other half was showing signs of regenerating. There shouldn't be strawberries growing wild in that trash, she told herself. It was too early in the year for them to fruit without being forced under cover, and they would never grow naturally in soil so abused as this. She mentally ran through the various cultivars that she knew of, and drew a blank, unless this was some kind of hybrid variety, but even so, what was it doing here?

Every inch of her skin crawled at the thought of setting foot on that plot again, but those berries were only a few feet beyond her reach – it would take just one step for her to be able to pluck the nearest one, and then she could find out what kind it was. Colin had been buried right up at the other end, where Ardwyn and Everett had built their shed – there was nothing that could hurt her here.

Before she could frighten herself out of it, Dennie made one large stride deep into the overgrowth, planted her foot, reached out with her right hand, grabbed the nearest strawberry off its stem, and reversed her step.

And lost her balance.

She wobbled, pinwheeling her arms desperately. She saw

herself collapsing sideways into nettles that were already as high as her head, every hair on every leaf full of poison, or else into the whiplike embrace of brambles. If not them, then there was bound to be broken glass and rusted metal hiding amongst the stems. She would be stabbed and impaled, and her blood would soak into the soil to be sucked up by the hungry roots of plants which had no business growing in God's earth. *Ah, but which god?* said a dry voice in her head, and in her terror she was sure that it was the voice of the Neary plot itself.

Then gravity reasserted itself, she reeled back to the safety of the path, and the Neary plot relinquished its nightmare grip on her body and mind. She ran back to her shed and fell onto her camp cot, sobbing.

Viggo came in and licked her until she felt better. She'd tied him up outside to stop him from getting into mischief but had left him enough lead so that he could get in if he wanted. When she felt more like herself she examined the treasure that she had won from her ordeal. For a wild strawberry it was large, unbothered by worm or beetle, and the colour of fresh blood. Tentatively she bit into it, and found that the flesh was very firm for a strawb, almost meaty in fact, and with a peculiar salty aftertaste. All told it was one of the most unpleasant things she'd ever put in her mouth. She spat it out.

'It's playing us for fools, my boy,' she said, scratching Viggo between the ears. There was too much going on that didn't make sense, and she'd had enough of it. There was still no word about Marcus Overton, Ben Torelli hadn't been seen for weeks, and plants which had no right to grow were fruiting out of season. Not to mention the unwelcome visitations from Sarah Neary. Dennie had been spending too many nights in her house and had let her watch slip.

'No more, my boy,' she said. 'No more.' She got up and went to check how much bottled gas she had for her camping stove and to air out her sleeping bag.

4

A PREMATURE INTERMENT

TOWARDS THE MIDDLE OF MAY, EVERETT ASKED MATT to use the tractor to dig another hole, just like the other two that had since been filled, in the field behind the long stone barn.

'I know what these are for, you know,' he said, as he flicked the levers that operated the back-hoe attachment, and the huge metal jaw with its square teeth scooped another chunk out of the stony soil. He'd carved out the first few feet and was working on deepening the hole.

'Do you, now,' replied Everett, barely interested. He had a shovel and was clearing out the loose rubble that kept sliding back in. Gar was collecting the larger rocks and carrying them over to the dry-stone wall to be used as material for repairs.

'I know what's in them.'

Everett squinted up at him. 'Is there a point to this

or are you going for some kind of suspense?'

'They're graves, aren't they?'

'No,' Everett said, and bent to his task again. 'Graves are for dead people. These are refuse pits for empty vessels.'

'You can call them what you like, but I've seen them. The bodies, that is.'

Everett stopped again, leaned on the shovel handle, and looked at him properly. 'Oh?'

'Yes. He showed me.' Matt pointed at Gar, who had dropped his rock and was ambling back over.

Everett stared at Gar, incredulous. 'You *showed* him?'

Gar shrugged. 'Ee ask.'

'He asked and you just showed him? Just like that?'

'Ee okay. Rust im.'

'I want you to know that I'm completely cool with it,' Matt went on hurriedly, before Everett's displeasure turned to him. 'I'm not going to tell. I mean, I figure that it's for their money, or because they pissed you off or something.'

'It's for neither of those reasons and you'd better keep your damned nose out of things that don't concern you.'

'But it does concern me, because of this.' Matt gestured to the tractor, the back-hoe, and the excavation. 'You've made it concern me. I'm an accessory now.'

'You weren't. If anybody had asked, you could truthfully have said that you were just following orders and that you had no idea what the holes were for, but you've buggered that up now, haven't you? You've made yourself an accessory.' Everett tossed the shovel up onto the grass and climbed out after it. He dusted his hands off and came over to the tractor cab, looking at Matt closely as if seeing him properly for the first time and considering what manner of creature he was. 'The only question is, what do we do about it?'

Matt was suddenly and uncomfortably aware that Gar had approached on the other side of the cab and that there was now no escape if he tried to make run for it. He began to suspect that this might have been a very bad idea. 'You let me help.'

'You were already helping, before you opened your big yap.'

'More! You let me help more! I can do more than just dig holes. I can do other things. You know... the rest of it.'

Everett's scepticism twisted his face into a sneer. 'And yet you can't even say it. What makes you think I'd trust you to do that? Killing rabbits and lambs is one thing. Killing a human being who knows they're going to die and seeing the knowledge of that in their face before you do it – that's another thing entirely, boy.'

'So tell me what I have to do for you to trust me!' he pleaded. 'Anything! I'll do anything!'

'What, like Oliver Twist?'

'Who?'

Everett shook his head, disgusted. 'Young people today.' He stared at Matt for an even longer time – considering, weighing, judging. 'No,' he decided. 'Gar, chuck him in the hole.'

'Wait!'

Gar's fist bunched itself in the front of his overalls and he was dragged from the tractor's seat. He kicked and thrashed but Gar held his feet a good six inches off the ground, and all he succeeded in doing was to twist himself from side to side like a worm on a hook, the overalls bunched up cutting into his armpits painfully. 'Gar!' he yelled. 'No! You said I was okay!' But Gar's craggy jaw was set, and he uttered not a word as he dangled Matt over the hole and let him drop. It was only about four feet deep by that stage, but it still jarred his ankles. 'Everett, please!' he wept, and tried to pull himself out of the hole. Gar stomped on his fingers and he felt several of them break, the cracking sound and flaring pain like fireworks jammed into his knuckles. He fell back, howling.

In the meantime, Everett had climbed up into the tractor and had scooped up a bucket-load of rubble from the spoil pile that Matt had only just excavated. Matt watched in paralysed disbelief as the pneumatically powered arm of the back-hoe swung towards him, directly over his face, and he raised his hands in a futile attempt to ward off the full capacity of soil and stones which was unloaded right onto his head.

Rocks hammered his skull, cracking his cheekbones and breaking his nose in lava-squirts of agony. He was smothered instantly, choking on earth rammed into his eyes, ears, nostrils, mouth. He couldn't breathe, let alone scream. Another load hit him in the hips and stomach, burying the bottom half of his body, twisting his right ankle outwards until it snapped and then he *did* scream, muffled by dirt. A rock mashed his guts, making him shit himself. Then another load, and another, weight upon weight as his lungs began to burn for oxygen and his chest tried to heave but the weight on his ribcage was too much to allow even that, until it felt like he should be squashed flat. He should be dead by now, or at least unconscious. Any form of oblivion would be a blessing. He tried to rage *Youfucker youcocksuckerI'llfuckingkillyou* and he tried to plead *I'msorryohGodI'msorrywhatdidIdo* and neither did any good. All he could do was squirm. His arms were still uppermost, from when he tried to defend himself from the falling debris, one above his head and the other across his throat, and if he pushed with that one the dirt seemed to shift a little, so he wiggled his broken fingers despite the pain and flexed his wrist and felt the dirt slide around and under them, giving him another half a centimetre to wiggle and flex upward some more.

The lava in his lungs and injuries was spreading outwards to engulf the rest of his body, bringing with it the promise of a swift burning and then eternal darkness, but he didn't want that now. He wanted to live. So he flexed and wiggled, flexed and wiggled…

The deserter stood over the pile of earth and wondered if he hadn't overestimated the boy. It had been several minutes now.

Next to him, Gar shuffled. 'Ded?'

'Maybe. I thought he was stronger than that.'

Gar sniffed. 'Shame. Ee good boy.'

A little soil trickled down the pile, but that wasn't unusual since it was still settling. Then the trickle became bigger, a gentle heaving in the dirt, and the deserter's heart leapt when he saw three fingers emerge like pale grubs, squirming weakly.

Gar uttered a deep squeal of joy and slapped the ground with both palms.

'Come on, let's get him out.'

Together they scooped away the soil and tossed aside the stones, pulled Matt clear of the hole and laid him on the grass. Everett rolled him on his side and cleared his mouth of as much dirt as he could. Matt was pallid and bleeding from a bad cut to his head, and had several breaks by the look of things. The boy retched for breath.

'You with me?' he said, slapping Matt's cheeks. 'You there, Matt?'

Matt groaned and spat mud at him.

'There we go.' Everett grinned. He and Gar slung Matt's arms over their shoulders and carried him back to the farmhouse, Matt moaning all the way and yelling when his injuries were jarred. Ardwyn met them at the door, looking surprised and concerned.

'What have you boys been doing?' she asked. 'Not playing too roughly?'

'Just a little rebirth initiation rite, nothing to worry about,' Everett replied as they manhandled Matt upstairs, screaming as his ankle slapped against each step. It wasn't easy with the three of them on the staircase; ordinarily Gar would have filled the space on his own.

'Is this a thing that we discussed?' She disapproved, as if it had anything to do with her.

'You said to test him. Can we talk about it afterwards?' he called back down the stairs as they climbed. 'Bit busy right now.'

Once they'd cleaned Matt up a bit and got him onto his bed, he'd recovered enough of his wits to glare at Everett and utter one hoarse question: 'Why?'

'Because you're a worm, Matt,' he replied, not ungently. 'I'm a worm too, and so is Gar here, and Ardwyn, and everyone else on this mudball of a planet. We're all just worms, squirming around over and under each other, trying to keep out of the mud for as long as we can. There is nothing else. Did you think you were going to die?'

Matt nodded.

'Did you *know* you were going to die?'

Matt nodded again. He was starting to cry now, tears mixing with the dirt on his face to form brown trails that actually did look a bit like worms crawling down his cheeks.

'Because it's one thing to know it here,' the deserter pointed to his head, 'and quite another to know it here,' and he pointed to his heart. 'If you're going to take the life of another human being, that's where you need to know it. You need to understand that it's them or you, that their death is necessary to keep you out of the mud for a little bit longer. You've got a chance here, with us, to keep yourself out of the mud for longer than most, but pity, empathy, all of those things – they just make the hole deeper, and I will not let you drag me down into it with you. This hand,' he continued, holding up his own, 'that pulled you out, will bury you again rather than let that happen. Do you understand this?'

Matt nodded and croaked, 'Yes.'

'*Where* do you understand it?'

The boy pointed to his heart.

'Good lad. Now then, I know you look and feel like a bit of a mess, but you are blessed in having eaten the first flesh, so you will heal quickly – not as quick as in the old days, admittedly, but hopefully in time to help out with this month's replenishment ceremony. Would you like that?'

'Yes.' Matt coughed again and groaned. 'I won't let you down,' he whispered.

'Well, good. Because now you know what the alternative is. Right, let's get those fingers and that ankle strapped up.'

'What was that all about?' Ardwyn demanded. The deserter was bundling up Matt's clothes – which he'd befouled and that Everett had needed to cut off him to tend his injuries – into a bin bag in the scullery by the back door.

'You said, "let's see if he has any qualms". I was just de-qualming the boy in advance. We don't have the time or the piglets for him to make a tusk bracelet and be properly initiated, so I took a bit of a short cut. Sometimes a short cut takes one down some rocky roads.' He opened the back door and went out to the skip where they were dumping the ordinary household waste.

'That's not what I meant,' she said, following him. 'I heard everything you told him – all that about worms and mud. Is that what you really think about what we're doing here? Is that all this is, as far as you're concerned?'

'Of course not!' He slung the bag in the skip and turned to face her. 'But it's what he needs to hear right now. Stick to go with the carrot.' He gathered her into a hug, and she let him, but he could feel how tense she was. 'Darling, we knew that reforming the church of Moccus would require some radical new practice, but the heart of it will always be the same. You're missing the old ways, and that's understandable.'

She pushed him away. 'Don't you dare patronise me,' she said.

He dropped his arms and stepped back. 'Fine. I'll talk to you as Mother, then. We need to move more quickly in fortifying our position in this place. Dinner parties are all very well, but you've been living the life of Riley and you know as well as I do how quickly this modern age works. You say no more until he rises again, but I estimate two, maybe three more sacrifices at most before people start joining the dots. We have to be wired in all round by then.'

'Your methods are brutal. They lack finesse.'

He smiled. 'I thought that's what you liked about me.'

'I thought you were talking to me as Mother.'

She allowed him to gather her into his arms again and kiss her. 'In the modern vernacular, I have some very serious issues.'

5

A BLOOD-PAINTED MOON

THE DECK IN FRONT OF DENNIE'S SHED WAS NOT much more than four wooden forklift pallets laid in a square; it had room for her folding chair, a small table and Viggo to curl up and snooze next to her on an old tartan blanket, where he was currently snoring. The sunset on that Sunday evening in late May had been glorious, and the sky still held its lingering citrine haze while low in the west Venus was leading the slimmest fingernail of a moon towards the rooftops of the houses surrounding Briar Hill Allotments. Dennie had dined on a boil-in-the-bag sweet potato casserole cooked on her camp stove. She had a mug of tea next to her, and was just starting to think about putting on her down jacket before it became too chilly when she saw Angie Robotham and David Pimblett walking between the plots towards her.

'Here we go,' she said to Viggo, who pricked his ears and raised his head to see what was going on.

'Hello, David!' she called, waving. 'Angie,' she added, with a curt nod. 'David, we haven't seen you around here for a bit. I hope everything is all right with Alice?'

'She's on the mend,' he replied. 'She's been home for a few weeks now, and the doctors are happy with her progress. Still not out of the woods yet, but we're getting there.' He was hanging back behind Angie's shoulder and fidgeting with his phone.

'So, just doing the rounds?'

Angie produced a thin smile. 'We just wanted to make sure that you weren't planning to do something silly like sleep out here again.'

'Or you'll tell on me to my daughter again?'

David ahemmed. 'There have been a few reports on the OWL of people hanging around here late at night, maybe trying to get in.'

'That's funny, I haven't heard anything like that.'

'Well, it's all on the app.' He had it open on his phone which he held out to her so that she could see for herself, but she wasn't remotely interested in whatever was on that tiny screen.

'Well, I have an app too,' she said. 'It's called talking to your neighbours, and nobody has said anything about people hanging around. The only dodgy types I've seen here recently have been other tenants – and yes, I include myself in that description. It's probably me they're reporting.'

'And what happens if you have another sleepwalking spell and end up hurting yourself?' asked Angie. 'I couldn't have that on my conscience.'

'Well then, I absolve you of your sins. Say ten Hail Marys and five Mind Your Own Businesses.' She punctuated her point with a slurp of tea.

'It is my business, Dennie. Your irresponsible behaviour is everybody's business. Every time something like that happens we have to file an accident report with the Council for legal and insurance reasons, and if the insurers see an uptick in incidents they raise their premiums, and the Council passes that on to us in the form of higher rents. You think it's just yourself but it impacts everyone, Dennie. Frankly, it's not fair. You're being selfish.'

'I'm being selfish? With every Tom, Dick and Harry suing for every stubbed toe and bee sting because they're too greedy to take responsibility for themselves? Rubbish. It's ambulance chasers who are pushing up the premiums, not people like me.'

Angie sighed as if from deep regret, as if she'd done all she could to be reasonable but had been left with only one last course of action. 'I think in that case we have to let the tenants as a whole make the decision about whether it's rubbish or not.'

Dennie didn't like the sound of this. 'What do you mean by that?'

'Just that I've done everything I can to persuade you to behave in accordance with the allotments' by-laws, but if you will insist on breaking them and threatening the well-being of all the tenants you leave me no choice but to put it to the next Association meeting. They might agree with you that it's rubbish, or they might even amend the by-laws to allow overnights, but I think it's more likely they'll decide that it's for your own safety and the good of all concerned to impose a cessation order on your tenancy.'

'You'd kick me off my plot? You wouldn't dare!'

'Not me, Dennie. The Association. Your neighbours. You're not really giving us much of a choice.'

Dennie got to her feet, joined by Viggo. 'Angie, let me spell it out for you very clearly. The only way you're getting me off this plot is if you come back with a squad of goons to physically pick me up and carry me off it.'

David, who had been watching this argument unfold with more and more visible discomfort, opened his mouth to say something, but Dennie cut him off. 'And if you say that you're all only thinking of my well-being I will scream, David. You're a lovely man and I pray to God that your daughter gets better, but I don't know how you let Angie talk you into this. I think you should both go now.'

Angie had made the point she'd come for, and David was only too glad to get out of the way, and they left without another word.

She subsided into her chair and Viggo laid his head in her lap. She scratched him between the ears. 'Kick me out, would she? You'll protect me from the big bad witch, won't you, boy? Won't you?'

'I told you she wouldn't,' said David to Angie as they walked back to the Pavilion. In a way, he was glad. He liked Dennie, and was ashamed of having lied to her – almost as ashamed of having faked those OWL reports, which she'd never even glanced at. 'Why are Everett and Ardwyn so keen that the allotments all be clear tonight, anyway?'

'They didn't say, and I didn't ask.'

'But aren't you curious?'

'Yes,' Angie admitted. 'But I trust that when it's something we need to know, we'll be told. Speaking of which, there's going to be another get-together at Farrow Farm next Friday. Will you be there?'

'I suppose so,' he said, though the idea of going anywhere near the contents of that barn made him cold inside, and it wasn't just the memory of how fundamentally he'd been humiliated.

'And will Becky and Alice be joining you?'

'I haven't decided yet.' He was even less happy about taking his wife and daughter anywhere near the place. The parcel of meat – the 'first flesh', Everett had called it – had been sitting in the back of the kitchen freezer since that night. Alice had come home four days later with a bloodstream clear of infection, a prescription for heavier antibiotics, and a new chemo port, and since then he'd been focussed on trying to get things back on what passed for an even keel for his family. As tempting as it was to use Everett's gift, he knew he couldn't do so without deceiving Becky and he feared that no matter how healthy his daughter might become, his marriage would suffer irreparable damage when his wife found out.

'Well, I hope you decide soon,' said Angie, patting his hand. 'I can't wait to see her well again. Besides, it's all very well us grown-ups being amongst the chosen, but it would be lovely to see some children too.'

As they walked on a voice shouted, 'Hey, David!' It was Big Ed. He was packing up for the evening, stowing a bag of tools in the back of his white hatchback. 'You going to the Pavilion?'

'Just five minutes, and then home,' he called back.

'Well, if you see that Ben Torelli, you tell him he still owes me six quid from that last game. I think he's hiding from me!'

David turned to Angie. 'Ben's not one of the, uh, gang, is he?'

'No, thank God.' She snorted with disapproval. 'He's probably smoked himself into a coma somewhere.'

David stopped. Torelli's plot was a few over from Big Ed, and from here it did look overgrown. Even the chillies, which were Ben's pride and joy. 'You carry on,' he said to Angie. 'I'll be along in a minute.'

He went to have a look.

Matt's newly mended finger bones tingled only a little as he gripped the steering wheel of Everett's blue van and waited for him and Gar to return. Aware that he was tensing up, he forced himself to relax. He looked at his watch: just after two. They'd only been gone a few minutes but it felt like much longer. He slid a bit further down in the driver's seat and pulled his hood further over his face, not that there was much danger of being seen. The lane was empty and the hedges were high on either side, creating a dark tunnel.

He didn't blame them any more. Straight after it had happened he'd been tempted to tell them all to get fucked and leave, and the only thing stopping him had been the fact that he couldn't actually walk yet, but after he'd had some time to think about it he realised that if he walked away then everything he'd been through would have been a waste. Worse than that, it was possible that what he had already been given could be taken away, and he couldn't face the prospect of having to deal with further humiliation from that bitch Lauren and her friends. He had friends of his own now.

He even kind of understood where Everett had been coming from; you couldn't trust this kind of work to just anybody. You had to be sure. Matt had passed the test, and so, far from feeling resentful or bitter about it he felt flattered – he'd shown that he could cope with anything they threw at him.

He looked at his watch again. The light of its dial was the only illumination; the van was switched off and there were no streetlights on this empty country lane. He was parked just to the side in a space made by a farm gate that Gar had opened by simply lifting it off its hinges, and the two of them had jogged off into the night across the field of maize towards the houses that backed onto it at the other side.

In one of those houses was the woman they had come for. The vessel, he'd been told to call it. Someone else who'd eaten the first flesh at the hog roast too, but had been chosen for this rather than to become one of the Farrow. Ellen Webster. She'd been a librarian, apparently, before it had been shut down. Matt had never heard of her but then he'd never set foot in the village library either so that wasn't surprising.

The watch was new yesterday – a G-SHOCK the size of a tractor tyre and all in black and wasp-yellow, partially a reward for his fortitude, Everett had said, but the practical purpose being that it wasn't a phone and didn't have a signal that could be tracked. Matt couldn't remember the last time he'd used his phone anyway. There was no point trying to keep up with the people who had once been his mates because they were doing nothing that interested him any more. Drinking, hanging around and trying to get girls to shag them? That was beneath him now. He was part of something important.

Movement in his peripheral vision jerked his attention back to the maize field. The first flesh had given him pretty decent night vision and he could clearly make out two figures walking back along the edge of the field, keeping to the shadows of the border hedge. The bigger of the two figures was behind, with a large bundle slung across one shoulder.

He started the engine, and then the back doors opened and Everett and Gar were sliding a long, heavy weight into the van. Gar climbed in the back and Everett came around to the passenger side.

'Holy shit!' said Matt. He knew he should be cool but excitement had got the better of him. 'Did you get her? It, I mean? Did you get it?'

'Yes. Let's go. Straight to the allotment. Mother will be waiting for us there.'

'Can I see it?'

'You can drive, is what you can do. So shut up and do it.'
He shut up and did it.

Dogs were so much like men, thought Ardwyn, as she
approached the old woman's shed. Give them any amount
of attention and they were your loyal friend forever, or
until some other cute bitch wagged a tail at them. She was
carrying a long plank under one arm and walking as slowly
and quietly as she could to avoid waking the dog. It was
possible that he was already awake, but she hoped that if so
he would be able to smell her and recognise her as a friend.
She gently wedged one end of the plank underneath the lock
hasp on the shed door and the other in a gap between two
planks of the decking, and then returned to her own plot to
prepare and await the arrival of Everett with the next vessel.

The tusk moon had long since disappeared below the
horizon, but she felt Moccus' presence around her all the
same, in the life growing from the soil, thick and green and
swelling. To think she had harboured doubts about this
place. It was perfect for the new church. For Everett and
the other men, Moccus was the razor-toothed warrior of
the deep forests, but he was also the first farmer, using his
tusks to plough up the earth for roots and so revered by the
earliest agrarian cultures as the bringer of crops and fertility.
When the little farmers of Briar Hill saw the bounty that he
would bring, they would flock eagerly to his worship, and
she would turn this sad little patch of suburban scratchings
into a new Eden.

* * *

Despite his improved eyesight it was still not easy for Matt to drive the van down to the allotment without headlights; they were lucky that it was close to one of the access tracks so he could get right up to the shed, but there were unexpected dips and bumps which caused the van to sway unexpectedly.

He hopped out and opened the doors at the back so that Everett and Gar could unload.

'Do you want any help with that?' he whispered. He couldn't take his eyes off the woman that Gar was carrying over his shoulder. Her head and torso hung down his back, covered in a large sack, but her pale legs and buttocks were naked to the air where he grasped them in front, and her ankles were tied with brown parcel tape. She was making a faint, muffled whimpering noise.

Vessel. She was the vessel. He had to remember that.

'No,' Everett replied. 'Stay outside and keep an eye on things. If anybody comes by, act like a burglar, chase them off or something. If the old woman over that way wakes up and makes a fuss, or that dog of hers starts barking, for God's sake make sure neither of them gets out until we're done here.'

'What if she does get out? That dog of hers is massive.'

Everett patted the jacket pocket where his Webley lay snug. 'You let me take care of that fucking dog. Honestly, I'm fed up with all of this pussy-footing around. I might just take care of her too. Can you handle this?' It was one of the very few times Matt had heard Everett drop the f-bomb. He must have been pretty nervous.

'I can.'

Gar carried the vessel around to the other side of the shed where the door stood open and he caught a glimpse of the floor having been folded back to reveal the black earth underneath. Mother was already there, and she had painted lines curving upward from the corners of her mouth – probably to resemble the tusks of the god, but as far as Matt was concerned she looked more like the Joker, and all of a sudden he was very glad that he'd been told to keep out. Both she and Everett scared the shit out of him sometimes, but at least he kind of understood Everett, whereas with Mother it was like trying to understand the moon.

Then the vessel was carried inside, and the door was shut, and he was safely outside in the darkness.

3:07

That's what her bedside clock says when the phone rings, jarring Dennie out of sleep. She fumbles for it and picks up, thinking that at this time in the morning it can only be one of the children. There's been an emergency; one of her babies is hurt. With her other hand she flaps at Brian to wake him up and then remembers that Brian has been dead for just over a year, and her heart lurches.

'Hello?' *she mumbles.*

For a moment there is just breathing on the line – harsh and thick, as if on the verge of sobbing or screaming. Great, she thinks, my first dirty phone call.

Then Sarah Neary's voice: 'Dennie?'

This wakes her properly, like a glass of cold water in the face. 'Sarah? Honey, what's wrong?'

More breathing. Thick swallowing. 'I think I've killed him.'

For a moment Dennie couldn't tell whether the clock display was the one from her memory or from now, in the shed. She must still be dreaming because Sarah was standing in the corner, facing away from her, except it couldn't be a dream because Viggo had just woken up too, and was whining his concern. It had to be real because Dennie needed the little emergency LED to see that Sarah was in the process of drawing something on the wall with her finger, and she'd only just started. In her other hand she clutched Sabrina, who peeped over her shoulder at Dennie as Sarah worked.

A line, curving out to the right and then back in again at the bottom, like a bow. Then another bow, starting and finishing at the same points but curving out further, so that the result was a crescent moon. Whatever Sarah was using for paint dripped and ran, but Dennie knew that it wasn't paint. It was blood from the wrists that she'd slashed in her prison cell twelve years ago with a sharpened toothbrush handle, and it was fresh on the wall of Dennie's shed.

Then Sarah turned to her and said: 'They're going to bring him back. You can't let them, Dennie.' But it wasn't Sarah's voice, it was Sabrina's.

Then she was gone.

Dennie woke up and found that she wasn't lying on her camp bed at all, but standing in the corner where she'd seen Sarah. The blood-painted moon was very real, however, and right in front of her. She was holding a pruning knife in her right hand, and her left forefinger stung like a bastard. When she looked down she saw that she'd cut herself in her sleep. She was the one who'd made the drawing on the wall.

'Do not tell Lizzie about this,' she told Viggo as she switched on her battery lantern and hunted out a first aid kit. 'She'll have me sectioned, and I wouldn't blame her.' She taped up the wound and switched the lantern off to save the battery.

Something moved in the window.

Don't be daft, she told herself. *It's because you moved the lantern when you turned it off and the shadows only made you think you saw something. Or it's your eyes readjusting to the dark. There's nothing out there.*

But there had been something out there, attracted by her light, peering in at her.

Her shed had only one window, no more than a couple of square feet wide, and it looked out across the south-eastern corner of the allotments – she'd oriented it that way to get the most of the morning light in the winter. The night was clear, and there were a few solar-powered lawn lights dotted around like earthbound fireflies, still charged from all the good weather. With that and the ambient light from the village streetlights, she could definitely see a figure walking between the plots. From this angle she couldn't see too many of her neighbours, but one of the few that she could see, albeit obliquely and through several others, was the top end of the Neary plot. There was the thinnest whisker of light coming from around their door, just like last time.

Viggo made a low hruffing sound deep in his throat. She shushed him. 'We're not scaring anybody off this time,' she whispered. 'And I don't much feel like being attacked again. I want to see what they're up to.'

Her window was top-hinged and only opened a few inches – to prevent burglars, ironically – and with it cracked she thought she could hear voices murmuring, though it was too far away to be sure, let alone hear what was being said.

'I wonder if…' She felt around the shelves, not needing any light to know where everything was, moving tins and boxes and cartons and bottles around like a game of three-dimensional blind Tetris until she'd uncovered the thing she was searching for. Back when the allotment had been a novelty for her young family, and ten-year-old Christopher had helped with the digging, he'd been fascinated by the robins that would come to inspect his handiwork, and this fascination spread to include the other birds – chaffinches, thrushes and sparrows – and so, because it seemed that this might become a hobby that would keep him outdoors and away from the television, she and Brian had bought him the *Observer's Book of British Birds* and a pair of binoculars for his eleventh birthday. Of course, the fad had lasted only a few months, and when she'd cleared out his room after he'd left home she kept the binoculars for the allotment, though she'd never used them to spy on her neighbours. Not until tonight.

It was tricky to get them at the right angle against the glass, and they didn't pick up any more light so focussing them was difficult too, but they did magnify what little she could already see and that was better than nothing.

'Let's see what you're up to,' she growled.

A hulking silhouette approached the door. The light from underneath it went out, then the door opened and the silhouette went inside, reappearing a moment later with a large bundle slung over its shoulder. It went around the side of the shed to the front, where she couldn't see, followed by two more silhouettes, one of whom lingered for a moment to lock the door. Then all three were gone. All the same, she stayed at the window, holding her breath as much as possible to avoid jogging the view, in case they came back.

Then she heard soft footsteps creaking on the boards of her own makeshift decking, and the breath escaped from her in a tiny, terrified squeak. Someone was standing outside. Inches away.

Viggo tried growling, but she shushed him again, her fingers curled tightly around his collar. She thought she'd be brave and defend her territory when it came down to it, but all she wanted to do was hide and freeze and wait for the menace outside her door to go away. This was different from confronting trespassers. There was something happening on the allotments that went far beyond a bit of vegetable theft and vandalism, and the last thing she wanted to do was see who, or what, was standing on her deck. Absurdly, what came to mind right at that moment was reading *Watership Down* to her children, and the way the rabbits had their own words for everything, such as the paralysing terror of an approaching predator. *Tharn*, she thought. *I've gone tharn.*

The footsteps paused, as if whoever owned them was thinking. Wondering what to do about her. Then there was a soft wooden scraping sound against the door. This was too much for Viggo, who barked a single warning shot. She shook him silent and he whined reproachfully at her as if to say *What am I doing wrong?*

There was a soft snigger from outside. It knew she was awake and aware of it. It would come in now and Viggo would be powerless to stop it from taking her and killing her and cutting her up and burying her under the brambles...

The footsteps receded, and were gone. A few moments later she heard the sound of a car or van engine, and a few moments after that the glare of headlights appeared on the road outside the allotments, fading into the night.

6

HOT POT

DAVID DIDN'T REALISE HOW MUCH ON EDGE HE WAS until the front doorbell rang, making him jump nearly out of his skin. He was in the kitchen chopping onions for dinner and nearly sliced his finger off.

'I'll get it!' called Becky from the living room, where she and Alice were hard at work on the long division questions that school had sent home for her. He freely admitted he was rubbish at maths and had been more than happy to leave them to it while he got on with the man's business of cooking and cleaning. Plus, it gave him a chance to think about what he was going to do about the whole Farrow Farm thing, and doing things with his hands always helped him to think more clearly.

'Dennie!' said his wife. 'This is a pleasant surprise! Why yes he is, please come in!'

'There goes that plan,' he said to himself, putting down

the knife and washing his hands at the sink.

When his wife ushered Dennie Keeling into the kitchen his first thought was of how tired she looked. He'd heard all about her sleepwalking episodes but had thought that maybe she'd been prescribed some sleeping pills or something, but it had been four days since he and Angie had tried to warn her off overnighting in her shed and it looked like she hadn't slept in all that time. He dried off on a tea towel and shook her hand.

'Dennie, hi, what can I do for you?'

'Sorry to trouble you at dinner time. I did say I could come back later but Becky insisted.'

'She's good at that. Cup of tea?'

'Go on, then. Twist my arm.'

While he was busying himself with the kettle and mugs, Alice came through from the living room with her mother and gave Dennie a hug. 'Daddy, can I play with Viggo?' she asked.

'Hey, troublemaker!' protested Becky. 'You already asked me that.'

'Whatever your mother said goes,' he replied. 'Which I'm assuming is a no. Sorry, honey.'

'I've tied the boy up outside,' said Dennie, and took Alice's face in her hands. 'And how are you doing, Looking-Glass Girl?'

Becky stroked the fine fuzz that passed for Alice's hair. 'We're taking it day by day. Over the worst of it, we hope. Probably still another six months of maintenance to go. Just so long as she doesn't pick up another infection.'

Alice was staring out of the kitchen window at where

the dog was sniffing around in the back garden. 'Mummy, if Viggo has puppies can we have one? And can we call it Kirk?'

That threw her mother. 'Well, I, uh, assume that if Viggo, becomes a, well, a daddy...' It also assumed that Alice would be well enough to be around animals, but David kept that to himself.

'Of course, you can,' said Dennie. 'And you can call it whatever you want.'

The tea had brewed and David passed mugs to Dennie and Becky. His wife took hers in one hand and her daughter's hand in the other and said: 'Come on, you, back to school.'

'Bye, Dennie!' Alice waved as she left.

'Bye, Alice.'

'We used to have a cat called Kirk,' explained David when they'd gone. 'He was a rescue cat, spent the first month of his life with us hiding behind the TV. Then, when Alice got sick we had to get rid of him because of the danger of germs. Granted, we were probably overreacting, but it was back to the rescue centre. I swear that cat knew what we were doing. The look of betrayal on his face...' He sipped his tea. 'Anyway, I would have thought I'd be one of the last people you'd want to talk to. You know, after last time.'

'Yes, it's about that.'

'Ah.' He steeled himself for an argument.

Dennie must have realised how he'd taken it because she was quick to clarify. 'Oh no, I don't mean like that. I know it was all Angie's idea. You at least had the decency to look embarrassed. No, this is about something different. Do you remember Marcus Overton?'

'What, the chap that went missing?'

'Yes. When was that? Have you got a record of it on that app?'

'There should be. Why? Have you heard something?'

'I don't know. I'm just trying to join some dots and I don't even know if they *are* dots.'

'All very enigmatic.' He took out his phone and scrolled through the OWL notifications. 'Here we are. Twelfth of April. We checked his shed and found nothing. Police broke into his house the same day and found evidence to suggest that he'd been missing for maybe a fortnight. Missing persons report filed. Nothing since, no credit card activity, no phone calls. I did actually ask at the station if there had been any word about a month ago. One of the officers there told me that phone and ISP records indicate his last use of the internet was dated the end of March, so if he has run away he's gone off-grid.'

'Can you remember the exact date?'

'The twenty-fifth, I think. *Oh shit!*' He glanced guiltily at the doorway to the living room in case either his wife or his daughter had heard that.

'What is it?'

'Ben Torelli!'

'What, Dopehead Ben? Plays dominoes with Big Ed down the Pavilion and always loses?'

'Yes! He's not been seen either! Ed asked me to remind him that he owed some money next time I saw him but I never did, and it all completely slipped my mind because, well, things have been a bit busy around here recently.'

Dennie sipped her tea. 'You're telling me,' she said drily. 'When was this?'

David racked his brains. 'Literally the same day that me and Angie came to see you. But he wasn't at the VE Bank Holiday commemoration, I remember, because Hugh Preston was there and I thought at the time, the two of them are both ex-servicemen and it was a surprise that Ben wasn't there to share in it.'

'Back at the start of May. So, nobody's seen him for, what, three weeks?'

'I'm sure he had a perfectly good reason, though I admit I didn't really know him very well to talk to. He was a bit of a loner.'

'Just like Marcus Overton,' she commented. 'Both solitary men, not many social connections, both easy to miss.'

'What are you suggesting – that they're linked? That they ran off together?'

'How would that work, a month apart? No. But I do think there's something very odd happening on our allotments. All right, thank you for that, that's useful. I have another question to ask and it's going to sound strange.' She was fidgeting with her mug, and he noticed that one of her fingers was bandaged.

'Dennie, trust me, it couldn't be as strange as some of the other things I've heard recently.'

'Oh? Want to share?'

He almost did. The secret of what he'd seen and heard at Farrow Farm had been stuck like a ball in the bottom of his throat for weeks now, choking him, and the thought of there being someone he could tell it to who wouldn't think him completely crazy or, worse, look at him with blame, was very tempting. Maybe he would, but not until he'd told Becky first, however badly she took it. 'Not really,' he replied. 'Go ahead.'

She was doodling in the condensation from underneath her mug, drawing it out into crescent shapes. 'Do you have a thing on your phone that tells you about moon phases?'

'Moon phases? I don't think so, but it shouldn't be too hard to download one. Why?'

'I'd like to know what phase the moon was in at the end of March and April, around about the same time we think Marcus and Ben disappeared.'

'See? That doesn't sound strange at all.' He tapped and swiped until he found an app called LunarLore which looked promising, downloaded it, and opened it. He entered approximate dates for the time she was requesting, and came up with the same result for both. His heart froze, and he was back in the barn at Farrow Farm, kneeling before the skull of a creature that should not exist mounted on the wall, and surrounded by crude paintings of the same exact shape as the one on his phone screen.

'David?' said Dennie. She touched his hand, and he recoiled. 'David, are you all right? You look like you've seen a ghost.'

He swallowed thickly. 'Waxing crescent,' he read. 'The growing portion just after the dark of the new moon but before it is half full. Sometimes known as a regeneration moon, or a rebirth moon.' He shook himself back together a bit more. 'Does this help?'

'I don't know,' she said. 'Like I say, it might not even be a dot to join. Are you sure you're all right? You look very pale.'

'I'm fine,' he replied, gathering their mugs and taking them over to the sink to hide the fact that he was very far from being fine.

'I'm sorry if I've upset you somehow,' she said. 'I think I'd better go. Whenever you want to tell me what's on your mind, you know where to find me. Thanks for your help.'

'Honestly, it's fine,' he said. 'It's nothing to do with you. I'd invite you to stay for dinner, but we're not eating veggie tonight, I'm afraid.'

'Bless you anyway for the thought. If I don't see you on your plot I might have a weed of those runner beans for you.'

'Dennie, you're a legend.' He watched her go into the living room and heard Becky seeing her to the door, after which Becky popped her head into the kitchen.

'ETA on dinner?' she asked.

He looked at the parcel wrapped in its white butcher's paper. He'd thawed it out and taken it to Partridge's to be minced, and it sat surrounded by chopped potato, carrots, onions, and all the ingredients necessary for a home-made 'lamb' hot pot to make his little girl healthy and strong.

The next waxing crescent moon was on the 22nd of June, which gave Dennie a little over three weeks to prepare. She made a rare foray into online shopping and ordered a rape alarm and a video camera with night mode, and while she was waiting for those to arrive she beefed up the security of her shed, installing heavy bolts top and bottom of the door. She packed two changes of clothes, a ten-litre plastic jerrycan of water, spare gas canisters for her stove, extra batteries for her lantern and enough tins and packets of food to last for several days.

Luckily, her opportunity to have a look inside the newcomers' shed came sooner. It would have been the simplest thing in the world to borrow a pair of bolt-cutters and just have at it, but then they'd know, and even if they couldn't point the finger at her to the extent of having her reported for criminal damage, *they'd still know*, and creeping around outside her shed in the wee small hours might not be the least of it. The problem was that the only times when it was unlocked was when one or other of them was working the plot, or at least pretending to. They'd got Matt Hewitson doing the occasional shift, though all he did was poke a rake around for a few minutes and then sit out with his headphones on, smoking and prodding at his phone. It was a case of waiting until he was there at the same time as his mother Shirley was home from her job behind the cash register at Homebase, and that was like waiting for the stars to align. But align they did towards the middle of June, and as soon as Dennie saw Shirley's car pull into her driveway she strolled with all the nonchalance she could muster up to the Pavilion and its ancient payphone, and dialled 999.

Her anonymous call having been made, she meandered back towards her allotment, stopping to smile and chat with the neighbours and trade advice on black-spot and greenfly and the eternal war on the slugs. She was talking to Fred Pline about his plans for the Anderson shelter when she caught a glimpse of blue flashing lights between the houses on Hall Road, and said with neighbourly concern, 'Oh, I wonder what that ambulance is doing outside Shirley Hewitson's place. Do you think someone should tell Matt? He's only just over there, look.'

Fred might have been in his seventies but he was nippy on his pins in an emergency, real or fabricated, and she watched him hurry over to the Neary plot, and the mime show that followed: Fred taps Matt on the shoulder. Matt pulls his headphones off and scowls. Fred gestures emphatically towards Matt's mother's house, which backs onto the allotments. Matt leaps out of his chair and dashes for the back gate.

Leaving the shed door open and unattended in his panic.

Dennie took a deep breath as she stepped onto the Neary plot and up to their shed. She didn't know how much time she had but it wouldn't be much. All she needed was one solid piece of evidence to take to David, or any of them, and say, 'Here! Look! I'm not paranoid! These people are up to no good!' She peered in. It looked like a perfectly normal gardening shed – a little on the large side, perhaps, and very neatly looked after. All the tools were hanging up, boxes of fertiliser and slug pellets were stacked on the shelves, bags of potting compost underneath, storm lanterns, paraffin, standard camp kettle and gas stove, mugs, folding chairs, and a rag rug on the floor. Absolutely nothing out of the ordinary.

In her imagination, Matt was currently watching his mother trying to explain to a very confused paramedic that no, she wasn't suffering a heart attack. Hopefully this was developing into a predictable mother/son argument, but it was equally likely that Matt was just about now realising that he'd abandoned his post and thinking that he should get back. Dennie couldn't risk it.

As she left the shed her foot caught on the edge of the rag rug and pulled it slightly to one side, and a gleam of metal from underneath caught her eye. It was a hinge, in the floor. Why would anyone put a—

Trapdoor.

She so desperately wanted to pull the rug away and open whatever was concealed beneath, but for the first time in weeks Sabrina's voice was screaming in her head *he'scominghe'scominghe'scoming* just like that time with the car crash, so she straightened the rug as best she could and slipped out of the door, around the corner, and off to her own plot without running and without looking back.

No voice shouted. Nobody stopped her. No pursuing footsteps or a heavy hand on her shoulder.

When she got to her shed she slumped in her chair, exhausted and slightly nauseous from the adrenaline while Viggo, who had been safely tied up, fussed over her. 'Put the kettle on would you?' she said. 'There's a good boy. I think we might just have got away with it.'

'Are you sure?' Everett's face was buried in his hands. He and Ardwyn were at the big kitchen table while Matt had not yet been invited to sit.

'Pretty sure. She was sitting outside her shed talking to that stupid dog like always.'

'How sure is *pretty* sure?'

'I don't know.' Matt shrugged. 'Like, ninety per cent? I don't get what the problem is. I was gone for like, three minutes, max. There's no way anybody could have gotten in without me seeing.'

Ardwyn sighed. 'She played you, Matt. That ambulance wasn't a coincidence. She knew exactly what button to press and she pressed it.'

'But she didn't find anything even if she did get in. Everything was still there when I got back.'

Everett slowly drew his hands down over his face like he was wiping it with a towel and stared at Ardwyn with eyes that looked utterly hollow and exhausted. 'Well, that's that, then.'

'Don't you dare say "I told you so",' Ardwyn said. 'As you've already pointed out, this was inevitable – it's just come a little quicker than we would have liked. I don't think we can rely on people dismissing her as a senile old woman for very much longer. She needs a lesson in boundaries, just like Mr Turner.'

'What?' said Matt. 'Do her dog?'

'No. That *will* attract the police. She'll need an accident. Something that can be blamed on her own stupid self.'

'Burn her shed,' said Everett. 'She can't spy on us if she's got nowhere to spy on us from.'

Ardwyn nodded. 'Agreed. Matt, make it happen. And do it from the inside, don't just go flinging a lot of petrol around and then lighting a match. The investigators can tell that kind of thing.'

'And what if she's in there at the time?'

'So much the better. Still an accident, but with more tragic results.'

'And the dog?'

'Take Gar with you,' said Everett. 'He could do with something to let off a bit of steam.'

7

3.07

THAT IS THE TIME IN THE MORNING OF THE 14TH OF *November 2007, when Sarah calls Dennie and in the flat, calm tones of someone who has gone through shock and out the other side into something resembling waking catatonia, tells Dennie that she's just killed her husband.*

Dennie says, 'Wait there. Don't do anything.'

Sarah gives an odd little laugh and hangs up.

Dennie throws on some clothes and drives to Sarah's house. It's close enough that she could make the journey on foot, but even in a place as quiet as Dodbury she doesn't like the idea of going out alone in the early hours. That two-minute drive is stretched out into hours by the chaotic turbulence of her mind. Is Sarah hurt? Is Colin actually dead or just badly injured? Will the house be surrounded by ambulances and police cars?

But the house is dark and quiet, unremarkable in its safe

suburban street. The first thing she notices as she pulls the car into the Nearys' drive and the security light goes on is that one of the front door panels has a splintered crack running down it. Sarah will tell her that it's because Colin came home from a drinking session with his mates having forgotten his keys, and she didn't wake up quickly enough to let him in, so he started doing it himself. A few days later Dennie will be back with Brian's old hand-sander, some wood-filler and a pot of paint to clear this up. There is a bigger mess to be cleared up first, however.

The lights are on in the kitchen around the back so she knocks on the back door and Sarah lets her in. Her eyes are glassy and unfocussed. She has bruises on her cheekbone, a black eye and a split lip, and a trickle of blood has dripped off the end of her chin onto the pink flannel of her pyjama top in a single ruby-red spot. Her belly swells with the tell-tale bump of Josh's new baby brother or sister. Dennie folds her into a hug to which she does not react, and for the first few moments is so concerned about her friend's condition that, amazingly, she fails to notice the body on the kitchen floor.

'Jesus Christ,' she breathes. She checks for respiration or a pulse, and finds neither. The only blood she can see is from his nose, which broke when he face-planted into the quarry tile floor.

Colin was a big man when alive, and stretched out on the floor like this he is a landscape from the cupboards to the doorway. He is face down, with one arm thrown above his head and the other pinned underneath his torso, and at first she thinks this is why he seems to be propped up a little on one side. She gets right down on the floor – not too close, because what if he turns his dead head and snarls or lashes out at her? – and peers into the gap underneath him, and she sees the knife handle jutting out of his chest. There is much less blood than she would have expected.

She crawls away from the body and holds Sarah again, the pair of them shaking.

'Where's Josh?' Dennie asks.

'He woke up with all the shouting,' Sarah replies in a lifeless voice. 'After I—' She stops, swallows, and tries again. 'After it happened I found him at the top of the stairs, crying.'

'Oh my God, did he see it?'

Sarah shakes her head against Dennie's shoulder. 'I don't think so. You can't see into the kitchen from there. I mean he might have, I don't know. I took him straight around to Michelle's.' Michelle was Sarah's older sister, who lived in Tamworth.

'At this time in the morning?'

Sarah's laugh is a small, broken thing. 'It wouldn't be the first time. I thought I'd just stay there and call the police, but then I thought, what if they take Josh away from me? Colin would love that; he always had to have the last word. So I thought, fuck him, and came back here to sort it out myself, but he's just too heavy. So, I called you. I'm sorry, I shouldn't have done that. I shouldn't have dragged you into this. Oh God, Dennie, I've fucked up, haven't I? I've really fucked up this time.' She clings to Dennie like a shipwreck victim, shuddering.

There really is only one thing Dennie can say. 'We have to call the police.'

This rouses Sarah. 'No!'

'Sarah, look at him! Look at what you did!'

'They'll arrest me and put me in a cell, and I can't face that, Dennie. I can't!'

Dennie doesn't know too much about Sarah's childhood, other than that it was bad and involved her being beaten and locked for hours in a cupboard for whatever crimes she was deemed to have been guilty of. She has learned this from helping Sarah on her allotment, seeing the way she wouldn't spend any longer than absolutely necessary in her own tool shed, and one incident when the wind blew the door shut so hard that it jammed while she was inside and she had begun to scream – the high-pitched animal wailing of absolute terror – and Dennie had opened it again to find Sarah curled up in a corner, sucking her thumb and sobbing. Dennie cannot understand why it is that some people, damaged for no fault of their own, will seek out relationships with people who damage them even more, but it's not her place to make other people's decisions for them, just to help them clear up the mess afterwards.

So she agrees to help Sarah clear up the mess.

She's not stupid. She knows this is a serious crime – almost as serious as the murder itself. After all, Sarah could reasonably claim to have acted in self-defence and got a relatively light sentence, whereas helping to destroy evidence of a crime and prevent the proper burial of a body is a conscious and deliberate act, but Dennie has a cunning plan.

Dennie goes back to her allotment and returns with two pairs of gardening gloves and a large sheet of thick plastic that she would ordinarily use to protect her planting beds from the winter frosts, and they use it to carry Colin out to her car. The simplest thing would be to drive him out into the countryside and bury him, but then there would be no way to prevent his body's accidental discovery by a farmer or a rambler. So they take him to the allotments instead.

It is nearly four in the morning and there is precious little chance of them being disturbed. In Sarah's shed they cut his clothes off (Dennie will burn these in her garden incinerator later, along with her gloves, her clothes and Sarah's pyjamas) and Dennie pulls the knife from his chest, and then the blood comes. His heart has stopped so it doesn't come pumping and spurting like in horror movies – it sort of oozes out of the two-inch slit, and it does this for quite a while, but they are able to catch it in the plastic sheeting and take it outside and pour it into the soil. Sarah whispers to Dennie: 'He gave me fuck-all but bruises when he was alive, he can at least give me some decent strawberries now he's dead.'

However, what autumn gives them in terms of more darkness, it takes away by forcing them to tackle the frosty ground, and Dennie quickly realises that they are never going to be able to dig a hole large and deep enough to bury the corpse in one piece.

She comes back with another knife and a pruning saw – the kind with the slightly curved blade and heavily serrated teeth designed to cut through small branches. She offers to do the job herself, but Sarah insists, so Dennie hands the tools over and goes out to hack at the ground while Sarah takes Colin apart at the joints. Years later, on the rare occasion when she is feeling strong enough to treat Viggo to a bone, she always feeds him outside because she cannot bear to hear the scraping and crunching sounds, and the smell of raw flesh turns her stomach. She is surprised at how calmly Sarah works at her grim task – she doesn't break down or betray so much as a sob, but dismembers her dead husband with a solemn intensity that is almost ritualistic.

The thin crescent of a waxing moon rises to watch the two women at their labours, and by the time they have buried Colin Neary piece by piece it is nearly six in the morning. Dennie calls in sick to work and stays with Sarah for the rest of the day, cleaning her wounds, watching over her as she sleeps and twitches in her dreams, and cat-napping herself when she can.

Six weeks later the police will find the decomposing remains of Colin Neary buried in his own allotment, and will arrest Sarah, who will steadfastly refuse to implicate Dennie in any of it. Sarah wants her to adopt the baby, but Dennie knows that isn't how those things work. Nevertheless, she's too afraid of what Sarah might do to herself and her unborn child if she refuses, so, to her undying shame, she lets Sarah take all the blame.

Right now, though, when Dennie finally returns to her own home, the first thing she does is go through her fridge and throw out anything that contains meat.

Dennie waited for the long shadows of the summer evening to stretch themselves over the allotments. Quite a few of her neighbours were taking advantage of the good weather to sit out on their plots in the lingering twilight, chatting quietly, having family barbecues, or just watching the day fade. According to her calendar the moon was waning, but she hadn't been able to see it because it had set during the afternoon and wouldn't be seen in the sky until the early hours of tomorrow morning. There was still a week before the newcomers did whatever it was they were going to do, which was also when she expected to have another visitation from Sarah and Sabrina – or at least the part of her mind that was using their shapes to try to communicate with her conscious brain. The strongest and most insistent of those times also occurred at the time of the waxing crescent, but that didn't help her because by then the deed – whatever it was – had already been done. What Dennie needed was for Sabrina to come to her in advance. Since that seemed unlikely to happen, she had decided to try to force the issue. She had spent an afternoon going through all the boxes in the loft looking for the actual doll, but without success.

'After all,' she said to Viggo, 'as the proverb says: if the bikkies won't come to the hound, the hound must come to the bikkies.'

Viggo thumped his tail on the floor of the shed hopefully, but since no bikkies were actually forthcoming he sighed tragically and went outside to have a sniff around.

The last of the summer twilight dwindled, and the hangers-on packed up and went home, leaving Dennie alone with the pipistrelles that darted after insects in the sky like scraps of storm-torn handkerchief.

She had to admit to herself that she had no idea what she was doing. It had been well over fifty years since she'd had conversations with her old rag doll, and the fact that she now knew she'd really been having conversations with herself wasn't helping. Maybe that was what ouija boards and crystal balls were actually doing – not contacting the spirits of the dead but opening lines of communication with parts of the human mind that knew things which were otherwise impossible to know. So, what was her ouija board? What was her crystal ball? What did she do to take her conscious mind off the hook and let in the echoes of the universe?

Well, digging in her allotment, obviously. It had always been the one thing she could rely on to calm her down when she was stressed. Whenever she'd had an argument with Brian, or the kids had been getting on her nerves, or the people at work had been feckless, she'd come down here and dig over a few feet of soil and somehow all the tension was grounded safely away like the atmospheric charge before lightning could strike.

Dennie took her favourite gardening fork and went outside into the gathering gloom.

She talked to Sabrina as she worked, in the hope that it might jog something. Nothing-words and nonsense-sentences like when she was little, a running commentary on what she was doing, ruminations on what tomorrow's weather might hold, trying to focus on her and yet not focus, to find the middle ground between being aware and zoning out, between being asleep and awake. She pottered between her rows of tomatoes, breaking up clods of earth and flicking out weeds, hardly able to see what she was doing and peering so intently at the ground that she nearly ran into Sarah, who was standing barefoot in the soil.

Slowly, Dennie raised her eyes.

Sarah was wearing the same flannel pyjamas with the single bloodstain and clutching Sabrina tightly. She stared around with wide, frightened eyes. Plainly she didn't know where she was or what she was doing here.

'Sarah,' Dennie said softly. Her head began to ache, as if she'd had too much coffee.

The dead woman's eyes snapped onto her. 'He's coming!' she whispered. 'It's not safe here! You have to go home!'

'Who's coming? Do you mean Colin? It's okay, honey, he's gone.'

Sarah's eyes resumed their urgent scanning of the surroundings, and now it seemed to Dennie that she hadn't been staring around in confusion but was looking for someone, or something. Something hiding amongst the bean poles and greenhouses. Something that terrified her. The headache was growing stronger, throbbing and pulsing in Dennie's skull. 'Please, Dennie!' she begged. 'It's not safe! You have to go home! They're bringing him back! He's coming!'

'Sarah, *who's coming*?'

The reply did not come from Sarah's mouth, though it was uttered in Sarah's voice. It came from the doll clutched in her hands.

'*He Who Eats the Moon.*'

Then something seemed to burst out of Sarah, or through her, shredding her form like smoke, something that was

339

huge and bristling and tusk-mouthed, that leered at Dennie and snarled in a voice that was an animal squeal in human words: *Go, and stay gone, you interfering old witch!* It might have done more, but at that moment there came the great full-throated baying of a hound and Viggo was there in front of her, feet planted, raging against the thing that threatened his mistress. Whatever the thing was evaporated, no more substantial than Sarah had been, and Dennie found herself alone with her barking dog in the middle of her allotment, shuddering at the pain of something that felt like a rail spike being hammered between her eyes.

Her nose and lips were wet. Had she been crying? She put her fingers to them, and they came away red.

She left the gardening fork where it was and stumbled back to the shed to find a rag to staunch the bleeding, gathering her things one handed with the other pressed to her face. No way was she going to sleep here tonight. Bolts and locks and fancy gadgets weren't going to help her against, against…

'He who eats the moon,' she whispered.

She locked up and hurried home. By the time she got there she had a thumping headache, so swallowed a couple of paracetamol and hoped that a night's sleep would take care of it. But she wasn't even granted that respite, because her phone rang at a little after two the next morning. It was David Pimblett, calling in his capacity as Neighbourhood Watch liaison.

Her shed was on fire.

PART FOUR

AGGRESSIVELY WEED

1

ASHES

DENNIE STOOD IN THE STROBING BLUE OF THE POLICE and fire appliance's lights, too stunned to weep.

By the time Staffordshire Fire and Rescue Service had responded to the call there was nothing they could do except stop it spreading to the other allotments, and by the time Dennie had arrived they were dampening down, and there was nothing to save. The nearest half of her crops were gone along with it – scorched by their proximity to the flames, ruined by the jets of high-pressure water, or just plain trampled on. Her precious grafted tomatoes had been annihilated.

The shed itself was little more than a scorched black platform covered in sodden ash and the metal debris of anything that wouldn't burn – she saw her kettle, some paint tins, the thin struts of a stunt kite that they'd taken up Kinder Scout one blustery weekend, and the melted lump that had once been her battery lantern. Her folding chair that she'd sat on for so many nights was a twisted skeleton of blackened aluminium, and the glass of her old cold frame, that she had built herself with panes scavenged from an abandoned plot, was a crust of shattered and blackened fragments that crunched beneath the boots of the firefighters as they moved to and fro. It had been her refuge, her bolthole in times of trouble – more of a home than her actual house, and it was gone.

Sian Watts had her arm across Dennie's shoulders, gripping tight, and Angie was on the other side, and despite Angie's recent harsh words she was glad of the company because she felt that without someone to hold her up she might end up like Lot's wife, who had looked back to watch her home destroyed and been turned into a pillar of salt as punishment for her presumption by a vengeful lord.

There had been a wooden panel beside the door where Christopher and Lizzie had chalked their names when they had been little and her shed had been not just a place for keeping tools but a playhouse, a castle, a Tardis. That was gone too.

That was when the tears came, and Sian and Angie held her up.

Eventually the emergency services packed up and left, and the residents of the surrounding roads who had watched either from their driveways or back windows returned to their beds. Angie vowed that first thing in the morning she would put wheels in motion to get it all cleared up and to sort Dennie out with a new shed, new tools, whatever she needed, and departed for her own home. Sian asked three times if Dennie wanted a lift home, or someone to stay with her, but took the hint after the third refusal and went her own way, leaving Dennie to stare at the wreckage alongside David Pimblett.

'They did this,' she told him, stating it as a simple, bald fact. She didn't feel angry, not at the moment. Her soul felt like ash. Anger would come later.

'They?' he asked. 'Who do you mean, they?'

'The newcomers. That Farrow Farm lot. Somehow they must have known I'd seen something and this is their way of punishing me.'

'Wait, that's ridiculous. There's absolutely no reason to think—'

'Come here.' She walked over to the sodden mess that had been her shed, and pointed. 'See that?'

'What, that? It looks like a storm lantern.'

That was exactly what it was. A faux-retro metal lantern with a glass bulb protecting a cotton wick fed by a reservoir of paraffin in the base. Except that the glass bulb was smashed and the whole thing was bent out of shape, either from the heat or from having been stepped on. The fire crew commander had pointed it out to them as the likely cause of the 'accident'.

'I don't own one.'

'Are you sure? You had a lot of stuff in that shed. Maybe you got one a long time ago and then forgot about it.'

She shook her head. 'Nope. I've never allowed naked

flames. Cooking gas aside,' she added, as he opened his mouth to object. 'That's controlled and switched off when it's not used and comes home with me. I never leave it in the shed. If I want light I have – *had* – my little battery lantern. No candles. Not even tea-lights. Despite the tendency of many people to think of me as some kind of semi-moronic old fart, I've always been careful about fire. Always. For God's sake, the bloody thing was insulated with Styrofoam! That thing,' she said, prodding the twisted object with her foot, 'came from the newcomers' shed.'

'How can you possibly know that?'

'Because I saw it there.' She briefly described yesterday's adventure, and finished by pointing out that the fuel reservoir of the broken storm lantern was missing its little screw cap. 'They want people to think that it was an accident, that I did it myself because I'm careless and stupid and not to be believed. Why do they have a trapdoor in the floor of their shed, David? What are they doing at the start of every waxing moon? Why are two people missing and nobody else seems to be concerned about it?' *What was the thing that attacked me? Who is He Who Eats the Moon?* But of course she couldn't ask that because then he really would think she'd lost it.

'Three,' he said, so quietly that she almost didn't hear him.

'Three? What do you mean, three?'

'Ellen Webster. She's a retired librarian, in her seventies, lives alone.'

'There's a surprise.'

'She was supposed to be running an adult literacy class in Abbots Bromley last week and didn't turn up. The organisers tried to contact her but had no luck, so put a request on the online community forum to see if anyone knows where she is. Apparently one of her neighbours went around but she wasn't home.'

'Dear God. David, we have to tell someone. *You* have to tell someone. They've already done a good job of making it seem like I'm paranoid and losing my marbles, but you're a police officer, for heaven's sake.'

'I'm only a volunteer.'

'It doesn't matter! They'll take you seriously! Tell me that you'll say something – or at least that you'll look into it. Please!'

'I will look into it. But don't expect me to go around kicking doors down and shouting "You're nicked, scumbag!" because it doesn't work like that.'

She took his hand and squeezed it. 'Thank you. Thank you for believing me – and for being one of the few people around here that I can trust.'

David saw Dennie safely back to her house and then went home, feeling sick at his own hypocrisy. He tried to tell himself that he hadn't deceived her, hadn't actually *lied* to her by omitting the fairly significant fact that he had shackled his family to the fortunes of Farrow Farm, but it didn't do any good. The only thing that allowed him to put it to the back of his mind was the fact that Alice – who had been looking and feeling a lot better since eating Daddy's magical hot pot – was going to have her blood tested tomorrow.

2

GIVING THANKS

'EXPLAIN THAT TO ME AGAIN,' SAID BECKY. DAVID
watched her biting the inside of her cheek and twisting her
wedding ring, evidence of a war being waged inside her: the
desperate hope that what the oncologist had just said was
true battling with the fatalistic certainty that somehow it
was a mistake, that it would turn out to be an equipment
error or a mix-up with another little girl's results or just some
inexplicably sick practical joke. There were no miracle cures,
they knew this. They were in it for the long haul. Through the
window in the doctor's office door he could see Alice playing
a card game with Gavin, her 'onkie' nurse, chattering and
laughing, brighter-eyed than he'd seen her in months.

'Frankly, I am at a bit of a loss how to explain it,' said
Dr Barakhada. 'But we've tested three separate samples
from Alice and had the results cross-checked and verified
by Birmingham Children's Hospital and there really can be

no doubt. Her count is a little on the low side still but well within the normal range for her size and age, and we can find absolutely no lymphoblasts in her blood at all. It's as if she's somehow leapfrogged the next eighteen months of treatment and gone right into complete remission.'

Becky glanced at David, her eyes swimming, and then back to Dr Barakhada. 'But that's impossible.'

He closed Alice's file and sat back in his chair. 'I don't like to use the word impossible, especially when it comes to kids,' he said. 'There is such a thing as spontaneous remission, but it is staggeringly rare – about one in a hundred thousand patients, though that may be a conservative figure – and it isn't really something you can hope for as a treatment option. There is some evidence to suggest that whatever mechanism is at work can be jump-started by an infection, which we know Alice had, but sometimes at the end of the day you simply have to throw your hands in the air and thank the universe for whatever it's doing. Kids bounce. Sometimes they bounce in unpredictable directions.'

Becky put her hands to her face and wiped away the tears that insisted on spilling free. 'So, what do we do now?'

'What I'd like to do now is take another bone marrow sample and see if that's clear too, and we should probably make an appointment to have her port removed. Remember that remission doesn't mean she can't suffer a relapse – she'll still need all of the standard follow-up. But for the moment...' He smiled and spread his hands.

'Thank you, Doctor,' said David, getting to his feet. It took a moment for Becky to join him, as if she'd forgotten how to make her legs work or she was still waiting for the bad news. She wouldn't get that from Dr Barakhada, he thought.

No, the bad news was that they were going to have to move house. David was going to get his family as far away as possible from the people at Farrow Farm. Somehow they were poisoning Dodbury, and if Dennie's fears were true then they were also capable of extreme violence. He knew that he was taking the coward's option in deserting his hometown, and he would tell the police about the thing in the barn eventually, but not until his loved ones were safe.

He had absolutely no intention of telling Becky any nightmare fairy stories about eating a dead god's flesh, and she wouldn't believe it anyway – no sane person would – especially not with *spontaneous remission* as an alternative. David didn't know how this first flesh business worked – whether it was permanent, whether it required regular consumption, or whether, as the doctor had said, the leukaemia would come back. If it did then they'd be no worse off than they were before. For the moment, Alice was cured, and that was the end of it.

'I can't believe it. I just can't believe it,' Becky kept saying as they left the office. She took his hand and gripped it tightly. 'Do you think there actually might be something up there looking out for us?'

'I really think there might,' he answered.

Lauren Jeffries would not normally have walked home through the park after work, but it was nearly midsummer and would be daylight for hours yet. It had been another unseasonably hot day and there were families all over the place – in the playground on the swings and slides, picnicking on the grass, queuing at the ice-cream kiosk, riding bikes and scooters, throwing bread to the ducks and splashing in the Pent Brook that fed into it. This was Dodbury, not some inner-city shithole. She'd played on exactly those swings and slides when she'd been that age, and when most of her friends couldn't wait to escape the village that they called the most boring zit on the arsehole of the country, she had got herself a nice little flat and a job in Free Range Travel on the High Street. Which was ironic, when you thought about it: helping other people find exotic locations to jet off to when she was perfectly happy here, thank you very much. Hopefully one day she would take a daughter of her own to play on those swings and slides, and the thought of it made her feel solid and centred and happy; her feet were on the earth, her head was in the summer breeze, and she was on her way home to a tuna salad and *Bake Off* on the telly. Maybe a drink with Pauline down in the beer garden of the Golden Cross if she was up for it.

She didn't notice the lads on the bikes until she was nearly at the point where Pent Brook exited the park over a short bridge onto Cathcart Road, because the park crowds had thinned but that tight little knot of a dozen or so figures on bikes with their hoods pulled up was still there, not exactly following her, but too close to be just minding their own business. When she had been little her dad had told her the story of the Three Billy Goats Gruff, and for years afterwards whenever she'd had to cross the bridge she'd always checked underneath it carefully for trolls first.

Lauren picked up her pace. Cathcart Road led onto Osier Road, which was just around the corner from her block of flats. Ten more minutes at most.

'Hey, love!' shouted one of the lads from behind. 'Where ya goin'?'

She heard sniggers from the others, but didn't turn around. Put her head down, and walked. They weren't going to do anything; this was Dodbury. They were just being a bit cheeky. It was what lads did.

Two of them whizzed past her on their bikes, one on either side, one of them close enough to brush the material of her skirt with his handlebars. They powered up to the bridge and parked right in the centre of its span. Now they were ahead of her and behind.

'Come on, love!' he shouted again. 'We just want to have a chat!' More sniggers.

This time she turned around and got a good look at them. They must have been about fourteen or fifteen, mostly white but there were a couple of black lads too. Nobody she recognised, but they were bound to be the younger brothers of the friends she'd grown up with, so not exactly strangers either. They all had their hoods up and one or two had buffs covering their faces, which meant that they had come for trouble because you didn't wear that kind of thing in this weather.

'Going skiing, are you then?' she shouted back, even though her heart was pounding. One thing she did know was that lads like this were brave when they were mob-handed, but they were maddened by your fear like sharks smelling blood.

The one who had yelled at her – red-faced and acne-ridden, with a scrappy little weasel's arse of a moustache – frowned in confusion. 'What?'

'Or are you just too ugly to show your faces in public?'

'Why you being so nasty, love, ay? We're just trying to be friendly.'

'Oh, just fuck off and go wank each other, why don't you?' she shouted, turned and marched towards the bridge. The two that were there had left just enough space for her to squeeze between them, and their unwashed clothes reeked of body odour and musky deodorant. *The trolls are on the bridge!* she thought, and in her head it sounded like an alarm.

'You've got a bit of a mouth on you, darling, haven't you?' shouted the Scarlet Pimpleface. 'A real rude bit of a mouth!'

The troll on her left leaned in and said, in breath that stank, 'Why don't you use that rude mouth on me?'

'Fuck off!' she spat, and scurried past, but not before he'd grabbed her bum, laughing.

She made it over the bridge and started running, and as if that were their cue they all started jeering and catcalling, pursuing her through the wooden park gate and onto Cathcart Road, fanning out on either side of her and in front so that she felt like she was being mobbed by crows, and she was trying not to cry.

Then a car pulled up in the road directly ahead – a canary yellow Astra that she didn't recognise – and the driver leaned out of the window.

'Hey, Lauren!' he shouted. 'Can I give you a lift?'

It was Matt.

'Oi, mate! Fuck off, yeah?' shouted one of the trolls.

'Seriously, Lauren, get in.'

Lauren had no love lost for Matthew Hewitson; he'd been a dick of the first order and under any other circumstance she'd tell him to get knotted, but right now he was the lesser of two evils so she hurried around to the passenger door, which he had already opened, and got in.

'Thanks, Matt,' she said as he drove away.

'Hey, no problem.'

He watched the figures grow smaller in his rear-view mirror. One of them waved. If Lauren was watching she'd probably just see it as sarcastic, but to Matt it was a wave that said 'job well done'. That had been the best hundred quid he'd ever spent. When this was all over he'd probably even buy Jason and his mates a round at the Golden, sort of as a bonus. She really did look terrified: flushed, out of breath, and almost on the verge of bursting into tears.

'Are you okay?' he asked.

'No, I'm not fucking okay!' she snapped. 'Those dickheads! Those absolute fucking dickheads!'

He drove in silence for a while, letting her compose herself. 'How are you doing these days, anyway?' he asked. 'I mean, generally, like.'

'Generally, like? When I'm not being harassed by kiddie perverts?' She shrugged. 'Okay, I suppose.' She looked around properly for the first time. 'You seem to be doing okay for yourself, car like this.'

He shrugged. 'I've met some helpful people. But are you well? You know – health-wise?'

'Why are you asking after my health? Why are you being weird?'

'You used to have asthma, didn't you?'

She gave him a strange look. 'What do you mean "used to"?'

'I mean that you don't have it any more, do you?'

That strange look had turned into a stare of outright suspicion and fear. 'How do you know that?' she whispered. 'I haven't told anybody that.'

He shrugged again. 'Lucky guess.'

She was paying more attention to what was outside the car now – the countryside that they were driving through. 'And where are we, anyway? This isn't the way to my place. Where are we going?'

'To meet my new friends. I think they'll really like you, especially Mother.'

'Like fuck we are. Let me out of the car!' She fumbled at the door handle even though they were still moving. 'Let me out!'

'I don't think that would be a good idea,' he said. The village roads had taken them onto the A38, which at this point was a dual carriageway following an old Roman Road called Rykneld Street. It ran straight as an arrow from Lichfield to Burton, a stretch infamous for joy-riding races, and he pushed the speed up to sixty.

Lauren left the door alone and took her phone out of her

handbag. 'You take me home right now!' she demanded. 'Or I am calling the police. I've fucking had enough of this.'

'Okay, sure, no problem. Taking you home now. Next intersection, I swear.'

And he did – at the very next turning he pulled left off the dual carriageway and headed back for Dodbury along the narrow country lanes. He didn't mind – it was the turning he had planned to take anyway, since it went by Farrow Farm. 'Sorry, I didn't mean to scare you. I just want to apologise for the way I treated you earlier this year,' he said. 'I was a dick. And also for, you know, beating up Daz. I should have been happy for you two, I know that now.'

'Yeah, well,' she muttered. 'Me and Daz have split up, so there's that.'

This was an interesting turn of events. 'Sorry to hear that,' he replied, feeling anything but.

'But you were still a dick.'

'I know. Believe me when I say that I want to make it up to you.'

She didn't respond to this; just stared out of her window at the passing trees and hedges.

'You're not going to ask me how I know that your asthma has cleared up?'

'I just want you to get me home,' she said without looking at him. 'This day has been weird enough already without adding to it.'

'It was the pork you ate at that hog roast on the allotments back in March.'

'Please. Stop talking.'

'And you weren't the only one. I've seen a man grow back a missing eye. I broke all these fingers and they healed in a week.' He waved at her with his right hand to show her. 'I was buried alive, and died, and then I dug myself out and was reborn. We've been blessed, Lauren. Miracles really do happen.'

She dug for her phone again. 'That's it,' she said. 'I warned you.'

He snatched the phone from her hand and threw it out of his window. 'No. Can't have that, sorry. Everett really *will* kill me.'

She stared, open-mouthed, then launched herself at him, screaming and scratching at his face. Her attack was so sudden and vicious that he nearly lost control of the car, ploughing up the grass verge and into the hedge on the driver's side. Its stiff branches made a screeching noise like fingernails down a blackboard as they did to his paint job what Lauren was trying to do to his eyes, but he wrestled the car back onto the road and then back-handed her – not as hard as he could have done, just enough to quieten her down. Her head flopped back against the head-rest, blood spilling from her nose. It was all right, though. She was just stunned. She'd eaten the first flesh, like him, and she'd heal quickly enough. Luckily these lanes were quiet and there was little chance that they'd pass anyone who would wonder at the sight of his passenger with blood all over her face.

'I'm going to take you to meet the people who gave us this miracle. They're a great couple, really. You'll like them. They've been together for a really long time, much longer than you'd think. Just like you and me can be together.'

She was quiet the rest of the way to Farrow Farm. At the gate he was a bit worried that she'd try to run away when he had to get out and open it, but she seemed to be very calm, like she was thinking over everything he'd said. He drove into the farmyard and parked. 'First, though, I want to show you what it's all about. So you'll understand when you meet them.'

She let him lead her to the door of the shrine, which he unlocked and opened so that she could see. He watched her expression change as her gaze travelled over the wall with its paintings of the tusk moon, the god's gleaming skull and the carnyx. Her eyes and her mouth were open in wonder, and he knew that this had been the right thing to do.

Then she was running off across the farmyard, screaming.

'*Help me!*' she shrieked as she ran. '*Somebody please help me!*'

'Oh shit.'

He gave chase, thinking, ironically, that now would be a really good time for her to have an asthma attack.

Somebody did appear around a corner of one of the outbuildings, and she ran faster towards him, sobbing with relief and joy. Gar scooped her up very neatly and clamped his other hand across her mouth to stifle the noise. As he approached Matt he nodded at the squirming, kicking girl under his arm. 'Yours?' he said.

'It's a long story,' Matt sighed.

* * *

The deserter listened to him explain what had happened, thinking that it wasn't the end of the world as far as he was concerned, but Ardwyn was furious. He knew better than to interfere. She sat in her high-backed wooden chair at the large kitchen table, exactly copying the way Mother had in Swinley, either consciously or not, while Matt knelt before her in penitence. The girl had been secured in the half-finished dormitory conversion, which had meant that the volunteers who had been working on it at the time were hurriedly sent home because Mother still wasn't prepared to risk their reactions to the use of human vessels. They had heard the girl's screams and they would be asking questions. This dressing down was necessary.

'This is not how we do things,' she said when Matt had finished, enunciating each word like spitting splinters of glass. She was trembling with a rage that the deserter had rarely seen.

'Well, I'm getting told pretty much fuck-all about how you *do* do things so you can't blame me if I make it up as I go,' he replied, sulky and angry.

The deserter clipped him around the back of the head. 'Oi!' he warned. 'Respect your Mother.'

'Sorry, Mother,' he mumbled. 'I know I fucked up.'

'I don't think you have the faintest clue about how monumentally you have fucked up, you stupid child,' she snarled. 'We're probably going to have to leave this place now.' She waved her arms, encompassing the farmhouse and everything around it. 'All of this, everything we've spent months building. Our *home*. And all because you couldn't keep it in your pants for some silly little village slut.'

'She's not—'

'*She's whatever I fucking well tell you she is!*' Ardwyn yelled, leaning forward in her chair and spraying the spittle of her rage on the boy kneeling before her. The deserter stepped back a pace in shock. He'd never heard her like this. 'Each member of the blessed that we bring into the Farrow is chosen for a reason! Do you understand that? Angie Robotham because she controls access to the allotments. David Pimblett because he can keep the police away from us. Speaking of which,' her glare snapped onto Everett, and he flinched. 'I rather think now might be a good time for us to know where our pet PC Plod is. Have we seen him recently?'

'I'll chase that up, Mother.'

'Do so. Quickly. I want no more fuck-ups.' The look on her face told Everett that she was holding him to blame for this as much as Matt. He'd brought the boy in, and convinced her that Matt could be one of the Farrow. This was his fuck-up too.

'And me?' asked Matt. 'What about me? Why was I chosen?'

'Honestly, I'm beginning to wonder that myself.'

'Because you're a born killer,' said Everett, trying to claw something back from this. 'A church needs its priests, its vergers, and its sextons, that's true, but it also needs its crusaders.'

'Those that become the vessels of Moccus' replenishment are chosen very carefully because they will not be missed,' Ardwyn continued, slightly calmer now, but with a steely patience. 'This month's vessel was selected long ago. We don't know who this girl is, what her connections are, how soon people will begin to notice that she's missing. We can't possibly let her go now that she's seen the shrine, and we have to assume that soon people will be looking for her, which is why we might have to abandon our home within weeks – *weeks* – of His rebirth.'

'All the more reason to convince her to join us!' Matt protested.

The deserter shook his head. 'I rather think kidnapping her, smacking her in the face and then tying her up is hardly going to win her trust.'

'No,' Ardwyn agreed. 'I think that boat has sailed. The best use she can be now is as a vessel.'

'But if we tell her that's the alternative, to be sacrificed, then she'll have no choice!'

'When you threaten someone's life they'll tell you whatever you want,' Everett said. Sometimes it was hard to believe that the boy could be so naïve. 'It's not exactly conducive to long-term loyalty either.'

Ardwyn got up from her chair and stared down at Matt. He tried to meet her eyes, but quickly surrendered. 'I understand why you wanted this girl,' she said, and he flinched as she began to stroke his hair. 'There's nothing wrong with that. But you'll have a long, long time as one of the Farrow to meet someone who will have already come into the church with open eyes and embraced the first flesh, and there'll be no need for all of these silly games. The word "sacrifice" that you use means to give up something precious to prove your devotion to the gods; if you really want this girl then you could have made no better choice.'

'In the old days,' said Everett, 'a man would raise a piglet as his own for years and then sacrifice it to Moccus in order to join the Farrow.'

'She's not a pig.'

'No, she's not,' said Ardwyn. 'She is a vessel for the replenishment of the first flesh, and as such she is sanctified above all animals. If you think about it, you're actually doing her an honour. But it's three days until the tusk moon – she needs to be watched, guarded and tended. Fed, watered, and cleaned. By you. That's your penance. Do you understand?'

'I suppose so,' he mumbled.

'That's my boy.' She folded her arms around him and pressed his face to her belly in an embrace that grew tighter, and then tighter still. 'But if you ever do anything like this again,' she murmured, 'you will be the next to have that honour, and I will use the knife myself. Do you understand?'

'Yes, Mother.'

Ardwyn gave it twenty-four hours before she went out to the half-converted dormitory to see the vessel – partially to make sure that Matt was fulfilling his duties, but also because she was curious. He seemed to be taking it seriously; the girl was tied securely, she had a bucket on one side and a bottle of water on the other. There was a plate of biscuits, but she didn't seem to have touched those. She watched Ardwyn enter, keeping absolutely still, her eyes huge.

'I wanted to say thank you.'

'Get fucked,' the vessel spat. Her voice was hoarse from hours of useless screaming.

'I know, I'm not so naïve as to believe that anything I say is going to make a difference to you. I'm not trying to comfort you or persuade you that this is a good thing or a necessary thing, because all you can see is that you're tied up in a horrible place by evil people, and I can't blame you for that.

'For thousands of years it was only the most perfect swine of the village that were chosen to be the vessels of the first flesh,' she said. 'We'd have a wonderful feast afterwards and give thanks to the beast for giving life back to our god, but of course the beast never knew what its role was because, well, it was still a pig at the end of the day. So the thanksgiving was really just for us, to remind us to be humble and not to take things for granted. But now...' Ardwyn knelt down before the vessel and stroked a stray hair back from the girl's eyes. She flinched, but that was understandable. 'Now you. Not just you personally, I mean, the ones that have come before and the ones after, and not even just this time around. You are all aware of what is happening. You are the legacy of our faith. You give rise to an entirely new form of worship for us. Can't you see how exciting that is? In time, members of the church of Moccus will volunteer happily for this honour!'

She realised she was becoming intense, because the young woman had started to cry again, so she gently thumbed the tears away and stood up. There was no need to distress her any more than necessary. 'So, when I kneel before you and thank you, it makes a difference that this time you actually understand. Even though I know you'd like to strangle me with that rope and run far away from here.'

She paused on the way out, looking at the biscuits. 'And try to eat something. You can't starve yourself and it might be some small comfort.'

3

HELL WEEKEND

THE KITCHEN CALENDAR IN THE PIMBLETT HOUSEHOLD had three columns: one for Daddy, one for Mummy and one for Alice. Alice's column was mostly filled with hospital appointments, and Mummy's had a lot of crossover with that, but for Daddy the three days from the 19th to the 21st of June simply had 'Hell Weekend' written through them in red sharpie. Hell Weekends were not common, but they cropped up whenever his shifts at the printers coincided too closely with his volunteering rota, and this was one of them. On the Saturday he was down for a night patrol with the regulars, and being Midsummer's Day meant that the night would be shorter and rowdier for it in the pubs and clubs of Burton-on-Trent. He was very tempted to call in sick, but he stood a better chance of finding out more about what was going on behind the wheel of a police car than by fretting at home. So on the way back from the print works he steeled himself for grabbing a shower, a change, a quick bite to eat, and then an evening of picking drunks up off the pavement as the token 'hobby bobby'.

As he got through the front door and hung his jacket up he was met in quick succession by Alice throwing a flying tackle at his waist and Becky shouting from the kitchen, 'We've got guests, so behave!' Alice ran back through and he followed her to find his wife enjoying tea and cake at the breakfast counter with Everett Clifton.

'David, what a pleasant surprise!' he said, smiling broadly. 'I was finishing up on the allotment and I thought I'd just pop around and say hello because we haven't seen you all for so long. Becky was just telling me all about your wonderful news. You must be so relieved.'

'Yes,' he said, rearranging the pieces of his face into a smile. 'It's quite the miracle.'

'Alice has an amazing future ahead of her, I can tell.'

Alice was posting fragments of cake into her mouth. 'Daddy,' she said around her fingers, 'Everett says that we can go to his farm to see their new chickens. Please can we?'

'Assuming that you've already asked your mother,' he replied, 'what has she said?'

Becky handed him a mug of tea. '*Her mother* has said that she's not sure because it's still early days, the doctors still have lots of tests to do, and it might be best for Alice to avoid germs for a little while yet just to be on the safe side.'

David offered a silent prayer of thanks to his wife.

'I'm sorry,' said Everett, 'but I simply cannot accept no for an answer. The fresh air will be good for her, you don't have to touch anything, and I can guarantee that there will be no contact with chicken poop.'

Alice giggled and said, 'Chicken poop.'

'Or indeed poop of any kind.'

'Poop!'

Becky took Alice's plate away before she could start licking it. 'Stop saying poop, honey. David, what do you think?'

'Well...'

'What I can guarantee is more of Ardwyn's famous walnut cake. I'm not a doctor but I do know the countryside and I can tell you that a visit to Farrow Farm would be one of the best things she could possibly do for her health right now.' He ruffled Alice's hair and smiled straight at David, but there was ice in his eyes. 'Your daughter is such a lamb.'

Images of Turner's lambs hanging on the fence – eviscerated, their intestines puddled and flyblown in the dirt beneath their mutilated bodies – sprang vivid in his memory. The threat couldn't have been clearer if Everett had taken the knife out of that cake and held it to Alice's throat.

'I can hardly refuse, can I?'

'Wonderful! We'll expect to see you very soon, then. Let's say next weekend?'

'It's a date,' said Becky.

After Everett had gathered his things together and left, Becky put it on the kitchen calendar. To Alice's column of reminders about tests, there was now added *Chickens!*

* * *

Although Burton was technically the main police station for the Needwood area it was closed on the weekends – because nothing exciting ever happened on a weekend, did it – and his shift was based at the police station at Rugeley. He changed into his kit and paired up with his regular for the evening, Sergeant Praveen Kaur, a veteran of some fifteen years whom he enjoyed riding with because she took him seriously and didn't treat him like some gung-ho amateur who was only in it for the nee-naw and the flashing lights. The early part of the evening was spent mostly attending to calls about gangs of kids hanging around parks and making nuisances of themselves, an argument between hikers and cyclists who had run afoul of each other on Cannock Chase – the broad swathe of heathland and forest that backed onto the town and was always busy with families on the weekends but especially so at the height of summer – and a callout to a pair of cars in a lay-by that the dispatcher had said were suspected to be full of people dogging. It turned out to be two families of neo-pagan crusties heading home from the solstice festival at Stonehenge who had stopped for a rest. The driver opened the window on an interior full of dreadlocks and facial piercings and reeking with patchouli, and asked if everything was okay, officer. Prav thought there was a good chance that they had some weed, but, after asking them to turn out their pockets and having a quick look around the vehicle, couldn't find any and wished them a safe homeward journey. They were resigned and polite about it, as if that sort of thing happened to them all the time.

'Bit of a stereotype, isn't it?' he asked as they drove off.

'Assuming that they were in possession because they're into sun worship and facial tatts?'

'David,' she replied. 'When some idiot comes at you with a knife do you want him to see your uniform and think "Oops, better not make assumptions here, let's just see if I can stab him first" or do you want him to take one look and back off because the way you're dressed sends a clear message about the kicking he can expect from you if he tries it? Everybody wears uniforms, whether they mean to or not, and those uniforms communicate messages about the kind of behaviour you can expect from the people wearing them – again, whether they mean to or not. They're stereotypes because they're sometimes true.'

He thought about the fact that the pagan cultists he knew wouldn't have looked out of place on the average village allotment, but didn't say anything; she'd have just thought he was being sarcastic.

Then around eight in the evening they got a call to say that Lauren Jeffries' co-worker, Pauline Marsh, was worried that she'd gone missing. Apparently Jeffries hadn't shown up for work at the travel agency that day and wasn't answering her phone, so Marsh had gone to her flat and found it locked up and her cat unfed.

'Chances are she's bunked off and spent the day at the beach,' said Prav. 'Weather like today? I would.' She drove them to Dodbury to hear from Marsh first-hand, have look at the flat and a chat with the neighbours, who predictably hadn't seen anything and knew nothing, and in the meantime the Police Search Advisor at Stafford got back to them with a GPS result from the location app on Lauren's phone. It wasn't pin-point, and the data was two days old, in which time she could have gone anywhere, but it was better than nothing. When Prav punched it up on the car's satnav, David's mouth ran dry; the kilometre radius of the search area included Farrow Farm almost dead centre.

'That's your neck of the woods, isn't it?' Prav asked.

'Yes it is. A bit closer to home than the beach.'

'She could be visiting friends, sitting on their back patio, having a drink and ignoring her boss trying to call her. So, it's just you and me unless it turns out to be something else. Didn't you have another misper here a couple of months ago? Older chap?'

He nodded. 'He was a retired headmaster. Never showed up.' *Him and the rest.*

'Ooh, maybe they've run off together.'

'Four months apart? I don't think so.'

'No, but think about it. He leaves first and sets up their secret love nest while she hangs around just long enough to avoid drawing suspicion because their families don't approve of the age gap. It's your classic autumn-spring romance.'

David just looked at her.

'Well, your sense of humour crawled under a rock and died, didn't it?'

If the search area had been urban the task would have been almost impossible, but here there were only a few country lanes to check – assuming that Lauren hadn't taken off cross-country and that her phone would be by the roadside – so it was a process of elimination, taking each road slowly and peering closely into verges overgrown with nettles, hogweed and Queen Anne's Lace. Even so, it was a staggeringly small chance that either of them would actually see anything. As they moved onto the lane that ran past Farrow Farm, David found himself becoming increasingly anxious; he didn't know whether he desperately wanted to find anything or not. With every glint of sunlight on a glass bottle or crisp packet his heart did a queasy double flip.

Then Prav gave a whoop. 'There you are, you little sod!' she crowed.

Two hundred metres up the lane they found a smartphone lying in the long grass, its screen dead. 'Rubbish batteries on these things nowadays,' she said, picking it up with an evidence bag. She went back to the car and called it in while he stood and scanned the fields of sugar beet on either side. They couldn't be more than a hundred metres or so from the gate to Farrow Farm.

'All right, POLSA's on it,' she told him when she was finished. 'We do a house-to-house in the immediate neighbourhood and see if the locals have heard or seen anything. It's still possible that she's been found and is being looked after by a farmer.'

'But you don't think that's likely, do you?'

'This is where I stop making assumptions and start opening my eyes.'

'Dave, good evening!' said Everett, all smiles, when he opened the door, then saw the uniform and Sergeant Prav.

'I don't think I've seen you on duty before. This is exciting.'

David was sweating, and not just because it was still the tail end of a warm day. Everett had never called him Dave before. It was a warning. David knew exactly how this was going to look to the Farrow, turning up with a cop the day after they had threatened him, but he couldn't refuse the Sarge, so he'd done the next best thing and suggested to Prav that he do the actual door-knocking.

'Hi, Everett,' he replied, hoping that he was projecting the right kind of neighbourly calm instead of the jittering nerves that were crawling under his skin. 'We're following up a call about a missing young woman by the name of Lauren Jeffries.' He showed Everett a picture on his phone, taken from Lauren's Instagram account. 'Her phone was found just a little way down the road and we're just asking around in case anybody has seen or heard anything.'

'Her phone?' Everett said in surprise. 'Well, that's a stroke of luck, isn't it? No, I'm afraid we haven't seen her. But if we do we'll be sure to get in touch.'

'Is there anybody else at home that we can ask, Mr Clifton?' said Prav.

Everett's eyes flicked to her and then settled firmly back on David again. 'No, it's just me here at the moment. How are the wife and kid, Dave?'

'They're good, thanks, good. Well, cheers for your help all the same.' He felt an absurd urge to laugh; this was ridiculous, a pantomime played out for the benefit of an audience of one.

'Pleasure. Looking forward to seeing you next weekend.'

'Likewise.' *Like fuck*, he wanted to say, but he stepped

back as Everett closed the door, turned to Prav and shrugged.

'Friend of yours?' she asked.

'We're allotment neighbours.'

'Huh. Small world.' She shrugged, looking at the list of nearby residences on her own phone. 'Right, who's next?'

As they walked back to the car, he thought of the outbuildings around and behind the farm, and especially the abattoir shrine, wondering if the Farrow had Lauren locked up in one of them. It was still an if, he told himself. He had no definite, actual proof that they were kidnapping people. All the same, as Prav drove them away he opened his window fully to get some fresh air, sickened by his own cowardice and fear for his family.

Halfway through the house-to-house they got a call to assist other units dealing with a fight outside a pub in Lichfield, and from that point on the shift was absolutely rammed with no way for him to concoct any sort of reason for getting away early, and it was four o'clock on Sunday morning and dawn was just lightening the sky by the time he got home.

He didn't even bother to shower – just went straight into the bedroom, switched the light on and shook Becky awake. 'Honey. Honey, come on, wake up.'

She lurched out of sleep in the hardwired reflex of a parent with a sick child. 'Is it Alice?' she mumbled.

'No. Yes. Sort of. Get yourself and Alice and go to your parents. Now.' He was dragging her go-bag – the one with spare clothes and toiletries in case of an emergency hospital visit – from the top of the wardrobe and onto the bed as she roused herself fully.

'Why?' She pulled herself up in bed and looked at the time. 'Jesus, David, it's four in the morning! What's going on? You're scaring me.'

'You just have to go, okay?'

'David, I am not waking up our daughter at this ungodly hour until you tell me what's going on.'

He stopped and took a breath, wondering how to put this in a way that wouldn't make her think he was going mad. 'I think Ardwyn and Everett are dangerous,' he said. 'I think they're hurting people and I think we might be in danger too.'

'That's ridiculous! They've been nothing but lovely and friendly to us since the day they arrived! What makes you say that they're dangerous?' Then she must have remembered that he'd just come off-shift. 'Oh Jesus, have you heard something from the police?'

'Becky, for God's sake, have you ever known me to overreact to anything?' He was trying not to shout, with only partial success.

'No, never.'

'Well then. There will be time to explain everything when you're safe at your folks'.'

As he said this, Alice appeared at the door, puffy with sleep and disturbed by the conversation. 'Daddy, what's going on?' she asked.

'Yes, Daddy,' echoed Becky. 'What's going on?'

David knelt down by Alice. 'It's a surprise holiday, darling.

Mummy is going to take you to stay with Nanna and Pops and I'm going to join you later.'

Alice's eyes lit up. 'Can we go to the beach?'

'Yes, of course you can. Go and find your best sand-castle building outfit.'

Alice ran back to her room.

'But aren't you coming with us?' Becky asked.

'I can't. I have to stay here and help sort this out.' *Because I should have said something before, but I didn't, and now if that girl dies it's on me.* But before Becky could round on him and make this any more difficult – because she was obviously confused and scared by his behaviour – he simply took her by the hand and said, '*Please.*' She must have seen the naked terror in his face because she just replied, 'Okay,' in a very small but calm voice and started getting dressed.

4

SUNDAY

At a little after eight the next morning Becky messaged David to tell him that she and Alice were safely at her parents' place in Southend. He called Dennie Keeling to tell her what had happened and then had to drive around for a while before he found a working payphone; all the pubs, including the Pavilion bar, were closed at this time of day and what few red telephone boxes still existed had mostly been converted into ATMs or miniature libraries.

'Hello?' he said to the police operator at the other end. 'I have information about the missing girl, Lauren Jeffries. No, I don't want to give my name.'

Ardwyn watched the police car pull up in the farmyard and had the front door open in welcome for the two uniformed officers before they reached it. Both were men, one large and with a beard like a shovel and the other slimmer, darker, and younger.

'Two visits in as many days?' she said. 'This is unusual.'

The officer with the beard must have been well over six feet tall. 'I'm Sergeant Ryland and this is Constable Lennox, Staffordshire County Police. Are you Miss Ardwyn Hughes?'

'Yes, officer,' she replied, demure and deferential. 'Can I help you?'

'We have a warrant to search these premises for a Miss Lauren Jeffries. Do you know her current whereabouts?'

'I don't even know who she is, officer. She's certainly not here.'

'Is there anybody else currently on the premises?'

'Only my partner, Everett, and our farm hand, Matthew.'

'Please take us to them now.'

'Of course.'

She led them around to the long stone barn at the back, the doors of which were wide open. Inside, Everett and Matt were putting the finishing touches to a second coat of whitewash that covered the sigils of Moccus. The slaughtering frame and chains had been removed and redeployed as ordinary-looking agricultural equipment about the farm, and the skull of Moccus, the carnyx, the moon-knife, and the vessel itself were all safely with Gar in the van, parked off the road and under heavy tree cover. The chest freezer was still there and plugged in, but as far as the police were concerned it should have been perfectly harmless. A lot could be done in ten hours if one were committed enough.

'As you can see we're in the process of converting the

outbuildings into bed-and-breakfast accommodation,' she said.

Sergeant Ryland raised an eyebrow. 'Really?'

'Yes – why, is there a problem?'

'Well, it's just that we have reason to believe that you're not the legal residents of this property. How did you get planning permission for that?'

She allowed her smile to thin; Ryland had obviously taken a dislike to her and there was no point trying to butter him up. 'I thought you were looking for a missing girl,' she said, 'not coming to evict us, because if so I'd very much like to see the court order for that.'

'Miss, you're squatting,' said PC Lennox. 'We don't need a court order.'

Sergeant Ryland merely grunted and went straight for the chest freezer. He opened it and shifted the parcels of frozen meat around, but there wasn't enough to either hide or comprise a human body, so he closed it again. 'It's all good, healthy, organic produce,' she said to Constable Lennox. 'Feel free to take some, if you like. It's perfect barbecue weather this weekend.' Ryland and Lennox had a good look around, but other than the freezer the building was completely vacant. The younger man peered at the large black stain on the floor where the god had been bled, but Matt had covered it with engine oil so that it looked like the remains of an old spill. He had even moved the rubbish skip on top of the refuse pits for the previous vessels in case the police were suspicious about the three grave-sized mounds of earth. The boy had worked hard to make up for his mistake in forgetting about the girl's phone.

'We'd like to look in the house now.'

They found even less of interest in there. Ardwyn, Everett, and Matt sat in the kitchen and listened to them roaming around upstairs, opening wardrobes and tapping walls. Then they went back outside again and went through the tractor shed, the tool shed, the garage, and PC Lennox even stuck his head into the new chicken coop. After a few more minutes of wandering around in the back field and talking quietly between themselves, they came back in and Sergeant Ryland said that as far as he was concerned it seemed to have been a hoax call. 'It's probably just some attention-seeking idiot who picked the name of your farm at random. On the other hand, do you know why anybody might have suggested that you had something to do with it?' he asked. 'Is there someone who dislikes you enough to do that?'

'Oh, the last thing I want to do is get someone in trouble,' she replied.

'Does that mean that you do? Wasting police time is a serious offence, especially when missing young women are involved. If we can chase it up and take this person out of the picture it's one less time-waster for the search coordinator to have to deal with.'

'It's just a bit sad and embarrassing, that's all.'

'There's no need for you to feel ashamed,' said PC Lennox, with what he probably thought was meant to be a reassuring smile.

'Oh, not me,' she said. 'You. The police, that is. He was here just last night with another one of your officers. He's a volunteer – David Pimblett.'

'D'you know him?' Lennox said to Ryland.

'Vaguely.' To Ardwyn he said, 'Why would Mr Pimblett claim that you had anything to do with this?'

'Like I say, it's a bit sad and embarrassing, what with everything that's been happening with his daughter, you know, the one with leukaemia? The poor man's under a lot of stress, we all understand that. But for some reason he and his wife seemed to take dislike to us right from when we arrived. We have neighbouring allotments, you see, and I don't like to brag but I like to think I have a greenish thumb, and we managed to make a lot of progress with our plot in a short time and I think he was just jealous. I mean it was easy to ignore to begin with – snide remarks, that sort of thing – and I even loaned him some of my tools, but then, well, some of our plants were damaged and Everett had to have some harsh words. We asked for our tools back and Pimblett claimed they were his and that we'd never loaned them to him in the first place, and that was when he turned really nasty, saying didn't we know who he was and he had friends in the police and he'd make sure that we were taught a lesson and such.'

'Didn't you make a complaint?' asked Lennox, who was buying every word.

'We told the allotments supervisor, Angie Robotham, in strictest confidence, but mostly we just tried to avoid the man. As I say, his family was already under a lot of strain and we didn't want to add to that, even if he was the one in the wrong.'

'That definitely sounds like an awkward situation,' said Lennox, who seemed to be taking a bit of a shine to her.

'I wasn't going to say anything.' She shrugged. 'But you asked me if there was anyone who disliked us enough, and his is the only name that springs to mind.' It would also divert the police's attention very conveniently away from her.

It seemed to have done the trick because Sergeant Ryland closed his notebook and tucked it away. 'Well, we'll certainly have a word with Mr Pimblett, just to be on the safe side. Thank you for cooperating so fully.'

'It's a pleasure to help,' she replied as he and Lennox returned to their car. 'I only hope that you find the poor girl.'

'We will, Miss Hughes. Don't worry about that.'

She saw them out of the gate, waving and smiling, and only when they had disappeared around a bend in the lane did she expel a huge sigh of relief. When she got back to the house, Everett was cleaning and checking his revolver with a face like thunder.

'What do you think you're doing?' she asked.

'Pimblett,' he growled. 'That's who I'm going to do. So much for *keeping the police away from us*. And after everything we've done for him. I'm going to hang his daughter from a fucking butcher's hook.'

'And guarantee that they come back with dogs and guns? That's not at all wise, my dear. Besides, nobody's going to believe a word he says – especially not if he's stupid enough to start babbling about ancient gods and miraculous healing. Conserve your energy for tonight's ceremony – after that there's only two more before our lord Moccus rises again and our church will see him in his glory. Already they give us all the alibis we need. I know you're angry, and you're right to be, but you're clever enough not to do anything to jeopardise the replenishment.'

As she was talking she was stroking his hands, calming him down, taking the gun out of them and putting it on the table behind her. Gradually, Everett relented. 'You're obviously just pandering to me,' he said.

'Yes. Tell me it isn't working.'

He put the gun away and pulled himself together. 'I'd better go and get Gar,' he said.

When he'd left, Ardwyn picked up the phone and dialled. 'Hello, Angie?' she said. 'I need you to do a favour for me. You might get a visit from a pair of policemen today – no no no, nothing serious – but here's what I need you to say...'

David spent the rest of the morning waiting to hear news of an arrest – of raids; the girl discovered, distressed but alive, excavations and grisly discoveries. He tried to distract himself by taking care of some odd jobs around the house. The garden, especially, was a disaster zone. For a start, the lawn hadn't been mown in months. When they'd first moved in, Becky had planted a load of colourful things like crocosmia and astilbe, but when he went out there he found that the flower beds had been taken over by holly, hawthorn, and hazel – huge glossy green monsters, their berries probably having been dropped in bird shit. The old plants of the English hedgerow had come back and were reclaiming their own. When the police finally did arrive, he was sweaty and covered in scratches from trying to rip them out, but they were proving to be stubborn.

The cops introduced themselves as Sergeant Ryland and PC Lennox, and as David let them in he stupidly thought that they had come to tell him the good news directly.

'I hear you're a Special,' said Ryland, peering around at the kitchen.

David put the kettle on and took out three mugs. 'Just once or twice a week. Usually weekends, you know?'

'Oh, I know. Bloody bedlam it is out there on a Friday night, isn't it? Tell me Mr Pimblett, what do you like about being a Special?'

'I don't know. The chance to help people, I suppose.'

'Yeah, but you must find it exciting. Riding with the nee-naw on, sorting out troublemakers, keeping the streets safe. Bit like Batman.'

'If you say so. What's this all about?'

PC Lennox took over at that point, and with a jolt David realised that this wasn't just a friendly chat. It was an interrogation. He left the mugs where they were. 'You were volunteering yesterday, weren't you?'

'Yes. Night shift, eight till four.'

'Following up a misper report. You went to a place called Farrow Farm.'

'Me and the Sarge went to quite a few places.'

'Yeah, but you know the people at Farrow Farm, though, don't you?'

'How do you mean?'

'Well, you're neighbours at the Briar Hill allotments, aren't you?'

David leaned back against the kitchen counter and crossed his arms. The kettle boiled and switched itself off, unattended. 'So?'

Ryland was flipping back through the past months in the kitchen calendar, but let it drop and turned back to him. 'So, we've just had a chat with Angie Robotham, the secretary of your allotments association.'

'I know who she is!' David snapped.

'Steady now. There's no need to be getting all upset.'

'Well, I wish you'd just tell me what this is all about!'

'All right then. Mr Pimblett, did you make an anonymous phone call alleging that the residents of Farrow Farm are responsible for the disappearance of Lauren Jeffries? See,' Ryland continued before David could react, 'they've told us, and Mrs Robotham has confirmed it, that you and they had a somewhat fractious relationship. That you even, on occasion, threatened to use your status as a Special Constable to intimidate them.'

'They said *what*? That's bullshit!'

'Now I understand the appeal of volunteering as a Special, I really do. It's exciting, you get to wear the uniform, maybe throw your weight around with people who deserve it. Maybe sometimes with people who just piss you off.'

David had been worried that he wouldn't be able to lie convincingly, but his indignation at the bare-faced cheek of the lies being told about him was very genuine. 'This is a load of bullshit! They're lying! I've never done that, and I never would. You can ask anybody.'

'I just told you, we did. Mr Pimblett, I wouldn't normally

get out of bed to follow up a report of someone making nuisance calls. I wouldn't even fart, scratch my balls, and go back to sleep for it. But when it impedes the search for a missing youngster – *that* I take seriously. And I take it especially seriously, not to mention personally, if it happens to involve some part-timer wearing the uniform that I wear every day and taking the piss by using it to pursue their petty personal vendettas.'

'Sarge, I'm telling you, I did not make that call.'

'Good, glad to hear it.' Ryland clapped him on the shoulder with a heavy, meaty hand. 'If by any chance you do hear anything about Miss Jeffries, you be sure to let us know, okay?'

'You will literally be the first person that I call.'

Ryland gave him a look as if trying to work out whether or not he was taking the piss, but then obviously decided to give him the benefit of the doubt because he collected PC Lennox and they both left. David tried calling Dennie again but there was no reply and, not for the first time, he cursed the fact that she didn't have a mobile. Still, there really only was one place where she was likely to be.

Dennie was seeing how many of her strawberry plants could be salvaged from the fire when David Pimblett turned up looking for her. A midsummer Sunday was peak time on the allotments, and it seemed that everybody was out in the sun, working their plots, which in many cases were burgeoning. It looked like Briar Hill was set for the best harvest for many years. A few had come by during the day to offer their condolences and help with the clean-up, but nowhere near as many as would have been the case a few years ago. She tried not to let her paranoia get the better of her, making her see everybody else as belonging to the newcomers' little carnivorous clique. David had told her whom he'd seen at their dinner party, and it was obvious that Ardwyn and Everett had been busy behind the scenes recruiting many more such 'volunteers'. On the face of it, everybody was all smiles and friendly banter about the size of each other's marrows, and she tried not to see sidelong glances and whispered conversations but couldn't quite convince herself that they weren't happening all around her.

'They won't believe either of us. You, because they think you're an attention-seeker with a bee in your bonnet for the newcomers, and me because I'm gaga.'

'We need hard evidence. We need to actually catch them in the act of whatever they're doing, and call the police then.'

'Oh, I think we have a pretty good idea of what they're doing.'

'You really think they're killing people?'

'I've seen the knife that they use to do it, and the skull of the thing that they're doing it for.'

'Well, if you want hard evidence, that's simply done. Come on.' She got up and marched off towards the Neary plot, spade in hand. David followed close behind. 'Have you got your phone?'

'Yes.'

'Good. Frankly, I don't give a toss any more about

whether they know I've broken into their bloody shed. If what I think is there, the cops will find it and it's done. If not, it's just you and me that's done. Either way I'm finished buggering about. Here,' she handed him the spade as they walked, 'you're stronger than I am.'

She'd worked her plot here for nearly forty years – she'd seen newcomers arrive and give up within weeks or else go on to become long-timers like herself with decades of their lives in this soil. She'd seen their sheds go up, come down, move, fall apart, and be replaced. She'd seen plots merge and split, seen the families in the surrounding houses grow and leave and be replaced just like the fruit trees that she'd seen grow from seed, blossom and fruit for year after year, and then die. She'd watched people making love on their allotment when they thought nobody could see them, and she'd helped a woman bury the corpse of her murdered husband in one of them. This was her land, and someone was poisoning it right beneath her feet, and she meant to do something about that.

As they approached the Neary plot she saw Shane and Jason ambling over from the other direction to join them. Shane had a rake resting over his shoulder, and Jason had a one-handed claw-trowel, and at first she thought they had come to help – or out of simple curiosity at least – until she heard David muttering angrily under his breath and remembered that these two were now members of the newcomers' chosen few. They were just a little bit closer and faster than Dennie and David, and were standing in the way of their approach to the newcomers' shed by the time they got there.

'Afternoon, David,' said Shane with a neighbourly smile.

'Dennie,' said Jason, nodding at her.

'How are things?' Shane added, still smiling. 'How's Alice doing?'

'She's good, thanks,' David replied curtly. 'Safely out of harm's way now.'

'Oh, that's fabulous! Really glad to hear it!'

David moved to step around him, and the rake came down off Shane's shoulder ever so casually, blocking his way.

'Where you going there, Dave?' he asked, more quietly.

'Not really any of your business,' David replied. 'Fancy getting out of my way?'

Shane shook his head, still smiling. 'Looks to me like you're set to do mischief to our neighbour's shed. I don't know why you'd want to do such a thing, but I couldn't let that happen. What kind of neighbour would that make me?'

'The kind that doesn't get his head kicked in,' David growled, and tried to push the rake aside but Shane got behind it, and he weighed a good couple of stone heavier.

'Oh, don't be so bloody stupid,' said Dennie, and started around Jason, who stepped to meet her and grabbed her by the arm. She found the claw-trowel's three sharp tines pressed against her stomach.

'Please don't do this,' he whispered. His grip was painfully tight. Was this the strength that he got from being one of those who had eaten the first flesh? Or it might have simply been that he was a good forty years younger.

Viggo's growl was the subterranean approach of something massive threatening to burst out and engulf the man. She could feel her dog trembling with fury through her grip on his collar, and she looked Jason square in the eye. 'You might want to rethink that, son,' she said.

Jason released his grasp.

'And I'll scream blue murder if you don't let us go right this minute,' she added.

'And what good will that do?' asked Shane. 'Other than involve innocent people who might get hurt? How many do you think there are around you right now who didn't receive Moccus' blessing that first time and who haven't since? Not many. Mother has been having *lots* of dinner parties.'

Dennie looked around. All of the allotment tenants she could see were just getting on with their normal Sunday; digging, raking, weeding. If anybody had looked this way would they see anything other than four neighbours getting together for a bit of a chin-wag in the sun?

'Someone will call the police,' she said, but didn't even sound convincing to herself.

'And what will the police see? A silly old woman with a history of erratic behaviour and a man who they've already had to talk to once for making hoax phone calls? You want to keep a close hold of that dog of yours, Dennie. If he goes for someone then we really will have to call the police and they'll have to put a bullet in his head.'

David snarled, grabbed the rake handle and tried to shove past him, but the strength of Moccus' blessing within him was matched by that in Shane, who easily held him at bay. Between them they gripped the rake like two of Robin Hood's merry men fighting over a quarterstaff. 'Seriously, Shane,' he said, 'what's happened to you, man? We used to be mates. You and Jase have babysat for us, for God's sake.'

Maybe a shadow of regret passed over Shane's face, like a small and fleeting cloud against the sun, but it was gone quickly. 'You know what's happened to me, because it's happened to you too. Why are you fighting it, David? Why are you fighting *us*? Mother and Everett have done nothing but help us from day one. We're strong, we're healthy, our lives have been turned around. I'm just trying to stop you wrecking their shed and you're acting like this is *Invasion of the Body Snatchers* or something!'

'Everett and "Mother",' replied David, 'are killing people. That's why. It's not exactly complicated.'

Shane laughed. 'Don't be ridiculous!'

'It's true. I can prove it. Just let me get into that shed and I'll show you.'

'Can't do that, I'm afraid. Mother's orders. Go home, David. Have a good long think about what's in the best interests of your family. There's going to be a big get-together tomorrow up at the Farm. Genuinely, I hope to see you and Becky and Alice there. Otherwise…' He shrugged. 'Might be best if you stayed away for good.'

He gave a gentle shove and David let go of the rake handle, letting himself be pushed away.

'Come on, Dennie,' said David in disgust. 'This is useless.'

They left, along with a Great Dane who was still rumbling with anger.

As they walked, Dennie asked him, 'What did Shane mean by "Moccus' blessing", David? What aren't you telling me about this?'

'You're going to think I'm crazy,' he said.

She laughed. 'I'm the last person to accuse anyone of that.'

He was looking at her with the kind of half-afraid, half-hopeful expression of a child who has been caught in the act of something shameful and doesn't know whether or not to tell the truth.

'I can't help you if I don't know what I'm dealing with,' she said.

So they walked, and he told her.

5

THE BONE CARNYX

DAVID AND DENNIE RETREATED TO HER HOUSE TO mull over their options.

'We need to go back there tonight and catch them in the act, then call the police,' she said. 'It doesn't matter what else has happened – if they get a call to say there's a kidnapped girl being attacked, they are going to turn up.'

David shook his head. 'It's still going to take them too long. Being so out of the way as this place is, and emergency resources being what they are, we'll be lucky if they turn up inside ten minutes. We could all be dead by then.'

'So we have to make sure that they're in the area, close enough to come at a moment's notice but not so close that the Farrow get spooked, and for a long enough time, because we don't know when it's all going to kick off. Maybe, I don't know, if they get a phone call from someone saying that they saw a girl matching the description walking along the A38 nearby or something. They'd have to drive up and down and then check out the side roads – that could take them quite a while.'

'And what if they ping the number that called them because they've already had one bogus call and realise that it's not coming from a driver but from an allotment?'

'Then don't be at the allotment! Take your car, drive down the road to a lay-by and do it from there. Use my phone; I'm squeaky clean as far as the police are concerned. David, it doesn't matter if they think it's bogus; they can't not investigate it. It's not like the boy who cried wolf. They're not going to sit there and say "no, we won't bother with this one". They might only send one car but they will send someone.'

'The timing is going to be tricky. The Farrow might choose to do their thing any time from when the last person leaves. That's a big window – four or five hours, possibly. The police might give up before we need them.'

'Maybe we can narrow it down. We know that they're obsessed by the phases of the moon, especially the waxing crescent phase. Have you still got that moon phase app thingy on your phone?'

'Right here.' David opened the app, and they peered at it.

'All right. Tonight is when it emerges, and they'll want to get rid of Lauren as quickly as possible so they'll do it tonight, but their tusk moon will be very faint; says here only one per cent. That might be enough for them, but I'll bet they'll want to push it as long as they possibly can to maximise whatever it is they're getting out of it. Sunrise will be four forty-six GMT on Monday morning, so factor in time to get tidied away before the sun rises and the joggers are up and about... I think they'll do it around four. So, you need to make your roadside call at, say, three-ish, half-three. I mean, obviously I could be wrong so we'll have to spend the night watching them just in case, but that's what I think they're going to do.'

David looked at her. 'Wow. Have you ever thought of a career as a military strategist?'

'They couldn't afford me, dear. What worries me is actually getting anywhere close to them. They've got their cronies watching the place twenty-four-seven, I bet.'

'You know what? I don't think so. From the way Shane was talking, he obviously didn't believe that Ardwyn and Everett are hurting people, so maybe the allotments won't be so closely watched as today. Maybe it will only be the trusted few.'

Viggo laid his head across her knees and sighed. 'The trusted few still outnumber us, though,' she said, absent-mindedly scratching him between the ears.

'Yes, but we don't have to actually fight anybody. We just have to get close enough to be absolutely sure of what's going on and then make the second call. At most all we'll need is a way of keeping them distracted for a few minutes.'

'That should be easy enough. I've got a big four-legged distraction right here. I think he'd like to distract someone's arm off. Wouldn't you, boy?' She scrunched up Viggo's jowls and kissed him on the end of his nose. 'Who's a distracting dog?' He whined and thumped the carpet with his tail, not sure what she was saying. He only knew that she loved him, and that was enough.

'Which still leaves us the problem of how to get close enough,' said David. 'There's only one gate in and out.'

'There are also houses around three sides,' she pointed out. 'Houses which have back gardens and back gates that let onto the plots. They can't possibly watch all of those.'

'All right then, were you thinking of one in particular?'

They'd been able to hear the sound of a late-night TV variety show on at a punishing volume through the closed front door of Shirley Hewitson's house, so it must have been something of a miracle that she heard them knocking. When she opened the door the sound of a crowd whipped up to manic intensity flooded out. She was in her pyjamas and dressing gown.

'Dennie,' she said. 'David. Do you know what time this is?'

'Yes, we do,' Dennie replied. 'Sorry about that.' They were treading a fine line between waiting for the allotment tenants to go home – which had taken some time given the long midsummer evening – and getting there in time to interrupt the Farrow's activities. The silver lining to it was that the night was so short and mild that David and Dennie wouldn't have to spend hours waiting around in the freezing cold.

'We've come about Matt,' said David.

Shirley's hand flew to her mouth. 'Oh my God! Is he okay?'

'Yes,' replied Dennie. 'As far as we know.'

'What do you mean *as far as we know*?'

'There's no easy way to say this,' answered David, 'so I'm just going to come right out – he's fallen in with some nasty folk, I'm afraid. Look, this is a bit tricky, and I don't think you want to be talking about it on the doorstep; do you mind if we come in?'

Shirley led them through to her living room and muted the TV but didn't turn it off. On the screen a pixie-like host in a sequinned jacket continued to gurn and cavort with some Z-list celebrities while the audience wet its collective self at the hilarity of it all. Shirley had a large conservatory full of houseplants and a sofa the consistency of marshmallow where she invited them to sit. Viggo stayed in the kitchen, eyeing some unwashed takeaway containers in case they tried to make a run for it.

'It's those people up at that farm, isn't it?' Shirley asked. 'They're one of those county lines gangs, aren't they?'

'Something like that, yes,' David said. 'And, well, I shouldn't be telling you this, but there's going to be a police raid on them tonight. They've been dealing out of their shed on the allotment, apparently. I heard it from some of the regular officers.'

'About bloody time. But what's going to happen to my boy?'

'That's what we came to talk to you about,' said Dennie. 'We think we can help him, purely on a sort of informal Neighbourhood Watch level, without having to involve the actual police if we can help it.'

David leaned forward conspiratorially, and also to avoid being eaten by the furniture. 'Shirley,' he said. 'I'm trusting you here. This is totally against regulations. If the police find out that I've been talking to you about this I'll probably end up going to jail for perverting the course of justice. But Matt's a good boy deep down, and I know he deserves a second chance. What we want to do is talk to him – that's all, just talk – to try and make him see sense. The problem is that we can't get anywhere near him at the farm and the gang will be watching the main entrance to the allotments, so we were wondering if we could use your back gate to sort of sneak in and have a quiet word with him before it all kicks off. Then we can bring him back here and when the police do their thing he's got a perfect alibi.'

'Of course!' said Shirley. 'Why didn't you just say so right from the start?'

'We don't know exactly when they're going to be there. It might be quite a while.'

'I should come with you! He'll listen to me!'

'You'll be right here, keeping the home lights on for him and a cup of tea,' said Dennie, and squeezed her hand.

Shirley brushed away tears and nodded. 'Yes. I'll be waiting up, don't you worry about that.'

She led them down to the fence at the end of the garden. It was heavily overgrown with ivy and the boards of its larch-lap panels had disintegrated here and there, but the gate was solid enough. She undid the lock and let them through into the allotment which lay on the other side. It was a bit wild just here – nothing like as bad as the Neary plot, but some of the nettles were almost at head height and there were a couple of tall buddleia bushes in full bloom that perfumed the evening air and offered excellent cover. They were on almost the complete opposite side of the allotments from the Neary plot, with the Pavilion between. It was a lot of ground to cover. Still, she knew the location of every water butt, polytunnel, glasshouse, and cold frame better than the rooms of her own house now. They might have burned down her shed, but this was still her home and her territory.

'Do you think you can get us there without being seen?' David whispered to her.

'Try to keep up,' she whispered back, and set off.

David followed her from shadow to shadow. As they paused behind someone's greenhouse he saw a lawn-edging tool that someone had carelessly left leaning against the wall – a four-foot wooden handle with a semi-circular blade as its working end, which he thought might be a good weapon, just in case, so he picked it up as Dennie beckoned him onward. Eventually they came within sight of the Neary plot and hid behind a tall bean trellis. The shed was closed and dark, and there didn't seem to be anybody guarding it. For the moment it was dark and still. There was no light from around the door, no murmuring voices, no furtive silhouettes skulking about.

'You'd think they'd have someone watching over it,' whispered Dennie.

'I know,' he replied. 'Let's hope they're getting cocky about having scared us off.'

The stars wheeled slowly overhead. Lights in the surrounding houses went out one by one as even the night-owls sought their beds. A breeze rattled some raspberry canes nearby. Viggo's ears and nose twitched and quivered at the furtive scampering of small creatures.

David found that if he concentrated he could see quite clearly even though it was dark; the shapes of the world stood out like cardboard cut-outs in a diorama, flat and shadowless. This seemed to be another gift of the first flesh. *I don't want this*, he thought, to who or whatever was listening. *Get it out of me.*

At half past two in the morning Dennie nudged David awake from a doze. 'Time to cry wolf,' she whispered.

He grunted and stretched. 'Has anything happened?'

'Yes,' she replied acidly. 'I watched it all happen but didn't like to wake you because you looked so peaceful, sleeping like a cherub.'

'All right,' he mumbled. 'There's no need to be like that.'

He took her phone and skulked off into the darkness while she settled back to watch the stars and wait.

It was a good thing for her old bones that the night was so mild. She was tempted to try to call up Sarah again, but she didn't want to risk a repeat of either the migraine or the entity that had come through her. Not here and now. Sarah's face and shape were just the outward clothing chosen by the part of her mind that as a child had spoken through her doll, and yet in spite of everything she still couldn't think of the word 'psychic' without a sceptical snort. Sarah and Sabrina weren't two separate things – they were part of the same being, part of herself.

It seemed like only minutes had passed but the next time she looked at her watch it was nearly three. Only the dog licking her hand had woken her from another fugue state, the longest one yet.

'Please no,' she whispered. 'Please, God, not now.' She felt like an ancient mariner shipwrecked on an ice floe in dangerously warm waters, watching bits of herself break apart and drift away with nothing but an abyss below. What was happening to her? What damage was she doing to herself with all of this? Sensing her distress, the dog nuzzled her, whining, and she stroked his head in gratitude.

Her hand froze.

The dog.

She couldn't remember the dog's name.

Panic grabbed her, squeezing her heart and scattering her already tattered thoughts. The dog! His name was... his name was... there was a man, tall and dark, with a beard and a shining sword, and she couldn't remember his name! She clutched the dog in desperation, and he was licking her face, and her hands found his collar and the metal name tag there and she fumbled for her little torch and flashed the light on it.

'Viggo!' she wept in relief, and hugged him tighter still, her face buried in his fur. 'Oh, Viggo, I'm sorry! I'm so sorry!' Viggo let himself be held as her shudders slowly subsided, and eventually she sat back, wiping her face. 'I'm sorry I scared you,' she whispered. 'But I'm scared myself, boy. I'm really scared. I think whatever this is, it's bad, and it's getting worse.' Cruelly, the one word that she wished she couldn't remember was the one that sat in her mind as heavy as a tombstone.

Dementia.

Just thinking it made her cringe physically. It had taken Brian's father, reducing him to a shambling scarecrow of a man who had lived for the last ten years of his life unable to recognise his own family. It was an old person's disease, but she wasn't old, she was only in her sixties, damn it – she might live another third of her life so far. To do so with her brain rotting from the inside out like a worm-eaten cabbage was her worst nightmare.

But there was something that could fix it, if David's story was to be believed. He'd shown her the scar on his leg, and Alice's medical results were pretty incontrovertible. If it was true, then Ardwyn Hughes had access to something that could make it stop. All Dennie had to do was go cap in hand, and what was the sacrifice of one's pride when it was one's very mind at stake?

Well now, 'sacrifice'. That was the word, wasn't it? Yes, all she had to do was swallow her pride, along with a bellyful of animal flesh. All she had to do was be complicit in a young woman's murder.

No.

'Fuck you,' she said. 'I'd rather die.'

3:07 came and went without a visitation from Sarah, and at first she was worried that something had gone wrong, but it made sense if the apparition really was a hidden part of her mind trying to warn her conscious self about something. This was one night Sarah didn't need to show herself.

'Consider me warned,' she whispered.

When Viggo started to whine she knew David was back, and moments later he settled down beside her.

'Everything okay?' she whispered.

He nodded. 'Shirley was asleep on her sofa so I didn't have to make up any sort of excuse. Called them. Even saw them on the way back here, which was pretty quick, to be fair. Just one car, though, but at least we know they're in the area.'

'Good. Let's just hope that the Farrow are doing the same.'

It was a few minutes short of four in the morning when Viggo's head shot up, and he jumped to his feet.

'Look,' she whispered, indicating the dog. 'Shh, boy, nice and quiet.'

A moment later they both heard the metallic rattle and the creaking of the allotment gate opening, then the soft crunching of tyres on gravel as the snub-nosed shadow of a van rolled down the access road with its lights and engine both off.

'Have you got your phone?' she asked. He nodded.

'Let's see if we can get closer.'

They left the cover of the bean trellis and skulked forward to hunker down behind a pair of large compost bins, by which time someone was opening the newcomers' shed and lighting a candle, and someone else was carrying a large bundle from the open doors at the back of the van.

A bundle that kicked and squealed.

'David...' she said.

He made the call.

'999, what service do you require?'

'Police,' he said, not even trying to be quiet. There was no point any more.

'Connecting you now.' A moment later a different call handler asked, 'What is the nature of the emergency and your location?'

'The location is Briar Hill Allotments, Dodbury, in Staffordshire. There's a girl being attacked. And they've got guns.' He let his phone fall to the ground with its screen glowing brightly while the handler was asking him lots of other questions, and stood up out of hiding because he knew that Everett or whoever it was in the shed must have heard him by then.

Two figures came towards him – Matt, small and fast, and Gar, large and lumbering. Matt was strutting with his chest all puffed up the way David had seen lads facing off against each other in pubs and bars, stabbing a finger and waving a knife in his other hand. 'You better fuck the fuck off right now, or…'

David never found out what the alternative was because he swung the lawn-edging tool up and around in a short arc that stopped as the flat of the blade smacked Matt in the side of the head with a dull *clang!* Matt uttered a single grunt and toppled sideways into someone's cabbages.

So much for having a quiet word, he thought.

Then Gar was on him. He was seized in a bear hug and immediately had the wind crushed out of him. Gar headbutted him and the world greyed away for a moment and he was dimly aware of cracking sounds and a flaring pain like sudden savage heartburn as several of his ribs broke. Gar's maw was opening for his face, far wider than any man should have been able to unhinge his jaw, and he was reminded of footage he'd seen of hippos fighting. Even the great razor-pointed pegs of ivory that passed for teeth were the same, but David wasn't sure that a hippo's breath could match the fetid stench that washed over him.

Suddenly the pressure was released as one of Gar's arms fell away, and Viggo was snarling and tearing, teeth buried deep in the boar-man's flesh. Gar squealed in rage and pain, staggering back with a hundred and fifty pounds of Great Dane clamped to his arm and worrying at him. David fell, gasping for breath and instantly regretting it; it felt like being impaled by burning spears. He fumbled on the ground for the edging tool which he'd dropped in Gar's attack. Gar drove a fist hard into the side of Viggo's head and the dog let go with a yelp, then aimed a kick at Viggo's stomach which sent him tumbling. He turned back to David and met the blade of the edging tool as it swept in under his outstretched arm and thudded deep into the side of his torso. Gar frowned down at the metal sticking out of him, as if confused about what it was doing there, then took hold of the shaft and twisted it to and fro, working it free as blood gouted from the wound. It pulled free with a thick sucking sound and he tossed it to one side, then came for David again.

'David!' Dennie was yelling and shoving at the shed door. 'They've locked it from the inside! Help me!'

He could barely breathe, let alone run, but he managed a

kind of hunched stagger. Gar made a clumsy swipe that was easy to dodge, and when David reached the shed he kept going, shoulder charging the door with more momentum than finesse. It splintered around the bolt and sprang open, but before he could see what was happening inside, Gar grabbed him by the jacket collar and hauled him back. He bit deeply into David's shoulder, and David screamed.

Dennie saw David lay Matt out and become enfolded in Gar's huge arms, and she let go of Viggo's collar.

'Get him, boy!' she ordered, but the Great Dane didn't need any encouragement.

She skirted the lurching and thrashing figures and made her way to the shed. Two voices were chanting with a third muffled and whimpering, and light burned all around the edges of the door; she pulled at the iron ring handle, frantic at the thought that they might have been too late to save the girl, but it wouldn't budge. 'David!' she shouted. 'They've locked it from the inside! Help me!'

He was there in a moment and barged it open. Then Gar seized him and their brawl resumed, leaving Dennie to confront Ardwyn and Everett alone. She stepped inside; Sabrina was fully awake inside her and she saw everything with Sabrina's eyes.

Mother was sitting cross-legged in the middle of a patch of bare soil where the false floor had been, chanting as she rocked back and forth with something across her lap that looked like an alpine horn made out of fused vertebrae. But she was altered; her beauty had become ancient and hard-edged, like a tree aged almost to stone. The earth in front of her was black and glistening, saturated with blood, and on the other side a girl was kneeling with her neck outstretched over it – tied, gagged, and held in place by Everett. The butcher had one fist in her hair and the other holding a black sickle-blade to her throat, and was grinning with teeth filed to bloodstained points. This was what Everett and Ardwyn really looked like, Dennie understood, in the place where the echoes came from, the place that only Sabrina could see. Lauren Jeffries turned pleading eyes to her.

'The police...' said Dennie, but that was as far as she got.

Everett's cannibal grin widened as he swept the knife across Lauren's throat.

David was being chewed. He was face down in the dirt under Gar's full weight, and the only thing stopping Gar from taking off his shoulder and left arm along with it was his jacket, which had so far resisted being torn. He actually heard one of the bastard's teeth squeal as it scraped his shoulder blade, like a carpentry nail being dragged along glass. Gar's breathing was full of gasps and crackles, and David hoped that he'd suffered a punctured lung.

Viggo came at Gar again, and he was forced to relinquish his human prey once more. Weakened as Gar was by his chest wound, the dog easily bore him to the ground, and it was all David could do to flop to one side as they came down right next to him like falling giants, with Viggo's forelegs planted on Gar's chest and his muzzle working at the boar-man's throat – worrying, tearing, flinging pieces of flesh, and fan-sprays of blood while Gar squealed and beat at him weakly and more weakly still until he wasn't moving at all. But Viggo kept snarling and ripping all the same.

David was dimly aware that somewhere Dennie was screaming, but there was nothing he could do about it.

That was when the allotments were bathed in blue flashing lights and the sound of sirens.

Dennie screamed, but it wasn't just her voice screaming. Sabrina was screaming with her, screaming *through* her, and for a moment she was there in the shed for all to see, raging and accusatory. Everett reeled in bafflement at the sight, letting go of Lauren, who slumped forward onto the blood-soaked earth, making hideous gargling sounds as her lifeblood jetted into it.

'What is this?' he snarled. '*What is this!?*'

Then police sirens split the night and a patrol car slewed to a halt diagonally across the neighbouring allotment. Doors slammed, radios barked, voices shouted.

'*The end for you,*' Sabrina told him. '*Mud and worms and nothing else, Deserter.*'

'*NO!*' He tossed the knife aside and produced a pistol, then shoved past her and out into the night.

'Everett?' cried Ardwyn. 'Everett, *don't you dare leave me*!'

But he was gone, and the door swung shut behind him. His pistol cracked once, twice, and there were more shouts.

Dennie fell to her knees by Lauren, whose terrified eyes were rolling in her shock-pale face. She was trying to say something but could only make wet sounds. Dennie clamped her hands to the appalling wound, her hands instantly slicked – thinking how *hot* the girl's blood was – and screamed, 'Help us! For God's sake somebody please help us!' The headache was building, harder and faster than before, and blood was pouring from her nose to mix with the gore.

'Your *God*,' sneered Mother. 'Your bloodless, impotent God. *Meet mine.*'

She raised the bone horn to her mouth and blew.

It was an act of pure desperation. Ardwyn had no idea whether four vessels would be enough. The replenishment had always required six to be complete, but that had been with swine. Human blood might be more potent, who knew? The bone carnyx might summon Moccus whole and entire, or not at all, or as some half-finished thing. She might be arrested, or even killed by men with guns. The only thing she knew for certain was that it was over, at least like this, and that she could not leave him in the ground to languish half-born. So she blew the bone carnyx and summoned her god to life – whatever form that took.

Dennie felt the ground begin to convulse and did her best to twist her body around to shield Lauren while trying to maintain the hold on her throat. The girl's shuddering was becoming weaker. Sabrina had disappeared, or retreated into her again, and the shed had resumed its normal dimensions as her sight left Dennie. Hands flailed upward through the blood-mired soil and something with arms and legs and a head but otherwise obscured by the filth that hung in clots from it, crawled like a lizard out of a swamp to stand, trembling and weak, at the edge of the pit.

'My... lord?' murmured Mother.

Its head swivelled towards her, and then back to regard Dennie.

Dennie knew those eyes. The last time she'd seen them, they'd been glazed with death and staring up at the shovelful of soil that she'd dumped on them in this very spot. The fact that they had subsequently been exhumed and reburied elsewhere didn't change the truth that this place was where the rootstock had originally been planted – all the innocent blood that had been spilled here since was the fruiting scion, and this hybrid thing that glared at her with Colin Neary's eyes above a tusk-filled muzzle was the result.

'That's not possible...' she whispered.

'Interfering old witch,' he snarled, and reached for her. 'Her blood is mine!' The creature wasn't reaching for herself, Dennie realised, but Lauren.

'You'll have to get through me first,' she replied, and something of Sabrina must have still been in her voice because the creature hesitated.

'You there, in the shed!' shouted a woman from outside. 'This is the police! Armed units are on the way! Step out now!'

'My lord Moccus,' said Ardwyn. 'There's no time. You must leave now while you can.'

Moccus uttered a squeal of rage and frustration, and fled the same way that Everett had done a moment ago. Someone outside screamed, '*Jesus, what the fuck is that?*' Moments later the shed door was pulled open and torchlight blinded them, and hands were dragging Dennie away while voices bellowed at her. She saw a female Asian officer bend over Lauren.

'It's okay, love,' Sergeant Prav said to Lauren, whose face was ashen, her sightless eyes gazing up at the ceiling. 'Help is on its way. You're going to be okay, you hear me? You're going to be okay.'

Then the rail spike hit Dennie right between the eyes and the world went away.

6

DESERTION

THE DESERTER DID THE THING HE DID BEST, WHICH was to run.

He burst from the shed and fired twice in the direction of the police lights to keep their heads down as he ran for the boundary fence that gave onto open fields. He saw Gar being savaged by the old woman's dog, but sped by without slowing down. *Sorry, chum*, he thought. Trying to escape in the van was out of the question. Even though these first two officers were easily evaded in the confusion, soon there would be helicopters, cars, and the most up-to-date surveillance technology. There was no way he could outrun them, so the next best thing was to do what he had done at Loos – hide, sink, go under, and try to come up safely on the other side. Even the furrowed ground of the plots reminded him of No Man's Land, the bean trellises like barbed wire in this light.

He clawed his way over the boundary fence and dropped

into nettles and brambles on the other side, fought his way clear of them and dashed off along the fence until it began to run behind houses, then met a hedgerow that he turned to follow downhill, deeper into the field.

Behind him, the screams and shouts faded. Midsummer dawn was drawing the world around him in dim pastels, and dew soaked his trousers as he plunged through another field, and then another, over stiles and past fleeing sheep and puzzled-looking cows.

When he emerged onto a narrow lane between high hedgerows he stopped, stood very still, calmed his breathing and listened.

No shouts or sounds of pursuit. Possibly the faintest hum of a helicopter but equally that could have been distant traffic. A blackbird was trilling its morning song. It was tempting to feel optimistic, except that behind and underneath everything was that rolling wall of thunder that had pursued him ever since he had dragged himself clear of the French mud. In the hundred or so years of his life since then, it had sometimes seemed very near and sometimes – usually when he was with Ardwyn – so far away that he could forget about it for a while. Right now it was so close it felt like a tidal wave at his back threatening to fall on him.

They'd soon be throwing a circle around the area and filling it with uniforms, so he needed to get out of that circle as quickly as possible now. He set off along the road in the direction where it seemed to curve a bit more, for no other reason than it might give a better chance of cover if the first vehicle he saw was a police car.

Headlights swelled ahead, and he hesitated. It might be the police, and they might not have their flashing blues on, but he thought that unlikely given the hue and cry that must be erupting now. If he hid and it wasn't then he'd have missed his chance.

So he stood in the middle of the road and thought *Well, if this is it, this is it.*

The car that screeched to a halt in front of him was a grubby white thing with mud all up the wheel arches, and by the time the driver had wound down his window and was shouting: 'What the fuck do you think you're doing?' the deserter had walked up to the passenger side, opened the door and pointed the Webley at him.

'I think I'm going to paint the inside of this car with your brains, chum,' he said. 'Unless you take me where I want to go.'

The driver – a potato-shaped man with a shaved head – gaped at him.

'I'll take that as a yes,' said the deserter, and got in.

'You can't… you can't…'

The deserter shut his door and pointed the gun right in the driver's face, thumbing the hammer back. In the enclosed space of the car its mechanism was very loud. 'Drive or die,' he said. 'Up to you.'

Pale and trembling, the man set off again. 'Where to?' he asked.

'For the moment, that way will do,' said the deserter, pointing his pistol at the road ahead.

As the light grew so did the vague stirrings of a plan to

keep heading north until he hit the Peak District and then try to get lost in its moors and valleys. There was a hut he knew, and maybe a gamekeeper who still remembered him. For all their technology there were still corners of the world blind to prying electronic eyes.

They came to a junction where their lane was crossed by a larger B-road, but with no signposts to tell him what lay in either direction.

'Which way?' asked the driver.

He didn't know. Nothing looked familiar. The terrified man behind the steering wheel was breathing very quickly and the stench of his sweat was nauseating. It was all the deserter could do to resist putting a bullet in him right here and now.

'Turn right here,' he said, because a decision had to be made, even if it was the wrong one. *If this is it, this is it.*

As the driver indicated and started to turn the steering wheel, flashing blue lights appeared to their right and a pair of police cars came barrelling down the B-road towards them. The deserter pressed the gun's muzzle into the man's doughy flesh above his hip. 'Now don't be doing anything silly there, chum,' he murmured. 'Just let them go by.'

But potato man must have had some steel buried in all that lard because he stamped on the accelerator and pulled right out in front of the approaching police cars. The unexpected lurch caught the deserter by surprise, throwing him back and against the door, and by the time he brought the gun to bear again the driver had yanked his door open and was jumping out, screaming: 'He's here! He's here! He's here!'

The deserter cursed and fired, and the man went down with a red splash between his shoulder blades. The leading police car skidded to a halt while the one behind swerved around.

The deserter leapt out of the car and ran off along the grassy road verge, hunting for a break in the hedge to his left that would give him access to the fields. There were plenty. He ducked through one, earning a nasty laceration across his face from a hawthorn bush for his carelessness, and down a muddy bank. He had no idea where he was running – he just headed for the nearest stand of trees in the hope that the cover might help him in some way, but he was barely halfway when he heard the burr of a helicopter and it appeared, hovering over him, keeping pace as he ran, communicating his location to ground forces. He fired off a round at it, aware that he only had two remaining in the cylinder, and the helicopter swerved and retreated to a more diplomatic distance. Down towards the trees the ground became more boggy, and he found himself near a cattle-feed station – a drinking trough and a metal pen where hay was dumped – and a wide area surrounding it had been churned to mud by countless hooves and liberally splattered with shit. It slowed him drastically; he sank up to his ankles and had to fight to drag his feet clear with every step. When he looked back he saw two black figures back up by the road, walking at a crouch with rifles raised, and an amplified voice from the sky bellowed: 'Armed police! Stop where you are! Throw down your weapon or you will be fired upon!' He screamed his defiance at them and fired off his last two rounds. The figures threw themselves flat to the ground and he thought *Ha! Let's see how you like grovelling like worms!* There was a rapid crackle of automatic weapons fire and all of a sudden his legs stopped working, dropping him face forward into the mud and shit, but he raised himself up on his knees and pointed his empty pistol at them and a bullet tore off the top of his head and that was that.

Matt heard the helicopter and distant gunfire and cowered deeper into his hiding place.

It was the ruin of an old Victorian pumping house right down by the river, built in the county's industrial hey-day when the Trent was used for miles along its length by hundreds of mills, factories, and farms, many of which had long since been demolished or abandoned to be reclaimed by woodland. Nothing much was left but the redbrick shell and half of the roof which had survived because of a rusting framework of scaffolding holding it up, probably from some past attempt to renovate the structure. The interior was a litter of overgrown rubble; ivy scrawled itself all over the scaffolding, hazel and buddleia bushes sprouted from the walls, their huge brush-heads of purple flowers thickening the air with perfume, while in the part that was open to the sky, whole birch trees had taken root in the floor.

His dad had shown it to him, back in prehistory on the rare occasion when he'd been taken fishing, and as far as Matt could tell, he was the only one who knew about it. There was no graffiti or drugs trash or used condoms to suggest that the local kids or junkies used it, probably because there was no road connecting it to town, only a farm track through several locked and rusted gates or a tricky path to be picked along the river's edge that disappeared when water levels were high. It was situated on an inward bend of the river with vegetation crowding the steep banks in either direction – too much of an expedition for a high or a quick fuck.

He sat in the corner, knees drawn up under his chin, and rocked back and forth, still shocked at how quickly everything had gone to shit.

Pimblett smacking him in the head like that had been a lucky shot, but he'd forgotten that the guy had also eaten the first flesh and a blow that he should have been able to shake off had hit him like a truck. By the time he'd come to his senses, Gar was down and having his throat torn out by the old woman's huge dog, while Everett was shooting at the cops and legging it for the field. Matt had crawled off between the plants and sheds and done his own disappearing act before things could get worse. He wondered why he'd never told Everett about this place, but judging by how easily Everett had bottled it that was probably a good thing. Maybe some part of Matt had always known deep down that Everett couldn't be trusted.

He didn't know what had happened to Mother. The cops would be all over the farm by now, so he couldn't go back there, and his mum's place would also be one of the first places they'd look for him. He had no food, no money, and only the clothes he had on. He felt like an animal – one of those rabbits, its head in the noose, pulling and pulling and strangling itself until someone like him came along and did it a mercy by breaking its neck. He felt lost and bereft in a way that he'd never known; even before Ardwyn and Everett, when he'd had no job and nothing to do except hang around the village, there had at least been home and Mum and the vague sense that something would come along once he finally pulled his finger out and got on with his life like everybody kept telling him to. But now...

He cried, despising himself for being a pussy even as the tears fell.

When he heard someone moving through the bushes outside, he picked up half a brick and got ready to go down fighting – but at the sight of the thing that appeared in the doorway he dropped it and stared, slack-mouthed.

It looked like the result of someone trying to do a jigsaw puzzle of a naked man, but with some of the parts jammed in upside down or back to front or missing, replaced by crude home-made pieces, or even pieces from a different puzzle altogether – one of an animal, perhaps, with coarse hair and tusks. It looked like a child had tried to make a man out of Play-Doh while blindfolded. It looked like the stone carving of a giant lost in the desert for a thousand years, sandblasted by storms until parts of it were blurred smooth or destroyed. It looked like all of these to some degree, except that none of them fixed him with its eyes like this, or spoke.

'I smelled you,' it said, and its voice too was only a rough approximation of human words. There were fragments of squeals and echoes of howls in it. 'You have my flesh.'

'Who... what the fuck are you?'

'I am...' It paused, as if the question had never occurred to it before. 'Unfinished. She brought me back too soon. You're going to finish the job properly.'

It came fully inside and slumped down to sit against the wall opposite him. It – he – looked exhausted, and no wonder if he'd travelled from Dodbury in that state. There was something porcine about the shape of his face that reminded Matt of Gar, and of the skull in the abattoir shrine.

'Are you... are you Moccus?' he whispered.

The figure considered this. 'I would have been, once,' he decided. 'Once I was also a man who was murdered just for trying to keep his wife in line. When I've reclaimed all that belongs to me, I'll know. What's your name?'

'Matt. Matthew. Hewitson. Sir. My lord, I mean.'

'Well, which is it?'

'Er, Matt, I suppose.'

Moccus tipped his head back against the wall, closed his eyes, and sighed. 'Matt, you are the Farrow now. Serve me and you will be rewarded.' He cracked an eyelid and glared, and even that much was enough to make Matt squirm. 'Betray me and I'll take what I need from you instead. You may be the Farrow, but you could very easily become the Herd. Don't forget that.'

'I won't. Sir.'

'Good.' The eye closed, and Matt was released. 'And now you're thinking, what kind of a threat is that?' Moccus murmured. 'Look at how sick and frail he is. He can barely stand.'

'No, honestly, I'm not.'

'Then you're either an idiot or a liar, because you should be. Give me your hand.'

Matt hesitated.

'I'm not asking you to cut the damned thing off!' Moccus snapped. 'Give me your hand!'

Matt complied. The unfinished man's flesh felt cold and clammy, and his fingers gripped Matt's hand weakly, but then Matt was running through a forest of trees the size of cathedral columns, sprinting at breakneck speed on legs that were like tree trunks themselves, his bare feet sending clods of earth and leaf mould flying, his lungs pumping like forge bellows, and his tusks were like sabres in his mouth. The small creatures of the forest fled before him, but one especially trailed a scent-ribbon of terror that maddened him with the desire to see it split open and bleeding at his feet, and he laughed at the joy of it, and his laughter was a boar's holler that shook the earth. Then it was gone and he was just Matt again, shivering and gasping like a junkie. It was like what Everett had given him, but the difference was like the difference between Red Bull and cocaine.

'Do you want that?' asked Moccus.

'Yes! Oh, fuck yes!'

Moccus grunted with satisfaction. 'Then you know what to do,' he replied. 'Protect me. Serve me.' He looked around at the derelict pump house. 'This is a good place,' he said. 'It will do for the moment, but we can't stay here. I can't wait weeks for the next tusk moon here. The police will find us long before that.'

'I don't know where else to go,' Matt admitted.

'I do,' said Moccus. 'Swinley. The Place of the Swine. Where they murdered me, over and over again. Where my children languish, hiding in the woods like vermin instead of the hunters that their blood demands they be. *My* blood. Matthew, take me to my children. I will place you at their head, and I will set you to eat the world.'

PART FIVE

HARVEST THE CROP

1

INTERVIEW

Transcript of video interview with suspect identified as Ardwyn Hughes.
Date: 23/06/2020
Duration: 5:41
Location: Rugeley Police Station, Anson St, Rugeley, Staffs.
Conducted by Police Sergeant Praveen Kaur.

In the video, Ardwyn Hughes sits at a police interview table on her own, having declined the services of a barrister. She is wearing jeans and a violet blouse with a lace-up neck, from which the laces have been removed, so that it opens quite a way down her chest, a fact which does not go unremarked by the tens of thousands of male viewers who will subsequently comment on it when the video is eventually leaked. Across from her are two police officers – one male, one female. The female officer who conducts the interview has two small strips of wound tape above her left eyebrow.

PK: I am Police Sergeant Praveen Kaur of Staffordshire Police, Needwood Neighbourhood Team. I would like to ask you some questions concerning the murder of Lauren Emma Jeffries at the Briar Hill allotments two days ago. You do not have to say anything but it may harm your defence if you do not mention when questioned something which you later rely on in court. Anything you say may be given in evidence. Do you understand this?

AH: I do.

PK: You were arrested in your allotment shed, shortly after a male killed Ms Jeffries by cutting her throat. Did you know this man?

AH: Yes. He was my lover.

PK: Can you tell us his name?

AH: I only knew him as Everett, though I'm quite confident that it wasn't his real name.

PK: Why do you say that?

AH *shrugging*: Because he told me that he stole it from a dead soldier in No Man's Land in 1915.

This takes the interviewing officer aback somewhat, and she consults with her partner for a moment.

PK: And you believed him?

AH: Everett was a deserter, thief, murderer, and cannibal, but he never lied to me.

PK: Do you know why he assaulted Ms Jeffries?

AH: Yes. I told him to.

PK: And why was that?

AH: Because our god needed her blood. Although to be

accurate, it wasn't rightfully hers, not since she ate the first flesh.

PK: Um, yes... So you admit that you incited him to murder her?

AH: Well yes, obviously. I'm sorry, I thought that was assumed.

PK: Several witnesses have alleged that you are also responsible for the deaths of three other residents of Dodbury. Would you like to comment on that?

AH: Not particularly.

PK: Why not? You're ready enough to admit attacking Lauren Jeffries.

AH: I see no point in denying what was demonstrably true and right in front of your eyes. I'm sure that if there are other people that you're looking for, you'll find them soon enough.

PK: But you've been very cooperative so far.

AH: Sergeant Kaur, please don't mistake self-possession for cooperation. I have no intention of helping you any more than necessary to avoid wasting time. Being in a cell was, yes, one of the two ways we thought this might go, but it's still not my preferred course of action.

PK: And what is this course of action intended to achieve?

AH: The resurrection of my lord Moccus and the establishment of his new covenant.

She says this with the calm reason of someone discussing nothing more controversial than the weather, and the two police officers share a look.

PK: Moccus...?

AH: He Who Eats the Moon. The First Farmer. The

Hunter in the Wood. He is a primordial fertility god, ancient even when the Romans arrived, and he has been worshipped on this island since before Christianity was born. We who are his followers are called the Farrow. We sacrifice him and eat his flesh, and in return he blesses us with health and longevity, but that which is taken must be given back, and so from those who eat his flesh some are chosen as vessels to return their gift and renew Moccus for the next cycle. At least, so it will be in the new church. We're evolving.

PK: So, you're saying that your cult practises ritual human sacrifice.

This is the first and only time that Ardwyn Hughes' composure breaks, as she flashes with anger.

AH: We are not a cult! We are a religion. We had a liturgy, prayers, we gave philanthropically to charitable organisations. We don't commit mass suicide or pray for deliverance by aliens or any of that rubbish.

PK: You'd think people would have heard about you by now.

AH: We have, by necessity, been small in number because there is only so much of the first flesh to go around. This appreciation of how much it is safe to consume is why we have survived for so long – while in contrast it is your civilisation's wilful greed and ignorance of the same which is why the world is in such danger. This earth, our garden, is burning – *literally* burning, from the Amazonian rainforests to the Siberian tundra. The glaciers are retreating, and as they go they are giving up their dead. There are plastics everywhere from the top of Everest to the deepest abysses of the ocean, and have even entered the fossil record. This is happening because of your greed and apathy; you are taking too much, much more than the world can provide, but even if you stopped taking everything tomorrow it wouldn't help because the damage is too severe. We must begin to put things back. We must replenish the world with our lives, our very blood if need be. We must give back what we have taken – *that* is the lesson Moccus has to teach us.

PK: And we're supposed to learn it by killing our own kids? I don't think so. I'm afraid you're not going to be in a position to teach much of anything for long time.

AH: That is because you think like a product of your dying culture, which knows nothing but to invade and proselytise, to send crusaders and missionaries to conquer with the sword and enslave with the word. I will be content to remain in my cell and let those who yearn for a better way to come to me as Mother.

PK: I don't think a prison will allow quite that many visitors.

AH: No, but they always allow phones, if only by their own negligence. My church won't be a building, and my message won't be by word of mouth. It will be online, everywhere and eternal. I told you, we have evolved; technology makes it inevitable. It's started already. You're helping me even as you sit there, mocking. (*At this point, AH looks at the camera and begins to address it directly.*) This video will be leaked – if not today then tomorrow, or in a year, or ten, but it will. And in any case, how long will they hold me for? Twenty years? I will preach to my new church from the darkness and when the term of my imprisonment has been served I will return to the world as young as the day I went in, and my church and my lord will be waiting for me. I have no fear of time or age or decay because I have been blessed with the first flesh, and this is my witness.

What happens next becomes the subject of furious online controversy when the video is inevitably leaked. Some claim that it's a hoax, nothing more than video and prosthetic effects, but many more are convinced of its truth.

AH stands up too quickly for the two police officers to stop her – she is preternaturally fast – whips the biro out of PK's fingers and then, to the horror of both, slaps her own left hand palm down on the table, raises the biro in her right, and slams the point of it through the back of her hand so hard that it goes straight through and impales the table underneath. The table can be seen to actually move as she then tugs her left hand free. She appears to be in no pain and is quite calm, unlike the police officers who are yelling for assistance. AH holds her wounded hand up to the camera in extreme close-up so that the biro's point can be seen protruding from her palm, and then pulls it back out. For a moment the hole is obvious – light can be seen through it – though it quickly fills up with blood, but then her right hand comes up to grasp her wrist and her thumb smears away the blood, and the hole is gone. She turns her hand over to show the back, and there is no entry wound either, no mark whatsoever except for a small dot of blue ink.

The video goes viral, of course, clocking up over two million views in the first twenty-four hours, while the hashtags #motherardwyn, #hewhoeatsthemoon, and #replenishtheworld trend for three days.

2

HOMECOMING

There were no signs for Swinley, and not even much of a road.

Matt had to abandon his car by the side of a narrow lane that was closely crowded by trees, parked as close as he could to their trunks but still afraid that it didn't leave enough room for anything else to get by and that he was going to return and find the side doors gouged open like a tin can by some dick of a farmer. It was night, and there were no road markings.

The locals had been worse than useless in response to his requests for directions. They either claimed to have never heard of a place called Swinley or just walked away from him as soon as they heard the name. Moccus' own instructions had turned out to be hopelessly vague, too, and he'd slept most of the way here, leaving Matt to work it out on his own. *On the road between Church Stoke and*

Minsterley will be a gate hidden in the trees, he'd said. Well there were three roads between that shitsplat village and the other, and he'd driven them all and he'd seen no gates. It wasn't made any easier by the darkness, night vision or no night vision. They'd stayed at the old pump house until the day had faded before sneaking back to where Matt had parked his car. The yellow Astra had been bought for cash, wasn't taxed, insured, or registered in his name so he didn't think it likely that the police would be looking for it. Dodbury was only sixty miles away as the crow flies, but he'd driven here along a maze of minor roads to avoid the ANPR cameras on the M54 and the A-roads, and that had added a good hour to the trip.

He'd been retracing his route along a steeply hollowed lane almost entirely enclosed by trees, trying to hold back the panic that was rising in his throat like vomit because the last thing he wanted to do was wake the figure in the passenger seat, when he'd felt a strange tugging at his guts. It was like the intake before a sneeze, or the pause before coming, and it rose to a peak and then just as suddenly tailed off. He stopped the car and reversed, and the tugging grew stronger again, and when he looked more closely into the dense undergrowth at the side of the road he saw the headlights gleaming on a metal gate that he'd missed the first time.

There was no putting it off any longer. He leaned across and gently shook Moccus. 'Sir,' he whispered. 'I think we're here.'

'I know,' he grunted, and Matt thought that maybe he hadn't been asleep after all. 'I can feel them. My Recklings. Take me to them.'

Matt helped him out of the car and to the gate. It was unlocked, and swung open on well-greased hinges more easily than its condition would have suggested, but opened only a very little way until it fetched up against a huge pile of logs and branches on the other side. It was far more substantial than to have all fallen by accident, but that made no sense because if this track was used regularly enough for the gate to be in working condition why barricade it off? Why not just lock it? The barricade was head-high and extended left and right into thick woods, with the sharp prongs of broken branches set very deliberately pointing forward so that it was like approaching a medieval fortification. Whoever built this was seriously uninterested in visitors.

And the second little pig built his house out of sticks, thought Matt. 'Little pigs, little pigs,' he muttered, 'I've come to nick your video.'

'I can't climb that,' said Moccus. 'You'll have to go and talk to them. Get them to dismantle this and let me in.'

Matt squeezed through the gap and picked a careful way over the barricade, snagging his clothing a couple of times, and dropped down on the other side. Just like the gate, the track was in a lot better condition than he would have expected from the crowded and overarching trees. It was solid tarmac, without potholes, but there was a light littering of leaves and twigs on its surface which suggested that maybe it had once been used regularly, but not for quite a few months.

With no other option, he began walking along the track in the direction of what he assumed to be the village of Swinley.

He soon became aware that faces were watching him

from the woods on either side. Just the flash of an eye or the gleam of a tusk, gone when he turned to look without even the rustling of a leaf. Moccus had told him to expect that his children might be wary or even violent, but drawn to the presence of the first flesh within him all the same. It must have been that which he had felt tugging on him as he'd driven past – their flesh calling to him, and his to them, bound and linked by the blood that they shared. They might have been born with it, whereas he had ingested it, but it still made them one in Moccus. Instead of feeling afraid of them as he walked, he felt instead a sort of kinship, as if meeting long-lost family for the first time.

'I'm not afraid of you,' he called out. 'So you might as well show yourselves. I've come with our father.'

Into the road ahead of him stepped a woman. She was barefoot and wearing only a floral summer dress against the night, but her elongated jawline and the tawny fur on her arms and legs told him she was not entirely human. She looked like she might have been Gar's younger sister.

'I am Sus,' she said. 'You smell like Farrow, but they're all dead now. Who are you?'

'Matt,' he replied, looking her up and down. 'Wow.'

'Save your mockery,' she sneered. 'Who is Matt and what does he mean by saying that he has come with our father? Answer before we gut you.'

'I wasn't mocking, honest! I'm just... I actually think you're pretty.' It was hard to tell who was more surprised at this statement – Sus or himself. She came forward, her bent-backward legs giving her a swaying, balletic movement.

'And will you still think I'm pretty when I'm eating your entrails before your eyes?' she asked.

Probably, he thought. 'I'm sorry,' he said. 'I've fucked this up. Let me try again. I've come with our father, Moccus. He's in the car, just down the road.'

Other figures crept out of the undergrowth to stand on the road around her. No two were alike – some were squat and muscular while others were slender, some went on all fours while others walked on two – but all of them shared the same porcine qualities that made them children of Moccus: tusks jutting from elongated faces, split hooves where fingers should have been, and bristling fur.

'Take us,' said Sus.

He led them in an eager, loping mob to the car, but when Moccus stepped out they fell back, dumbfounded at the sight of him. Instead of the giant figure they had expected, here was something that looked like a tattered coat on a stick.

Sus's hand went to her mouth, and she shook her head in swift denial. 'No,' she whispered.

Moccus laid his hand on her cheek. It only had three fingers and she flinched from its touch. 'Daughter,' he said softly.

'What…?' Tears were spilling down her cheeks. '… How has this… you're…'

'I am home,' he said. 'Will you take me in and heal me?'

She bowed before him, and the other Recklings followed her lead.

They dismantled the barricade and carried him into the village. Matt couldn't make out too many of the details but he got the impression that the village was deserted and partially ruined. Moccus was taken to a large barn-like building and laid upon a bed of rags and straw, and the Recklings crowded around him, telling him of themselves and what had been happening in Swinley in his absence. Sus took Matt to one side while this was happening. 'There are still a few cottages left standing that you might be able to use for yourself,' she said. 'Don't worry about the owners. They've all… gone. I would get comfortable if I were you.' She nodded at the adulatory mob. 'This could take a while.'

The following day Sus showed him around the remains of Swinley.

The hedgerows were overgrown and the fields were untended – some dotted with the long-rotted and partially eaten corpses of livestock, others with their crops lost to weeds. A herd of small muntjac deer bolted from them, dashing through a broken fence and back into the woods. There seemed to be few cottages or farmhouses, but those he saw were either broken open to the elements or fire-gutted shells. He had found one that still had some food in the larder – stale bread and cheese, but as breakfasts went it was better than nothing.

'It didn't happen all at once,' said Sus as they walked. They were accompanied by a male Reckling who introduced himself as Griskin. He wore the rags of a once-expensive suit, but with his head hunched so far forward that it was below the level of his shoulders, and though his arms were disproportionately short, they ended in claws that were long, black and wickedly curved. 'When Mother Ardwyn and the butcher stole the carnyx it was like a beehive that someone had stamped on. Fury. Disbelief. We watched because there was nothing we could do. Some of the Farrow came and said "find them for us", and a few tried, but we never heard from them again. Then the equinox came and we felt that He Who Eats the Moon was summoned, but not for the people here. They were not able to renew themselves with the first flesh. The oldest died first, as the sicknesses that they had kept at bay for so long caught up with them, but there was nobody living in Swinley who had not outlived a normal human lifespan, and within two months they were all dead. Some of them took their own lives. Some tried to escape to the outside for help.'

'What happened to them?' asked Matt.

Sus looked at him sidelong. 'We couldn't let them draw attention to us.'

Griskin chuckled quietly.

'Some of the buildings caught fire,' she continued. 'The people who live in the neighbouring villages must have seen the smoke, but nobody sent help. I think they were glad to see Swinley burn.'

By now they had reached a small church with a square Norman tower. Sus paused before she opened the door. 'We put the rest of them in here,' she said. 'It's what we think they would have wanted.'

The sweet, thick stench of decay rolled out of the church as she opened it and led him inside, and he had to bury his nose in the crook of his elbow to keep out the worst of it. The

Recklings had gathered all the corpses of the Farrow that they could find and put them here, having removed their clothes and placed them in positions of copulation as if indulging in one last and eternal orgy. The midsummer heat had not been kind to any of them. All were bloated, and many had burst, spilling their insides over each other. Flies, disturbed at their feast, swarmed up in great buzzing clouds from upturned faces and gaping jaws, while rats scuttled away under the pews.

Matt reeled from the sight and clawed his way out to the fresh air, retching.

Sus and Griskin joined him a moment later.

'We are his children but those were his faithful,' she said. 'It's different for you. If you're going to fight for him, then fight, but don't be surprised if this is the reward you get. That's all I'm saying.'

Later that morning Moccus called the Recklings to him. Now that Matt saw the barn in daylight he noticed all the traps and rabbit snares hanging from the walls, and he nudged Sus. 'Did Gar live here?' he whispered.

Sus scowled. 'Gar betrayed us. He helped Mother Ardwyn and the butcher steal the bone horn, and that killed this place.'

Matt shrugged. 'He was good to me. Taught me stuff.' He was surprised to find tears prickling at the corners of his eyes. 'The old woman's fucking dog chewed his throat out. I'm going to kill them both for that.'

'Shh,' she said. Moccus was speaking.

'Even though the next tusk moon is some time away we must still move quickly,' he said. 'There is a threat to me that must be destroyed.'

'What threatens you?' asked Sus.

'By now the police will have found the carnyx and the knife, and therewith the means to both bind and kill me.' Moccus growled – it was a weak, pained sound, but they all felt it vibrate through the ground, nonetheless. 'I will not suffer that again. I will not be their meat again. I will be a man.'

'But the police have guns and dogs and helicopters and all that,' Matt pointed out. 'They're basically an army.'

'So are we,' said Griskin, and there was a murmur of approval from around.

'You are aware that you're talking about attacking *a police station*, right?' Matt protested. 'That's a counter-terror-level response, right there. We're talking drones and satellites and fuck knows what else. That's a pretty big kick-me sign on the arse for someone who says he wants to lie low for a month.'

'Do you think that I have not had enemies in all the long centuries before?' Moccus replied. 'Or that this place has not learned how to hide itself from the outside world? You have been here less than a day; you know nothing. Your arguments are noted but it is my will that you do this thing. Does that suit you? Will you defy me so soon?'

Matt bit his tongue. 'No, of course not. But how are we meant to find this horn and knife? They could be in any one of who knows how many places.'

'Start with the police stations. You will know when you are near the carnyx – it calls to my blood and my blood will respond to it. Remember how you felt the presence of my children before you saw them?'

'Fair enough. And transport? This lot are definitely not going to fit in my car and I'm pretty sure that the trains don't do group saver tickets for things not of this earth.'

'There are many farms in Swinley,' said Sus. 'A few of them have cattle trucks. They are old but they should still be working.'

And that was how Matt found himself driving a 1958 Leyland Comet cattle truck east along the M54 at 1 a.m., with a cargo of excitable Recklings peering out through the wooden slats of the high-sided vehicle at the lights of houses and oncoming traffic. Sus was in the passenger seat of the cab, navigating with an old-fashioned A-Z, since he didn't want to risk the authorities being able to track his phone's GPS.

'This is not how I imagined my summer was going to go,' he muttered.

The police station in Burton-on-Trent was sandwiched between the main works of Molson Coors Brewing on one side of a busy A-road and the loading and delivery yards on the other, and in between there were plenty of lay-bys and yards where a vintage cattle truck could sit unnoticed amongst all the container lorries and forklifts. Moccus had been right – Matt had felt something tugging at him as he'd driven slowly past the station house. He was just glad that it was still in the old Victorian premises rather than one of those corporate complexes on a new estate outside town where county councils liked to stick all the emergency services under one roof. It meant that security might be a bit less tight.

He jumped down from the cab, walked to the back of the truck and unhitched the rear panel, letting it down into a ramp. Inside, the cattle compartment was full of shifting shadows and eager whispers.

'Come on then,' he said. 'Let's do this.'

3

NIGHT SHIFT

Sergeant Praveen Kaur should not have been back at work.

The problem was that the Briar Hill incident was throwing out so many offshoots in terms of just getting statements from everyone, never mind any of the forensics, and with staffing having been hacked back year after year because of budget cuts, it was all hands to the pumps, as the Chief said. He'd made the right noises, of course – told her that if she wanted to she could take whatever time she needed to cope with the aftermath of what she'd seen in that shed – and she had no doubt that he meant it, because Chief Inspector Connors was a decent man, but all the same she could see him wondering how he was going to cover her absence even as he said it.

So no, according to any right-thinking person she shouldn't have been in the office collating witness statements in the early hours. She should have been snuggled up in bed after a Thai takeout, a bit of a cry, and a long conversation with her Auntie Raisa (although 'conversation' might have been stretching it a bit) about why policing was far too dangerous a job and what was wrong with starting a family, anyway. But then she'd have had nothing to distract her from remembering the thing that had come out of the shed.

The problem was that Prav was not a right-thinking person, at least as her Auntie might consider such things. Prav liked this. Collating and filing and organising helped to defuse the chaos, whereas sitting around at home in her slippers watching daytime television just let the chaos spread unchecked. She could have hung around at the allotments with the scene-of-crime crew but she'd only have been making a nuisance of herself and not actually contributing anything. Coming in after the front desk had closed meant that she could work uninterrupted by members of the public coming in to complain about their parking tickets or with things needing to be signed. And it wasn't as if she was on her own. Spencer, the duty sergeant, was downstairs, and Ryland and Lennox were on patrol, which meant that they were in and out of the station all night.

The wheels were turning, and as long as she was helping to turn them, she could see this ride through to the end and sleep happily when it was all dotted and crossed.

After that disastrous interview, Hughes had been transferred to the station at Watling Street in Stoke, since the custody suite at Burton had been closed over a year ago because there wasn't enough money to refurb it. Everett

Clifton had been shot dead in a field. Dennie Keeling and David Pimblett were all in hospital, she recovering from some kind of seizure, while he was recovering from his mauling at the hands (and teeth) of that huge unnamed assailant that everyone in the station was calling 'Chewie', though never to the media and *definitely* not in earshot of the Chief. There was no question of Viggo being destroyed, since he had obviously been defending his mistress against a violent attacker.

No, these two, physical injuries aside, weren't the ones making all the work. It was the list of names that Pimblett had supplied – the ones who he accused of having been accomplices to Hughes and Clifton – that needed checking out. It seemed like he'd named half the tenants of the Briar Hill allotments. What the hell had been happening there over the summer?

That had not been a fun interview either – though not for anything he'd said or done during it, so much as the exchange that had happened after she had put her notebook away.

'When you and I went to that farm,' she'd said, 'you already suspected that the girl might be there, didn't you?'

David's eyes were guarded as he replied, 'What makes you say that?'

'Because if you didn't know then and only found out later, you wouldn't have made the call anonymously. You'd have given your name. You didn't give your name because you didn't want to have to explain why you failed to report that you thought she was at the farm very first thing. So. Why didn't you say anything?'

'Because they threatened my family, okay?' he said, probably thinking that he sounded defiant. 'I had to make sure that my wife and daughter were safe first. I told the police as soon as I could.'

'Which gave Hughes and Clifton enough warning to move her somewhere else, obviously.'

He fiddled with his hospital bracelet, avoiding her eyes. Most of his torso and left arm were strapped up and according to the doctors he was lucky that they were still attached to each other. He must have been in considerable pain, but he'd told her that he wasn't taking any morphine at that moment because he wanted to give her as clear an account as possible. She had to credit him with that, she supposed, but all the same she couldn't not pursue it. 'You knew that Lauren was probably being raped and tortured as we stood there on the doorstep getting fobbed off by that bloody woman – and you *let* us get fobbed off.'

'Yes!' he said, and when he looked at her again she saw how haunted he was by that decision. 'And all I could see was it happening to my little girl instead. What was I supposed to do? What would you have done?'

'I'd have trusted the person sitting next to me in the car,' she retorted. 'You should have trusted me, David.'

'Ardwyn chose the people around her – the Farrow – very carefully. Tenants on the allotments who could cover for her, me because of my volunteering with the police, basically anybody she thought might have had influence and could help her. Maybe even you, for all I knew. I couldn't take that risk. Are you going to put this in your report? Have me charged with perverting the course of justice or whatever?'

Prav sighed. 'No. What good would that do? You helped save the girl in the end and that's got to count for something. People like Ardwyn Hughes become strong by making people like you and me distrust each other. I'm not going to give her the satisfaction.'

And with that she had left David to heal what he could.

The playlist that helped her concentrate came to an end and she removed her headphones, thinking that it might be technology's way of saying *that's quite enough for one night*.

She heard something fall over downstairs.

Prav left her desk and went to the office door, which opened onto a short hallway and the staircase down to the ground floor.

'Spence?' she called.

There was the sound of something being dragged.

He'd probably decided that he needed to go looking for something in one of the cells, which were now being used as general storage and overspill for the evidence room. Even though the custody suite was out of commission, Burton was one of the few stations left with a front desk where the public could hand in lost-and-found, because knives and drugs didn't need to be fed and monitored in case they choked on their own vomit or pissed on the floor. Spence was in his sixties; whatever he was trying to move, he was likely to give himself a hernia.

'Do you need a hand with anything?' she called as she went downstairs.

She saw Spence in the long corridor that ran from the

front desk to the back door. He was lying on the floor, face down, being dragged backwards by something that made no sense. For a start, it had no arms or forelimbs, just a pair of thickly muscled legs with knees that rose over its back as it crouched by Spence's head. It was dragging him with a whiplike tongue that was wrapped around his throat, and he was leaving a streak of red on the floor.

The thing looked at her, opened its mouth and *squealed*.

That was when she saw that the door to what had once been the cellar of the old Victorian building was open. Normally it housed just the boiler and electrics, but something simian with a pig's face launched itself out of there, jabbering at her, and all of the other doors in the corridor were open, spilling forth creatures that looked like they'd stepped straight out of a vivisectionist's nightmare.

Prav ran.

She didn't run without purpose, though. She dashed for the back of the building, towards the changing rooms. There was a rack of personal radios permanently on charge, and she grabbed one, pivoting left down a side corridor and towards the unused cells. Something close behind her skidded on the polished floor as she took the corner too sharply for it to follow and crashed into a bank of lockers, screeching. She didn't look back to see what it was, simply yanked open the first cell door that she came to, praying that it was being used for storage, and threw herself inside. She saw boxes, a filing cabinet, two old desks stacked on top of each other, and a huddle of broken office chairs. She tipped the filing cabinet over as the door was shoved from the other side; it landed with a crash, drawers flying open and spilling old property records everywhere, but it stopped the door opening more than six inches. A hand snatched through the gap, except it wasn't a hand, it was a pig's trotter with a thumb. A yellow eye peered at her through the viewing slot in the metal door, and something half-snarled, half-squealed: '*Goan tah eeechooo!*'

'The fuck you are.' Prav shoved the desks towards the door too, and upended them onto the filing cabinet, then began throwing boxes onto her makeshift barricade. When it became clear that no amount of pushing from the other side was widening the gap any more, she took out the radio.

'All units, all units! This is bravo zero! Burton central is being attacked! Over!' Despite her best efforts to remain calm there was no disguising the panic that was creeping in at the edges. 'All units, all units!' she repeated. 'This is—'

'Bravo zero, this is mike three,' said Mick Ryland's voice on the other end. 'Prav, is this a joke?'

'No, it's not a fucking joke, Mick!' she screamed. 'Some fucking I-don't-know-what-the-fuck-they-are have broken into the station! They got Spence! They got him on the fucking floor!'

'Bravo zero acknowledged,' Ryland replied, clipped and professional. 'On way, five minutes.' There was a brief pause and then: 'Hang in there, Prav, we're coming.'

When she turned back to the door, whatever it was that had been trying to get through was gone, but she could still hear sounds of things being thrown around, doors crashing open, and furniture being upended from elsewhere in the station. She sidled up to the gap and peered through. There was a man and a woman in the corridor. At least, the man was definitely a man. The woman was… different. They were having a conversation, and then he turned around and Prav saw that he had Everett Clifton's black sickle-knife stuck in his belt and that hideous bone horn thing in his hands, and he was grinning like it was Christmas morning. She recognised him from the information supplied by David Pimblett; it was Matthew Hewitson.

And he saw her peering out.

Prav gasped and ducked back into the room, but it was too late. Hewitson came to the door. He looked down and around at the barricade and gave the door an experimental push, and when it didn't move he shrugged. 'It doesn't matter,' he told her. 'We've got what we need. It would have been fun watching you wriggle, but hey.'

'There's a patrol car on the way,' she said. 'They're going to be here in minutes.'

'So that's a whole…' He performed an elaborate pantomime of counting on his fingers. 'Two more cops? That's almost worth sticking around for. But sorry, no. Places to do, things to be, you know how it is.' He disappeared, but then came back for a moment. 'There is one thing you can do, though,' he said. 'You can tell the rest of the herd that our lord will take what is owed to him.'

He went away again, and didn't come back. The noises of destruction faded too, to be replaced soon afterwards by the welcome music of police sirens.

4

VISITING HOURS

'HELLO, STRANGER.'

David looked up from his phone as Dennie approached his bed. It was the start of visiting hours on the ortho ward, but he wasn't expecting anyone; Becky had rushed straight up from her parents' when she'd heard about the attack three days ago, but had gone back yesterday after collecting more of her things from the house. As far as she knew he'd tried to stop an abduction-murder, which was more than enough to be going on with.

Dennie came around to his good side and gave him a lopsided hug. She moved slowly, and he saw how gingerly she took each step, as if afraid of what the floor might do underfoot. 'How are you getting on?' she asked.

'I feel like I've been chewed up and spat out,' he said.

'Funny, that.'

'You?'

She so-so'd and perched on the edge. 'Lizzie's been looking after me. I've been sleeping a lot. Other than that, mostly raging migraines and nosebleeds.'

He winced. 'Because of…?'

'I think so. As far as I can work out, whatever it is in my brain that makes me see Sabrina – the bit that *is* Sabrina, if that makes sense – wakes up when it needs to, but when I try to wake it up deliberately, well, pop.' She mimed a little explosion underneath her nose.

'Cripes, that's not good, is it?'

'No, indeed.'

Footsteps approached, and they turned to see Sergeant Kaur appear on the ward, headed for them.

'Huh,' David grunted as she arrived. 'Come to give me another bollocking, have you, Sarge?'

'No,' she replied. 'I've come to ask for your help.' She nodded at Dennie. 'Both of you, actually.'

She wasn't in uniform, he noted, and she looked tired. Now that he looked at her properly, she looked absolutely wrung out. He sat up straighter in his bed, wincing at the twinge in his shoulder. First flesh or not, he was still in a bad way. 'What's happened?'

She pulled up a chair and slumped into it. 'Last night,' she replied, 'or should I say more accurately, early this morning, I had a surprise visit from a Mr Matthew Hewitson.'

'*Shit.*'

She snapped her fingers. 'Yes. That. He broke into the police station in Burton-on-Trent and stole two objects from the evidence room. One was a certain curved knife, and the other was an ugly horn thing made of bones.'

'Did he hurt you?' Dennie asked.

She produced a tired smile. 'No, he didn't. I managed to find somewhere to hide. Which was just as well because he had brought lots of friends with him.'

'What do you mean, *friends*?'

David listened as she tried to describe the creatures that had raided the station, but when she asked if either of them knew anything about them he had to confess his ignorance. 'They sound a bit like they're related to Gar, but I never saw anything other than him. Jesus, there's *more* of the bloody things?'

'It's pretty obvious to me that this whole business is a long way from being over. The problem for me is that I can't tell anybody on the force about what I really saw because if I do they'll send for the men in white coats.'

'Maybe you should *trust* them a bit more, because that always works,' he said. It was a low blow, he knew, but she deserved it.

'Self-righteousness doesn't suit you,' she said. 'Hewitson also said, if I've got this right, the rest of the herd should know that their lord would come to take what was owed to him. Do you have any idea what that means?'

'David and I worked out that the Farrow were conducting their sacrifices at each new waxing crescent moon,' Dennie said. 'They'd already done three. Lauren was the fourth, but we must have interrupted the process before it could be finished because what came out of the ground was... was...' She stopped, frowning.

David and Prav waited for her to continue, but she didn't. She just sat there looking puzzled, her lips moving slightly as if trying to form words that wouldn't come. Her fingers were making little snapping motions that were becoming increasingly irritated, and with horror David saw a small bead of saliva forming on her bottom lip, getting ready to fall. He couldn't let that happen – couldn't let her actually start drooling on herself – so he reached out and laid a hand gently on hers. 'Dennie, are you—'

'I'm fine!' she snapped. 'I don't need you mollycoddling me, Brian Keeling! I was going to say that I think what came out of the ground was not what they were expecting.' She looked from one of them to the other. 'What are you two staring at?'

He almost said *You just called me Brian*, but couldn't bring himself to do so. It would have humiliated her.

'Nothing,' he said. 'So, look, we've got no way of knowing how many more sacrifices there should have been to do the job properly. At least one, by the sounds of things. They're going to try to finish it somehow.'

'So, what's this herd that he mentioned?' Prav asked.

'Everybody who ate the meat that Ardwyn and Everett provided at that hog roast they hosted back in March,' he said. 'Except they called it the first flesh—'

'Hughes used that phrase in her interview.'

'I know. I saw the video.'

Prav grimaced. '*Everybody* saw the video. There's a data officer somewhere answering some very awkward questions, I hope.'

'Well, it's the flesh of their god.'

'What do you mean *their god*? You can't eat a god's flesh. A god isn't a physical thing that you can cut up.'

'Yes, and human-boar hybrids don't attack police stations in the middle of the night to steal sacrificial knives.' Before she could protest he went on. 'Prav, this stuff is real. The first flesh is real. I know, because my daughter ate it and it cured her leukaemia. I ate it, and I should have lost my arm but it's already getting better.' He waggled his fingers at her from inside their cast. 'I mean, I saw a man's bloody *eye* grow back.'

'Everybody who ate the first flesh is marked,' said Dennie. 'If Ardwyn decided that they could be useful, they were recruited into the Farrow. If not, they were the herd, and their blood could go back to the god. Whether you believe any of this or not, Matt Hewitson absolutely does, and someone who was at that hog roast is going to be murdered at the next crescent moon.'

'Like either of you, or David's daughter.'

'And thank you so much for saying that out loud,' David muttered.

'Not me,' said Dennie. 'Veggie. Sorry.'

'So, was it a big do, this hog roast? Or a small, intimate gathering of easily locatable friends and neighbours?'

David grimaced. 'It was pretty large. The allotment tenants mostly, but also some of the locals from the neighbouring houses, plus friends, relatives.'

'Great. So that means it could be any one of literally dozens of people.' Prav rubbed her face with her hands and yawned, but paused and her mouth snapped shut. 'Hang on, though,' she said. 'How did Hughes decide who to approach and who to sacrifice? If she was new to the area she wouldn't have known everyone by name.'

David cast his mind back to the events of that Sunday afternoon, as best he could. 'She did do an awful lot of chatting and mingling,' he said. 'Everett was the one who took care of the food and drink. Which makes sense, if she was sizing up potential victims right then and there.'

'Let's hope she made a list.'

He snorted. 'What kind of idiot would write down a list of all the people they intend to kill?'

'Oh, only loads of mass killers. They write long manifestos and keep diaries of grievances against everybody they think has done them wrong – school bullies, government officials, pop stars, girls who won't shag them, and yes, it's always men. Hughes strikes me as a very methodical but also very arrogant person; frankly it would surprise me if she didn't have it all written down somewhere. If she did, and it was at her farm, it'll be in evidence. Uniform have been searching the place for the past couple of days, and everything's coming to Burton while they sort through it. I'll have a look when I get back. Trust me, it'll be there.'

'Great then, job done,' said David.

Prav squinted at him. 'Are you being sarcastic?'

'No. I'm serious. If there is a nice convenient list of potential victims then we don't have to do a thing about it except pass it on to your lot and let them do their job. We can't protect them any better than the police can, surely.'

'David,' said Prav, 'let me tell you how police protection

works in the real world. Technically, you are an informant of an organised crime group. No, don't laugh, that's the closest equivalent to your situation: you were drawn into a group with threats of violence and you've worked to undermine them and now the lives of you and your family are at risk from reprisals. Your case, if you're lucky, is dealt with by the UK Protected Persons Service. They give you and Becky and Alice fake identities, relocate you away from anybody who knows you – friends, relatives, Alice's grandparents. And you all have to live with the psychological stress of knowing that the group could find you at any moment.

'The PPS might only look after the person being directly threatened, though, so let's say it was just you who ate this first flesh and not your family. That would be you being separated from your wife and daughter, potentially for the rest of your lives.'

'That's ridiculous,' said Dennie. 'They wouldn't do that.'

'Of course, they do that! What's cheaper for the government: a flat for one snitch or a semi-detached house for his family? Now, scale that up to however many people we're thinking of here – thirty or so? How many of them are voluntarily going to leave their loved ones? Of the ones that do, where do they go? The PPS is geared to handle individuals, not groups; they're not going to put everyone in one nice, easily defendable building, they're going to split them up all over the country. And none of them is going to have armed cops outside their door twenty-four-seven. It's the anonymity that's supposed to be the security. And that's to protect them just from ordinary, run-of-the-mill crims.

'What I saw come out of that shed, and then what attacked the station – that was not normal. I'm not qualified to say what I think it was, but you tell me that it was a half-resurrected god? I say okay, why not, it's as good an explanation as any. You say that a psychic hallucination of your dead neighbour led you to the cult's farm? Again, okay. So, here's the problem with normal police protection: if this Moccus person is what you say he is, who's to say that he can't do that too? Maybe he can, I don't know, sniff out their souls or something.'

'She has a point,' said Dennie.

Prav went on: 'We can't assume that the police are any more qualified to deal with this than you, and to be honest I'm not happy putting my colleagues in the way of something that they're not equipped to handle. They might even make things worse by separating Moccus' potential victims and making them easier to pick off.'

'So, we can't protect them,' said David bitterly. The beast's flesh was in his loved ones, and it was his fault.

'In a nutshell, no.'

'Well then, we better hope that the police find Hewitson pretty bloody quickly.'

'Oh, they will. It's just a matter of time.'

'Time that we don't have,' Dennie objected. 'If I was him I wouldn't be sitting on my hands for three weeks waiting for the next tusk moon before I nabbed a sacrifice. I'd take as many as I needed as soon as possible and then keep moving them about until it was time to use them. He knows he's being hunted. He's going to act fast, if he hasn't done so already.'

'If someone else had been abducted we'd have heard about it by now,' said David.

'Not necessarily,' Prav replied. 'I bet quite a few of them will have seen that video and got out of town already. Communication between different county forces can be dodgy at best, and if there is another misper report they won't necessarily connect it with—'

David felt a sudden terror hollow him out, and he grabbed for his phone, moaning a string of denials.

'David?' asked Dennie. 'What's wrong?'

'Becky,' he muttered, past a lump of panic that was growing in his throat. He stabbed the contact icon for her. Her smiling face expanded to fill his screen, a shot taken at the beach in the south of France on their honeymoon, above another icon that said *Calling…*

'David,' said Prav, 'there's no way that he could know—'

'Shut up! Who's to say what he can't do? Your words!'

Calling…

'Oh Jesus, honey pick up the phone, please pick up, *please…*'

Calling…

Dennie tried laying her hand on his but he shook it off.

Call ended. His phone hung itself up. She hadn't answered.

With trembling fingers he found the number for her parents and called that. It was answered in a few rings by Naomi, his mother-in-law. 'Hello, David,' she said brightly. 'How are you doing? Rebecca told us all about—'

'Is she there?' he cut across her. 'I need to speak with her if she's there. Please. It's important.'

'Of course, I'll just go and get her,' she said, with that cool politeness that told him she objected to his tone. As if he gave a toss. If Becky was there he'd apologise with flowers and grovelling.

A few moments later, Naomi came back. 'I'm terribly sorry, David, but she's not here. I think she must have popped out to the shops with Alice. Shall I get her to give you a ring when she gets back?'

His throat was so tight he could barely speak. 'Yes please, that'd be great.'

'I'm sure she's absolutely fine,' Dennie said, but he could tell that even she didn't believe it.

They sat in silence, lost in their thoughts while the business of the hospital bustled around them. When David's phone rang again, it made them all jump. He snatched it up; Becky's picture was back and *Incoming Call* flashed at him.

'Oh, thank God!' he said into it. 'Honey, are you—'

'Hello, David,' said Matthew Hewitson. 'How's the family?'

If his earlier panic had felt like being hollowed out before, this felt like the entire room had been evacuated like a bell jar, every particle of air sucked out to be replaced be a vacuum that roared in his ears. If he hadn't already been sitting in bed he'd have fallen to the ground. He heard himself whispering, 'What have you done with them?'

'Now come on, be fair, you were warned.' Hewitson's voice was cheerfully smug. 'You were given something miraculous and you threw it back in our faces, so it's only fair that you should make up for it, don't you think?'

'Fine, so let it be me, then. You don't have to hurt them.' Somewhere in the background he could hear Becky and

Alice, their muffled voices crying out against whatever was gagging them.

'You're right, I don't. But you killed my friend.' The false cheeriness was gone now. 'You and that old bitch and her fucking dog. You fucked up the only good thing that ever happened to me. So no, I don't have to hurt them, but I'm going to have fun imagining your face when I do.'

He cut the call.

The dead phone fell from David's hands, and he turned to Dennie and Prav. 'How do we find him? I don't mean the police. I mean, right fucking now. How?'

Dennie uttered a huge sigh that seemed to come up from the soles of her feet. 'Sabrina,' she said.

Prav looked at her in alarm. 'Wait,' she said. 'Didn't that nearly make you pop a blood vessel in your brain last time?' She turned to David. 'You can't ask her to do that.'

'He doesn't have to,' Dennie replied.

5

GUNS AND DOGS

IT WAS FOUR IN THE MORNING, AND DENNIE WAS running away from home.

She knew every creaking stair and grumbling floorboard, and Lizzie was flat out, bless her, exhausted by the last few days dealing with the police and doctors. Dennie, on the other hand, had never felt better, which was ironic given what the doctors had actually said.

They'd shown her CAT scan images of her brain, pointed to blurs and blobs on it which didn't make any sense to her and talked about things like 'infarcts', 'transient ischaemic attacks', and 'vascular dementia'. The upshot of all of this seemed to be that it wasn't just her nose that was bleeding – her brain was too. High blood pressure wasn't helping, and she had been sent home with all sorts of advice about lifestyle changes that might help to bring it down, such as avoiding sources of stress and anxiety.

Dennie was not in the least bit anxious about setting out to confront whatever Colin Neary had come back as. It was the right thing to do. It was necessary. If she'd acted sooner back when Sarah was being beaten she wouldn't have killed him, he would never have been buried in that allotment and the Farrow would have left them alone. Dennie wasn't naïve enough to believe that it was all her fault, but she owned a part of it, and putting that to rights made her feel more centred and steady than she had in years.

Nevertheless, she was under no illusions about what such a confrontation was likely to do to her. Still, what of that? What was worse than spending the next ten years slowly being stripped of her ability to talk, to think, to even perform the most basic tasks like eating or going to the loo? Having everything shredded away to be left as nothing but an echo of herself? Better to die.

Sneaking out of the house without waking up Lizzie was a doddle, but there was no way Dennie was going to get past Viggo so easily. When she reached the kitchen he struggled up from his huge cushion by the back door and limped towards her, whining. He had suffered four cracked ribs in the fight and his torso was strapped up from shoulder to hip.

She shushed him and tipped a few biscuits into his bowl, stroking his head while he munched.

'Sorry to do this to you, boy,' she whispered. 'But you're in no shape to come with me this time. Besides, I need you to stay here and look after Lizzie for me. Can you do that?' She was crying now, and he looked up, whined, and licked the tears off her face. 'Yes, I know you can, because you're a good boy, aren't you? You're the best boy there is.'

She unlocked the back door and eased it open. Viggo's tail began to wag at the prospect of a surprise night-time walk, but she made him sit and stay, and the hurt in his eyes was almost too much to bear. 'Look after my baby girl, all right?' she told him. 'I've got to go look after someone else's.'

She eased the door closed and set off down the garden path, and even without looking back she knew that his nose was pressed against the bottom of the door to smell her for as long as he could.

That afternoon David found Mark Turner out in a wide field dotted with dozens of black plastic-wrapped cylindrical bales of silage. He was driving a tractor with a pair of five-foot-long bale spikes attached to the front like fangs, impaling each bale, lifting it, and carrying it to be deposited on a long trailer with the help of his son Darren. As David approached he shut off the engine and jumped down to say hi and shake his hand.

'How's the arm?' he asked. David's left arm was in a sling, but that was more for show. It was a bit stiff but basically fine.

'Oh, getting there, getting there,' he replied, and nodded at the bales on the trailer. 'Summer been good to you?'

'On and off. What can I do for you, Dave? Bit of a long way out to come just to talk about the weather.'

'Yep. It's been a strange year. Got those squatters out from next door. Still a shame about those lambs, though, hey?'

He watched Turner's face turn crimson. 'What the fuck do you want, David?'

463

'It's about what you want, Mark. Do you want the scumbag that did it?' David didn't know for certain that Matt had killed and mutilated those lambs himself, but given who he'd been living with and what they'd done, that hardly mattered.

Darren hopped down from the trailer and came over. 'It was Matt, wasn't it?'

'Do you want him?' David repeated.

'Of course, I fucking want him,' said Turner. 'So do the cops, apparently. Are you telling me that you know where he is?'

'No,' David admitted. 'But I know a woman who does.'

'Well, are you going to tell me, or is there something you do want after all?'

'That depends. How many shotguns have you got?'

Mark Turner's eyes widened.

Dennie sat in the passenger seat of Mark Turner's huge green Defender, with Turner himself driving. Behind her were David, and Turner's son Darren, and following behind them was Prav in her own car. Right in the very back of the Defender were two excited farm dogs who had been introduced to her as Hob and Bella. She felt a bit guilty that they'd been brought along on this expedition when her own Viggo was with Lizzie, but if Prav knew her business there wouldn't be any fighting and nobody would be in harm's way. All Dennie had to do was actually find the place where Matt had holed up and Prav would call it in and they could just let the police do their thing. She wasn't sure that involving the Turners was either necessary or a good idea; 'Just in case,' David had said.

She couldn't say that he was wrong, but there was something about the way the men sat in grim silence without even the usual witless banter that made her think they weren't going to be satisfied with letting the authorities handle it. Even Prav had brought along a Taser and got hold of some stab vests. The shotguns were racked safely in the back with the dogs, but that didn't make her feel much safer.

Prav had not been happy about the guns.

'What exactly do you think we're going to do?' she'd demanded. 'Charge in there like a SWAT team? It's just asking for trouble!'

'Well, I don't know what your definition of trouble is, but kidnap and murder definitely do it for me,' David retorted. 'I kind of think that boat has sailed, don't you? Besides, are you forgetting the bit where you've already been shot at?'

'No, David, I am not forgetting that. And I'm not keen on it happening again. I especially don't want to get accidentally shot in the back by a pair of trigger-happy bloody farmers!'

Mark looked at Daz and raised his eyebrows. 'None taken,' he said to her.

'People like Matt Hewitson don't respond to diplomacy,' said David. 'Going in without a show of strength is just an invitation to get the shit kicked out of us. Anyway, nobody's forcing you to come along. But if you do,' he added, 'you're not a sergeant and you don't get to go around treating everybody else like they're idiots.'

'Good,' she shot back. 'That means I can punch you in the face and not get sacked when you turn out to be wrong.'

'We have to find them first,' Dennie pointed out. 'After

that you can all be as childish as you like.'

'Any idea of where we're going yet?' asked Turner. They were driving out of Dodbury and they'd soon hit the A38, whereupon he would need to know whether he was turning left or right.

'Shh,' said David. 'Let her think.'

'I still don't see why she couldn't have just pointed it out on a map,' said Daz.

'Do you want to find this bastard or not?' David replied.

'If you'll all just kindly shut your traps for a bit,' Dennie murmured. She closed her eyes and thought about Sabrina, trying to recreate that feeling of being both simultaneously distant yet focussed, of being outside her own body and yet deeply inside herself. *Come on*, she said to Sabrina silently. *Don't be afraid. And don't worry about me either. I know what this will do to me, and it's all right.* Sabrina had always been a bit panicky, anxious about often being the bearer of bad news. *It's not your fault. None of this is your fault. But I need you now, more than ever.*

The Defender slowed and stopped at the road junction. Vehicles flashed past on the wide dual carriageway in front of them. 'Going to need a decision now,' said Turner.

Still Sabrina didn't show, and Dennie began to be afraid that either she couldn't, because Dennie wasn't strong enough to summon her and some part of her brain was too broken from having summoned her before, or because Sabrina was simply too scared. Dennie decided to try a more direct appeal to the shade of Sarah Neary that she wore. *Sarah, I'm so sorry I couldn't help you more back then, but I need you to help me now because I'm going to do something that I should have done much earlier – and maybe if I had, you'd have left Colin and you'd both still be alive and none of this would have happened. I need you to help me find him, because I'm going to give him a bloody good piece of my mind.*

Behind Prav, a car horn beeped. In the mirror she saw Prav gesticulating rudely to the driver behind.

'Look, Mrs Keeling—' Turner started.

She felt Sabrina's arrival as a sudden pressure in her brain, as if a part of it deep inside was squeezing tightly. She opened her eyes and looked through the windscreen to see Sarah standing on the other side of the dual carriageway, looking back at her with tears in her eyes. Slowly, Sarah turned and started to walk away along the road.

'That way,' said Dennie, pointing.

The headache began again, and she thought this one might be the worst of all.

David thought that if there was a method to Dennie's navigation, it wasn't one that a waking, rational mind could comprehend. She led their tiny convoy a wandering route through mazes of narrow country lanes before taking them along the M54 for a couple of junctions and then off again along A- and B-roads with no apparent destination in mind except that the trend was always west, out of Staffordshire and into Shropshire, through the outskirts of the West Midlands urban sprawl, and down into the Severn Valley before finally out the other side into the uplands of the

Welsh Marches. For the rest of them it felt longer than the two hours that his watch claimed, and for Dennie herself it must have been worse. As the journey lengthened it took its toll on her; her nose bled continually, she began to nod as if dozing, and her speech became slurred. More than once his concern almost overcame his desperation to find Becky and Alice, and he tried to make them stop so that Dennie could have a rest, but every time this roused her into a fierce denial and a determination that they keep going. By the time they were winding along yet another lane, this one somewhere between a village called Pennerley and another simply known as The Bog, he thought she'd actually passed out, but then she sat bolt upright and cried, 'Here! He's here!' and slumped back in her seat, groaning.

Turner looked at the trees that crowded close on either side. 'This place?' he said. 'I don't see anything.'

'All except for that gate,' Daz pointed out.

His father stopped the vehicle. It was a humid day of another unseasonably hot summer, and the heat seemed to push itself into the car along with a heavy silence. Prav pulled up behind, got out and started unloading the stab vests from her boot. 'Right, let's go and have a look,' she said.

'Wait a minute,' said Turner. 'I thought you said we'd just find the place and then call the cops and let them sort it out.'

Prav gestured around. 'That gate could be anything. We need to be sure. We've got one shot at this; if we call the cavalry and we're wrong they'll never believe us again.'

David was checking Dennie; she was flushed and sweating, and he didn't like what he heard of her breathing and pulse.

'This is not good,' he said. 'I think she's overdone it.'

'Well, we can't leave her here,' said Prav. 'Not on her own and unprotected. We'll get her to a doctor as soon as we can.' Under her breath she muttered, 'We might all bloody need one soon.'

Daz took a set of bolt-cutters and opened the gate, while Prav showed them how to put the vests on. The Turners had their shotguns, while she was carrying her Taser with an extra cartridge clipped to the handle. *And what have I got?* David thought. The first flesh, that was what: Moccus' blood poisoning his body. So, the god wanted it back, did he? David would be more than happy to oblige.

Prav got into the Defender with them, leaving her car on the road, and they swapped positions – David replacing Dennie in the passenger seat while she was sandwiched protectively between Prav and Daz. They were surprised to find that it was not a dirt track on the other side of the gate but something more like a tarmac driveway. It was covered with leaf-litter and tree branches that had been crushed and splintered as if somebody had driven over them without going to the trouble of clearing them away properly first. Mark took it easy, crawling along as his passengers stared out at the foliage that encroached closely on either side. The engine's low rumble and the crunching of its tyres through debris only made the silence beneath the trees seem deeper.

In the back, Hob and Bella were restless, growling and whining as if they could smell something that they were simultaneously terrified of but also wanting to rip to shreds.

'Dogs are spooked,' said Daz.

'Probably the things that attacked the station,' replied Prav. 'I bet the woods are crawling with them.'

'There's a cheery thought,' said David. 'Please do not open your windows or feed the animals.'

The trees started to thin and he saw fields appearing between them, and then buildings, but it all had an overgrown and dilapidated look – he saw ruined walls and half-burned cottages and wondered what this place had been.

Then a curve in the road straightened and he saw the church. It too seemed perfectly ordinary, with its square Norman tower and crumbling gravestones, and a man was sitting on a bench in the shade of the lychgate, eating an apple.

'Yep,' said Prav. 'That's one of them.'

Matt Hewitson looked up as they approached, flicked the half-eaten apple into the long grass of the overgrown graveyard, and stood to meet them, wiping his hands on his trousers. There was a placid smile on his face which could have meant anything.

'That was quick,' he called. 'Where did you—'

But David already had his door open; he leapt around the truck bonnet and punched Hewitson in the face. 'Shut the fuck up,' he snarled. 'Where are my wife and daughter?' Prav was yelling at him, and he knew it was a stupid move, but even he hadn't realised he was going to do it until it had happened.

Hewitson fell back, cursing, hands to his face, but when he straightened up he was smiling again. 'Fair enough,' he said, massaging his jaw. 'I suppose I had that coming. Sure, you can come and see them. Word of advice, though?' he called to the rest of them who were still in the truck.

'Keep those dogs on a leash when you get out.'

'Or else what, you little shit?' shouted Turner.

Hewitson shrugged. 'Or else they'll get eaten.'

'Never mind that, where are Becky and Alice?' David demanded.

'Up that way,' said Hewitson, nodding at the wooded slopes that surrounded the village. 'It's not far but we have to go on foot.'

'It's just me,' said David. 'Nobody else.'

Hewitson shook his head. 'Not happening. You want to see the little ladies, you come with your friends.'

'Why?'

'Because my boss says so, that's why. Look, if you don't want to see them, that's fine, just get back in your big-ass four-wheel drive and go home.'

'You don't understand – we have an old woman who can barely walk.'

Hewitson blinked at him. 'Now what on earth makes you think I give a fuck?'

David turned back to the people in the vehicle. 'Are we going to do this?'

Prav was checking the cartridge on her Taser. 'Well, I'm definitely not going to sit here and let you toddle off on your own with that psycho, if that's what you're asking.'

'We didn't bring these along for decoration,' said Turner, patting the butt of his shotgun, and Daz nodded.

'I can walk,' grunted Dennie. Her face was pale now rather than hectic, but David didn't know whether this was an improvement or not. 'Old woman, is it? I'll old woman your arse, Brian Keeling.'

David traded worried looks with Prav. 'Is she…?'

Prav shook her head. 'I don't know. I just don't know. The stress of getting us here, maybe?'

Hewitson led them through the graveyard and along a path into the trees on the other side that sloped uphill. David and Prav helped Dennie between them, with Mark Turner in front and Daz behind, each of them with a shotgun in one hand and a tightly leashed dog in the other. Hob and Bella were more restless than they had been in the car. The sense of being watched by unseen eyes was even stronger, and combined with the airless heat it made David's head swim.

'Guns and dogs,' said Hewitson as they walked. 'How'd that work for you last time?'

Turner bristled but Prav laid a hand on his arm. 'Don't. He's just trying to provoke you.'

'He's fucking succeeding,' Turner growled.

'This is where it all began, you know,' Matt continued, unconcerned. 'The cult of Moccus. Mother always said it was a church, not a cult, but let's not fool ourselves. Maybe one day when everything's settled down this will become a place of pilgrimage, but at the moment it's dead. Time to find a new home, make a fresh start. Just a few loose ends to tidy up first.'

'What, like us, you mean?' David asked.

But Hewitson just laughed.

'David?' asked Dennie. Her voice was trembling, and she was looking about her in confusion. 'Are we there?'

'Yes, Dennie, you got us here.' He patted her arm and smiled, even though he felt like screaming.

6

THE CLEARING

THE PATH LEVELLED AND WIDENED OUT INTO A clearing dominated by the ruins of a large stone column in the centre that had fallen and broken into chunks. On one of them, Becky and Alice sat huddled close together, watched over by another woman – or something that looked a bit a like a woman, anyway – but David was paying no attention to the details because he was running towards them, blinded by tears.

Or at least he tried to. He fetched up against Matt's outstretched palm and it was like running into a wooden beam end-on.

'Not so fast there, chum.'

'Daddy!' screamed Alice, and when he looked the female creature had a knife to her throat and Becky was being held by something with preternaturally long arms and a leering porcine face low down between its shoulders. Then from the trees around the clearing emerged a crowd of squat, loping shapes, and Mark Turner shouted: 'What the fuck are those things?' Prav was yelling something and the dogs were barking furiously and straining at their leashes.

'Everyone just cool your shit!' bellowed Matt into the noise, which abated slightly. He had his fist curled over the front edge of David's stab vest, holding him. Once he had their attention he added, with less volume, 'There is no need for this to get stupid! This is a parley! You get violent, we get violent, everybody loses. Now calm the fuck down!'

David didn't know how he was supposed to calm down when his daughter was sobbing in the grip of something that held a knife to her throat with fingers that weren't entirely human, and his wife was pleading at him silently with confused terror, but somehow he managed it.

'You have guns and dogs,' said Matt. 'We have numbers. I kind of think it'd be fun if we all just got into it but my lord doesn't wish his children to be harmed, which I'm sure you can understand, so we parley, get it?'

'Parley?' David swallowed thickly. 'About what?'

From behind the still-standing base of the column emerged a figure that could only have been Moccus. Dennie's description of the half-resurrected god didn't do justice to the appalling state of him; surely such a thing couldn't live – or if so, it was only by sheer brute force of will. He would have been tall if he hadn't been stooped over a great cavity in one side of his torso. He would have been human if one side of his face hadn't been a denuded boar's skull. He was holding a tattered coat close around himself as if trying to ward off a chill, despite the heat.

'Colin Neary,' breathed Dennie. She was leaning on Prav. 'Dear lord, what happened to you?'

Moccus fixed her with a glaring amber eye. 'I rather think you know what. You helped, after all.'

'I'm sorry,' said Prav in disbelief, 'Colin what-now?'

'It's a long story,' said Moccus. 'Thank you, David, for bringing this old witch to me. I won't waste your time; my terms are very simple. Dennie Keeling comes with me, and you get your wife and child back.' He shuffled towards Becky and Alice, supporting himself on the broken stone as he went.

David wasn't sure that he'd heard right. 'Dennie? Why do you want her? She's not one of your chosen.'

'No, but she *interferes*,' Moccus growled. 'She pokes her nose in where it shouldn't go. She sees things she shouldn't be able to see.'

'He doesn't like that I can find him,' said Dennie, and uttered a laugh so dry it sounded like a cough. 'As if it isn't actually killing me, anyway.'

'You didn't poke it in far enough, though, did you?' he sneered. 'You never actually went so far as to call the police when you knew that Colin was beating Sarah. You just made useless comforting noises and cups of tea while he did it again, and again, until it was too late. And why?'

'Shut up, you foul creature.'

Moccus laughed. It sounded like something being drowned. 'Why? Because if Sarah had actually done something about it then you would have had nobody to comfort, would you? Rattling around the empty old family home with just that desperate waste of a husband who you never really had anything in common with except the children, at least until he had the decency to drop dead in his own driveway…'

'Shut up.'

'… and the doors that you close because you can't bear the echoes of your children's absence.'

Dennie gasped.

'Oh yes, I see things too. You needed Sarah to fill those echoes, and you let Colin beat her because it drove her closer to you.'

'That's not true! Don't you dare put that on me! You beat her! You're the monster!'

'We're all monsters, my dear. It's just a matter of degree.'

By now Moccus had reached his wife and daughter. 'David, you would never have come if it weren't to save your loved ones and you would never have found me without her, and once I have her nobody ever will. Possibly you're thinking that this is all a trick and that when you hand her over I'll just take these two anyway. Well, just to prove that I am a…' he paused, considering, 'man of my word I will remove the first flesh from your loved ones and renounce my claim on them. Since they will be of no use to me there will be no reason for me not to return them to you. Don't worry,' he added, seeing David struggle afresh against Matt's grip. 'It won't kill them. The hurts that have been healed will stay healed; only illness and age cannot.' A smile twisted the ruin of his mouth. 'But it won't be pretty.'

'David?' cried Becky. 'David, what's going on? What's he going to do?'

'Daddy! Don't let him touch me!' screamed Alice.

But Moccus had laid his hands on them.

Immediately they fell to the ground, writhing and spasming, vomiting up gouts of bloody bile – or at least that was the nearest David could get to understanding what was coming out of them. It streamed from his wife's nose and eyes like ectoplasm and evaporated into the air. It came out of his daughter's mouth in sinewy strings that crawled up Moccus' arm, blending and merging with the half-formed flesh, regenerating it, covering naked muscle with skin, plumping it out and filling the holes in his frame – not completely, but by the time the last of it had voided itself out of the girl's spasming system, Moccus was considerably more finished than he had been a moment ago. It seemed to go on for hours, even though it really could have been only a few moments, and when it was finished Becky and Alice were huddled against the stone, clutching each other and shuddering – but very much alive.

Moccus spread his hands. 'You see? Now, if you will simply surrender Mrs Keeling to me without a fuss, you can take one of them and go home.'

'How is this even up to him?' Prav protested.

'It's not,' said Dennie. 'Of course, I'm going to go with him.'

Prav uttered a short, hard bark of contemptuous laughter. 'Oh, that's not going to happen.'

'Wait,' said David. 'One of them?'

'Of course,' said Matt. 'We're meant to trust that you won't call in the cavalry as soon as we leave? Uh-uh. We give you one of yours as a gesture of good faith, we take

Dennie and the other one, and once we're safe and sound we let the other one go. And we all live happily ever after, like baby lambs.' He looked at Turner and winked.

Prav sighed. 'Oh, you stupid dickhead.'

Bellowing, Turner threw himself at Matt, and it all went to shit.

Matt swatted Turner away, but in doing so Turner lost his grip on both gun and leash and Hob leapt for the one who had attacked his master. Daz saw his dad knocked flying, let go of Bella's leash and raised his own shotgun while Bella lunged for Matt too. David saw the female creature that had held a knife to his daughter's throat bend towards where Alice and Becky lay clutching each other, still shuddering from the effects of Moccus' exorcism, and he leapt at her, screaming, 'Get the fuck away from them!' The female loosed a cry exactly like an enraged boar, mouth agape and grinning with tusks, and turned to meet his charge, swinging her knife. The stab vest turned it, and his momentum carried him into her, slamming her to the ground. His hands were around her throat and he squeezed with the strength of the first flesh while she clawed at him; the vest caught some of her attacks, but she was gouging at his arms too, and his blood was running down them and onto her face.

'Oh, you stupid dickhead.'

Prav levelled her Taser on Moccus and fired; the twin barbs struck him squarely in the chest, and the pistol crackled as fifty thousand volts surged along its wires. Moccus looked down at them with a frown like a man seeing a bug crawling on him. He plucked them out and tossed them away.

'Or we can do this,' he said, and came for her.

Gibbering things were coming out of the trees and a shotgun was barking and Dennie was at her back, hands over her ears, screaming. She dropped the Taser, flicked out her police-issue baton, dropped her centre of gravity into her knees and squared herself to meet the god.

Mark Turner picked himself up, and looked around for his gun. Daz was blasting at the things that came running out from the bushes. A few yards away, Hewitson was staggering about with Hob locked on his arm and Bella ripping at his thigh. As Turner's fingers found the smooth steel of the gun barrel, Hewitson plucked Hob away by the back of the neck as if he'd been nothing more than a puppy and flung him at a stone block the size of a fridge. Hob bounced, shrieked, and fell limply to the ground.

'You little fucker,' he grunted, and grabbed up his shotgun.

Dennie cowered amidst the noise. With trembling fingers she fumbled at the gardening utility pouch on her belt and took out the little foldaway pruning knife she habitually carried. Its blade was only two inches long, but it was the only weapon she had.

No, it isn't, said a familiar voice, and the rail spike slammed her between the eyes.

* * *

The female creature had stopped clawing at David's arms and instead was pushing at the ground as if trying to dig her way into it. He realised she wasn't trying to hurt him any more, just get away, so he released his grip and she scrambled out from underneath him and fled for the safety of the tree-line, clutching her throat. He threw himself over to where Alice and Becky were cowering. He clutched them both in his arms and kissed them.

'Stay here,' he said. 'Don't move.'

'Don't go,' Becky moaned. Alice whimpered into her shoulder.

'I'll be right back, I swear.'

He picked up the knife that the female creature had dropped, and went to help Prav.

Matt shook the other dog free and charged at Daz. Half a dozen Recklings were dead or crippled from his gun, and the rest of them looked like they were ready to break and run. Sus had already legged it. In the dark, and with the element of surprise, they could be vicious little bastards, but in broad daylight with a man shooting at them their natural animal cowardice was taking over. He needed to do something about that.

He ran up to Daz and ripped the shotgun from his grip, flinging it away. Daz swore and punched him in the face but it was a grazing blow, easily shaken off. The first flesh was in him, and he was untouchable. He laughed and dropped Daz to the ground with a fist to the guts, and then kicked him a couple of times for good measure.

Matt turned to the Recklings. 'Well, come on, you chickenshits!' he yelled. 'Take him!'

The Recklings fell on Daz with tusk and claw.

Prav tried to sidestep Moccus' charge, but he was fast – God he was fast – had all that shuffling been a sham or was this a last-ditch burst of energy? It didn't matter either way, because she wasn't quick enough to avoid the tusk on the boar-side of his face; it was razor sharp and as he passed, it slashed through the stab vest, the t-shirt beneath, and her flesh beneath that in a bright line of red agony. She got in one solid whack with the baton as he went by, but didn't think it had done him much harm. Then he was past, and behind, and she turned, and this put Dennie in front of her, pointing her little pruning knife at him. It was like seeing a mouse trying to fend off a cat with a toothpick. Out of the corner of her eye she saw a thrashing heap of creatures where Daz had been, and red, too much red, and Mark Turner screaming as he turned his shotgun to bear on Hewitson. The gun barked, and Hewitson's shirt turned crimson, but he just looked down at it and laughed.

Sarah has the kitchen knife in both hands as Colin comes at her. He's drunk and angry – angry about so many things. Losing his job, the bills, the fact that she's going to have another baby when he thinks they could barely afford the first one. Four-year-old Josh is awake, she can hear him crying upstairs, and she's tried to calm Colin down so that he's not making so much noise but he's just not having it. He's clipped her a couple of times already and from the look in his piggy little eyes he's settling in for more, and all of a sudden she realises that she's just not having it either. She doesn't want to hurt Colin, but she's finally had enough of him hurting her, because it's not just her he's hurting, it's the baby inside her too, and she suspects that if his beating causes her to lose it he won't shed a tear.

She genuinely doesn't know whether he runs onto the knife or she shoves it into him. All she knows is that once it's there, it's not coming out, and so she hangs onto it while his rage turns to surprise, and then fear, and then terror, and then nothing.

Moccus threw himself at the old woman with the puny little knife, except that she wasn't an old woman any more, and the knife wasn't puny at all – it was large and it was bright and when it went into him it hurt like the remembrance of an old death.

Oh, it *hurt*.

David plunged the knife deep between Moccus' shoulder blades, and for a second he thought he saw a much younger woman standing where Dennie had been, but then the god died and the first flesh died along with him. David was seized with a sudden savage cramping low down in his guts that doubled him up, screaming. It felt like he was being twisted in half. He fell to the ground as the cramping spread out through his torso and into his limbs as if clawed things were swarming in his guts, snapping and shredding every inch of the way – and as it went, his body expelled the first flesh from his every orifice and even the pores of his skin.

Prav clutched at Dennie as she fell. Her nose was pouring blood, her eyes had rolled up to their whites, and as Prav eased her to the grass she began to spasm as if she was the one who'd taken the Taser shot instead.

'Dennie? Dennie, can you hear me?'

But the only response Dennie made was a guttural throat-deep keening, and she began to foam at the mouth.

'Oh Jesus, Dennie, don't do this.' Prav lifted her head and screamed, '*Help me! For God's sake please somebody help me!*'

The Recklings fled at their god's death and Matt fled with them, taking advantage of the confusion and the fact that Turner had thrown his gun away and was cradling the mutilated body of his son, weeping.

He'd never personally gone cold turkey from heroin but he knew people who had, and this felt like it might be close. He was virtually blind, his legs refused to hold him up, and it felt like every single one of his internal organs was trying to vomit and shit itself out of him simultaneously.

The Recklings had fled and Moccus was gone. He'd felt the death in his blood. He was nothing now – worse than nothing because of the knowledge of what he had lost. He ran deep into the woods and lay and let his body purge itself of the dead god's flesh, and hoped that it might carry on dissolving, turning inside out and vanishing like a worm into the mud.

But even that mercy was denied.

Before long, he became aware that he was being watched.

Sus was standing over him, bruised and tattered, and she was holding a very large rock in both hands, raised above his head.

'You brought this on us!' she snarled.

'Wait—' he said, holding up his hands to ward off the blow. It was all he had strength left for, and it wasn't enough.

Sus brought down the rock, hard.

Sus gathered those of her kin who still had enough wits to follow, and led them up into the deep woods and out of Swinley as the sound of sirens grew.

7

ECHOES

'SHE'S HAVING ONE OF HER LUCID PHASES,' DENNIE'S daughter had said. 'But please don't tire her out.'

David went through to the back garden where he found Dennie working on her new vegetable plot. She'd dug up half the lawn into rows marked out with small wooden stakes and was busily sowing something out of a packet, prodding the seeds into the soil with her forefinger. It was August, a time when things should be ripening, but with the Briar Hill allotments either closed or abandoned it seemed that this was the next best thing. Lizzie had told him that the doctors' advice had been that the exercise and the mental stimulation would be good for her, so Lizzie had let her get on with it. It was a poor shadow of her old plot, he thought.

Viggo lay panting in the sun nearby, watching his mistress carefully. His bandages were gone and he was as mobile as ever: too much of a handful for Dennie these days, so it was her daughter who took him for his walks. He bounded up with a *hruff!* of welcome and licked David's hand. Dennie straightened up, saw him, and beamed.

'David!'

'Hello, trouble.' He smiled. He tried not to notice the lopsidedness of her own grin, or the way her left hand was curled as she hugged him.

'What brings you up this way?'

'Oh, there are a few things with the house that need doing. Solicitors, estate agents, stuff like that.'

'So, you're really selling up, then?'

'Yeah. It's for the best. Me and Becky will split the proceeds and there should be enough left over for me to get a flat or something nearby so that I can visit Alice.'

'How is she after... after everything?'

He sighed. 'Well, the leukaemia's returned and she's back on chemo so that whole bloody circus has started up again.'

'Oh, David, I'm so sorry.'

'No, don't be. Given the alternative, it really is for the best.' He almost asked Dennie how she was, but it was quite obvious and he didn't want to upset her. 'Are things... quiet for you?'

She gave him a sharp look. 'Do you mean have I had any more visits from Sabrina?'

'Subtle, huh?'

'As a brick.' Dennie swatted him, then sighed. 'She's gone. Or at least, she's back deep now, deep inside where she belongs, and I'm at peace with that. Though I sometimes think—' she started to add, but then stopped.

'Think what?'

'About what would have happened if I'd taken what the Farrow were offering.'

'More people would have died, that's what. Anyway!' he added brightly, since horror and disease and his foundering marriage were the last things he wanted to talk about. 'What you got going in here, Mother Nature?'

She took him by the hand and showed him. 'Spring onions over here, spinach over there, the odd turnip or two if I'm feeling adventurous.' She looked around as if afraid of being overheard. 'Maybe even something medicinal for the old, you know,' and she made a whirling screw-loose sign with her finger beside her head.

David laughed. 'You'll get arrested!'

Dennie's expression was all wounded innocence. 'Me? A harmless old bat going gaga in her own back garden? Nobody would be so cruel.' Then her face clouded. 'Nobody would... would...' Her eyes wandered up to his. 'What was I saying?'

He glanced back to the house, where Lizzie was watching through the kitchen window. She saw his look, and her shoulders slumped in a sigh. It had only been with great reluctance that she'd let him see Dennie in the first place; she still blamed him for what had happened. *Get in line*, he thought. 'You were telling me what you had planted out,' he said as cheerfully as he could manage. 'Spring onions and spinach?'

'Oh, don't be silly, Brian,' she scowled, turning away. 'It's entirely the wrong season for spring onions and spinach.

Now what did I do with...' She drifted away, hands fluttering, looking for something that probably wasn't even there. 'What did I do with...'

Then Lizzie was there with her arms around her mother. 'Come on, Mum,' she said. 'Let's go have a cup of tea, hey?' As she guided Dennie carefully away, she turned to David over her shoulder and mouthed *Sorry*.

'I should go,' he said.

Lizzie nodded and led the echo of her mother back towards the house.

He went back to Briar Hill to have a last look at his old allotment. The Farrow plot was still surrounded by fluttering police tape, and while a handful of his neighbours' allotments were still being tended, many more had been abandoned and were overgrown by weeds. It didn't seem likely that the Association would be able to lease his out to new tenants. This place was poisoned.

The earth hid horrors, he knew that well now. It soaked up blood and pain, fear and hatred, and it didn't take very much effort to dig that all back up again. But as he walked down to his shed and back, scuffing at the soil with his shoes, he thought about all the memories he and Becky and Alice had made here – the time when they had wrestled those old railway sleepers into place to make the raised beds, the time when Alice had chased butterflies, the picnics and Easter egg hunts, the frosty mornings and the long slow summer evenings – and he hoped that maybe the soil soaked up love too, and friendship, and family.

So he found an old plastic flower pot, and he scooped

up a handful of earth and filled it. Whether his daughter ended up with a garden of her own or just a window box, he would sprinkle this soil in it and pray that whatever she planted there would grow strong and true.

EPILOGUE

'THIS IS WHERE IT HAPPENED,' SAID THE MAN, STEPPING into the clearing. His small entourage of four followed, bundled in thick coats and gloves against the snow. Two were women and two men, but all were young, in their twenties or late teens while their leader was older, in his forties. They all carried backpacks and snow shovels over their shoulders.

'There were remarkably few casualties,' he added, 'but only if you count the cost in lives.'

He led the group through the knee-deep snow to the centre of the open space, where the fallen remains of the great stone column were larger hummocks in the otherwise uniform blanket of white, and they set to clearing the snow with their shovels. This February's Beast-from-the-East had been harsher than the last few, and though more bad weather was forecast for later in the day, for the moment the sky was

490

an icy blue. Trees had encroached over the years, and there had been a discussion about using them to string up some kind of shelter like a tarp over the top, but he had said no – it was better that they were exposed to the elements. On the cleared ground they laid waterproof groundsheets and thick woollen blankets atop those.

'With He Who Eats the Moon dead but not consecrated,' he continued, 'the first flesh died with him and was rejected by the bodies of those that had eaten it. Fairly uncomfortable, but in the end not much worse than a bad case of food poisoning. For Ardwyn Hughes though, the last survivor of the old Swinley church, it was a bit more serious.'

As the younger members removed their clothes, the older man took from his backpack the objects that he carried, placing them carefully on the stone block as if it were an altar. One of them was a large bronze bowl. The other was a black sickle-shaped knife, its blade broken but still gleaming.

'When the prison guard went to check on her the next morning, she found a corpse that looked like it had been dead for weeks. I have no idea how old Ardwyn really was. The injuries that the first flesh had healed stayed healed, but time is a wound that can't be fixed, I suppose.'

'Though it does come back around,' suggested one of the young women.

He thought about this. 'Yes. Yes, I suppose it does.' When melting polar ice had killed the Gulf Stream in '31, the islands of Britain had reverted to a climate more in keeping with Iceland or Norway, which some romantic souls were calling a new Ice Age, though this conveniently ignored the fact that there were no more ice sheets or glaciers left and the land was instead being inundated with rising sea levels and catastrophic flooding. The 'Neodiluvian', was its proper term. Fifteen years on, people were still arguing whether it was settling down or speeding up.

'There are wounds that can't be healed, though, and maybe shouldn't.' The man removed his coat and jacket and rolled up the sleeve of his right arm, exposing an underside that was scored with ranks of old, parallel scars. He took up the ancient sickle in his left hand. 'This may work, or it may not, but either way we will at least have tried,' said Joshua Neary, and put the knife to his flesh.

'Now, shall we begin?'

ACKNOWLEDGEMENTS

WHEN PEOPLE ASKED ME WHAT I WAS WORKING ON and I told them it was a story about improbable horribleness on an allotment, far more than I was expecting replied either with an enthusiastic, 'Ooh! I've got an allotment!' or a wistful, 'You know, I've always wanted to get an allotment,' or a furtive sidelong glance as if afraid of being overheard and a, 'Let me tell you what really goes on down our allotments.' If I'd wanted to, I could have written a book of handy hints, tips, and shaggy dog stories for allotment holders, and one day I might, but in the meantime the people I need to thank for letting me pick their brains, weed their plots, and put up their sheds are: Mike and Debs, Dan, Julian, Arwen, Ju, Sharon, Lindsey, Megan, and my Dad. May your strawbs be fruitful and your plots be ever slug-free.

I may have taken some liberties with historical details. While the lands of the Cornovii were around that part of the Midlands, there's no evidence that they worshipped a boar-headed god. Moccus was a real god, however – or at least as real as gods go – worshipped by the Lingones people around Langres in France. However, boar worship was very real and very widespread, so it's not inconceivable that such cults might have existed in ancient Britain. Any glaring holes in this or the details of the WWI chapters are entirely my fault, for which I hope the history nerds will forgive me. Find me at a con and put me right; I'll buy you a beer. But no pork scratchings.

The cultivation of my own plot (see what I did there?) would not have been possible without the keen eyes of Cat Camacho and Jo Harwood at Titan, and the encouragement and support of my agent Ian Drury at Sheil Land.

But last and forever to Eden for her gay apples, Hopey for her priapic cacti, and T.C. for being Mother.

J.B., January 2020

ABOUT THE AUTHOR

JAMES BROGDEN IS A PART-TIME AUSTRALIAN WHO grew up in Tasmania and now lives with his wife and two daughters in Bromsgrove, Worcestershire, where he teaches English. He spends as much time in the mountains as he is able, and more time playing with Lego than he should. He is the author of *The Plague Stones*, *The Hollow Tree*, *Hekla's Children*, *The Narrows*, *Tourmaline*, *The Realt* and *Evocations*, and his horror and fantasy stories have appeared in various periodicals and anthologies ranging from *The Big Issue* to the British Fantasy Society Award-winning Alchemy Press. Blogging occurs infrequently at jamesbrogden.blogspot.co.uk, and tweeting at @skippybe.

For more fantastic fiction, author events,
exclusive excerpts, competitions, limited editions and more

VISIT OUR WEBSITE
titanbooks.com

LIKE US ON FACEBOOK
facebook.com/titanbooks

FOLLOW US ON TWITTER AND INSTAGRAM
@TitanBooks

EMAIL US
readerfeedback@titanemail.com